The Decline and Fall of Air Arcadia

A Novel

Former Captain

Former Captain™ Press

*This book is dedicated
to the
men and women
of
Air Arcadia*

Author's Note

Writing fiction, the author can just make stuff up. That's convenient, especially when reality doesn't cooperate. For example, we don't normally think of corporations as having thoughts and opinions, even if they are airlines. But a thinking, feeling airline is handy if you are trying to portray characters who give it their working life. Those characters think and feel, and their lives are touched and changed by their devotion to their work. So it's nice to invent a conceit where that devotion doesn't necessarily mean that they're nuts.

I did work for an airline. After I retired I realized that I loved her and wanted her memory to survive. My head was filled with characters and stories, inspired and related by hundreds of friends and colleagues over many decades. To do justice to them all would take dozens of books. Instead I let their memory ferment, and I forgot. Reality and fact faded in my head and gave way to what my experience meant for me.

This book is a work of fiction. No character is real, and no event occurred as described here. Rather, this novel is about the idea of an airline and its people during the last quarter of the twentieth century. The events are common to most airlines of that era, and the characters are fictional archetypes. Nevertheless, I hope that they are accurate enough so that airline people will recognize something of themselves here. After all, this book is dedicated to them.

The
Decline and Fall
of
Air Arcadia

In the Beginning

In the beginning was Arcadia, a land so vast that its ends were mapped only from the sea. Caught between ice and independence, its middle was largely empty, hospitable only along a southern fringe. Competing conquerors vied to prise the land and its riches from the custodian tribes.

Centuries passed in parochialism as the conquerors remained aloof from revolutions and from each other. Arcadia's Backward Party finally patched together this uneasy family of loyalists with steel rails and spikes, proclaiming a monopoly for private enterprise. A half-century later the Forward Party echoed their achievement, stitching the patches still closer with airplanes and radio beacons, and proclaiming the rightful place of government.

To this day adherents to disparate faiths, fatherlands, mores, and mother tongues sit uneasily together in parliament, struggling to frame the issues of the day in terms of Backward and Forward, public and private. The story of Arcadia has been and still is a story of technology sent forth to link the unwilling. Railroad and telegraph, aircraft and radio range, radio and television: these are bribes which tempt the tribal children to travel and listen.

This is the story of a particular Arcadia, as she is known to herself and her people. To the wider world she was Trans Arcadian Air Lines, later known as Air Arcadia as she morphed from public to private and still later passed from publicly held through bankruptcy to privately traded. Is it any wonder that we are confused? She herself is confused.

But do not be put off by trying to comprehend financial arrangements to which only the gifted are privy: there is plenty here for our unremarkable intellect, plenty to engage our limited attention. This is a story of how technological wonders – the original aircraft and radio ranges urged on us by the Forward Party – were forged in the crucible that is our Arcadia, with its mountains and lakes and ice and plains but mostly its weather, its extremes of heat and cold, water and ice and snow, clouds and fog in undreamed-of combinations, winds of a strength only associated with the open ocean; how these technological baubles, thrown into the crucible and sparked into a life of their own, continued to develop along with the other Arcadia, the airline they made possible, and, as life itself so often does, moved in directions not predictable in their genetic code.

It is also a story of Arcadia's pilots – one, I would venture to say, that we might rather not know. As we sit for hours in a space too small after surrendering our human dignity in a full-body scanner, we would rather think that the worst is over, that all we must do is endure until our arrival at the gate. And usually this is so. But the reality is that we are packed into a small aluminum tube hurtling through space, held aloft by forces created when the wings divide the atmosphere into separate paths. We are breathing air that enters through the engine intakes and is packed together by thirteen or more successive compressor stages. Our aluminum tube is kept separate from others like it by the pilots' collaborators and colleagues, the Air Traffic Controllers. Finally, our fragile tube, after hundreds or thousands of miles in the clear and in solid cloud or rain or snow, shrugs these trailings of atmosphere off her wings and emerges at that exact point where the runway is there before her, her energy and her velocity vector in three dimensions adjusted so she can flare and land and dissipate the remaining energy with drag and braking and reverse thrust within the confines of the runway. This feat of navigation is accomplished – and here I am going backwards through history – with the help of GPS, IRS, INS, ILS, VOR, ADF, and the Radio Range. To this day our orientation in space is maintained with the help of gyros, both mechanical and now with those which to all appearances are virtual: beams of ruby laser light are the only movement as they race in opposite directions around a triangular crystal racetrack, their interference patterns speaking to us of minute accelerations.

Yes, you may say. That is all well and good. But why should we dwell on these matters? Do we have to know anything about the protocols involved? And do not the airplanes these days land themselves?

You are right of course. Many of them can – in the right conditions and on certain runways – land themselves. Some airplanes are even designed to be pilot-proof. This knowledge is reassuring, because we are human and we understand what it is to be human and we would rather not trust our lives to something as fragile and fallible as humanity. We would rather put our faith in impenetrable technology. But just as your cellphone occasionally drops a call, so from time to time there is a crash and people lose their lives.

Perhaps we would rather not know. Certainly the management of airlines and aircraft manufacturers would rather we do not. A yellow tape goes up around a crash, in every sense of the word. Move along. Nothing to see here. But every real pilot understands and accepts that the job, the job he loves, is to keep that crash from happening. The responsibility is his and his alone. Should he (or she) survive his career he also understands that it is not just his superior skill but also luck that bore him here.

And so, dear reader, traveller, trusting passenger, beware. Do you really want to know how sausages are made? Do you really want to shed your illusions and see those who are, for those hours in the aluminum tube, your last line of defense against an untimely death? Do you really want to see them in the context of their messy humanity, a humanity not unlike your own?

But if you would know more about Arcadia – the airline Arcadia – you have no choice. To know her you must know something of her world, her airplanes, and especially her people. For what is she without them?

I am thinking especially of the pioneers, the legends whose stories were passed around as we flew the line in the early days. Knowing the stories added to the surprise when you would occasionally run into one in the flesh, say on a Sunday layover in Calgary where Cicero would command fine repast of chips, carrot and celery sticks and whatever else could be negotiated and brought to the table so beer could legally be consumed, or on a half-hour ferry flight from Ottawa home where, the airplane safely put to bed, Cubby would drag you to a grubby tavern in industrial Dorval that you never knew existed.

It was exciting to meet them, and more exciting to fly with them. Nevertheless, retaining a degree of caution was a good idea then and is a good idea now. For example, if you choose to read on, it might be as well to ask that you reserve judgement on these assholes. You see, in those days the rules for instrument flying were being written, and the assholes were the authors. Their instruments were basic; their radio aids primitive. So they improvised their own Standard Operating Procedures, their own Minimums, and their own Minimum Equipment Lists. Instead of Approach Plates they likely had headings from Farmer Jones' barn.

But they didn't always share their knowledge. It was still, to some extent, every man for himself. You built your own trade brick by brick. No one could tell you how to do it. You did it your way, the right way. You were the captain, you were God, and your word was the law.

§

Arcadia – 1954

The sun is just up on what promises to be a fine, hot June day. The 1950 Mercury convertible has cleared downtown Montreal and is heading west toward Beaconsfield and eventually, Hudson. Aside from the gang of four men weighing down the Merc, only the birds are awake. Cicero, the driver, has been holding forth as only he can.

"…and to cap it off, my good man, my landfall was within inches of the plan."

Cicero is wheeling the Merc around the Dorval circle. He looks like Thor the Large discovering Iceland: his long blond hair and matching moustache blow in the wind; his six-foot-six frame, still mostly muscle in those days, holds his head well above those in the back seat. Beside him Big Bob, almost his equal in size, is slumped slightly sideways so he can hang his arm, and occasionally his head, out into the breeze.

"My navigator, although an amiable enough chap, was I must say nevertheless far from my equal in intellect, and I could see plainly that in his recommended heading from forty west he had failed to consider the gyroscopic effect of the earth's rotation …"

In the back seat Cubby's blood begins to boil.

"You're so full of shit Cicero your eyes are brown."

"Did I hear a voice of dissent from the cheap seats?"

"You couldn't navigate your way out of a wet fucking paper bag."

This is not just talk. Cubby is known for carrying his own sextant.

"Those in the peanut gallery would be wise to be seen and not heard, like the small children they are."

That wakes up Roy the Boy. Beside him Cubby keeps needling Cicero.

"After some of the stunts you've pulled, Cicero, I'm surprised you still have a driver's licence, let alone a pilot licence. I'll bet the only type endorsement you have is for the Salt and Pepper Shaker at Belmont Park."

Looking at Cubby, you wouldn't give him the longest odds against Cicero the Bulk. He is five-foot- eight and wiry. But Cubby is Basque; uncompromising smuggling outlaw ancestors have been honing their fiery temperaments for centuries so they can pass their secrets on to Cubby. He always claims he can't help it: he doesn't want to make trouble but sometimes his blood just starts to boil.

"My good fellow, you have had a snootful. You would be well advised to keep your opinions to yourself."

The Mercury kicks up dust as Cicero runs wide coming out of the circle.

"Yeah, and who am I afraid of, you pompous assholes up front? Look – you can't even stay on the road. If you were an F/O worth shit, Bob, you'd have taken control by now."

Cicero's neck is turning red. The Merc weaves as he swings his right arm, trying to clip Cubby in the back seat. Cubby ducks and Cicero's swing continues further than he intends, finding Roy the Boy's temple as he sits up to see what is going on. Now the Merc is on the shoulder, running through gravel and grass. Cicero stomps on the brakes, bringing the car to a stop with a buck and a wheeze, stalling the flathead V-8. He has forgotten the clutch.

Cubby is out first, leaping tidily over the side. Big Bob opens his door with a heave, almost nailing Cubby, and then lurches out of his seat, leading with a left. Cubby dodges, feints, and taunts:

"Can't hold your liquor, Bobby. Now you gonna take on the little guy?"

Cicero, red-faced with the effort to retain some dignity, gets out and stands up. As he turns he comes face to face with Roy the Boy.

Roy earned his moniker in sports. He especially liked contact sports; although hockey was his main love he played football and rugby as well, and earned a reputation as a good player and a fair player. He is one of those large men who, rather than taking perverse pleasure in beating up those smaller than himself, instead became a stickler for fairness: a check or a block has to be legal; sneaking in an extra move out of sight of the referee is anathema to him. Indeed, Roy has no need to go beyond the legal. If an opponent's nasty move comes to his attention, he is quite capable of sidelining the miscreant while keeping within the rules. In the Air Force the name Roy the Boy stuck because as his team-mates grew older and wiser in the ways of the world, Roy maintained his boyhood faith in the natural justice of things. Still, he never seems quite aware that the agent of justice is himself.

Roy's face still smarts as Cicero turns, obviously enraged, and looks him in the eye. Beyond his throbbing temple Big Bob is a peripheral shadow, struggling to move fast enough to lay a hand on Cubby. One on one there. Fair enough. He holds Cicero's gaze, waiting him out, even though it is obvious that Cicero has already lost control. Cicero lunges, trying to pin Roy against the side of the Mercury. Physical contact can not be avoided, but Roy ducks and pins Cicero's knees against the rear wheel well. The momentum of that large upper body and that swelled head takes charge, rubbing the blond moustache along the rear fender and down into the gravel.

Cubby runs around the front of the car, staying clear of the drunken Big Bob and determined to come to the assistance of his team-mate. Roy holds up a hand to stop Cubby, nodding toward the big blond on the ground.

 "Time out!"

The Merc's left taillight lens, which had looked like half a smile, is broken. So, it appears, is Thor the Bore's nose, which is distinctly lopsided and bleeding profusely. Cicero rises tentatively, feeling his nose, mumbling sonorously.

"Fucking bunch of goons! Cretinous sons of bitches! Brawling bastards!"

Meanwhile Big Bob is earnestly trying to hold his end up. He circles the other way around the convertible, appearing behind its rounded rump and taking in the blood on his buddy's moustache. He looks up at Roy.

"You!" he accuses. "You!"

Roy the Boy holds up his other hand.

"Time!" he commands. "Easy!"

But Big Bob is beyond imprecation. He is in the La-La Land of the very drunk, each breath of cool air a gift, each successful movement a surprise. He advances steadily, ponderously toward Roy, his sleepy gaze trying to focus on the task at hand. When he feels he is within range he begins to concentrate, the effort plain on his slack features.

Again Big Bob leads with his left, lunging with the effort of the hard punch. Roy steps to the right and then as the punch goes by pivots to the left, wrapping his arms around Bob from behind in a bear hug.

"Easy, I said."

Big Bob grunts, trying to dislodge Roy by simply stomping around in a circle. Roy's toes are dragging in the gravel, but he is not a rider to be dislodged easily. Still grunting fiercely, Bob trips and falls face-first into the gravel, Rider Roy still attached. Although his arms hurt, Roy knows he has to watch his back and shoots a glance over at Cicero.

The Big Blond is still trying to get up. He has almost succeeded, but he has a rider of his own: Cubby has Cicero in a two-arm headlock and is still needling him.

"Oughta get you to a doctor, my good man."

Cubby's voice takes on a smarmy sincerity. He twists his head back and forth as if examining the damage.

"That patrician nose of yours is in danger, Cicero. In fact you look like a fucking bum. No one is going to listen to your bullshit now."

For a few heartbeats time seems to stop. Cubby gazes speculatively as blood drips from the big blond's chin. Wearing an ironic smile Cubby takes his left hand from the headlock and grabs enough hair to twist Cicero's head around for a better look. Their eyes lock. Another few heartbeats go by and the big Viking suddenly relaxes, slumping into a sitting position. He starts to laugh.

"Truly this is a fine morning," he pronounces.

Blood is still dripping from his chin and being shaken loose from his moustache as he laughs. Through the magic of booze, brotherhood and a night on the town – or perhaps it is just Basque trickery – the tension of a week of flying has been released.

"A great day for a ride in this fine vehicle. Anyone for breakfast?"

Table of Contents

Table of Contents

Part I

Every man's work shall be made manifest:

for the day shall declare it,

because it shall be revealed by fire;

and the fire shall try every man's work

of what sort it is.

1 Corinthians 3:13

Arcadia

Pebble in the Pond

Toulouse, France – January, 1988

Months in Toulouse and Miles is still nowhere.

"Pedro, we're going to be flying that bird back home in a week. There isn't much time left."

The supper dishes have been cleared away, but Pedro's carafe isn't empty. He swirls the wine in his glass.

"So – we're going to draw lots to see who gets to be captain? We can do that in thirty seconds."

"This is serious, Pedro. We have a mission."

It is almost as if Pedro isn't an Air Arcadia guy at all. The traitor swirls his wine again, tips it up, and drains the glass.

"Right. We don't want to bend anything on the way home. Looks bad."

Miles's exasperation creeps redly up his throat.

"I'm talking about the Standard Operating Procedures. The SOP's."

"Yeah. You've written them. Single-handed. And they're horseshit."

"Jesus."

Miles pushes his chair back. It makes a noise against the floor. It is a noise he doesn't recognize, a French noise. French floor, French chair. He doesn't get up. Pedro holds him steadily in his gaze.

"Fact is, Miles, there's no fucking way I'm going to sign on. Haven't you been listening to our instructor?"

"Jules? A bit full of himself, don't you think?"

"Sure. He's French. What the fuck do you expect?"

Miles does not smile. Pedro carefully pours the remaining wine into his glass.

"I don't see what Jules has to do with our agreeing on procedures. And we've got to agree."

"Says who?"

The colour has crept up into Miles' ears.

"Jesus, Pedro. Management, that's who. The Standards Committee. And they want procedures that are standardized with the other airplanes."

"But the SOP's don't have to be identical, Miles. The airplanes aren't identical."

"Where they can be they should be."

"I'll tell you what, Miles. You could fix your draft real easy. Just take out all the memorized drills. The Electronic General Actions Director has all that shit covered."

"So?"

"The point is, Miles, that with your procedures the pilot is fighting the EGAD. It's like both pilots trying to do the same task and nobody's flying the airplane. Remember the L-1011 that landed in the everglades? Three pilots trying to change a light bulb?"

"You can't tell me memorized drills aren't good."

"Sure they're good. But the Bus has them memorized much better than our boys can and she's gonna present them to you on the screen whether you've got them memorized or not."

"I don't see what that has to do with anything."

"It has to do with assigning tasks, Miles. And on this airplane you have to let her be one of the players."

Miles pushes his chair back again as if he is going to make a move. He doesn't.

"So. That's what Jules is lobbying for?"

"See, that's what you don't get, Miles. It's not political."

The irony jumps out at Miles. Of course it's political. Everything is political. And this guy, this Air Arcadia envoy and representative, is in bed with the enemy.

"Jules works for Bus Industries, not for Air Arcadia. You work for Air Arcadia."

"Yes. And our job is to help keep our boys from pranging one of these things. We have to write SOP's that do that. Yours don't."

"Oh, come on . . ."

"Talk to Jules about the Mulhouse crash."

"You mean the airshow flyover . . ."

"Attempted flyover. Fly over and settle gracefully into the forest."

"So?"

Pedro drains his glass, considering a man who can dismiss a crash, total hull loss, and death.

"Three people died. If that machine had been as you say just like the other airplanes then a hundred and thirty-seven people would have died. You know what? The guy who designed this airplane was trying to make it pilot-proof. And he did, more or less. The guy is a fucking genius."

Miles shrugs.

"No, really. I'm not being facetious, Miles. The airplane is fabulous. But it's not perfect. Look at what happens when it comes into conflict with Mulhouse Captain Asshole, who thinks he knows how to do a low pass just like in any other airplane but he hasn't thought it through and he doesn't know his systems so the auto-thrust is in *IDLE* and his punishment is that the envelope protection doesn't let it stall and the high alpha routine puts his power up for him but it's too fucking late the engines take seven seconds to spool up from idle so it settles gracefully into the trees wings level at the slowest possible speed and saves his sorry ass so he can go to court and go to jail."

Pedro involuntarily sticks his right arm behind him, trying to shake off a strange tingling.

"And what is it, Miles? Ego. Blind ego. Thinking you know what you're doing when you don't. Thinking you've made the perfect machine when it's just as perfect as you are and no more."

The tingling is running down his neck. He brings his hand up to feel for wetness.

"Pedro, you just don't understand how the head shed thinks. You haven't been around . . ."

"No. You're right. I'm just a fucking pilot. Then Instructor. Then Chief Instructor on the TriJet. So I don't know shit about the subtleties of vice-presidential intrigue."

"Jesus, Pedro . . ."

Pedro stares at his hand. It is dry.

"Miles – I'm here for a reason, just like you."

Miles stands up.

"I need some shuteye."

Pedro pushes his empty glass level with the empty carafe.

"OK. What the fuck. Goodnight."

§

Ship 201, resplendent in Air Arcadia colours, backs slowly into a parking stand below the third-story window wall. Miles watches as the tug disconnects. The brilliant blue day surrounds him in his lookout, but there is no glare in the room. His eye is caught by a lander on 32 Left. Air Inter. Also a Bus. One of the first, probably. His eye comes back to ship 201. He is going to fly that pretty bird today. Going to be the first to fly it. First Air Arcadia pilot, anyway. Well, except for Pedro.

Miles feels a trickle from his nose and reaches in his pocket for a tissue. Wipes. There is some blood. He turns back to the flight planning room.

"Bonjour, Miles. Where ees he, Pedro? You have seen eem?"

How long has he been here?

"Bonn jour, Jewels. No, now you mention it. Didn't see him at breakfast today."

"C'est pas grave."

Jules walks toward him, his footfall light on the carpet. He is small and elegantly dressed, dwarfed by the twenty-foot ceiling. Miles has trouble imagining him as a pilot. Jules glances at his wrist.

"One hour twenty-two before start. We have time. You have seen zee programme for today, Miles?"

"Yes, thank you. I have a copy."

Miles waves the sheets of paper. Not 8 1/2 by 11, they have an unfamiliar aspect ratio. Centimetres, or something.

"Jewels, I have a question."

"But of course."

"I see our first approaches are visual with autopilot and auto-thrust off."

"Yes. This ees to see she ees really an airplane. Before we get into all zee magique."

"I'd like to see some auto-lands."

"Yes, yes. You will, Miles. As many as you will want."

Jules steps up to the flight planning desk and re-arranges some of the paperwork he has set out. He selects a sheet of sequence reports and offers it to Miles.

"As you can see, mon vieux, we have a perfect day where to begin our work. Passage of cold front. Northwest winds fifteen gusting twenty. Visibilité incroyable. Beau, beau, beau. Later we will do auto-land on one-four right. But not today, évidemment."

"Trying to jigger the schedule, Miles?"

Neither man has noticed his approach. Pedro plunks down his own wad of paper on the chest-level, sloping desk.

"So, how do we start? Maybe CAT III auto-lands with a twenty-knot tailwind?"

"Jesus, Pedro."

"You know, just to see if the airplane can do it? That would show the test pilots a thing or two."

Jules holds up his hands.

"No, no. Eet is fine. I explain to Miles we will do as much as he will want. Later on, when ze wezzaire. . ."

He lowers his hand to shake with Pedro, clapping him on the shoulder with his left.

"Bonjour, copain. Bien dormi?"

"Pas tellement. Je lisais."

"Ooh, dommage." Jules cocks his head. "Comment vas-tu?"

"Oh, ça va aller." Pedro turns to the stack of papers he put on the desk and fishes out a book. "Hey Miles – you read that book I gave you? This one?"

"Yeah. I had a look through it. Pretty technical."

Jules inclines his head again to read the title.

"Ah, oui. Handling the Big Jets. Je le connais. Excellent."

"C'est un Anglais, Jules."

Jules laughs.

"Oui. Mais quand-même, c'est – comment dirait-on? – la Bible du métier."

"Yeah. I was reading it last night, Miles. After our little discussion."

Miles doesn't bite. He is studying the flight plan.

"So Jules. Where is the practice area?"

"West and northwest. Seexty kilomètres."

"I still think we should start with a coupled ILS to 32 Left. It's an automatic airplane. That's how it's going to be used on the line."

"Still putzing around with the schedule, Miles. You should be ashamed."

Miles does his best to ignore Pedro. This airplane is a tool for the airline. It will be used to fly ILS's ninety percent of the time.

"No – I explain. Ees important. You see, Miles, when we use ze auto-thrust we must aware ourselves of ze mode."

"The mode."

"Oui. If you are do an approach eet must be *SPEED* or *OFF*. We start with *OFF*. First you see what ze pilot do, zhen what ze airplane do."

"I told you yesterday, Miles. Captain Asshole. He had his auto-thrust in **IDLE** mode. That's why he pranged. You would do well to listen to our instructor."

It is not only annoying, it is embarrassing. Pedro is fighting with him – and in front of a stranger.

"Excuse me, Pedro. We both work for Air Arcadia and we have a mission to accomplish. Please pull yourself together. If you can't be civil you'll have to recuse yourself."

"Sure. So you can do exactly what you want. So you can take back those lame procedures you've written. Why the hell do you think they sent the two of us in the first place?"

Miles' neck is red. He shrugs.

"The airplane requires a crew of two."

Pedro stares at Miles, his face florid, acne scars showing strongly in whitish relief.

"OK, I'll tell you why they sent us. For you, it was a kindness. They already fired you from that job – director of whatever the fuck it was. This was your chance to stay in the game and demonstrate you could be reasonable. Or maybe it was just thank you for services rendered."

Pedro notices a small trickle of blood from Miles's left nostril. He feels he can taste it.

"Me, it was balance. They know it's all politics to you. That it's all about where you wind up in the company. Me, I'm just a fucking pilot. I think that technical shit is important. I think standards and safety are important. I think it's a matter of fucking life and death."

Pedro pauses for breath. Jules lift his hands.

"Messieurs, messieurs, je vous prie . . ."

"Non, Jules. Je ne vais pas lâcher."

Miles wipes his nose with the back of his hand, but he doesn't look.

"That's outrageous! And here, in front of Jewels!"

The blood is no longer a trickle.

"You want me to back off. To disappear. Well, I'm not going to give you the satisfaction."

Pedro takes a rasping breath and moves closer to Miles, invading his space, face to face.

"I'm going to do what I came here to do and that's to make God damned sure we take back an SOP that's simple and unambiguous and make sure our pilots have the essential knowledge that Jules here is giving us and not let it get diluted by passing through your fucking corporate correctness . . . through your blind, self-seeking fucking . . ."

He stops.

"Ooh, mon dieu."

Jules has looked back to his friend. It is as if nothing has changed, except everything has changed. Pedro's face is slack. The animation that makes Pedro who he is has drained away.

Miles feels the blood running down his neck but he, too, is struck by the larger thing happening to Pedro. Whatever it is, Pedro looks surprised. As they watch, his eyes lose focus and glaze over as the spirit passes from him.

Jules manages to catch him. They both wind up on the floor. Jules hasn't extricated himself.

"Miles. Vite. Téléphone. Zero. Wait for ze tone. Zhen fifteen. One-five. Pass me ze phone."

Jules is still on the floor but he has got his leg out from under Pedro. He lays Pedro's head down gently and grabs the bloody receiver from Miles.

"Merci, Miles. Allo? Secours médicaux?"

Miles looks around at the day streaming in through the slanted windows and the blood on his hands. At last we've got somewhere, he thinks.

It's a Hard Rain

AIRLINE HONCHO

March 28, 2003

Air Arcadia CEO Confident

OTTAWA - Boy Wonder, CEO of Air Arcadia, today responded to questions concerning the government's review of the 'pension holiday' the company has been enjoying during its merger with the former Arcadian Airlines.

"Our pension fund is is excellent shape," Mr. Wonder affirmed. "I am confident the regulator's investigation will confirm, and that the government report will reflect, my confidence in our funding of future obligations."

Cameron

NEWLY SPAWNED RIVERS are coursing down Vancouver streets, overwhelming the drains and finding their way across roads and over curbs. Cameron is waiting for the light at Davie and Granville, vainly trying to stay dry under a canopy that isn't a canopy. The light changes. He runs the last block to the Swamp Pub.

He pushes in through the door and stands there, dripping and peering around the room.

"Sir, I'm afraid we've had to close these tables by the window."

She has reddish hair and freckles. Standing between the brass rails of the waitress station, she points at the water running down the inside of the window and dripping onto the tables and the floor.

"Would you like a seat at the bar?"

Speakers over the bar play celtic music. It is loud enough to almost cover the noise of the water dripping from the window wall and from Cameron himself. Wet, wet as the sea, the dripping coasts. The music is coastal, too, our Maritime music, Arcadia's own Bluegrass, singing of fishing and family and being broken by work, the work we can't do without.

"Or up there if you prefer . . ."

She is a Maritimer, if Cameron has the accent right. She has come three thousand miles from home to find the same salt air and soaking rain.

She gestures up the steps to the right of the bar.

"Cameron! Over here!"

"Rod!"

Cameron has to recover his balance as he looks up, disoriented by Rod's voice. It is the same voice he heard when they met, thirty years ago. Memories flood his thoughts. He stares up the steps at Rod's table.

There's Rod, who he met at St. Hubert before they joined Air Arcadia. And Jean-Luc, who was a student pilot there, a kid earning money by packing groceries at Steinberg's.

Thirty years have slipped by. A year from now Cameron will be sixty and that will be it. Retirement. His career over.

He walks up the three steps. Rod gets up with an easy grace and walks around the table to embrace him.

"Cam! Glad you're here. Hey, where's your F/O? What's the matter – did you piss him off?"

Everyone laughs except the third pilot at the table. Cameron tries not to struggle for the name.

"Yeah, who you wit'?" asks Jean-Luc.

"Trefor. He's up visiting his Dad. Somewhere on Horseshoe Bay. Didn't sound too happy about it, but he hasn't been up there this month and he's had three layovers here."

Rod finishes pouring a glass for Cameron.

"They're separated, right?"

"Tref's parents? Yep. Long time."

"Ouais. C'est la mode. Separate, divorce." Jean-Luc raises an eyebrow, presumably to indicate disgust. "Mes parents n'ont jamais eu de chance, hostie."

"How do you mean?"

It is the third pilot, the First Officer. The name pops into Cameron's head. *Courtley.*

"Mon père 'e drop dead, tabarnac. L'avait quarante-six ans."

"Oh, I'm sorry . . ."

"C'est normal, hostie. 'E work too 'ard. Dey don giv 'im no fuckin' respect. L'a crevé son coeur."

"Sorry . . ."

"C'est ma mère qui nous élevait. Me and de five h'odder."

"You were six kids?"

Jean-Luc laughs.

"'Garde-donc, Courtley. C'était normal dans ce temps-là." He looks around the table with a little smile. "Beside, now it me gonna get divorce."

Rod and Cameron glance at each other and back to Jean-Luc.

"No!"

Jean-Luc laughs again.

"Ouais. She find out."

They are aware of a loud noise at the entrance. Heads turn. Freckles and a dark-haired girl are at the waitress station at the bar, staring at the door.

". . . sure know how to make a guy feel at home. Jesus! And not just like I'm back east, I'm at sea and it's a rough fuckin' day! Beer! You got any beer?"

Cameron can see Freckles is smiling broadly. A dark-haired waitress has joined her. Both girls are edging closer, giggling.

"Must be the Swamp or I'm dreaming – where else would there be two such beautiful girls at the bar? Am I in love or is it just the music?"

Like Bird of Prey and Cubby and Cicero before him, Bad Dog has become a legend.

The girls gesture at an empty seat at the bar beside them. The legend lurches, and like a drowning man grabs one of the brass rails.

"Beer," he says. "Bring me beer."

A strong gust rattles the windows on the side street, calling attention to the wet tables and the water on the floor. Bad Dog gazes in mock horror.

"You're mermaids! Mermaids of the Swamp!"

Of average height and sturdy build, he is not handsome but he radiates force and confidence. More than once the military haircut and the blustering facade have made Cameron think of an officer trying to pass as a Marine Drill Sergeant.

"Shit! Just when I find love in the Swamp."

Bad Dog's piercing yellow eyes have found Cameron's table. He turns back to the girls.

"Sorry, ladies. I see my buddies are here."

Bad Dog bounds up the steps.

"Geez, I'm glad you guys are here to save me. I think I was falling in lust. O, mon hostie de tabarnac – Jean-Luc – c'est-tu possible?"

He waves dismissively at the pitcher of beer on the table.

"What're you guys, a frikkin' tea party? Rod? Cameron? Bloody Anglophones, stands to reason . . . but Courtley – hostie – t'aurais dû mieux soigner ton commando, tabarnac . . ."

The girls are still watching Bad Dog with fascination. He turns to them and holds his right hand aloft with two fingers up, waving them in a circle.

"Bring on the beer!"

He pulls up a chair and sits down.

"Where're you in from? asks Rod.

The answer is a few seconds in coming. Bad Dog has been pouring his first beer from the pitcher already on the table. He chugs it and burps loudly.

"London. Flying with a fuckin' Blue guy. Tried to kill me."

He pours himself another beer and drinks half of it at a gulp.

"I ditched him."

Bad Dog is distracted by Freckles coming up the stairs. She is blushing. He watches with appreciation as she re-arranges the table to make room for two more pitchers of beer. Rod waits until Freckles starts back downstairs to the bar.

"You ditched him?"

Bad Dog inclines his head and puts on a treble voice.

"You going out for supper, Bad?"

It is as if he has a puppet on each hand. He turns back to the Bad Dog puppet and his own voice.

"Oh, I dunno, pretty tired, going to take a nap first. Maybe I'll see you."

He grimaces.

"Nap – are you kidding? After twelve hours in a fuckin' airplane? First priority: dump. A good dump. A mega-dump. I just can't shit right until I re-pressurize, and then . . ."

He chugs the rest of his second pint.

"Beer."

He puts it down.

"It's good we got a party going here. Take my mind off all the crap."

"So what did this Blue guy do?" asks Rod.

Baddy jerks forward.

"Fuck, man, it's more what he didn't do. To be fair, it could happen to anyone, you're so fuckin' tired and punchy after all night over the Atlantic. London gives us a hold and they want 190 knots . . . ennaway, I'm waiting for him to call for flap but he thinks he's light or some shit. Thank God he gets the 190 straight and level, 'cause we're about 12 degrees nose up . . ."

Bad Dog holds up his right hand with thumb and forefinger almost touching.

". . . and we're that far from the shaker, I swear to God – a fuckin' cunt hair away, and so I say – Mr. Diplomacy here, all nice and sweet: Would you like some flap, Jim? Might make the attitude a bit more comfortable."

Bad Dog makes a face.

"What I didn't fucking say was ya better hang something out

before you start your turn or this sucker's gonna stall."

He sits back. Rod shakes his head.

"What did you do?" asks Courtley, eager for gossip.

"Didn't do a fucking thing. See, it's not that I mind the fuckup. I mean, we all fuck up, right? So I give him room. I give him a chance, and – nothing."

Courtley looks blank.

Bad Dog sits forward and puts both elbows on the table.

"My point is that he still hasn't made it right with me. He's had the whole layover, and all day today, and he's never brought it up. That's what pisses me off. So I ditched him."

"Aie, t'es ben sage, toi. I'd 'ave jus' h'ask him where he learn' to fly."

Bad Dog locks eyes with Jean-Luc. They both start to laugh.

"Fuck, it's good to be with you Red bastards," says Baddy. He looks at Cameron. "Say, Cameron. D'ja have a good time last month?"

Cameron chokes on his beer. Jean-Luc claps him on the back.

"That good, eh?" Bad Dog puts his own beer on the table.

Cameron's mind is racing as his face flushes red.

"Ah, you mean, with last month's, um, student?"

"Yeah. Don't worry. We're not going to tell tales out of school." He looks around the table. "You guys aren't here for a minute." He lowers his voice. "Cameron, you know I do some union counselling . . ."

"Yes . . ."

"So, did you spend any time with this guy talking about keeping a low profile?"

"Yes. Hours. Over beer. I called it keeping a thin file."

"Good. Good for you."

Bad Dog waits until the table's attention relaxes, then turns to Cameron and whispers.

"He was really steamed about your making him wear three stripes. Good fuckin' job."

He looks around the table.

"So how's everyone doin'?"

"Ai, là," Jean-Luc snarls. "Da 'ole hairline goin' to shit in a bucket, hostie."

Bad Dog snorts.

"Good to see we're all so keen. How would you anglos say that?"

Cameron takes the bait.

"Ah, maybe, hell in a hand-basket?"

Jean-Luc and Bad Dog laugh. The laugh spreads to the anglos. Bad Dog looks pleased.

"So now we got a quorum, what stupid fuckup are we going to complain about?"

Rod is the first to stop laughing. A cloud comes over his face.

"You guys know Chutzpah, right? I'm worried about her . . ."

"I wouldn't worry about Chutzpah," says Bad Dog. "She's not going to take shit from anybody."

"I know. But last week in Toronto she pulled me aside in the hall. Asked me if dispatch ever hassled me about putting on more fuel."

"Tabarnac, dey 'assle us h'all about fuel."

"That's what I said. But get this: a bigwig from the head shed pulled her into the office and told her they were watching her. That if she knows what's good for her she'd better not make any waves with Dispatch."

"I don' believe dat. Not Boss Boss."

"No. It wasn't Boss. Shit, I'd quit tomorrow if I thought it was Boss Boss. It was some free-floating asshole. You know, not on any airplane? Director of something?"

"Not la Barnacle? Hostie, I tell you, if it was la Barnacle I'll punch 'is fuckin' face . . ."

"No such luck, Jean-Luc. Some other asshole. I just can't believe they'd threaten her. You figure they start with her 'cause she's a woman?"

"I tell you dat's not de woman I would mess wit', hostie."

"So I wonder who else they've been hassling," says Bad Dog. "Do they mess with Training Captains, Cameron? You know, set an example and all that shit?"

"They haven't said anything to me. But I retire in a year. Then they're rid of me."

"Rod?"

"No. Dispatch will always try to argue. It's a pain in the ass. But I get what I want." Rod smiles around the table. "What about you, Baddy?"

Jean-Luc is the first to laugh. Then the whole table is guffawing. Bad Dog takes the opportunity to drain the pint in front of him. He fills it up again from the pitcher.

"I'd like to know who they're hassling," he says. "Because I've heard a few stories. From other airlines, too. Minimum gas. Not a fucking drop extra."

"Why do they want us to carry minimum gas?" Courtney asks.

"Money, moolah," Bad Dog replies. "Gelt."

"How does that save us money?"

"Four percent per hour," offers Cameron. "That's what it costs to carry any weight, including gas."

"Four percent?" Courtley has the blank look again.

"Hostie, Courtley, 'garde donc, c'est sur le plan de vol, tabarnac."

"Pas de blague?" manages Courtley.

"It's called Estimated Zero Fuel Weight Correction." Cameron continues his seminar. "EZFW CORR."

"Courtley," Bad Dog snaps, "For fuck's sake. Just look it up. And report back."

Cameron and Rod are caught between decorum and laughter. They exchange glances.

Rod's hair is mostly grey now. He doesn't look any older, Cameron thinks. But there is a change, something hard to pin down. Maybe it's retirement: when they joined it was purely theoretical. Now it is taking on flesh and rushing toward them.

"Oh, and another thing," says Rod. "Chutzpah says they have a list. I think that's what really pissed me off. Can you imagine having a goddamn list?"

"Who has?" asks Cameron. "What for?"

"Dispatch. They have a list of troublemakers."

"Pilots who want more gas."

"Yeah."

A bitterness has crept into Rod's voice. The table is silent. The drip of rain and conversation from other tables creeps into the foreground.

"How the hell did we get here?"

Cameron is taken aback. This is not the Rod he knows. It is not so much the words as the tone of his voice that has stopped conversation.

"First the strike, then the merger. Now we're losing money hand over fist. The last time anything made sense was when Horace Homer was here."

Cameron breaks the silence.

"Yeah, the strike. Because the Ministry of Movement was making war on the pilots and management knew nothing about it. What a stupid sequence of events. And Miles started it with his brainless procedures."

Cameron's offering sinks like a stone. It is a rare thing. Beer-lathered pilots with their mouths closed. Bad Dog pushes his chair back. It scrapes the floor and shrieks.

"You guys know Bird of Prey?"

"Who's that?" asks Courtley.

"You're too young to know. Retired before you were born."

Rod and Cameron nod. They remember Bird of Prey.

"He's the guy that got me into this business," Bad Dog continues. "Bird took zero shit and didn't give a shit. He flew his way. Somebody did something stupid – which was all the time – he would say, *Should fire the useless fucker. Fire him.* The next generation – his senior First O's – when it was their time they would grumble about erosion of Captain's authority. But Bird had the stuff."

"What about Cam and me?" asks Rod. "His junior F/O's."

Cameron is still trying to parse the question, which seems uncharacteristic to him. Bad Dog snaps back.

"How the fuck should I know? You tell me."

Bad Dog grabs the pitcher, fills the glasses, and waves to Freckles for more. Suddenly his expression changes.

"Fuck, he found me!"

He stands up and beckons at a figure hesitating near the door.

"Jim! Over here!"

Baddy sits down, smiling widely but muttering out of the side of his mouth.

"Well, so much for bitching about Blue guys all night…"

Cameron is curious. He has never flown with a Blue guy, although the airlines have been merged for three years. Maybe he won't have to. He doesn't want to. To feel the clash of the cultures, to try to finesse around it. Something else making it harder to maintain a professional approach on the flight deck.

Jim arrives and is introduced. They find him a chair. Small talk starts up. There are awkward silences.

Suddenly Bad Dog sits up.

"Hey guys, just imagine for a second – I know, it's a stretch – but just gimme a minute and imagine Bad Dog as your president. Bad Dog succeeds Boy Wonder as President of Air Arcadia. *What would I do?* you're asking."

Courtley leans over to pick up a peanut.

"You're not going to eat that, are you?

Courtley drops the peanut.

"Ennaway, what I wouldn't do is have all these chicken shit little airlines running around pretending NOT to be Air Arcadia. I mean, for Christ's sake – Twist, Snap, and Jive – that's not airlines, it's fucking deodorants."

Boy Wonder has dreamed up Twist, Snap, and Jive to be the no-frills leisure carrier, the low-cost point-to-pointer, and the collection of regional carriers.

Bad Dog is working himself up into a rant. There is colour in his cheeks.

"I mean, for fuck's sake, look at Starbucks expanding into Arcadia.

They're all over the world and they make the most expensive coffee known to man. But it's not the best coffee. Tim's is the best fucking coffee!"

As it gathers steam his rhetoric recalls that of Cicero, prankster and brawling drunk, now long retired.

"Tim's is fucking breakfast central. Tim was a hockey player and Arcadians love hockey, so we're loyal. Tim's is a fucking national monument, like Mount Rushmore to the Yanks. I don't care where you are or what time of the day it is when you're going to work, you can always stop at Tim's and get real coffee and muffins. Not this designer shit."

"So what does dat 'ave to do wit' . . ." interrupts Jean Luc.

"Aie, donnes-moi une minute, hostie . . ."

Bad Dog pauses to allow the drip of rain outside to be heard again.

"We're loyal. We LOVE Tim. So does Tim try to be Starbucks?"

He looks around the table.

"NO!" he roars.

People at other tables are looking at him.

"Of course not. Tim's are the best at what they do."

Jim nods. He looks more relaxed.

"So as our president, I think I can rest my case," Baddy concludes. "Just do what you're good at. Just keep on being the best fucking airline in Arcadia."

The sound outside has become more of a roar than a dripping. Jim speaks up.

"Bad, do you think that's Boy Wonder's business plan?"

Bad Dog's manic mien vanishes.

"You mean, it sure as fuck isn't that best airline in Arcadia shit."

Jim sighs. He looks like an accountant, but no one feels like laughing.

"Well, yeah . . ."

There is a gap in the exchange, as if Baddy can't get his breath.

"It's OK, Jim. We're not going to take offence. So he doesn't give a flying fart about our being the best airline? I hear you." Baddy takes his breath. "But what does he want? What does the fucker want?"

"Could be it has nothing to do with our interests. Or even with the company's interest."

Cameron finds himself staring at Jim. He glances across the table. Bad Dog looks like he has just swallowed an insect on a dare. He swallows again like a dog trying to keep something down.

"Fuck! I was just thinking of my brother."

"Tabarnac, you never tole me dere's anodder Dog, hostie!" Jean-Luc chortles.

"Oh, fuck off, Pepsi. Gimme a chance."

"What does your brother do?" asks Rod.

"He's an uneducated, jumped-up Pepsi. Just like me. But he's a craftsman."

"Il fait quoi?"

"Bain, il peut tout faire. Flooring. Plumbing. Moldings. Installation. He does it all and he does it well. Because he loves it. He couldn't do a fuckin' shoddy job if he tried. So two years ago, he's hired by this design company. Mostly kitchens and bathrooms. They have the latest Computer Aided Design software and connections with dealers and all that shit. But when my brother comes along they've got all these fucked-up installations. So my brother starts to work with these guys they've got, and they're not bad guys, but they're labourers, not tradesmen. You know, give me fifteen bucks an hour and tell me what to do."

"Et quinze minutes pour un café puis un smoke."

"Oui. Exact. So he winds up trying to train these guys. Some times it works, some times it doesn't." Bad Dog nods his head toward Cameron. "The Training Captain can tell you about that. Still, he saves their sorry asses. And for a couple of years it's perfect. He can do good work and not worry about money."

"The company does well?" Rod asks.

"Yeah. They're up to three, four installer teams. My brother has bought a big house in the West Island."

"So what happens?" asks Cameron. He is trying to put this together with what Jim said.

"They lay him off," replies Bad Dog. "Fire his ass. He's the first to go. 'Cause he makes the most money. Then the guys he's trained."

"I don't get it," says Rod. "Doesn't the company depend on those installations not being screwed up?"

"You know, we're all a bunch of dumb shits," says Bad Dog. "I didn't get it. My brother didn't get it. It was my brother's wife figured it out."

"So don't 'old h'us in suspense, hostie."

"They're going to sell. They build up the business. It looks great. Then they trim back expenses. Get a year when the balance sheet looks great. Then they unload the company."

Jim the accountant nods.

"Yes," he says. "Extract the value after it's already gone."

The rain on the window is suddenly deafening. In their table's unaccustomed silence it is as if people at other tables, too, have stopped talking. Freckles and the dark-haired girl are struggling with the water downstairs. The world feels fragile.

"It has nothing to do with our being a good airline," Cameron ventures. He feels like he has been punched in the stomach.

"I don't know – don't get me wrong – but, maybe," says Jim.

"Fuckin' A," says Bad Dog.

The rain sounds like a speaker: a big woofer connected to a powerful amplifier. The input has just gone open and there is a powerful hum. Now the hum starts modulating in waves: wet waves, attacking the windows.

"We're doing what we do," says Rod. "We don't control the world."

"Brother," says Bad Dog, "We didn't in Bird's day. Firing or not firing whichever asshole it was."

A sudden gust blows a wave of rain down Davie. It looks like surf. The Swamp Pub is a frail ship.

Strike!

Montreal – September, 1998

Cameron

IT IS ONE OF THOSE DAYS Montrealers have in mind when they say September is the best month. Air sings in the lungs at each breath. The sun is warm on bare arms. Cameron walks up the circular drive, aware of each blade of grass. The grass fades as he looks up.

Bruno is holding a clipboard and blocking access to the school. There are more papers and folders on the card table behind him.

"You gotta sign in. Even though I know who you are, Cameron. Security."

"That's new . . ."

"Well, we can't take any chances. There's lots of press around. I gotta see your card. Write down your number. Then you get this . . ."

Bruno holds up a badge. It has Cameron's name, rank, and aircraft, as well as today's date.

Cameron takes out his wallet. He is embarrassed by how long it takes him to dig out his card. He looks furtively at the line forming behind him.

"Don't worry, Cam. Everyone's the same. But if you don't mind I think I'll give a heads-up to the guys in line."

"Sure . . ."

"OK, guys. Listen up. You'll make this process much faster if you get out your union cards and have 'em ready to show me."

Cameron signs the attendance sheet and Bruno hands him a 5 ½ x 8-inch manila envelope full of papers. He wanders down the hall to the gym. It is already half-full. Cameron finds an empty folding chair about half-way back on the right wall. The first sheet in the envelope explains today's security. Cameron's eye is caught by the last paragraph: it asks each member to be alert to the people around him in the room. To check the badge of anyone he doesn't know personally. To challenge anyone who seems suspicious.

Then there is a three-page analysis of why they are considering the present action. Cameron scans it. Yes, there it is, among other bullet points: recurrent Simulator failures.

"Messieursdames. Ladies and gentlemen. Votre attention s'il vous plaît. Your attention please. My name is Born Leader. I'm your Master Executive Council chairman. There is a lot to cover today, so let's get moving. We'll start with a look at the agenda for today's meeting. You can see there is time planned for your questions and comments. If there is a point you want to bring up, please line up behind the microphone in the center aisle. I would ask you to keep your comments brief."

§

"My name is Doug Fields. I'm a Captain on the Bus. The Ministry Of Movement is failing guys on the Bus for the flimsiest of reasons. Just the Bus, not the other airplanes. I haven't failed a ride yet, but my friends all tell me that it is just a matter of time. I'd like to point out how stupid that is. Our competence and our confidence are assets. The company is just pissing it all away."

The room comes alive with murmurs, then breaks into applause. Doug's cheeks redden slightly as he returns to his seat. The next speaker takes his place at the microphone.

"Hey. Fern Enthuser. Captain on the BigTwin. You Bus guys are just a bunch of wimps. If you don't want to fail all the time, why don't you just bid a real airplane?"

A deadly silence falls. Still, Fern looks satisfied as he regains his seat.

"Jean Luc. Premier Officier sur le Bus, et je vais le dire en englais. If you can add, you gonna see dere are more of us Bus guys, hostie. Votez oui! Vote yes on da strike!"

There is a chorus of grunts, whispers, and scattered applause.

The next speaker drones on in French, making his point several times over. Born Leader waits politely until he pauses for breath.

"C'est certain, Louis. Je dirai qu'ils seront pas nombreaux qui ne sont pas d'accord avec toi. But perhaps you could yield the mike to the next speaker ..."

"Oui. Oui. Merci."

Louis makes his way back to his seat. His seat-mates stare straight ahead.

Born Leader is good at keeping the meeting on track. The line at the microphone gets shorter. Soon it is time for the wrap up. Here, too, the chairman doesn't waste time.

"In your handout you'll find everything you need to vote on-line. The computers at Air Arcadia Pilots Association Headquarters are ready to go. The deadline is midnight tonight. Ladies and gentlemen, by tomorrow at this time we could be on strike."

§

The union office in the terminal building has never been so full of

29

pilots. They crowd around a church-basement table loaded with cartons of donuts and a large coffee urn.

"Moaner. D'you buy all this for us?"

"Sure. I do you guys a favour once in a while."

The door to the inner office rattles, then opens abruptly.

"A-shift. Line A. We're on duty in ten minutes."

Pilots with coffees make space for Bad Dog. His uniform is pressed and spotless; his shoes glow with spit-shine, the creases in his trouser legs are as sharp as he is in the cockpit. His voice is big.

"We're going to line up for inspection. Outside in the hall."

He opens the door. Steps out. Looks up and down the hall.

"All clear. OK, lose the coffees. Get your hats. Line up along this wall."

Pilots line up for the wastebasket, taking a last chug or two. Brush themselves off. Straggle out the door to find a place along the wall.

"Tu n'a pas compris, Jean-Luc? On n'est pas ici pour bavarder, hostie."

Jean-Luc gives the Sergeant a sheepish grin and gets into the line beside Cameron. They are stretched along the inside wall of the fourth-floor hall, shoulder to shoulder.

"The order doesn't matter, guys. Just do it. Stand straight. Eyes front. We're not going to go downstairs and look like fuckheads."

The military guys try to bring it back. Cameron tries to remember movies he has seen about the military.

"Rod – what part of eyes front do you not fucking understand?"

Rod straightens up and looks at the wall.

". . . and the hat. Lose the lean."

Rod straightens his hat.

"You're not Captains in this line. There is no seniority. There is no authority except for yours truly. Understood?"

"Yes."

"Yeah."

"OK."

Baddy swaggers down the line. He stops in front of Cameron, who is doing his best to stand straight and look at the wall.

"Cameron!"

"Yes?"

"Yes WHAT?"

Cameron combs desperately through his experience.

"YES SIR," he says, as loudly as he dares.

"Fucking right."

Bad Dog continues down the line, stopping momentarily in front of anyone showing the least sign of sloppiness or attitude.

"In five minutes we are going downstairs. We will be in public view. We may be on TV. We will look at no one. We will speak to no one. We will look straight ahead and walk."

He paces the line some more.

"You have no doubts."

Cameron's mind fills with his own doubts. *We're not doing this for our customers. Not for the company, that's for sure. Even our fellow employees. No matter their solidarity. They're just laid off without pay and they get nothing. This is for us.*

"Not in this line."

He's right. No doubts. Banish the doubts.

Bad Dog continues his pacing.

"You will speak only to me, and only if addressed. I will speak to the public and the media only if absolutely necessary and refer all questions to Born Leader."

He continues walking the line and looking us in the eyes, daring us to look at him or to look aside, daring us to loose our focus on the far wall.

"Born Leader is our spokesman. Our only spokesman. Understood?"

The hall sounds like an echo chamber.

"Yes es ss sir essir!"

Baddy paces to the head of the line and turns.

"You will follow me down the stairs. When I give the signal we will march directly to the designated area. It is about 40 feet. You will follow me around the circle. We will be marching counter-clockwise as seen from above. The perimeter is marked with small x's of red tape on the floor. When I step aside you will close the gap and keep walking."

He has his hand on the knob of the stairway door.

"After ten minutes I will join you and call a halt. I will give the order for about face. You will pivot on your left heel. I will call, *Line A, march*. Then we will be marching clockwise. Our shift is thirty minutes. Any questions?"

Silence. Baddy opens the door.

"LINE A, MARCH!"

§

It is hard work. People are watching. With eyes front you catch only glimpses of your surroundings. You can't look, so you think harder. You ignore the fixed stuff and try to remember the new stuff flashing by in your peripheral vision.

Bad Dog is marching alongside Cameron.

"LINE A, HALT!"

"LINE A, ABOUT . . . FACE!"

Cameron pivots. *Shit, left heel! At least I didn't collide with Bad Dog.*

"LINE A, MARCH!"

Something is happening about twenty feet away, over toward the elevators. A media scrum is developing around Born Leader. There are tripods with extensions and TV lights on top. A boom mike is being wielded by a guy in navy blue sweats and sneakers. *Just keep marching. Don't look.*

Suddenly the lights come on and bathe the scrum in washed-out white light. Born Leader is being interviewed. There is an occasional flash from a still camera.

After what seems like no time at all, the bright lights are out. *Wow, those TV interviews are short. But he'll come across. In whichever official language.* Line A continues the clockwise march. Cameron tries to sneak a peek at the clock.

My feet hurt. How much longer?

Cameron is aware of a solitary flash behind him. He glances over at the guys coming the other way. They are looking around, losing the eyes front discipline. Another flash.

As he rounds the second right turn the TV lights come on again and he is looking straight ahead at Boy Wonder.

Cameron has to turn right again. Behind him in line, where Cameron was twenty seconds ago, Rod catches the moment, his head held proudly straight.

Maybe Rod can fill in the blanks for me. Boy Wonder out here on the Departures Level of the Terminal? What is he, VP of Inflight Service?

Bad Dog is marching alongside Cameron again.

Left heel.

"LINE A, HALT!"

"LINE A, ABOUT ... FACE!"

Cameron pivots on his left heel. It feels good. He has managed to be at one with his brothers in arms.

"LINE A, MARCH!"

Only ten minutes to go.

The lights are out. The media people have got what they want.

The last ten minutes are long. Nothing is happening. Finally Bad Dog is back, walking with them. Cameron stays in line as it leads him out of the circle and back to the stairs. They climb, thinking of coffee and donuts.

Voices

Montreal – October, 1998

Boy Wonder

THE NEW CEO PACES his still unfamiliar corner office. He feels like he has been thrown to the dogs.

It has been his life's ambition to run an airline and here he is and this is all he wants to do. Run it as best he can, just as Horace did. But Horace didn't have this life-threatening force bearing down on him. Horace didn't have Ziggy Birnbaum and the Jade corporation trying to take it all away the minute he stepped into the job.

I am real, you know.

Boy peers out the big northwest windows, toward 24R. Nothing. Just heat shimmers above the runway.

Horace did a heck of a lot in his five years. But he also had opportunity in that bilateral. He saw the opportunity and he took it. He brought this company into the modern age.

Boy! Puppy! Listen!

Panhandle Pete had it right, back then, talking to Congress. What'd he say? *It will be a goddamn miracle if anyone makes any money in this business ever again.* Something like that. His foresight didn't stop the U.S. Congress from de-regulating the airlines, though. And we haven't made any money since, not any of us, at least not for more than a month or two and anyway it's been one at the expense of the others, a zero-sum game or worse. Yeah, he saw it, all right. He saw the bankruptcies. Except he didn't mention the frenzy of mergers and acquisitions, all supposedly in service of those elusive profits. Those profits are gone. And now Horace is gone too.

So is Father. But I am here, Boy. Talk to me.

Boy stares determinedly at 24R. He walks out to the corner of the room, where the windows meet, and looks northeast. A Boing BigTwin is over the approach lights.

I'm hearing things. Do I go to a doctor?

He watches the flare, the core exhaust from the JT9-D's joining and augmenting the heat shimmer on the runway. He waits while the puffs of smoke from the tires drift away.

I haven't got time. Besides, it's too risky.

Boy wheels around, challenging the office space.

"OK, I'm talking. And I feel like a fool. Who are you?"

The room is stubborn, unyielding. Boy sits down behind his desk, thinking how he will arrange the office.

Arcadia, Boy. I am called Arcadia.

Boy sits still, looking at his hands on the desk.

I am the airline.

"And you can speak to me?"

Boy says it in his head; he tries not to move.

Yes, Boy. I speak to all my presidents. I always have. Sometimes they hear. I still talk to Father.

He thinks over what he knows: the 1930's, the beginning of Trans Arcadia Air Lines.

"Your father – the Minister of Everything."

Yes.

Boy sighs. There is too much to do.

I knew about the debt. I saw how Southern Gentleman let it creep up in his two years at the helm. Heck, the stock price is half of what it was a year ago. I'm ready to deal with that. But this Jade thing? It came out of left field. A takeover bid? In my first month here?

And I don't know my way around the government up here. Not well enough, anyway. I need help. I'll start with Larry Tennyson, our legal guy. He's Arcadian born and bred.

You miss Horace, don't you?

"Yes. But I knew he was going to go."

Southern was supposed to be here longer. Isn't that so?

"Yes. The strike. It came out of the blue."

It blindsided us all. But it was my opportunity. Sure, it was too soon. But who ever said this would be easy sailing? The job is a test, everyone knows that. Hell, life is a test. And now I'm hearing voices.

Just me, Boy. You hear me because I am real.

Do I have to answer? She said *sometimes they hear.* Maybe I'll be one of those who doesn't.

I'm not sure that's what you want.

And why not? Why the hell would I hear if I had a choice?

We're in crisis, Boy. Southern didn't hear me.

Starry Skies was brilliant. Worldwide consortium of airlines. Southern was right to join. Now the whole world has our back.

You don't screw around with Air Arcadia, boys. Starry Skies gonna mess with you. Gotta keep that in mind. Things are global now.

Boy looks around. The office is reassuringly real.

Except there's also the other consortium. World Unity. World Unity and Starry Skies, battling it out for world dominance. God, the arrogance of our business world. Wonder what Panhandle thinks about that. I'd love to go down to Texas to one of his barbeques. Chat a bit. Just don't have time. Besides, that would just be fun and he knows Congress but he doesn't know the government up here.

You can chat with me.

"You said Southern didn't hear you. Who did? Besides your father?"

Ben, sometimes. Chauncey, often. And Horace. Bless him.

It's hot. Boy loosens his tie, shifts in his chair. Think about what's different in Arcadia. The Forward Party and the Backward Party. Crown Corporations becoming publicly traded companies. The Ministry of Movement with its finger in many more of our pies than the FAA down down south. And Minister of Movement David Punctilious. There's something about that sucker. Gotta be careful. Can't run my airline fighting him.

Otis Lemming took my Ben away.

Otis Lemming. Another Minister of Movement. That's history. Took my Ben? Ben Plat, she means.

Boy grabs the thick binder and checks the index. He leafs through. December, 1975. Ben Plat eased into retirement. He reads. Closes the binder with a sigh.

Be careful of MOM, Boy.

But Air Arcadia has always been the darling of the Forward Party. Carrying the mail. Carrying the Members of Parliament back and forth to their ridings. Joining this vast country together, and all that nonsense. Except – is that still the way it is?

There was a clue two weeks ago. Minister Punctilious was carefully circling the subject without really saying anything, as only he can. Baffling the people and the press. At the time it seemed like the Government was going to let Pacific Airlines International, the Proud Goose, go down in flames. Let their debt drag them down, out of the picture. Leave us to compete with BestJet.

Boy drags out another binder. Finds the text of the speech.

Reading it again it is obvious. *Made in Arcadia solution.* That's the clue. He's a politician. Is he going to let good Arcadian jobs vanish on his watch? Hell, no. Momma Minister is gonna get in the picture, break up the fight, impose some truce that pisses us all off. Made in Arcadia.

But not for Arcadia.

Yeah. See what she means. Not for her. And Ziggy Birnbaum was in on it. Shit! Ziggy is hooked in to the Forwards. He's got Patriot's money behind him and all of World Unity's, for that matter. Hell, Ziggy and his Jade Corporation are just a front for that money, the Arcadian face of it, so Punctilious can either look the other way or change the law. So much for the Forwards covering our back.

They used to. In Father's day.

"Yeah. So who can be trusted? "

You can trust me.

Pub Story

Vancouver – January, 2000

Rod

ALBERTA'S SNOWY LANDSCAPE is still visible through the cockpit windows, but the Rockies a hundred miles ahead are not. Instead a wall of cloud greets Air Arcadia 129 as an occluded front creeps through the Okanagan, over Banff, and down the foothills.

"So if we get in through all this muck, Ramrod, where will you drag my old bones for a drink?"

Rod returns from his reverie into the presence of his old friend. He has been basking in the warmth of it, the pleasure of flying with Brendan again for the first time in thirty years.

"I thought you were going to drag me. Isn't the F/O responsible for that part of the operation?"

"Jasus, old man. You forget that I'm new at this airline thing. I'm not yet intimate with every pub in every town."

"Well, I'm ruling out the Beer Garden. On your behalf, by the way. Plenty of pilots, but no Guinness on draft."

"Yes, I see. Although it's possible I could perhaps be persuaded to . . ."

". . . go without? When there are any number of places . . . hey, what about that place Cameron took you? On your line indoc."

"Oh yes. Down in Yaletown. But it was summer. We sat outside."

"Not gonna do that tonight."

"No."

It is almost time to pay attention. The Top Of Descent arrow is approaching.

"Perhaps you'd like to check my handiwork, Ramrod. I don't want a mistake of mine distracting you in this weather."

In answer Rod calls up the FLT PLN page on his MCDU. Booth 5 STAR. ILS 08L. He flips over to FLT PLN page A. All the STAR constraints are there: VITEV at or below FL 210; LANNE at or below 16000, BASRA at 230 Kts or less. Brendan has added constraints at each waypoint to reflect the Minimum Enroute Altitude for that segment.

"Nice. Thank you, Brendan."

"My pleasure, old man. Still, I'm curious to see how you're going to separate the Cumulo-Nimbus from the Cumulo-Granite on the radar."

Rod chuckles and turns on the radar, adjusting it to catch the mountain tops. He flips through the RAD NAV page and the FUEL PRED page and the PERF CRUISE page. Just for fun, he hits the DES FORECAST prompt. Brendan has wind entered at four different levels, including four thousand feet where they are likely to be on downwind.

"Wow, look at these winds. How they back around. Not east until we get down to four."

"Yes. I played with the cabin descent rate. I hope you don't mind."

Rod glances over. 280 feet per minute.

"I thought, with the restrictions and all, why not even it out?"

Rod looks more closely at the predicted crossing altitudes. A couple are very close to the restrictions.

"Very cool."

Rod picks up the ATIS: 200 Broken, 300 Overcast, visibilty 3/8 mile in moderate rain and snow, temperature 2, dew point 1, wind 110/18G24, altimeter 28.91, ILS 08L, CAT II operations in progress. RMKS CLG RGD. He glances back at the four thousand foot wind: 160/45. He interpolates and makes up a number to keep in his head for base leg: 140/40. Base leg will be at three, or maybe descending to two, depending on traffic. They will be on vectors, but it's nice to have an idea ahead of time.

He presses the EGAD Status button. All systems are go.

"Nice job, Brendan. You'll have to be careful, though – people might think you're a geek."

Brendan looks over to see Rod grinning at him.

"Ah, Jasus, Ramrod. You know I'd show off for no one but yourself."

Laughing, Rod launches into his approach briefing.

". . . we may be picking our way around some buildups out over the water, by the look of it. And with the viz at 3/8 we'll set up and brief for a CAT II, just in case. But if we have the appropriate visuals before hundred above I'll disconnect and do a manual landing, just so you can blame me. Config 3. Autobrake LO. Normal reverse. And let's remember the altimeter is two eight nine one. Let's enjoy this then we can go drink beer."

"I'll call a hundred above and Decision. Indeed: 28.91. And amen."

"Here comes Top Of Descent."

Rod sweeps his right fist down, thumb pointed at the throttles.

"Descent, please. And Pre-Descent Check."

§

As expected, they are held at eight thousand until BASRA, just east of English Bay. Then they have to get down in a hurry. There is no one ahead of them and Approach is anxious to get them turned in.

"Air Arcadia 129, cleared to three thousand, slow to 180 when reaching."

Rod pulls the speedbrake handle back and calls for Flap 1. In his head is the VFR view: the mound of the Simon Fraser campus sliding beneath them; Belcarra and all of Indian Arm off their right wing; downtown and English Bay ahead. The engine and airframe anti-ice are on. Out of six thousand the turbulence begins in earnest. It is not eyeball bounce intensity, but close. Rod turns his display lighting up a notch. He visualizes the mountain tops north of the city rising above them: Mt. Seymour, Grouse Mountain. The radar is contouring these and others, to the right of track. There are a few similarly-contouring blobs on the track.

"You were right, Brendan. Tell him we will deviate three miles south of track at VARSY. Oh, and if he wants to turn us in from three south of track, that's OK. Big south wind here. Flap 2."

They are skirting the blob at VARSY, levelling at three. Suddenly there is a burst of heavy, noisy precip.

"What the heck is it? Not hail, I don't think."

Brendan inspects his windshield wiper bolt.

"It's Jasus slush, Ramrod. Flyin' fockin' slush."

"Air Arcadia 129, descend two thousand, slow to 160, turn left heading 150."

"Gear down, Landing Check."

"Air Arcadia 129, turn left heading 110 to intercept, cleared ILS

CAT II 08L, hold 160 to DULKI.”

“We’re gonna be inside DULKI, but that’s OK. LOC alive. LOC. Flap 3.”

“Flaps 3, Vapp 139.”

“Glideslope.”

“Air Arcadia 129, tower at DAWG one one niner dezimal fife fife.”

“Roger. Air Arcadia 129, tower at DAWG. See ya.”

Rod waves his thumb over the throttles.

“By the DAWG. Love that. Dawg.”

“Air Arcadia 129 by DAWG.”

“Air Arcadia 129, Vancouver Tower, cleared to land runway 08L, altimeter two eight eight niner, wind one one zero at two zero gusting two eight, RVR 2600, lights strength fife.”

“Roger Air Arcadia 129, cleared to land runway 08L, two eight eight nine, OK, Dawg was 1320, altimeter two eight eight nine, Missed Approach 2000 set.”

It is still rough. But the ceiling is indeed ragged; whitecaps are intermittently visible. One of the log booms flashes by underneath. Then the vista begins to open out. With their almost ten degrees of drift, it would be quite disorienting to the unprepared.

Rod already has his head turned ten degrees left. He glances up. A pretty picture.

“Autopilot Off.”

The cricket chirps. *Bleet bleet bleet.*”

“Roger. Hundred Above.”

“Roger.”

“Decision.”

"Visual. Landing."

Brendan gets his eyes inside to cover Rod. The LOC and Glideslope are still nailed. He looks up. In one motion that seems unrelated to the turbulence, Rod flares, pushes the nose smoothly left to line up, and lowers the right wing a few degrees. The power comes off. The attitude is as if frozen. The touchdown is announced by a slight settling as the spoilers come up. Brendan glances down at the wheels page. It is true. Ten little green arrows point upwards from ten little lines: the five spoilers on each wing.

Rod selects reverse. Brendan moves his eyes to the upper screen.

"Reverse Green."

Rod selects a moderate reverse thrust, more by sound than numbers. The decel light blinks a few times and stays on, indicating that 80 percent of the LO BRK deceleration target has been reached.

"70."

Rod is already moving the reverse slowly to idle. The Autobrake eases in, maintaining the target 5.6 ft/sec/sec deceleration rate.

"Air Arcadia 129, first high-speed if able, contact Ground one two seven dezimal one fife."

"Well, Ramrod, 'twill be my own self buyin' tonight. That was a work to behold."

§

"You know, we might try this place, Brendan."

They are on their way to Yaletown, walking through the wet and slush. A couple of blocks south of Granville, a Guinness sign hangs in a window.

"Must be new. Never seen this place before. The Swamp Pub. What do you think?"

"Guinness, sure enough."

"We'll stop for a beer. See if they have food."

"Command decision, Ramrod. After you, old man."

§

The L-shaped bar is someone's very fine handiwork. A medium-dark wood with a beautiful grain pattern glows under the coasters. A set of draught pulls sprouts from the bar to their right. Pints of Guinness and Okanagan Pale sit half-empty in front of them.

Rod takes a sip of his Okanagan and catches the bar girl's eye. He moves two fingers in a circle.

"Jasus, Ramrod. Get me far enough into the pints and I won't be needin' me supper."

"No fear, Brillo. We'll eat after this."

He gestures to their right. At end of the other wing of the bar three steps lead up into a larger room where food is being served.

"We can even take these up, if you like."

"Sure and maybe. But let's be done with the subject, such as is is. You were sayin'?"

Rod sighs.

"Whatever I say about Enrico will be too much. But with you, Brendan . . ."

Brendan waits him out.

"Well, I have to admit I was surprised. Not because I didn't think he could do it. He can do very well if he puts his mind to it. But I knew they were gunning for him, is all."

"Yes."

"And they send him out with Ice Pick . . ."

"Yes. Do you know the man?"

47

"Yeah. He was on our course. Good guy and all, but . . ."

"Tough?"

"You mean as a checker?"

Brendan nods.

"Yeah. I would think so. Serious type."

"Takes himself seriously, perhaps?"

Rod snorts.

"Yeah. Not a lot of laughs."

The music has been subliminal until now. Somehow the song intrudes. It is Stan Rogers singing *Make and Break Harbour*. The beauty of the old ways, and their passing, catches both men at the throat. The image of the Cape Islander, tacking for home on a fair breeze but with an empty hold. And the singer.

"Borne away with the cod, he was."

"What, Brendan?"

"Stan. By our own airline."

"Yeah."

The song ends. *Old nets hung to dry.*

Brendan drains his pint and pushes it to the back of the bar. He pulls the new one closer on its coaster, an outsized cargo on a small barge.

"My turn to say too much, now."

He inspects the head on his new Guinness.

"Pretty, is it not?"

Brendan puts his pint back on the coaster. A trace of foam remains on his upper lip.

"I heard from an old friend, Ramrod. Derek. Military. After your time. Mechanic. Good one, too."

"He called you?"

"Yes. The day before we left on this cycle."

An Acadian fiddle tune begins. It seems to re-energize Brendan.

"Thing is, I have never heard him so upset. He poured his heart out to me."

Brendan takes a gulp from his Guinness.

"You see, Derek joined our airline before I did. Based in Calgary. Has family there. Always been an Albertan. So Cold Lake was sort-of home, as well. Anyway . . ."

Brendan tells the story. It is a sad one. Rod shakes his head in disbelief.

"So the ELAC he installed was unserviceable?"

"Just so."

Rod looks stricken.

"You're right of course, Brendan. It's buried. Ninety-nine percent. Enrico passed. He's not going to spill anything. And as for Ice Pick . . ."

"He could lose his job. As could anyone who was in it with him."

"Yeah. Still, Derek has nothing to worry about."

"Agreed. But that was no comfort to the poor man. I told him he would keep his job and his suffering was a message from Our Lord. When he had pondered on it sufficiently he would be absolved."

Their pints sit empty in front of them. Rod twirls his glass.

"Brendan – don't you feel it? That something has gone?"

"Our integrity. As a group."

Brendan pushes his coaster and its empty cargo to the back of the bar.

"Jasus. As an airline, when it comes to that."

Rod waits.

"Well, then. When one of us tears the fabric, it doesn't stop there. T'would take a great leader to put up new canvas or sew up the wound."

"So Brendan. Is Boy Wonder up to it? Is he that leader?"

"Smart he is, that's sure enough. And well intentioned, I believe."

Brendan pushes back his stool.

"But I fear not, Ramrod. Shall we go eat?"

Ignorance is Death

Cold Lake, Alberta – June, 1970

Rod

AT SEVEN HUNDRED THIRTY KNOTS the east practice area is a blur. He eases up to clear the last hill on the low-level run. Trees flash by underneath.

That's it for the day. Rod pulls the nose further skyward, still in afterburner. What a boot in the butt! He is tempted to keep it lit and point her straight up but that is not his mission today. He pulls the throttle out of the burner gate and rolls the wings vertical into knife-edge flight and lets the nose fall to the horizon. Rolling level he pins her at 6000 feet on a 260 heading and calls Cold Lake for landing.

"Blue Two, turn left two two zero."

"Blue Two, heading two two zero."

"I'm setting you up for a right base 31R, Ramrod. You gonna be OK with that?"

"Blue Two, affirmative."

Now the problem is to lose energy quickly enough. Thrust idle.

She's still a dart, just whistling along, well above her max lift/drag speed. Rod pulls up and climbs a couple of thousand feet to convert some of that kinetic energy to potential energy. It is enough to slow him to V_{FE}, Flap Speed. He selects flap to the middle notch, T/O Lndg, and puts the gear down through slowing through V_{LO}.

Now she's as slow as you want to get without Boundary Layer Control and sinking like a stone. Rod is thinking *take final flap at least 1500 above ground to get the BLC working early* and counting seconds in his head to figure the lead he needs for spool-up time and thinking *shit this is when you really don't want that afterburner nozzle to stick open*, when it happens.

His hand is on the flap lever and the windshield is suddenly full of prairie and brush. Because he has rehearsed this and only because, he knows what this is and what to do. He snaps the flap lever up, out of the back notch and into the middle notch. He slams the throttle forward past the burner gate. He is not quite inverted so he goes back the way he came, using right aileron and rudder until he has blue above. He pulls the nose up and retracts gear and flaps. He starts to breathe again as he punches through ten thousand feet climbing like a rocket.

"That was a pretty good show, Ramrod. You OK?"

"Cold Lake, Blue Two had a BLC failure. Gonna need to set up for a partial flap landing."

"Blue Two, Roger that. 31R is yours, Ramrod. Take all the room you need."

Rod can feel his heart pounding as he thinks through the landing. No BLC on the left side, obviously, so he'll use the T/O Lndg position on the flaps and a speed 40-50 knots above normal. Drag chute, for sure, but wait for the chute's max speed. It's going to be tight.

He is heading east to give himself plenty of room and plenty of time. His eye has caught that hill at the end of the low-level run where he was just minutes ago and his thought *start the right turn* doesn't have a chance to form before the fireball blooms.

"Cold Lake, Blue Two. Got a fireball out here at the end of the run. Don't see a 'chute."

§

The mess is half empty, even though Friday evening is well in progress. Rod looks around. Perhaps it is the fine June weather and the long light keeping pilots outdoors, admiring the sky. He walks slowly through the room.

At once he is aware of the kinky copper hair, glowing in the light of the low-angle sun. Brillo has his back to him.

Rod approaches the table.

"Brendan, I'm sorry about Kozy."

His friend jerks upright in his chair as if startled from a dream. Rod touches his shoulder.

"I know you guys were on course together in Moose Jaw."

Brendan jerks his shoulder away. His chair scrapes the floor.

"Dammit, Ramrod!"

His voice is strangled, awkward.

"Accidents are shit! Can you not let a man mourn?"

Rod takes a step back and lets a few moments pass. The fire dies down. He nods at Brendan.

"Hey, I'll get us a beer."

Rod strolls away toward the bar. His withdrawal leaves a hollow feeling in Brendan's chest. It has been the week from hell.

Normally TGIF at the Officers' Mess is a landmark in Brendan's week, something he looks forward to. And not just for the beer.

Sure, he does like his ale, but . . .

Monday. Kozy clips the trees at 480 knots. Blizzard of paperwork, brass on his case. Monday Monday. Brendan shudders.

. . . it's not the beer, it's his people, the pilots of 417 Squadron. At the end of the week he can step outside of rank and enjoy them. Forget the brass and the paper. But tonight . . .

Monday Monday. Can't trust that day. Ramrod is my best instructor. What would I do if he . . .

Suddenly Brendan knows what he is feeling. He puts his hands on the edge of the table and pushes himself upright. *Fool. You're a fool. Kozy wasn't the first. Rod was the first and he survived.*

Death and non-death in one day. Both have pulled him to pieces. A friend gone and a friend still here. Brendan closes his eyes and says the *Our Father* in his head. *Fool. You work for them.* He looks around the room at the earnest discussion, the beer, the laughter.

The perfect posture registers unmistakeably, even way out in Brendan's peripheral vision. Perfect posture carrying two pints. His best instructor, and every drill instructor's dream. Tall and sandy-haired, Rod's good looks are tempered by cragginess. *Makes him look serious,* Brendan thinks. *And he is. Still, it's that posture landed him his handle.*

Brendan pushes himself upright. He looks awkward.

"Forgive me, Ramrod. I've not been myself today."

"Of course, Brillo." Rod smiles and puts down the pints. "This will help."

"In fact, I've not been myself all week."

They sit, penitent.

"I'm sorry, Rod."

They lift their beers. In Brendan's mind his pint merges with the chalice he helped bless as an altar boy.

"Nectar of the gods, transform us, give us strength."

Rod is used to these mumblings. He taps Brendan's glass with his.

"I've been talking too much about crashes."

Of course he has! thinks Brendan. This week Rod has studied all the Starfighter crashes he can get his hands on, including the CF-104's here at Cold Lake. Kozy was the eighteenth on the base.

"You've been talking and I haven't been listening. Until now. So tell me about them fockin' crashes. And about your Boundary Layer Control goin' south."

"Yeah. Well, I don't know what got Kozy . . ."

Rod speaks slowly, re-visiting the event.

". . . but I know that I'd be dead too if I hadn't been ready for that BLC thing. If we didn't have the procedures we do. Like take final flap at 1500 AGL and keep your hand on the lever. The roll is so fuckin' fast Brillo you wouldn't believe it. You don't have time to say, *What the fuck?* You have time to recognize it and do exactly what you have thought through on the ground."

"So you rehearsed it?"

"Yeah, in the cockpit. To get the spatial stuff."

"I'd better be doin' some of that myself. Save my own fockin' arse."

"Yeah. Stick around, OK, Brillo?"

"Fockin' right." Brendan looks pleased. "So what's goin' on with this Jasus airline, anyway?"

An almost-new Air Arcadia DC-8 has recently crashed after an attempted landing at Toronto with the loss of all on board. It has been all over the radio and TV and newspapers for the last few days. More so now than even the day after the crash. It is because the voice recorder has been found and its evidence has erased all doubt.

"This is not the first DC-8 they've pranged, if I can remember."

"No. It's the third."

"So – why are they fockin' up?"

"Guys get to think they know what they're doing, flying the props. Then this big jet comes along. A lot of assumptions have to change. And some of these guys are not young."

Brendan flashes forward to an unknown future where the two of them, still friends, are no longer young. The thought is strangely comforting.

"Oh, alright then, Ramrod. Tell me the tales. The three of them."

Rod shifts forward in his chair, the teacher emergent.

"OK, the first one. Takeoff from Dorval. Initial climb. Slams into the ground in Ste. Thérèse at 480 knots."

"Like Kozy."

"Well, same speed. Only problem is, that's 140 knots above the DC-8's max operating speed.

"So. Why?"

"Accident report says maybe pitot icing, maybe vertical gyro failure, maybe an unprogrammed and unnoticed extension of the Pitch Trim Compensator. But the PTC is supposed to be fully extended above 395 knots. So it might have been unnoticed – it was found fully extended – but it certainly wasn't unprogrammed."

"Wait a minute, Ramrod. The report said maybe this, maybe that . . ."

". . . actually what it said was the cause could not be determined with certainty, but the things I mentioned, which were put out as theories, could not be ruled out."

"So they're just dodgin' the bullet."

"Yeah. I guess. But they also found the horizontal stab at more than 1.5 degrees nose-down. That's full nose down. More than full nose down."

"So it took a dirty dive?"

"Hit the ground at fifty-five degrees nose down."

"And it a transport plane, and all." Brendan takes a sip of his beer. "Trying to fly like a fockin' Lawn Dart. So this pitot icing and vertical gyro and all the rest they're talkin' about is just to say why else would they run the horizontal stab all the way down?"

"Yeah. Exactly. Except it doesn't make much sense. I mean, you got two pitot systems. Two vertical gyros. Two pilots."

"So. What?"

"You'd be accelerating. That can be disorienting in itself. And you'd be trimming nose down. "

"Yes. A runaway stabilizer that they couldn't or didn't stop." Brendan glances at Rod and raises an eyebrow. "How are you knowin' so much about the DC-8, anyway?"

"Yeah. Dunno. Maybe I got a buddy who joined the airline."

"So you're a regular Sherlock Holmes, readin' accident reports. And now you've got a fockin' hard-on for crashes."

Brendan puts down his beer, his face red.

"I'm sorry. I'm being an arsehole. I'm supposed to be listening to your tale. So what was that second one, a training flight or some such as I recall?"

"Yeah. Instructor doing Checkouts on Type. Three aboard. Instructor thinks he's a test pilot."

"That's a serious charge, Ramrod. I wouldn't want to be standing on the carpet defending it."

"Word has it they were doing an approach with two engines out on one side, and I can't find a Vmc, a minimum control speed, for that condition in the manual. Has it even been flight tested? Did they have the other two engines at idle, or were they really shut down? So as they slow for the approach – they gradually run out of rudder – then they get a bit low or slow or both and the poor klutz flying pushes the power up and they flip on their back in the blink of an eye . . ."

"Steady, steady." Brendan breathes deeply, looking at Rod. "So she flipped on her back? On approach?" He shakes his head. "That's nasty. That's fockin' nasty, a big beautiful ship."

"Yeah."

"What are they goin' to say about the likes o' that? Let me ask you something. Would there be a certain lack of detail in the report?"

"You're right. All it says, is failure to abandon a training maneuver under conditions which precluded the availability of adequate flight control."

For a moment Brendan's hair glows psychedelic red. Rod breathes out through his nose, letting the anger escape his body. Then the remains of the sun are gone for the day. Brendan's hair dulls as the incandescent bulbs of the Mess take over, conferring a glow upon the polished wood of the tables and bar.

Rod watches as Brendan takes a generous gulp. The glass is nearly empty.

"These accidents. They weren't necessary."

"Nor Kozy, either. May his stupid arse rest in peace . . ."

Kozy's youth, cocky or not, was all he had. Better lay him properly to rest.

". . . he was on his planned track."

"Yeah. He was."

"… and planned airspeed and planned radio altitude."

"I know. I've been looking at the data."

"… and there's this two hundred-foot ridge. Two hundred fockin' feet, Ramrod! With trees on top. And he doesn't pull up quite, quite fockin' enough!"

"Yeah."

"… and he's climbing when he hits the trees. Ten feet from the top. Only there's too many of 'em." Brendan pushes his chair back and stands up. "My round. Then we'll figure out Kozy. And your fockin' DC-8's, too."

Rod looks around at the Mess. *A good crowd.* He looks out at the ramp. It is now quite dark. *Better have something to eat soon.* There are pools of yellow on the ramp under the light standards. *Where was Kozy's head?*

Rod is still staring at the patterns of light on the ramp when Brendan plunks down two foaming black pints.

"Here, Ramrod. Tell me about Kozy."

The Guinness is good. Almost like food.

Brillo has always been fun. Getting promoted but not getting too serious, staying one of the boys. But he was serious this week and he's serious tonight.

"Wasn't that he was trying to be a hero," Rod starts.

"Why not?"

"Because he was on profile."

"Yes."

"So he comes to the pull-up …"

"And?"

"… and he's got to pull some G's. Theoretically, in the profile, it's not more than three. And no negative. Just zero or so on the push-overs."

"So?"

"So maybe he's afraid of a pitch-up?"

Brendan is briefly quiet. He is not drinking, either.

"Don't we drill it in, on training? How the Zipper has no wing?"

"Don't go mishandling it."

"Yeah. Don't pull past that burble. Feel for the burble."

"Or it can go on rotating into a high alpha. Instead of flying."

"Right. So do you follow your training in the heat of the moment?"

"Yes, yes." Brendan nods. "You've been trained not to pull too hard. So you don't."

Brendan has abandoned banter. Rod presses on.

"And the new mission. Fly in low-level and supersonic over East Germany or somewhere, under the radar, lob a nuke and then get out."

"Perhaps this is not a mission for the Lawn Dart?"

"Well. Maybe with the right training."

Brendan is nodding as he looks at Rod.

"The time to think is before."

"Yeah, Brillo. Exactly."

Brendan follows Rod's gaze out to the ramp. A CC-115 Buffalo is pivoting into its parking spot, the left prop already slowing.

"Your thesis on the second DC-8, God help us, is they didn't know their ship. V_{MCA} with two out, and all. Didn't think about it in advance."

Brendan watches the Buffalo's right prop. It is quiet enough in the room so he can just catch the sound of the combustion pressure collapsing when the fuel is cut off and the descending whistle as the turbine winds down. He turns back to Rod.

"So it was more like boys. Dare ya. Watch me."

"Well, yeah."

"They just fockin' did it. And died."

Rod sighs. His exposition has gone home. Brendan crosses himself.

"Requiem aeternam dona eis, Domine."

Rod shoots him a glance.

"Latin, old man. May God grant their sorry arses eternal rest."

On the ramp the Buffalo's door is opening. In the pools of yellow light dark lines have formed leading toward the door: airmen in dress uniform. It looks odd, out of place on a summer night. Puzzled, Rod peers out at the spectacle.

"What the heck?"

"High mucky-mucks from NDHQ. Heard some scuttlebutt about it. Supposed to be secret."

"Then why the welcome?"

"Maybe our base commander wants to impress."

"So why are they here?"

"Could be just what you were talkin' of, old man. The low-level nuke lob job."

"Do you think Kozy's thing figures in?"

"Could be, could be." For a moment Brendan seems preoccupied, looking out the window at the scene on the ramp. "We gotta go eat, Ramrod. But first, your third crash. With the spoilers, and all. So what is it that we take away from that sorry mess?"

Rod sits forward again.

"The voice recorder transcript is so sick. They argue. They go back and forth. They wind up confusing themselves."

"So explain it to me. Since neither one liked what was in the book and neither one had any understanding of why it's safer to arm those spoilers with some air underneath you, what inanity did they come up with?"

"The First Officer liked to arm and extend them on the ground."

"Arm and extend. Both."

"Yes."

"Well at least that would be middlin' safe."

"Yeah. Unless you bounce, or you think you're on and you're not. And it's using up precious runway while you screw around."

"And the other? The Captain?"

"He liked to arm them on the flare."

"Well, and again there's no harm done, at least as long as he only arms them."

"Right. That's true. And they'd been doing it that way for months." Brendan shuts his eyes.

"I can see it now clear as a bell."

"They're doing the Before Landing Check. It's a call and response. The First Officer calls. He says, *three green, four pressures, spoilers on the flare?* It's a question. Almost like a tease. He's just back from vacation. So he has to revive the argument they've been having for months. My way? Or maybe your way?"

"It's supposed to be *spoilers armed*. Period."

"Of course. But now they're back and forth. Captain says he is giving up. He is tired of fighting it. First Officer is laughing. Laughing, Brillo!"

Brendan waits, watching the emotions play on his friend's face. Rod presses on.

"And the Captain says, *All right, give them to me on the flare!*"

"Mary and Joseph. I can see it."

"Worse, Brillo. It's worse. Sixty feet above the runway, double, triple the flare height, he says . . ."

"Who says?"

". . . the Captain. He says, *OK.*"

Brendan sighs. Looks down at the table.

"And Lord save us the First Officer arms and deploys the spoilers in one motion. As he had been used to doing."

"Yes. And then he says, *Sorry, Pete. Oh, sorry, Pete.* Then they hit the ground so hard the number four engine falls off. Then he says, *Sorry, Pete.* The Captain has pushed the power up to try to save the sink, but now as they bounce they're flying again, the spoilers have retracted because the throttles are up and the wing is still there, for the moment, just not the engine so they're climbing . . ."

"And that's another suck-in . . ."

"Yes. They don't know the wing is trailing flame and they get to three thousand feet and the tower is talking about landing on runway twenty-three because there's debris on thirty-two . . ."

"Their fockin' number four engine . . ."

"Right. And then there's more explosions. First some more wing panels. Then the number three engine is gone. Still flying, believe it or not . . ."

"Talk about two out on one side . . ."

"Fuck. Yeah. And then with the last explosion the whole outer end of the wing is gone."

"And any remaining lateral control with it."

Brendan mumbles to himself. It sounds like Latin. He looks up.

"What are we takin' away from this mess?"

"Know your airplane. Think about why you're doing what you're doing."

"And don't be makin' shit up in ignorance."

Brendan pushes back his chair and stands up. The Honour Guard, or whatever it was, has disappeared. The ramp is back to pools of yellow light.

"Have you worked up a hunger?"

"Sure," says Rod, "Now you mention it."

"I hear there's a prime rib tonight. Myself I have a wonderful hunger. In fact I'm starvin' altogether."

Dan's Story

St. Hubert, Quebec – 1972-73

Cameron

SUMMER IN ARCADIA is a mad place. Expo '67 set off a rush of manic energy which is still going strong in this summer of '72. Downtown barely clothed young people rejoice like cows let out of the barn. At the airport Marshall is on the phone constantly, making and erasing appointments on his big sheet which has all the airplanes on it, cramming each one's day full with names of students and instructors. Twelve, thirteen, fourteen hours he books in June. *As long as there's light we fly,* he says. Then in the afternoon a thunderstorm might roll through and that makes a mess of Marshall's sheet as he erases and re-schedules and juggles and picks up the mike to bark at some student who's not parking his aircraft in the right slot or to confirm something he already knows with some instructor just because he can.

All day Cameron's next student has already done the pre-flight and the aircraft is gassed up and ready and he's barely got time to remember the student's name. Then they're taxiing out again to join that madhouse circuit on 24 Left with maybe ten aircraft doing touch-and-gos where the student is mainly learning radio work. Increasingly Cameron has been leaving the circuit to fly the five minutes to Beloeil and teach at the grass strip where the student can think about flying instead of talking on the radio. He asks Marshall to schedule someone ready for a dual cross-country at noon so he can eat his sandwich and apple on the way down to Bromont.

At eight-fifteen with the light fading and the sky in the west going red he finishes with his last student, this little smiley guy Jean-Luc who has come directly from his shift bagging groceries at Steinberg's. The kid is super-keen but Cameron sees him only every once in a while because Jean-Luc has to work a lot of shifts to pay for an hour of instruction especially since half of it is going to Maman to help pay the rent.

Then Cameron is driving home into what's left of the red sun and because it's Friday Leslie has asked an old friend over and prepared the nicest meal she can with their pennies and they laugh and drink glasses of wine from the gallon of Ben Afnam they bought at the Regie des Alcools de Quebec Liquor Board and Cameron's face has fallen into his plate before dessert and he's snoring and their old friend laughs some more and says, *That's our Captain.*

§

In the winter there are blizzards which shut down the school for days. And you can't fly at night; night is a separate rating in Arcadia and who would want to teach primary at night anyway, it's a whole different ball game. Of course there are beautiful winter days when the ramps have been cleared and the snow carefully brushed off the airplanes and the crosswinds are not too strong to teach landings but by four o'clock it's dark again. Cameron is lucky if he gets an hour or two of instruction on a winter day. At least he's not laid off like most of the other guys from the summer. In the winter his tasks expand to include just about anything that needs doing around the flying school. He shovels and brushes off snow and helps the mechanics move airplanes around and drives the gas truck and cleans toilets and if he's lucky gets an hour every now and then to shoot the breeze with old Albert, the owner's uncle who flew The Hump at the end of World War II with the Flying Tigers.

§

With the equinox comes hope of change in Arcadia. Cameron thinks of the earth hurtling around in its orbit and sees the days changing, lengthening at their fastest, the sun every day climbing higher, creeping around buildings, rising and setting more to the north. And yet in April the odd blizzard still pushes through, teasing skiers and municipal snow removal budgets. But with the next sunny day the drains are open and the gutters running with melt; jackets are open and gloves in pockets and there are smiles where last week there were none.

Cameron's days are starting to fill up on Marshall's big sheet. Twin work has been rare but that's nothing new. The snow banks are receding onto the grass along with winter's doubts. Cameron has finished his scheduled students for the day and is looking forward to a cup of coffee and the cookie he saved from lunch. At almost four o'clock the sun is still well above the hangars and the light has that golden glow that happens in early spring when there is still snow cover and the trees are bare. *Maybe I don't want to teach forever. Maybe I do want a job with the airline.*

Marshall looks up as Cameron enters the building.

"Locked up Juliet Tango. Tied her down."

"Thanks. She's done for the day." Marshall looks down at his sheet, then back at Cameron, as if what is on his sheet is a surprise to him. "I've got some twin work for you. A whole course."

"Wow, thank you!"

"Yeah. A military guy. Air Force."

"And he needs a multi rating? He doesn't have one?"

"Oh, I don't know. Some Ministry of Movement thing. You can sort it out with him. He just wants the rating as soon as possible. I've booked you every day. In NBD. Starting . . ." Marshall turns around to look at the clock on the wall, ". . . in fifteen minutes. At four o'clock. When Bix gets back with the airplane."

"The guy is here?"

"Where'd he go?" Marshall looks around, squinting, pointing. "That's him, on the ramp. Name's Rod."

Cameron follows Marshall's gaze outside. There he is. A tall fellow, his own age.

As he crosses the ramp Cameron is thinking about Dan, his friend and mentor at his first instruction job who said, *Cameron, multi-engine instruction is the most dangerous thing you'll ever do in aviation*, and Dan knew what he was talking about because he had survived an inverted flat spin in a Twin Comanche. At higher altitudes a twin's V_{mc}, Minimum Control Speed, falls with the engines' power output and eventually meets the stall speed. So get it high enough and slow enough with power out on one side and it will flip on its back before you can say *What the fuck*. And for good measure the dumbbell effect of the engines on the wings gives you a lot of rotational inertia so the spin recovery is difficult.

Dan was lucky because although he was in the back seat his very experienced boss and mentor was in the right seat, and with quiet determination the boss got that inside engine unfeathered and running even though they were upside down with dust floating in their faces. *I've never been so scared in an airplane before or since*, said Dan who is a good Catholic and can't swear without giggling.

Rod has seen him coming and greets him with a smile.

"You must be Cameron. I'm Rod. Pleased to meet you."

Cameron shakes the extended hand.

"Marshall gave me the tour. I thought you might be a fit. I hope you don't mind."

"Of course." Cameron tries to shake off embarassment. "Marshall didn't give me all the details. But you need a Ministry of Movement multi-engine rating? I would have thought, being in the military . . ."

"I'd have one already? Yeah. Well, I have a few hours on twins but not much. So it's quite legit that MOM wants me to get a rating."

"What did you fly? If you don't mind my asking."

"I started with the CT-134. That's what we call a Beech Musketeer. Then into the CL-41, the Tutor, for advanced and aerobatic. Then the CF-104. The Starfighter."

"You're a fighter pilot?"

Cameron's admiration is written on his face. Rod nods.

"The 104 is a single-engine?"

"Yeah. So's the Tutor. So I don't have a lot of multi-engine experience."

"But the 104. There have been a lot of . . . of crashes. It must be a dangerous . . . a difficult airplane . . ."

"Yeah. Sure. But multi-engine planes can kill you just as dead." Rod smiles. "So I hear."

Cameron relaxes.

"True. My friend Dan . . ." he begins.

Cameron shares Dan's story. Just in the last month MOM has lost a Twin Comanche with three aboard in an almost-identical scenario. Cameron is impressed that Rod knows all about the accident, more that Cameron knows himself. They are still talking about it when NBD taxis in and shuts down at the end of the line.

"That our bird?"

"Yup. She's a dog, but a good old dog. Wanna go check her out?"

"Yeah. Looking forward to it. I think this is gonna be fun."

Cameron isn't sure. He has never flown anything larger than a Navajo. How will he teach Rod, who has been flying the CF-104?

But Rod makes it easy. By the time they have strapped in Rod has already asked many questions, including, *Critical engine? What's that?* inviting Cameron to explain 'P' Factor, the angle of attack of the down-going prop blade. Cameron's confidence re-emerges as they discuss the mechanism of constant-speed props and the Apache's lack of unfeathering accumulators.

NBD becomes a precision instrument under Rod's caress. He brings out her shy charm. As the speed slides back on approach Rod catches it precisely, easing the power up so subtly it's beautiful. It is as though NBD is flying solo, doing it all by herself. He is making her look good.

"I gotta say you're not having too much trouble with the transition," Cameron says as they shut NBD down for the day.

"Thanks." Rod is finishing the tail tie-down. "But hey, an airplane is an airplane." He stands up and smiles. "Just a little slower, is all."

§

The next day they are going over the MOM-approved drill for engine failure. Cameron knows it has to be verbatim so he is rehearsing it with Rod.

"*Mixture, Pitch, Power, Gear Up, Flaps Up,*" intones Rod. "*Check for fire.*"

"*Fire, No Fire,*" Cameron interrupts. "Believe it or not, they actually want you to say that. I know it's stupid . . ."

"No, no. That's fine. I gotta get it right. How is it? *Fire, No Fire. If Fire, Fuel Off, Throttle Back, Feather. If No Fire,* what is it, *check fuel on main tank? Tank with fuel in it?*" Rod laughs.

70

"Yes. You've pretty well got it. It's just that they like it word for word."

"Hey, that's how I want to get it. Drills like this saved my butt more than once in the Lawn Dart."

"Really?"

"Yeah. Made my own up sometimes. Where there were none. You don't have time to think it through when things go for shit. You just react. So you want to make sure your reaction, you know . . ."

Cameron nods.

"That's how you survived the 104."

Rod smiles.

"Sure. That and some luck."

§

On the day of the ride, they fly over to Dorval together in NBD. Cameron is along because technically he is needed, at least on the way over, because Rod isn't yet legal. He brings a book to read while Rod is out with the examiner. They park NBD on the old ramp, up near the buttons of 10 and 06 Left. It seems small now for a DC-8 and impossible for the new B-747, but this was the main terminal ramp twenty years ago and North Stars parked here. MOM has some office space and a small lounge in what may have been part of the old terminal. Now it seems like a shack.

Cameron keeps a low profile in the lounge. When the examiner comes out, Cameron doesn't recognize him. That is unsurprising since two MOM multi-engine people recently died in the Twin Comanche crash. Maybe that's why this MOM guy looks so serious. Cameron can't help watching because the contrast with Rod is a story in itself. He struggles to remain impassive as Rod gets to his feet, towering over the examiner, his quiet confidence so different from the Mom guy's bustling officiousness. Rod, he notes, is polite but not overly deferential. They are exchanging observations on the wind and ceiling as they go out the door.

The book Cameron brought along is *Handling the Big Jets*, by D.P. Davies. Cameron is fascinated with the multitude of changes the jet transports bring with them. He pores over V_1, balanced field length, lift and drag curves, dutch roll, deep stall, and much more. He has begun to read accident reports and think, for example, of what could have caused the first B-727 crash, the one that wound up in Lake Michigan. Human error, of course. But what else? The three-pointer altimeter? The slow spool-up time of the engines? He has begun to imagine himself flying these machines.

Today he is reading the chapter on asymmetric flight training. Cameron closes the book, thinking about the task of training pilots on a new jet. How much training do the airlines actually do? Davies implies that the airlines may not be doing enough and that their pilots may not have the deep knowledge of their airplane that he deems necessary. Could he, Cameron, even get hired by an airline, let alone become a Training Captain some day?

He hears the off-beat rhythm of a twin turning on the ramp with asymmetrical power, the pilot using one engine's thrust to pirouette more elegantly into a parking position. Could that be Rod already? Cameron looks at the clock on the wall. *My God, it has been an hour. A bit more.* Cameron opens the book randomly as cover.

The door to the ramp opens and Rod and the examiner enter the lounge. Cameron is looking for signs. Although he has known Rod for only a week, there don't seem to be any bad vibes. Clearly, he passed. But there is something.

They disappear into the MOM inner sanctum. Cameron goes to the window. There she is. Perhaps not pretty but neatly parked. He goes back to his bench and opens his book again. It falls open at the rear flyleaf. Cameron pages backward through the index. Chapter 11. To airline pilots. To training captains. *Airline flying really is money for old rope most of the time.* He reads on. *Fifteen points for training captains.*

Rod emerges from the inner sanctum. Catches his eye. Winks in a way that wouldn't transmit to the room. Shakes hands with the examiner. Walks toward Cameron. They head for the door to the ramp. They walk around NBD, looking at all the things you have to look at. Rod wants to check the oil in the right engine. Cameron waves Rod onto the wing to take the left seat. Rod steps through and Cameron follows, stepping into the right seat and closing the door. The engines fire up. Rod is reading back an IFR clearance. When did he file? Before they left St. Hubert? No matter. They have a squawk code and a departure frequency. Rod twists his wrist on the throttles and they pivot out of the parking place. They are rolling down the new ramp toward the threshold of 28. The wind has picked up from the north-west and Cameron, trying to be useful, has scribbled down the ATIS. He also digs into his flight bag and pulls out their cleared departure. *Heading 300. Climb to 3000.*

As they level at three thousand they are vectored. Right turn, heading one zero zero. They are heading back over the thresholds of 24 left and right. Cameron looks down at aircraft on the approach. This is fun. Approach control is calling traffic for them. **NBD, traffic, three miles, two o'clock, squawking 1200.** Cameron finds him, low over Nun's Island. **NBD, turn left, heading zero six zero.** Somehow you feel more important with an IFR clearance, with the controller calling VFR traffic for you. Like an airliner. They are crossing the river near the Victoria Bridge. Vectors for an ILS 24R at St. Hubert.

Rod turns his head and calls above the engine noise.

"Mind if I do the ILS with one at idle?"

"Sure," Cameron grins. "You got the rating."

"Why don't you pull one back and surprise me?"

"OK."

NBD, turn right heading one fife zero. Base leg. *Catch him on the intercept. Highest workload.* **NBD, turn right heading two one zero, cleared for the ILS 24 Right, contact tower now one one eight dezimal four.** *Any second now.* The localizer needle moves off the stop. Cameron reaches with his left hand, finding the stalk of the left throttle and pulling it smoothly back to idle. NBD's song changes, but it is only her engine note. Rod has nailed the left yaw before it can develop and is already rolling into the right turn to intercept the ILS. And here is the glideslope needle, coming down from the top of the instrument.

"Glideslope," Cameron calls.

"Thanks, buddy."

As the glideslope comes down Rod puts the gear down and goes through the GUMPS Check. *Gas, Undercarriage, Mixture, Props, Switches . . ."*

"Three Green. One in the mirror."

He reaches down and winds on some rudder trim, taking the pressure off his right foot.

Decide that you are going to fly the airplane, and not let it fly you, Davies advises airline pilots. That is what Rod is doing. *I can do that too.* Davies also says *personal enthusiasm for the job is beyond value. It generates its own protection.*

As they taxi in Cameron has a feeling of well-being, the glow of a job well done. Even though Rod did it. But there is also a surprising sense that this is not an ending but a beginning.

"Here. You wanna steer? I'll help push."

Cameron has found a nose-wheel bar that fits the Apache and attached it. He hands it to Rod and stands in front of the wing. Rod eases NBD backwards onto the grass between the tie-down ropes.

"If the flight back was any indication, I'd say you aced it."

"Yeah," Rod smiles. "Well, good enough, I guess."

"And there's a story, I think."

"Right. Yeah. I've been thinking about it. Still digesting it, maybe."

"Something about the MOM guy."

"Yeah. We had a few discussions."

"You mean you had an argument?"

"Well, no. But he asked me to feather it. You know, throttle back, feather. He wanted it really feathered. I thought about what you said. About no unfeathering accumulator. I thought, OK, it's April, it's not that cold. Besides, I could land it like that, I felt sure."

"So you feathered it."

"Yeah. And we flew around for a few minutes. He was vectoring me. Giving me airwork. Climbs. Descents."

"OK."

"So then he says, OK, good, we'll head back and land."

"Uh huh."

"Then after a couple of minutes I say, shall we start it up again? We can leave it at 14 inches to simulate feather."

"What'd he say?"

"We went back and forth a bit. I said I was sure I could land with an engine feathered, no problem. But I said I thought it would be safer with it running, even at idle. I used that old saying about the superior pilot."

"Superior pilot?"

"You don't know that one? *The superior pilot uses his superior judgement to avoid having to demonstrate his superior skill."*

"Holy shit." Cameron laughs uneasily. "And?"

"He said, OK, start it up. So I did. I pushed the prop and mixture up, left the throttle at idle and cranked it. It fired right away. Shook like a bugger until the prop unfeathered, but that didn't take long." Rod looks at Cameron. "I hope I didn't do something wrong."

"No, no," Cameron laughs. "Shit, you got your rating. And we're here and NBD is tied down. Survived again." He holds up his book. "That's what the author of this book says. I was reading about asymmetric flight training. *Sure, do it*, he says. Even with two out on one side. On the B-747. *But with the engines at idle. Fuel on.*"

"That's really interesting. Could you show me?"

Cameron holds the book out to Rod. He examines it and hands it back.

"Where does he talk about two engines out training?"

Cameron leafs through the last part of the book. He can remember the passage he is looking for near the top of the left-hand page.

"Here."

As Rod reads the noise of aircraft in the circuit and the occasional car on the road seem louder to Cameron as he sees Rod's eyes take in the passage and then keep going. He smiles and turns to watch a Cessna 150 turn final. The little mosquito is being blown off course by the northwester and has to correct back to the right. Cameron watches the rest of the approach and landing. At the flare, as he or she pushes off drift with left rudder, the Cessna drifts downwind. Then the right wing comes down a bit, stopping the drift. Cameron turns back to see Rod turning another page.

"Yeah. This is great. You do training. But first you have to know the numbers. Then you train safe. Engines at idle. Fuel on."

"Yes. I liked that, too." Cameron pauses for a heartbeat. "Rod, why don't you take that book? Borrow it. I've almost finished it anyway."

"Really?"

"Yes, sure. Read it. Maybe even before you go on course."

Rod seems at a loss.

"That's very good of you."

Rod has the book in his right hand. He shakes it, vertical, spine down, like a pointer, looking at Cameron.

"Say, Cameron – you thinking about the airline?"

"Yes."

"You know, there's a course starting May 7."

"A week Monday."

"Yeah. And word is, it's not full yet."

"Are you . . ."

"Yeah. I had the interview with Captain Carillon. He said, you get the multi rating before then, you start course. So I plan on showing up."

"Wow. Congratulations!"

"Look. Cameron. You're interested, right?"

"Sure. I've applied everywhere. Had interviews. Got one Monday with Air North. For the ice patrol job."

"But that's for Second Officer, right? On the Electra?"

"Yes."

"Cameron, this course at Air Arcadia is for First Officer on the DC-9 and it's not full. Just over a week to go, and they need a few more. They want guys like me with military jet time. Figure we'll transition easier. But I know who's coming out of the military and

I think they're coming up short."

"You think . . ."

"Look – I don't know, but I think it's worth a try. You've got a university degree, right?"

"Yes. But not in anything relevant."

"In what?"

"It's a B.A. But my major was music."

"I see what you mean. But it doesn't matter. All they want is the B.A." Rod sees Cameron's doubtful look and adds, "Really."

"But I thought they had to call you for an interview. They haven't. Not so far."

"Yeah. That's the way it works. Supposedly. But I'll tell you what – got a pencil and paper?"

"I think so," Cameron breathes, searching his pockets. "Yes. Here."

"Captain Carillon does the interviews. But Ingmar schedules them. She's his secretary. A looker, too. Ready to copy?"

Rod pulls out his wallet and fishes out a scrap of paper. He reads the number to Cameron.

"That local gets right to her desk. It's her line."

He smiles at Cameron.

"The rest is up to you."

Adulthood

AIRLINE HONCHO

January 9, 1961

Epitaph for the Minister of Everything

The man known as the Minister of
Everything
Was an accomplished doer of deeds.
He abandoned academe to build grain
elevators.
He made a harbour in Port Arthur.
That was the first age.

To make things happen in Arcadia
The Forward Party anointed him.
He won a seat in Parliament.
He was the first Minister of Movement.
He was fruitful in his ministries.
His first-born was brought forth,
The Airline.
That was the second age.

Two decades the Forward Party remained
in power.
The Man remained minister
of something or other.
The Man sired progeny.
In each new ministry he brought forth.
That was the third age.

The War called for action
For factories and munitions and armour and
aircraft.
All these he caused to be brought forth in
profusion.
That was the fourth age.

The Peace called for Reconstruction,
For transition from arms to innovation.
Swords were beaten into plowshares
Tanks and armoured vehicles into
electronics
Drill fields into airports
Transports into airliners.
All these things and more the Man
conceived
All these things he made.
That was the fifth age.

From the War came ideas
Jets and Radar and Broadcasting.
And the Man saw that they were good
And incorporated he them
Each according to his kind
And there were sea-ways and harbours
And mines and mills
And grain came to market
And ore to smelter
And there were railroads and airfields
And pipelines.
After six ages he rested,
The Minister of Everything.
And he saw that it was good.

Then the Backward Party called loudly
Saying he was over-reaching
That ideas can be bought from others
That jetliners are too risky
That pipelines are too expensive.
The Minister lost his seat.
The Backward Party formed a government.
The Minister rested in peace.
That was the seventh age.

Arcadia

You are gone, Father. You are gone and I am grown. I grieve, Father. I grieve for you, for our country and for how it will be without you. But as I grieve, I can see that it is also for me, your daughter, your firstborn. For I am no longer young.

In my infancy when you were my president I was giddy with possibility. Our great country was at my feet and under my wings. Now suddenly I am alone. Now when the cold North Atlantic is under my wings I feel small in a way I never felt before. I am conscious that I am a link not just between Vancouver Island and The Blessed Rock but also between Our Arcadia and the larger world. My purpose has expanded even as my certainty has evaporated. Is this what responsible adulthood is, Father?

Should we have doubt? Should there be uncertainty?

I have been thinking much, Father, in the days since your passing. In my youth you were strong and certain and to all appearances had no doubts.

Until the Backwards took thy seat. Then our world fell apart. The supersonic fighter cancelled, just last year! And three years ago our Jetliner – the first, Father! – was cut up. Cut to pieces like the fighter. And I am not without blame.

At the time it seemed right. The Backwards were crying out about my involvement in the Polar Star. Up here in Arcadia, we should have instead bought DC-6's and DC-7's. Never mind developing an Arcadian airliner, one that worked for our needs. They had a song and dance about how it was not appropriate for me to be involved with the development of an aircraft. But it was fun, Father! The flight guidance part of the autopilot so we could hook it to a glideslope! Brand new, and how we need it in our country! The remote-sensing compass. The exhaust crossovers to try to cut the noise. And then we – I and my people – got involved with the Jetliner as well. Stage length, payload, that kind of thing. But the outcry only worsened. So reluctantly (no matter what you may have heard from our own nay-sayers) I got out. Decided that helping develop a jet was too risky. I felt badly for a year or so, Father. Then the Comet started exploding in mid-air.

For a while I was smug. Let others take the risks of development. Wait until it is safe before you jump on board. The Backwards may have a point. So I have been content with my Polar Stars and my beautiful Connies.

But with the years regrets have returned. Don Rogers, for example. Not that he said anything to me. He is too kind a man. But I heard. I heard of his pain as the Jetliner was attacked with saws and axes and hammers and pieces were falling on the hangar floor. I imagine the tears as they formed in his soul. How his beautiful mistress of seven years and four hundred forty hours was hacked cruelly to pieces though no fault of her own. Regrets for myself as well, Father, for I could be flying the Jetliner now on many of our shorter North American routes. And she had round windows from the start! She never had those square windows that caused the Comet to explode!

I think of your life, Father, and remember it with pride. Send me some of your strength. I feel I may need it. Rest in peace.

On Course

Dorval – May, 1973

Cameron

THEY ARE THE ONLY people in the room.

Cameron isn't going to say anything, but their eyes meet. Cameron gets up and walks the couple of paces separating them. He holds out his hand.

"Hi. I'm Cameron."

"Cameron? I am pleased to meet you. My name is Ernst."

Ernst is a pleasant-looking blond boy. Average height and build. German, or at least European, by the cadence of his speech. What is unusual is his openness.

"I am here for an interview. For the ice patrol. Second Officer on the Electra. Are you as well?"

"Yes," says Cameron. He looks for something to say. "So, do you know how many they're hiring?"

"Yes. I believe they hire eight on this course. For next Monday."

"Did you hear anything about qualifications? About what they want? Like minimum hours?"

"Yes. They are asking five hundred hours. Instrument. Commercial. Multi-Engine. I have eight hundred hours," Ernst smiles. "And you?"

Cameron has no feeling he should hold anything back. He is not even surprised that he doesn't.

"I've got about two thousand hours. And some instructor ratings. Do you think we have a chance here today?"

"Yes," Ernst nods, smiling. He is bubbling over. "Yes. I am very hopeful. Very."

They both turn as a door opens on the other side of the room. A kindly-looking middle-aged man is holding a sheaf of papers. He looks at them for a few seconds.

"Mr. Ernst Zander?"

"Yes, sir." Ernst turns and smiles at Cameron. "Wish me luck!" he whispers.

The door closes. Cameron returns to where he was sitting. His left hand fishes for a magazine on the end table. He wants it more for cover, for distraction, than for information. It is a Flight International, the British magazine. He leafs through it. A picture of an L-1011 being towed from a hangar catches his eye. The hangar has Lockheed written in big letters over the doors. The news blurb is titled, First Air Arcadia TriStar. Cameron reads it. *The first TriStar will arrive in February and fly the Toronto-Miami route.* Cameron checks the cover. January, this year. *Then in March it will fly Montreal-Toronto-Vancouver.* He reads to the end. *Air Arcadia will approach the end of the 1970s with about 30 TriStars, 50 DC-9s, 40 DC-8s and a handful of 747s.*

The Flight International sits on his lap but Cameron is lost in a reverie. He is nowhere. Not at St. Hubert, instructing. Not at Air North, although he is sitting in their offices. His life until now is just that. There is no future. He cannot imagine his past continuing. He cannot imagine tomorrow or even later today.

The noise of the door opening brings Cameron back to the present. *How long has it been?* The kindly man is beckoning Cameron into his office. Ernst strides toward him, beaming.

"I start Monday, Cameron. See you there for sure!"

In the office Cameron watches from his seat across the desk as the kindly man reads, moving papers in a file. After what seems like an age, the man looks up.

"This is difficult," he begins.

Cameron feels his eyebrows go up.

"Difficult?" he croaks.

"Yes. I'll get right to the point. Your qualifications. They are too good."

"Too good?"

"Look, I understand. It must seem ridiculous to you. I would hire you in an instant. You have everything we want and then some. But there is a marketplace out there. You also have everything Air Arcadia wants. You are right in their profile."

"Air Arcadia?"

"Yes. You see, if I put you on this course and train you, then this month or next month, it doesn't matter, Air Arcadia will hire you away from us. The investment in your training will be lost. We're a small outfit. We can't afford it."

Cameron feels he has been punched in the stomach. He straightens, trying to undo the sensation, rising from his chair.

"So you're not hiring me," he manages.

The kindly man is rising too, holding out his hand.

"No," he says. I'm sorry."

§

The old Jaguar is not pretty, but Cameron is blind to its shortcomings. He has put it together from wrecks and the lovely mechanical bits are all he sees. He loves the walnut dash and the black starter button. He loves the long-stroke six with its three SU carburettors. He loves the beautiful aluminum castings covering the twin overhead cams. But most of all he loves the Laycock de Normanville electro-hydraulic planetary overdrive.

The song of the six dips in a glissando as he flips the switch at speed on Côte de Liesse.

"Eeeeeeeyaaaahhh."

The exhaust settles into a comfortable burble as The Jag cruises along, somewhat above the speed limit. The Montée de Liesse exit is coming up. He leaves his foot on the gas and flips off the overdrive.

"Aaaaahhhyeeeeeee."

Once the revs are up he takes his foot off the gas and the compression of the big six pulls the speed back. He turns off, following the road as it does a 270 to the right and through the underpass. He goes up through the gears and burbles along Montée de Liesse. At the end he turns left on Côte Vertu. Buildings disappear and the sky opens out. The Jaguar is now heading 240 degrees, running between Dorval's two runway 24's. A mile or so ahead is a group of buildings and hangars. Air Arcadia.

Cameron is doing what he has to, moving because he must. The Jag seems to understand. It growls to a stop at the guard shack, perhaps because the barrier is down.

"Good day, sir. What is your business, please?"

"I'm here to see Captain Carillon."

"Do you have an appointment?"

"Uh, not exactly . . ." Cameron takes his wallet out and fishes for the piece of paper. "If I could call this number, uh, this local, and talk to Ingmar . . ."

The guard dials.

"And what is your name, sir?"

Cameron hands his ATR licence to the guard. " . . . she'll have my file right there in front of her."

The guard disappears inside his shack, talking into the phone. Cameron's heart thunders in his chest. *What the heck is he doing? Is he going to get arrested?*

The guard reappears, without the phone. He nods to Cameron. The barrier goes up.

"If you'll just park in there for a minute, sir, I'll write up a pass for you."

The Jag glides through the gate and into the slot the guard indicated. Cameron shuts down and gets out, standing beside the car. Ahead, to the southeast, are a group of low buildings. They seem to go on forever. In the distance a long line of external trusses is outlined against the sky. To the southwest, much further away, he can see the terminal building with the tower sitting on top. To the northwest is just sky. From somewhere under that sky a long rumble is building in volume. A DC-9 lifts off runway 24 Right, leaving a faint trail of black smoke. The noise is intense.

"Here you are, sir."

Cameron is startled. He hasn't seen the guard approach.

"Ingmar says to come right up." He hands Cameron a visitor pass. He is careful not to let it blow away in the wind. "Got it?" He is pinching the pass together with Cameron's licence and the piece of paper with Ingmar's number.

Cameron takes the papers. "Yes, thank you."

"Do you know where it is?"

"Uh, no . . ."

"OK, Flight Ops Headquarters, C-206. It's written on the pass. See that building there?"

Cameron looks where he is pointing, to a low building beside the road.

"That's the simulator building. The ground school building. You want the building to the left. See, there's a connecting passage. The entrance is just there. Go up, through the passage, and the stairs up are at the other end. Your car is OK there if you won't be more than an hour."

Cameron gives the Jag a pat for reassurance as he sets off. He is still moving ahead. The world hasn't come to an end. He hasn't been flicked away by a fingernail or been crushed like a bug. He is walking toward that connecting passage, the glassed-in breezeway between the buildings. Once he is in the door and up the stairs he sees where to go. At the end of the glass passage, on the left, an open stairway leads up. There is a sign on the wall: *Flight Operations Headquarters*. Glass doors at the top of the stairs open onto a little vestibule with a couch. There are end tables with magazines. On his left is a large space with four secretaries at their desks. The nearest one looks up as he enters.

"Good morning," she says. "And what can we do for you today?"

"Good morning," Cameron echoes with a confidence which surprises him. "Ingmar told me to come right up."

"Well, in that case, go right over and talk to Ingmar."

She gestures at a desk behind her and to her right. A striking blond girl is seated behind it. Cameron walks over.

"You must be Cameron?"

She is holding a file. He nods. She gets up from her chair.

"Come along. He'll see you now."

She walks a few paces, knocks on an office door, and opens it a head width.

"Captain Carillon? He's here."

It is a replay of the scene at Air North less than an hour ago. Cameron sits across the desk from Captain Chris Carillon. The captain is reading Cameron's file, nodding from time to time and occasionally mumbling. The captain is tall and slender and has a beaked nose. He is well dressed in civvies but the effect is uncertain. At times he gives off an air of military precision and discipline. Then something in the way he moves or holds his body makes him seem like a bumbling boy.

"Medical," he mumbles. "Good."

Cameron's field of vision has opened out. There is still no future, but that doesn't seem to matter as much as it did a half-hour ago.

"Some multi-engine instruction, I see."

"Yes, sir." Cameron doesn't want to draw attention to how few hours of it he has.

"Any of it recent?"

"Yes sir. Last week. Did a whole course."

"Good. Good." Carillon's body makes an awkward movement as he turns to look out the window. "Just talked to another of my pilots on this course. Got his rating. Good thing."

"Yes, sir." Cameron's mouth is on autopilot. "Last week's course. I was flying with a pilot who is going on course here." *Course. Course. Awkward. Why did he bring that up?*

"Were you? Good. You know, I'll bet it was . . ."

The Captain shuffles his files, looking for the name he has forgotten.

They clear up that it was indeed Rod.

"Yes. Yes. Like I said, I spoke with him this morning. Said he enjoyed the course. Good. Good. You know, we needed him to be on this course. I'm glad you ..."

The Captain shuffles his files, looking awkward. He finds what he is looking for and suddenly straightens in his seat, looking military and proud. Like Rod, Cameron thinks.

"... you see, this course next Monday," Carillon twists slightly to look at the calendar on the wall. "The seventh. It is a DC-9 First Officer course." The Captain turns and looks at Cameron. "Would you like to be on it? Could you start that soon?"

"Yes, sir." Cameron's eyes widen as he nods. "Absolutely!"

"Good. Good. You'll have to do well, though. You see, we need you all this summer."

"I'll work hard, sir. I won't let you down."

"Good. Excellent." Captain Carillon stands up and holds out his hand over the desk. "I'll be watching your progress. Ingmar will give you the details. See you Monday."

§

Monday the guard directs him through the gate and into the main employee lot. He finds the entrance he used last week and goes upstairs. This time he turns right into the simulator building.

On his right a glass wall looks out over the simulator bays. Cameron brushes the hip-level railing with his hand as he walks along, looking for an open door on his left. He finds one and enters tentatively, edging along the back of the room. He counts fourteen desks. A few are already occupied. At the front of the class is a small, grey-haired man. He waves to Cameron.

"Come on up. I'll show you your desk."

In a minute Cameron is studying the folder of papers having to do with the course and with today's schedule. This morning appears to consist of welcomes by various speakers, followed by a coffee break and something called 50 and 500.

The grey-haired man clears his throat.

"Gentlemen, welcome. My name is Wally. This is the Air Arcadia Pilot Course of May 7, 1973. I will be with you for the first two weeks. During that time we will study the 50 and 500 Manuals. They are our Bible."

He holds up two volumes. They could be Bibles except for the colour. The pages are half-size: 5 ½ by 8 ½. The 3-ring binders are green with *Air Arcadia* embossed on the front. There is a transparent pocket on the spine where you can slip in a card with the name of the volume.

"In a few minutes I will be handing out your personal copies. You will put them in their binders and together we will put in a few transmittals. Assemble them. Put your name in them. Guard them with your life. Your career may depend on it."

As they assemble their personal copies, Cameron sees that the 50 and 500 are Air Arcadia's Standard Operating Procedures, an essential part of the airline's Operating Certificate. Wally speaks sternly of what he expects of the class. There will be exams. Morse code. New York and Chicago Terminal Areas. And of course the Bibles.

Then it is time for the speakers. Captain Carillon is first, welcoming them to the *Air Arcadia family*. He assures them that the course will be *no cakewalk*, but when he says that he is confident that by summer they will all be First Officers on the DC-9, he sounds like he means it.

Next is a large, peaceful-looking, dark-skinned man named Rajan. In two weeks time, he explains, he will join them to teach the technical subjects: jet certification and field performance, and the DC-9 in particular.

As Cameron makes a tick mark beside Rajan's welcome, Wally announces the coffee break. *Be back here in twenty-five minutes.* As Cameron stands up to go he realizes Rod is beside him. He is holding out *Handling the Big Jets.*

"Thanks for the loan, Cameron. Great book."

He was expecting to see me here.

"You can keep it longer if you like . . ."

"No need," Rod goes on. "I've already ordered my own copy. Wanna go for coffee?"

§

The last speaker of the day is from the union. He is short. Although not plump, he gives an impression of roundness. In repose he appears genial, his face flushed like a favourite uncle.

"Good afternoon and welcome aboard, gentlemen. My name is Beau Brown. I'm a First Officer on the DC-8 and I'm here on behalf of our union, the Arcadian Air Line Pilots Organization."

Beau writes the union name on the blackboard.

"I say our union because as soon as you guys finish this course you will be given a seniority number and you will be members in good standing of AALPO. I will be passing out inscription forms and in due course you will receive your union cards in the mail."

In big letters, all caps, Beau writes SENIORITY under the union name.

"Seniority is now a big deal in your life. You may not have prepared for this. You may not have thought about it at all. Or maybe you have. Anyway, you guys are a special case, being direct intake DC-9 First Officers. You may feel that you don't even need a union. Hey, you're jumping seniority already, going direct to DC-9 F/O."

Beau's face is flushed. His geniality is morphing into intensity.

"You see, for your first two years, while you're on probation, the Company can do anything it wants with you. Including paying you $800 per month."

The room declares its presence with a few audible exhalations.

"Didn't know that, huh? Yeah. You get out on the line, the Flight Attendants gonna be making more than you. Think about that."

Beau turns. Gestures at the blackboard. At where he has written the union's name.

"That's why we have a union. You know that bump on the 747? Over the cockpit? Know what that's for? Bloody right. To allow space for the Captain's wallet."

Beau allows that to sink in.

"Formula Pay. That's what it's called. We get paid by weight and speed, among other things. These jets, they're heavy. And they're fast."

Beau turns again and points at SENIORITY.

"So you guys are real fortunate. Jumping seniority to fly the DC-9. Good for you. But what the Company giveth, the Company taketh away. After two years, you'll start to get paid real money. And you'll have to bid your equipment like the rest of us. That's why we have a union."

Cameron is trying to keep up with Beau as he ricochets around. *So we may get kicked back to DC-8 Second Officer.*

"Seniority. It decides everything. Every month you bid for your block. What routes you're flying. Who you're flying with. Yeah. First O's and Second O's can bid to fly with Captains they like. Or not, if they don't. That's called the Twitchell Bid. 'Nuff said. Ennaway, you guys will be on Reserve for awhile. Twice a year there's an

Equipment Bid. Decides what airplane you're on and what seat you're sitting in. Then in March there's the Vacation Bid. You guys can forget summer vacation for awhile. Or having Christmas off."

Beau senses he may have taken this too far.

"But believe me, in the long run you guys are going to love seniority. You work in most corporations, it's the asshole who sucks up to the boss that gets the promotion. Or maybe it's the geek who takes work home at night and has no life."

He paces back and forth, thinking of the joys of seniority.

"We park the airplane at the gate, we're done. Shut 'er down, take our brain bags, and go home. No office politics. No worries. When our number comes up, we get our chance to make Captain."

Cameron feels whipsawed by this guy. *But I like that last bit. Sounds democratic."*

Beau moves on. More bullets are added to the blackboard list. Contract. Negotiations. Working Conditions. Now he has written Pilot Advisory. It seems pilots sometimes get into trouble. Things happen in their lives and they get stressed and it shows up in their work. That's when the union can help with arbitration and counselling.

"I'm almost done, guys. But before I go I want to leave you with some statistics. In case you've underestimated this job. You're young. Full of piss and vinegar. You all have thirty-some-odd years of career ahead of you before you hit retirement at age 60. Before you start taking your . . ."

Beau turns and writes PENSION on the blackboard.

". . . it's a good one, too, thanks to your union. Take your best five years of pay. Average it out. More or less half of that. Pretty damn good."

Cameron cannot imagine retirement, more than a generation away.

"But here's the deal, guys. Know how many of us make it to retirement?" He writes the number on the board. "No, really. These are actual, current statistics for this group. Twenty-six percent."

Beau pauses and looks around. The potential DC-9 F/O's are shifting in their seats.

"You want to put up your hands and ask, right? Isn't it twenty-six percent don't make it?"

More shifting. No hands.

"No. It's not. Twenty-six percent do make it. The rest get sick and die, wig out, or drink their way onto GuhDip."

Beau turns and writes General Disability Insurance Protection on the board.

"That's who pays you if you're too sick to fly. If you lose your license. Another reason you need your union."

Beau tosses his chalk in the air. And catches it.

"I'm done, guys. Welcome aboard."

Beau turns to go. He takes a few steps. Then he pivots back toward the class.

"Just one more thing. If you do make it to retirement. If you're in that twenty-six percent. Know what your life expectancy is?"

The class is silent.

"Two more years."

Captain Past Peak

Autumn, 1973

Cameron

THE SUMMER HAS GONE BY in a blur, the passage of time obscured by learning so intense that reflection is erased as it arises. Especially the first time flying the actual airplane, the real aluminum thing with touchable tires and rows of empty seats as they enter from the bridge, the airplane loaded with fifteen thousand pounds of kerosene for their proposed two-hour session of mostly touch-and-goes at Dorval, the unreality of the real, cramped cockpit and sitting on the jump seat built into the door frame with his knees on either side of the pedestal and how he has to spread them apart further so Rod or Al Lank, their instructor, can reach back to open the pneumatic cross-feeds or center the rudder and aileron trim and it's all like in the simulator and what they have been studying since May but never before have there been the smells and sounds and the amazing kinetics of it, not just the acceleration because they're so light, no passengers or cargo, just gas, but also the lateral forces as they taxi, the feeling of being ahead of the nosewheel, and then the elevator-like rising as they rotate on takeoff and you can feel the main wheels disengage from the runway far behind

97

you as the wings take up their task and hear the rush of air as the nose-wheel doors open and close as the gear comes up and the acceleration that feels like sinking, it's a function of body angle versus angle of attack as the flaps and especially the leading-edge slats retract and he integrates all of that with what he knows, which is quite a bit with his two-thousand-plus hours of flight.

Then the unreality as they stop on the taxiway after an hour and he and Rod change places and he is in the seat, the seat with the yoke now between his knees and the rudder pedals adjusted to his shorter legs with that pull-knob on the bottom of the panel and they turn onto the runway and Al says *you have control* and he says clearly *I have control* and pushes the throttles up to 1.95 EPR and he feels the kick in the butt which is more now because in the hour they have burned six thousand pounds of kerosene and he is a little slow with the nose-wheel steering through the pedals because he doesn't know how much force it will take and doesn't want to over-control and Al calls *Vee One* and *Rotate* and he does and their little compartment rises to room height before the main wheels way back there stop trundling and they are flying. He is flying. Cameron is flying a DC-9.

Sure, it is an airplane like any other. And the controls, the tab-operated ailerons and elevators have a familiar feel. But also not. The power-to-weight ratio is like nothing he has ever experienced. They are cleaned up and at three thousand feet it seems before he has taken two breaths and like, say, a Bonanza but way more so the power has to come back, way back, to level at three thousand without busting the speed limit in the control zone, two hundred knots, and as he pulls back the throttles he feels he is pulling the rug out from under them because he is pushing over to level off as the power comes back so it is not just that the acceleration stops but also the phenomenal rate-of-climb stops so to achieve straight and level flight at three thousand the acceleration vector has to go from major push in the butt to semi-weightless for a few seconds before equilibrium.

Cameron is in the moment and for the moment more than he has ever been in his life and the hour flashes by. Then they are at the loading bridge again and saying goodbye and Cameron is vaguely aware of Rod bantering politely with Al and he gets a feeling perhaps Al is a bit of a boozer but whatever, he sure is grateful for today, he's going to make it, he's going to fly the line, the line checkout is next week and he goes home and it's mid-afternoon and he says to his wife I'm tired and he goes upstairs and lies down and he's out cold until dinner.

§

The block awards are posted at one end of the bulletin boards in the briefing room, a long, narrow space with a door to the hall at each end. The bulletin boards are on the hall wall and on the window side a long counter divides pilots from dispatchers and crew schedulers sitting at desks but you can talk to them, they're real people and they'll come over to the counter and shoot the breeze or give you a briefing on your route or hand you a copy of your pairing, your trip, if you're on Reserve and they just assigned it to you over the phone. To Cameron's right along the bulletin board are Company notices and letters from Chief Pilots and NOTAMS and weather maps for the various areas: Intercity, Trans Con, Maritimes, USA, North Atlantic and Europe all aligned more or less in front of the dispatch desks dealing with that area. The long narrow space is about three pilots deep; they are confined there as if in quarantine and there is just room for the standing-at-the-counter pilot, the reading-the-bulletins pilot, and the walking-between-them-trying-to-get-to-the-Maritimes-dispatcher pilot.

Cameron finds the DC-9 First Officer Award List and looks at Reserve and he's not there. He doesn't panic because this happened last month too and he wound up getting a block, not on Reserve at all but the whole month planned out and not bad flying either.

Some pretty senior guys on Reserve this month, though. Don't know why they'd choose that unless maybe they wanted to try to pass flights and sit at home or something. He looks up at the block list and sure enough, there he is on Block 27. He riffles through the stapled stack of 8½ by 11 sheets and finds Block 27. Not bad. In fact, pretty ace flying, most of it Maritimes, plenty of days off because the flying is productive, packing the hours in when you do go to work. Cameron glances up at the DC-9 Captain Award List to see who he's flying with and it's Captain P. S. Peak Employee Number 64371 and he gets just a slight sinking feeling, not real worry or pain but just a slight unease as if there's something that he doesn't know, maybe, because Past Peak is who he has been flying with this month, all month, and it's OK, it's wonderful to be flying the line and especially to have a block so Leslie knows ahead of time when he will be working but it hasn't been exactly joyful now he thinks of it.

It's not so much the flying as – what? The layovers? Those have some pain associated with them; Cameron is still trying to figure it out: what should be and what maybe maybe shouldn't be and what is his fault, after all he's new and has a lot to learn, and what possibly is not his fault. Thinking of it Cameron realizes the impossibility of ever talking to Past about something like how he bids or especially his home life: Past hasn't mentioned a wife or girlfriend and certainly not kids and somehow just the thought of bringing it up gives him a shiver and why would that be? With the other Captains he has flown with (not that many, if you get right down to it) home life or at least where you grew up or something would be high up on the list after finding out what your flying background was and how senior you were.

Cameron checks his mail drawer for the usual stack of amendments to the 50/500 and the DC-9 Manual and the 580 Route Manual and lugs his flight bag and suitcase out to the parking lot. Driving the old Jag is soothing and pleasurable, like flying the DC-9 but without the pressure to learn. There is traffic at this hour and in the stop-and-go before the bridge Cameron's thoughts wander around exploring all of his two-and-a-half months of line experience, the flying and the layovers and the captains, mostly the captains because they set the tone; the whole cycle, the two or three or four days of work with layovers in between, the feeling, the impression of the whole cycle seems to emanate from the captain because it's his approach to the airplane, the job, the weather, the dispatchers, the flight attendants and the ramp guys, and to you, mostly to you, the First Officer, it's his take on all that and how he handles it that molds the experience for you.

Who was it that first month, near the end of the month, nice guy, big bear of a man, a Newfie, Harry, Harry Johnson, he's F.D.R. Johnson on the list, he was kind to Cameron, both kind and demanding, teaching Cameron now realizes all the time, like when they were taking off in a strong crosswind and Cameron wasn't aggressive enough on the rudder pedal steering and she tried to weathercock; he didn't take control or reprimand but instead called enthusiastically *Hang on to 'er, Cammy* and he did and will ever after because now he knows he can and it's burned in and there are many more learnings like that to come.

Harry and the other guys that first month-and-a-half, Cameron thinks, replaying it, they all talked about or at least mentioned airmanship; Cameron has stored it away, not knowing a definition, just an initial feeling, but really how could you not know what it means, obviously it is some kind of skill relating to this job, something that will seep slowly into the blood over time, and now he thinks of it, it was Harry who made the analogy with the crew of a square rigger and seamanship, the equivalent in their line of work.

Tacking a square-rigger on the open ocean, Harry said, required hundreds of coordinated movements, executed with precise timing. The seamen who crewed those vessels understood each maneuver instinctively, getting cues not just from commands but from the rig itself – the luffing of a sail, the slackness of a line, the subtle heel and torque as the vessel began to change course. But this instinct didn't appear overnight. Over years a crewman's understanding grew and he would rise through the ranks, serving in just about every position on the ship.

So Cameron does know what airmanship means, thanks to Harry; the picture of a young seaman climbing the ratlines and edging out along a yard with the wind freshening alarmingly and gusting, his feet supported on that other line strung beneath the yard and him reaching, groping for his buntline and on signal heaving with his fellows to furl the sail smartly; that picture sticks in his mind and informs his learning as no precept possibly could.

Now that he has flown a month with Captain Past Peak Cameron is piecing together a picture of the man. It is not something he can do with a casual ease because the layovers, where one might expect to be able to relax and relate to one's crewmate on a personal level are instead more rigorously choreographed than the flights. With the others it is occasionally the brushoff *See you at pickup* but more often *Wanna go for a beer and a bite? How long do you need?* But Past is always military, hierarchical. *Knock on my door in 15 minutes. Wear a tie.*

Then it's straight to the bar. It doesn't seem to matter if the bar has a nice atmosphere or a particular clientele but it never has music or entertainment. The beer comes regularly and quickly. Past is demanding and can be withering in his scorn if the waitress is not there at the moment he requires another beer. Cameron struggles to keep count so he can pay every other round.

There is no conversation. Cameron's duty is to listen to Past's jokes, which are always shaggy dog stories. Laughter at the punch line is required. The presence of the waitress for the delivery of the punch line is engineered by piercing looks, waving of beer bottles, and extension of the setup, which fattens with the beer count, digressing further and further from the subject and leaving the punch line orphaned. Being there with the laugh requires more and more concentration, although after four beers and an endless saga of an adventurer hiking the Himalayas, Cameron feeling rather foggy and trying desperately to pay attention, he knows to laugh when Past says without inflection *When the Foo shits, wear it.*

"Waitress! Another round!"

"Ah, Past, I'm on hold for awhile . . ."

"Lily-liver! Which reminds me – waitress!"

"Yes, sir. I'm here."

"Another beer. My friend here's not drinking."

"Yes sir. One beer."

"Which, as I was saying, lily liver – what is it? Lily-white boys, dressed in green-oh."

Past starts by humming to himself to remember the tune.

"Mmm, mm, mm, mmm, mmm, Green grow the rushes, Ho."

The waitress arrives with his fifth beer and he manages to pay her without missing a beat.

"Come on, Cameron, sing!"

Cameron mouths the words, at least the ones he can remember. After four for the Gospel makers Past pauses for a second and raises his beer:

I'll sing you five, O
Green grow the rushes, O
What are your five, O?
Five for the beer the jolly good beer . . .

It goes downhill from there. The twelve apostles remain forgotten. Seven beers gone and in full voice Past has switched to *Ninety-nine Beers on the Wall* and is richly amused. He is down to eighty-seven when the big guy appears at their table and suggests that now may be the right time to go get something to eat.

As they are eased out the door Cameron tries a fence-mender.

"Yeah, actually, I'm hungry. Should we . . ."

"There isn't a decent restaurant in this town anyway. No. Not hungry."

Past tries to stomp away and can't quite pull it off.

§

Cameron pays attention again as the traffic gathers speed and he rolls across the Victoria Bridge. The steel grating under his tires whines and the car darts from side to side an inch or two. It is terrifying the first time but if you just relax and go with it you don't lose control – it just feels like you're going to. Even so Cameron pays attention until his Michelins once again find solid asphalt.

Waiting for the left turn arrow off the boulevard his mind turns back to the cramped flight deck with Captain Past Peak. Small things the captain has let drop over the last month or so are beginning to add up.

Like Rod, Past was a fighter pilot. His time in the forces was fifteen years earlier so he flew the F-86 Sabre, not the Widow Maker. Cameron has already met a couple of others from that crowd. They left the military in a herd in 1959 and 1960 and joined the airline just in time to be in the famous layoff of 1961. Their stories and their personalities are molded as much by what they did during the layoff as by their time on the Sabre. Past is the exception: the layoff and anything which came after the Sabre are irrelevant.

Cameron can't get his head around it. For Past Peak being an Air Arcadia DC-9 Captain is a comedown, a demotion, a bummer. For Cameron it is his life's ambition. But the stars came into alignment for Past in the military. He qualified for fighter training and then was posted to Germany. Somehow he became friends with a German Baron. Once he was in the Baron's circle life was good. Fly the Sabre. Drive out to the castle for supper. On days off go hunting in the woods with the Baron and his party. Past was part of the nobility. Only the best food and wines. Only the company of the crème de la crème. Cameron thinks of Past mentioning that he attended most of a Ring Cycle at Bayreuth. That level of erudition seems a stretch for Past. But then there is the singing.

Cameron's attention is on the Jaguar again as he threads through downtown St. Lambert, almost home. But beyond the few blocks of shops there are only stop signs, and Cameron's attention drifts back to the flight line.

§

He is flying an approach to Stephenville. It's an NDB approach out over the bay. They are in solid cloud under Instrument Flight Rules. They have been cleared for the approach and are on their own, since there is radar (and radar vectoring) only at major cities in Arcadia. Certainly not out here on the west coast of Newfoundland.

Cameron, still short on experience, blows it. He crosses the beacon outbound still descending to the Procedure Turn Altitude at 250 knots clean. In cloud and bumping around, he realizes the airspace implications of being fast. Past is saying nothing. Cameron checks his chart. Phew! The 25-mile safe sector altitude is the same as the procedure turn altitude, and 25 miles is six minutes, maybe five with the wind, so one minute is OK, and now his mind is really working fast, and he's got to get down and slow down and track the beacon outbound and gauge the wind and drift and get dirty and remember to call for the right checks at the right time and not move his head and he's starting to sweat but he's got the tracking, he knows it's a crosswind from the south, and fairly strong because although the drift starts at less than five degrees it's now quite a bit more because of course when he left the beacon he was doing 250 and now he's got it back to 160, where he should be, with slats and flaps 15 and he's in the procedure turn to the north and he does exactly 45 seconds, by the book, but on the way back in realizes that – shit! – with that south wind he should only have done 40, maybe 35 seconds but, no sweat, he hasn't bust the airspace, it'll just take longer to re-intercept and yes, here it comes, finally, inbound track of 104 degrees, nail it – start at a 110 heading to allow for the wind – and yeah, not bad – better make it 115 for awhile – remember you have to get gear and final flap, and as you slow you'll need more correction, all this while you're *Leaving 3400 for 1900,* to cross the beacon inbound at 1900, the 115 heading is OK as they slow to 128, final approach speed, Vref + 5, power up to nail 1900 feet – don't sag! – and it's taking a long time to get to the beacon, yeah, he can still hear it in his headphones, DitDahDahDah, Dah, JT, that's it… of course, it's that damned 250 knots over the beacon outbound and a tailwind and now they're doing roughly half that and there's a headwind, no wonder… God, it sure is bumpy in these clouds… engine anti-ice on? Yes! Phew… no airframe ice… concentrate, don't blow it now… here comes the beacon, power back to 1.4 EPR, the approach target, 700 feet per minute down, don't forget the timing, and – steady, watch the tracking, it's backwards now, drag the tail of the needle – add some power, get that vertical speed back to 700, *One Hundred Above* (that's about the first thing Past has said) and Cameron sneaks a peek and sees the runway, it's OK, they're in good shape, just slightly right, take off some correction, not too much, don't go north of 104 degrees, it's visual, you can see what you're doing… *Minimum, Runway In Sight.* Looking good now. *Landing!* Cameron says, a little breathless. Gentle left rudder, right wing down a smidge, and *errck* there's those right wheels on, and it doesn't skip . . . *Buckets!* Reverse operating, spoilers are up, wait for 100 knots with no brakes to make sure the main wheels have spun up, then gentle braking . . .

I have control. Past taxies into the terminal and they shut down. Cameron is feeling bad about the approach but good about the landing, the locus of every pilot's ego. Past calls in the purser.

"Yes, Captain?"

"Approach bumpy enough for you?"

"Well, yeah, it was pretty bumpy . . . and it seemed to go on for awhile . . ."

Past jerks his thumb in the direction of the now-apprehensive Cameron.

"This is the so-called pilot who was responsible for that. Way too fast over the beacon. Our paying passengers had to sit through all that. It's a wonder the airline isn't broke."

"Yes, Captain."

§

Cameron realizes he is parked in front of his house. He is sweating and his cheeks are burning, just like they were that day two weeks ago in Stephenville. The engine is off but the little round key is still in its slot in the center of the walnut dash. He pulls it out and puts it his pocket.

Something suddenly makes sense. Captain Peak is near the top of the Captains' list, whereas he, Cameron, is at the bottom of the First Officers' list. There is only one way that twice in a row he could wind up on a block with Past Peak. Most of the other First Officers have been bidding around him.

Cameron thinks of Beau Brown and his briefing on that first day of class. The Twitchell bid. He will look into that.

Ville Émard

Quebec Province – the 1970's

Enrico

RIGHT HERE IN ARCADIA, hidden away from downtown Montreal, from the West Island, from the Plateau, nestled behind, hidden and fortified by LaSalle and Parc Angrignon to the west and south, divided from Verdun and the Douglas Hospital by the Aqueduc de Montréal to the east, and isolated by the Lachine Canal on the north, Ville Émard is almost a secret. Generations of Catholic immigrants have planted themselves here, raising their families in cold-water flats and their tomatoes on trellises in the small yard between the kitchen door and the lane.

In the fall truckloads of California grapes arrive and the men make wine, using no added yeast or sulphites but controlling the fermentation with home-made heat exchangers. Boys as well as girls learn to cook using the fresh vegetables culled near the kitchen door. A boy wandering down a summer lane with the vague intention of spending his allowance on a Dilallo Burger down on rue Allard would be distracted by someone else's Mama calling him *eh, caro figlio, veni gustare!* And he would have to go have a taste of eggplant parmigiana or osso buco and the Dilallo Burger at the end of his lane would be forgotten, his allowance still safe in his pocket and destined for the savings account which becomes essential when at sixteen he is suddenly aware of Viscounts and the occasional DC-8 flying right over his lane which happens only when the wind is strong from the northwest and Dorval is landing on runway 28.

Bad Dog

Further west, in a walkup in Dorion, a high school boy, barely fifteen, is climbing with determination. It is past midnight. Each time he lurches against the confining walls of the indoor stairwell he pauses and regains his poise with exaggerated dignity. At the top it takes some fumbling with the key to unlock the door. It is dark after all. Magically the door opens. It is Mom in her nightgown and robe. She has been worrying, awake. His breath is overwhelming. *Baddy! Have you been drinking?* Bad Dog looks Mom in the eye, his head attentively tilted slightly to one side. He smiles, radiating charm, good cheer, and undeniable inebriation. *Mother, you don't know the half of it!*

Enrico

He finishes polishing the windshield with the special plastic polish. Remembers to drag the step-ladder over to its parking spot beside the gas pump. Now the fun part. He gets into the pilot seat, fastens his belt and closes the door. He cracks the side window so he can stick his elbow out. He is a pilot. He remembers the book his Papa used to read to him when he was little. Pilot Small. Pilota Small. Pilota Small had a white scarf that trailed back from the open cockpit of his little airplane. The town, the cars, the people, and the cows in the pasture all looked small when he flew over them. Pilota Enrico checks outside, calls *Clear!* and starts the Cessna 150's engine. He rolls away from the pumps, heading for the flight line. He remembers to check that the wing tips have clearance on each side. There are several tie-down spots open on the grass. Good. He can taxi right in, swinging through one and back into the adjacent one so he doesn't have to shut down and push it in backwards. No too much power, though – he got shit last week for blowing dirt around. Something about how it dings the props.

It has been a good summer job out here in Cartierville. Washing airplanes. Gassing them up. And best of all, taxiing them around. He has been saving money. Soon he will have enough to take flying lessons.

Bad Dog

She is an ungainly girl, her figure as revealed by the one-piece bathing suit not one that would turn heads. Obviously though she is very much loved by Dad. Every day he is there to pick her up. Lately he is even there early to watch her progress. She is doing well: during the brief Arcadian summer she has come from barely treading water to swimming efficiently and with good power, especially in the crawl. Baddy is thinking he will recommend her for the lifesaving course. He will have to remember to talk to her about that, to see if she's interested. Better do that before mentioning it to Dad, although he would surely be pleased to know she's doing well.

Next week, the last week of the summer course, Dad is there for every lesson. Bad Dog has asked "Pumpkin", as Dad calls her, if she would be interested in the lifesaving course. She would. Today might be the day to bring it up with Dad.

It is a fine day. The early September sun seems low at four-thirty, the slanting light yellowish and friendly, warm and teasing on the skin. The lush green of early July is gone. The leaves have not turned but their intention is suddenly evident in this late light. Next Monday is Labour Day.

Bad Dog has vaulted out of the pool where he finally got Pumpkin to see how the arm starts at the sternum and how if she stretches (he was in the pool in front of her, just out of reach) and includes the clavicle in her stroke she can touch him. She is reaching further now as he stands dripping on the concrete pool deck, her arm looking more relaxed as it stretches forward above the water, the thumb now leading the entry at almost full extension of the arm. Better. Much better. That's where the power is. She's getting that tension, too. The pull-through even and slower, not thrashing, wasting energy.

Pumpkin touches the wall at his feet and looks up.

"That's it, Clarisse! Well done. Were you counting strokes?"

"Yes!" she smiles. "Eighteen! Never done it in less than nineteen!"

"That's your new power. Good job. Do another four lengths. See if you can keep it at eighteen. Then you're done. Go get dressed."

Pumpkin sets off. The first few strokes aren't quite there but then Baddy can see the body-memory kick in and she gets it again. Good. As he moves sideways, watching her, changing the angle slightly so he can see her clearly, his feet move out of the puddle he has made and find warm concrete. The sun is generous on his shoulders and chest. He is proud of her.

Suddenly he is aware of Dad at his side. His eyes, yellow as the sun, taking him in. The acne-scarred face, chin at Baddy's eye-level, gives him a start but that quickly fades because there is a peace there, too.

"Clarisse is doing very well, sir. See that stroke? She's got efficiency and power, now."

"You've taught her well."

"She has learned well, sir. And with your permission I will recommend her for the Lifesaving Course."

"She interested?"

"Yes, sir. We talked about it earlier this week."

"Good."

Dad watches Pumpkin do a flip turn at the far end. Surprisingly graceful.

"So . . ." the raptor eyes look back at Bad Dog. " . . . what about you?"

"Me, sir?"

"Yes. What are you going to do with your life?"

In truth, Baddy hasn't had anything to complain about.

"Oh, I don't know… I'm just finishing my Phys Ed Degree. Teach high school, I suppose. Coaching, maybe."

"You ever thought about flying?"

"Flying?"

"Yeah, for the airlines. The big jets."

"Well, sure . . . I'd love to . . . but I'm just a poor boy. Could never afford it."

Baddy waves at Pumpkin, who is heading for the changing rooms. The light is turning gold as the sun drops. He can feel it on his body competing with the dry breeze. Dad is looking him in the eye. It is like the sun and the air, making him feel alive.

"If you really want to do it, show up at my house tomorrow after breakfast . . . no, come eat breakfast. Eight o'clock. I'll teach you."

Enrico

He is staring with amusement at the vending machines above the urinals, taking it all in as he consummates this well-deserved pee. For the row of urinals, there is a matching row of chrome machines with twist handles, slots for two quarters and plexiglass-covered billboards about five inches square. There are little slots on the bottom where condoms come out. All manner of condoms. Ribbed. Lubricated. Unlubricated. Flavored. Sensitive. Dick in hand, he smiles his toothy smile, imagining an act for each one.

He zips up and washes his hands, Mama's voice in his head. *Lavare, Enrico. Sempre lavarsi prima gustare.* He washes well with soap because it is before lunch. Maybe a long lunch. They are in the Auberge des Trois Folies in Val d'Or. It is cold outside and snowing. Fucking prehistoric. Uncivilized.

Enrico has never been this far north. Never grow a tomato in this godforsaken dump. Let alone a grape. See why Mama talks about the old country. *Mai in Campo Basso*, she says.

He walks back into the big dining room, squinting as he finds Roger in the far corner. Fucking Englishman. Snooty Accent. Getting some hours today, though. Twin time. Instrument time. It's all going in the logbook.

He is surprised to see a large carafe of wine on the table. And two glasses. Roger has not waited for him. He has already toasted the morning.

"You're going to like this, Enrico," he says, waving the menu. "Good selection of pasta. Quite comprehensive."

Enrico reads it and winces, visualizing each item: the dried-out parmigliana, the far-too-coherent lasagna, the rubbery veal.

"Not that hungry, Rog. Think I'll have a burger."

"Good choice. Enjoy. Here …" he waves the carafe. "Have a snort, sport."

"Dunno, Roger. I mean, we're on duty …"

"Five o'clock departure, old man." The carafe still waves. "Plenty of time for it to wear off."

The meals arrive. The burger isn't bad, and the fries with it are terrific. He is reaching with his left hand to cover his wine glass when he becomes aware of movement across the room. He squints. Sure enough. Table of four men. Two heads turning toward them. The guys they flew up here this morning. The carafe is still waving as Rog tries to persuade.

"No thanks, Rog." His hand is still firmly over the glass. "Enough for me."

"Huh," says Rog, pouring his own. "Some red-blooded stallion you are."

Time goes by. They linger over coffee. It has stopped snowing. The carafe, severely depleted, is still on the table. He looks across the room and squints to be sure. The table is empty.

He stares out the window. With the visibility lifting the architecture and layout of this frontier town can intrude. He is not impressed. From beside him comes gentle snoring. Rog has his feet up on the chair around the corner from him. His head is tilted back and to one side.

He sits with his cooling coffee. Maybe that's why the old man sent him along today. To keep an eye on Rog. Heck – not my problem if the guy's a lush.

Back in the can, he gravitates to the urinal on the near end. Ribbed. He is smiling again. A stallion, plus ribbed. Bet she likes that.

He walks back to the table, hands unwashed, still thinking about ribbed. He is already seated when he realizes Rog is not there. The carafe remains, almost empty. Roger's coat, too. And his own cold coffee. He sits down and takes a sip. Didn't see him in the bathroom. Where has the fucker gone?

He looks around. The dining room looms threateningly around him. He looks at his watch. Be dark in an hour. Outside the snow has started again. Why would anyone live here? Fucking Siberia!

The cold coffee is empty. As empty as the room. He looks around. Maybe I should go look for Rog. Oh, piss on it. He'll show. His coat is here.

§

In the cab to the airport Roger is silent. I guess we're going. He's still pretty pissed though. He must be. They pull up outside the FBO. Rog pays the driver and they are alone in the snow.

"It was the old man. Said to bring the airplane back. Empty."

"Those guys? They're not ..."

"No. They're getting someone else."

Roger turns to enter the FBO. He turns back.

"So. Enrico. You want to fly back?"

"Sure ..."

"You got twin? IFR?"

"Ah, no. Workin' on 'em ..."

"No matter. I do and you're sober. So we're legal."

"Got my pilot license."

"Exactly. I'm Pilot in Command and it's your leg. Go sweep the snow off Triple Charlie and make sure they've gassed her up. I'll file the Flight Plan."

It is getting dark. He borrows a broom and gets to work, working up a sweat despite the howling wind and cold. Now just the walkaround. *Fuck!* His fingers stick to the gas tank tab. And there are three more of them. *My finger won't fit under that tab with my gloves on. Fuck!*

He remembers last summer arriving home to his own Mama and the smell of simmering tomato sauce and the noise of his most important person and first love pounding the veal cutlets and his mouth watering already as he announces *Mama I got my license I'm a pilot, Mama!* and she *Oh, Enrico mio, pilota, pilota! Caro mio, figlio unico, you are pilota! The best pilota! You will be the best pilota del mondo! Oh, caro Enrico, veni assagiare!*

Middle Age

AIRLINE HONCHO

December 13, 1975

Scandal at Air Arcadia

Chairman and CEO of Air Arcadia Ben Plat was eased into retirement early this month following a breaking scandal at the airline involving alleged six-figure payments to travel agencies for undisclosed favours.

Minister of Movement Otis Lemming explained that public corporations must expect closer scrutiny that private ones.

Sources close to Minister Lemming say he had privately expressed anger as the scandal broke in the press, claiming that Mr. Plat was effectively working for him anyway and would have to take the fall.

The structure preferred by the government for state corporations is to have a political chairman. The problem now, as it has been in the past, is to find a technically qualified president.

Arcadia

IN THESE SHRINKING DAYS of Advent they have taken my Ben from me, Father. I am not naive. I understand there can be corruption in my corporate body. People are people. But Ben was not a bad man and rooting him out as the Ministry did will not help. How would you have handled it?

I must tell you, Father, I am angry. That the Minister could think he knew better than I how to root out corruption. That he could indemnify his own fat ass by humiliating my president and taking him away from me.

There is more, Father. I have been thinking about my charter. Perhaps it is adversity and the dark times but my subservience to the railroad has been bothering me. I know I belong to the Crown, but to the railroad?

Fifteen years you have been gone. More like twenty since the Backwards took your seat. I know you were wounded, Father. I know the rebuke was unjust and clouded your last days. My Ben feels the same.

AIRLINE HONCHO
June 17, 1976

Air Arcadia CEO Injured

Air Arcadia President Chauncey Tinker was injured today when he stepped in front of a car after a tense meeting at the airline's head office.

Tinker is reported in stable condition at the Royal Victoria Hospital. Hospital staff describe him as conscious but perplexed that he could have walked into busy Dorchester Street traffic as witnesses have reported.

Aides to Air Arcadia's CEO were tight-lipped as to the agenda of today's meeting.

Arcadia

SUMMER SOLSTICE AND more trouble, Father! My Chauncey wounded in battle!

But I understand his distraction. He had been firing one of our vice-presidents. That self-smitten smartass had stranded hundreds of our passengers in Barbados for days. Why, Father? Why, so his shell game of financial manipulation could make his department's budget look better.

So my indoctrination into middle age continues, Father. I am at once hurt by what I do not expect and sick at heart because I expect it. Is this what sophistication is, Father? Some sort of cynical knowing?

I did feel right about changing my name. Trans Arcadia Air Lines has served me but now the sleeker Air Arcadia feels right. And Chauncey has been speaking with the Ministry about separation from the railroad. I am one step closer to my dream of independence.

Captain? My Captain?

The Maritimes – October, 1976

Rod

"Rod? Dick in Crew Sked."

"Yeah Dick. What's up?"

"You don't wanna know. You really don't wanna fuckin' know. This place is a zoo."

Rod decides not to bait Dick. Another time, perhaps. He has been sitting at home on Reserve for four days and it's time to fly. Don't jinx it.

"Been a quiet week for me. You got something?"

"Have I got something? You're gonna love this. Deadhead to Torbay. Layover. Then tomorrow some good Maritime flying. Five legs home."

"Sounds good. When does it leave?"

"That's the thing, buddy. Deadhead on 602 at 1430."

Rod looks at his watch. Shit! It's almost one! Sked Dick is still talking.

" . . . thirty-hour layover. F/O just booked off."

"OK, Dick. I can get there. Who's the Captain?"

"Thanks, buddy. You saved my bacon . . ."

Rod interrupts, trying to sound neutral.

"Dick, I gotta get moving. You'll have the deadhead pass and the details upstairs?"

"Yeah, buddy. Thanks. I owe ya one."

§

Rod is eating breakfast. The big dining room of the Hotel Newfoundland is mostly empty. Rod's table is under the east windows. The wide window ledge is about chest high on Rod if he is standing up; sitting at the table he can't see out. Last time he ate breakfast here – what was that? two years ago? three? – was with Harry Johnson.

On the list he's F.D.R. Johnson. Someone said it really is for Franklin Delano Roosevelt Johnson. Harry? Must be Newfie humour. We were sitting over there, near the middle of the room. He pointed at this window ledge with a smile, sort of sheepish, looked funny on that big bear of a man.

"See that ledge there, boy? Stood up there. Thirteen years old. Made a speech to the Rotary."

Then he chuckled. Made me feel good. I think I laughed, too. Then, was it that night? The approach in Moncton.

I remember the wind was favouring runway 24, the short runway. Before descent I briefed Harry for a visual approach to runway 24, using the words right out of the manual. It was a clear night. 100-mile visibility. Piece of cake, I thought.

He didn't say anything until we were on the downwind leg, about five thousand feet above the city. The lights of the airport were ahead; the lights of the city disappearing underneath us. Beyond the airport was – just blackness: the first lights in that direction, after the Northumberland Strait, would have to be on Prince Edward Island. All I saw out there were the stars on the horizon.

"You done a lot of these night visuals, boy?" It sounded like 'buy.' "You ever heard of the Black Hole?"

"No, Harry."

"OK then, boy. You see how dark it is out there? When you turn final you won't have any visual reference that's reliable. On this runway there's no glideslope and no VASI, so you've got to make your own. At night, always have something. See, now we're passing the end of the runway? What's your DME from the VOR? About six? OK, use that. Then use the 1 in 3 rule. At 700 feet per minute, it takes 3 miles to lose 1000 feet. That's your glideslope."

We were on base leg. I was calling for flaps and gear, treating it like half of a military overhead. I knew I was in good shape, but when I rolled out on final there were no lights at all, at least not between us and the airport. I was high! I knew I was high. How could that be? Then I hear Harry.

"Lookin' good, boy. See, 2 DME at 1300, that's 1100 AGL with 4 to go. Actually, yer a cunt hair low. Check to five hundred feet a minute for a bit - should be 1200 at 3 – we're getting' there – OK, about 6 plus 2 is 800 at 2 to go, perfect, hold 700 feet a minute and you've got 'er."

I thanked him while we were taxiing in.

"I was sure we were high, Harry. Just can't trust the visuals, eh?"

"That's right, boy. Black Hole's the same as the transition from instrument to visual in fog. You tend to duck under. That's why you always need a glideslope. If you don't have something, make yer own."

§

Outside it's a drizzly Newfie morning. On the rock not much separates the landlubber from the sailor – the driven mist smells of the sea and cloaks the vision wherever you are. Rod thinks about the need for a takeoff alternate. They most likely won't be able to come back in here and land this morning.

In the cab Captain Roscoe isn't saying much. His face is buried in the Financial Times. Didn't say much when Rod called him last night, either. Just *Good, see you at pickup*. At the airport they make their way behind the counter into the radio room. Roscoe just snorts as he looks at the weather. He signs the flight plan, then nods to Rod and mumbles. Something like See you up there or See you on board.

Rod heads out onto the ramp. He feels more alive out here with the drizzle stinging his cheeks. Cheerful, red-faced ramp guys call out greetings as he does the walkaround. The high-set horizontal tail fades in and out of view as he looks up to inspect it. He thinks of the takeoff – how everything is going to disappear on rotation. How an engine failure will be flown entirely on instruments, even with the mains still rolling on the runway.

Rod climbs back up the air-stairs into the cramped galley/entryway. He smiles for the girls but declines a coffee.

He settles into his seat. He is aware of Roscoe turning to look at him and swivels to meet his gaze. Only there is no gaze to meet. Roscoe is looking not at Rod but a point six inches in front of Rod's nose.

"Why don't you start?"

"Sure, OK."

There is no small talk in the cockpit. Rod is thinking how Roscoe doesn't know him from Adam and takeoff here is critical and the weather in Halifax is going to be minimums and blowing.

They pick their way out to runway 29. Roscoe asks for the runway lights to be turned up all the way and says, *You have control.* Rod aims carefully between the two or three lights he can see on each side and as he starts rotation moves his head firmly inside, onto the instruments, waiting for the lurch that doesn't come, the swinging in the HSI rose that would signal engine failure. Cleaned up, with gear, flaps and slats retracted and the critical engine-failure segment behind them, he carves left over the Bell Island he can't see but knows is there.

He amuses himself by using the radar for navigation, like Harry showed him, picking out St. Mary's Bay, Placentia Bay, The Burin Peninsula hanging out into the Atlantic *Like a dick*, Harry said with that sheepish smile, *Pointing at St. Pierre and Miquelon.*

Roscoe rustles in his Flight Bag. He finds an apple and chews, studying the Financial Times propped up on the yoke. The galley girl knocks discretely and pokes her head in. She seems to know not to make small talk. But Roscoe accepts a coffee and so does Rod.

More rustling in the Flight Bag turns up cheese and crackers from a previous crew meal, still in their EZ-peel pack and rustling cellophane, respectively. Roscoe munches, sipping his coffee.

The radar is picking up the eastern shore of Cape Breton: Glace Bay on the north, Louisbourg on the south and Main à Dieu on the east really looking like Michelangelo's limp-wristed hand of God, pointing at Scatarie Island.

Rod asks permission to get some weather from Sydney Radio.

"Sure. Go ahead." Roscoe waves a hand in Rod's direction.

The Halifax weather is 200 feet overcast, ¾ mile visibility in rain showers and fog, wind from 160 at 15 gusting to 25 knots. An ILS on runway 15.

There have been a few incidents on this runway in Air Arcadia. Rod tries to remember everything he has heard about it. Guys lose it below minimums, after they break out. Downdraft. The terrain pitches sharply downhill north of the approach lights and the air follows. With this wind there'll be a big sinker starting right around 300 feet.

Rod briefs the approach by the book, then adds, "Could be a downdraft over the lights with this wind. I'll be ready."

"Good, good," says Roscoe.

The descent is normal until they reach the beacon outbound. As they descend through 3000 feet on the procedure turn the turbulence turns on like a switch.

Not much showing on radar. Just showers. Must be a wave from that terrain dropoff.

Coming up on the Hotel Zulu beacon Rod calls for Flap 40 as the glide slope comes down to meet them. The marker starts to beep in his headset. As the ADF needle swings from 147° to 327°, he waves his left thumb over the throttles and calls:

"Hotel Zulu."

Roscoe is right there:

"1980. Two niner eight six inches set."

And keying the mike:

"Air Arcadia 613, by the beacon."

"Roger Arcadia six-one-three, cleared to land runway 15, wind 160 variable 180 at 20 gusting 35, runway wet."

It is bumpy enough so that it is difficult to focus on the instruments. Not eyeball bounce yet – where the G forces distort the eyeball – but Rod reaches over and turns up his instrument lights.

Better. Wind's pretty steady here. Ten-degree drift, more or less. Be ready for the sinker.

Rod cups his left palm behind the throttles, ready to push, cutting down the reaction time.

OK, steady. Any second now . . .

"One hundred above." Roscoe's slightly querulous voice.

"Rog . . ."

Wham! No doubt about it. Airspeed down ten knots. Left palm pushing the throttles up to 1.65 EPR. Nose up a couple of degrees. Not too much. Back on glideslope. Ease nose down a hair. Back to 1.4 EPR. Tracking OK.

"Minimums. Runway in sight."

Rod sneaks a one-second peek. There it is, where it is supposed to be, ten degrees left of straight ahead. He looks back inside.

Sagging under! Pull gently. A little more power.

"Lookin' good." Roscoe is still with him.

"Landing."

Rod's eyes are outside again. He flares, eases the power back, pushes the DC-9 parallel to the runway with his left foot on the rudder, and eases the right wing down a few degrees to keep from drifting left off the centerline. He feels for the runway with the right main gear. There! Hold steady. Now the left main is down too, the ground spoilers up. He takes his hand off the throttles and calls:

"Buckets."

The nosewheel is down. Roscoe selects idle reverse and takes his hand off the levers. Rod pulls to 1.4 EPR and feels the reverse thrust bite. They are through the intersection with Runway 24 and rolling up the hill. The visibility is worse up here. Below 100 knots he tries the brakes. Not great but OK. Rod continues light braking, slowly bringing the reverse thrust back to idle, hanging on to the centerline.

"**Air Arcadia 613, can't see you up there, cleared a 180 back, call**

Ground 121.9 when clear."

Rod has slowed the DC-9 to a walk and selected forward idle.

"OK, I have 'er."

Roscoe uses the tiller wheel down by his left knee to execute the 180-degree turn on the runway. Rod picks up the mike.

"Roger, Air Arcadia 613, we're cleared a 180, ground when clear."

Rod has that slightly breathless feeling from adrenaline as they do the shutdown check. He volunteers to run upstairs and get the flight plan.

"Anything special you'd like, Captain?"

Roscoe waves his hand abstractedly.

"No. Weather's bad. They'll give us enough gas."

Fifteen minutes later Rod is back on board with the flight plan and the new forecasts and actuals. He has managed to sneak in a pee and some human contact with the people in Station Operations Control. Running up the stairs has calmed his adrenaline rush. He settles back into his seat. It is fifteen minutes before departure. Time to do the cockpit check. Roscoe looks up from his newspaper and stares at Rod's left ear.

"Want to do another?"

"Ah . . . sure," says Rod.

§

The turnaround in Moncton is just long enough so they can balance a tray on their knees in the cockpit and eat a hasty lunch. The Captain gets the logbook. It makes a pretty good table. Roscoe has a newspaper propped up on the yoke as he eats. This time it is yesterday's Wall Street Journal. He seems to have a good appetite. He is clearing his tray with dispatch. Rod is too keyed up to be really hungry, but he finishes his entrée and pokes at his dessert.

Roscoe leans across the pedestal and eyes Rod's tray. He holds out his hand, palm down and fingers dangling. It looks like the crane bucket in one of those carnival games where you try to move a prize into the chute.

"Mind if I take your cheese and crackers?"

As the cheese and crackers disappear into Roscoe's flight bag, the hand approaches again.

"You going to eat that salad?"

Rod shakes his head.

"The dressing? It's blue cheese. I like that."

The Captain looks up from stowing his provisions. He is staring at Rod's windshield wiper bolt, as if looking for icing.

"Want to fly this one?"

"Ah, sure, why not?" Rod says, feeling a bit impertinent.

Rod thinks he should slap himself to get his mind back on the job. He takes a deep breath. The latest sequences show that the cold front has speeded up, but probably not fast enough for Saint John, their next stop. Saint John is flat on its ass. Freddy, their final stop in The Swamp, could bust open any time now. But Saint John is still in the warm sector. They are calling it 100 and 1/8, but they have two solid alternates and Roscoe wants to go. It will be an ILS to 23.

The approach to 23 is scary. Maybe not if you have never done one in VFR conditions where you can see the ground sloping up to you from the airport, trying to grab you before you are ready, before there is a runway underneath. And maybe not in cloud, either, if you are so busy your scan doesn't include the Radio Altimeter which reads just over two hundred feet for all of those agonizing last seconds when you are trying to keep those needles nailed and decide . . .

"A hundred above," says Roscoe laconically. "Keep 'er coming."

Rod's heart is pumping. He stops breathing. He is painfully aware of the ground flashing by unseen beneath them. So close to their wheels . . .

"Minimums," breathes Roscoe, barely audible over the white noise. "No Cont . . . wait . . . lights in sight . . . looks good . . ."

Rod can't help himself. He sneaks a peek. Just for a millisecond. Approach lights, whipping by under the nosewheel. Then they are gone. He is back inside, on instruments, keeping it steady as she goes. Then he is outside again. White lines under the nosewheel, looming out of the grey. In his peripheral vision, barely there, are the two lines of runway edge lights. About four of them on each side.

"Landing?" croaks Rod.

"Yes, yes," says Roscoe impatiently.

Rod has already flared unconsciously, as if with his autonomous nervous system, using the peripheral runway lights as guidance. Now he snaps the throttles closed. Plunk, they are on. Firm, but nice.

"Good boy," says Roscoe.

Rod is exhausted. He has flown three legs in nasty weather, mostly by hand. Roscoe hasn't cracked a joke or even a smile. Nothing personal, either, not even the basics.

As they taxi in and his heart slows down, Rod begins to feel annoyed. What have they just done? Was it anywhere near by the book?

Rod realizes he has been running on adrenaline instead of thinking.

True, I'm not the Captain. If someone reports us, it won't be me who has to answer for it. Well, unless Roscoe gets into really big trouble. Then I would have to go before the Board of Inquiry and answer embarrassing questions, like: *Do you think First Officers are just along for the ride?*

Four runway lights! That's eight hundred feet! The minimum visibility for the approach is ½ mile, or about 2600 feet. And the technique we used – without a word of briefing – was a sort-of, half-assed, PMA.

The Pilot Monitored Approach, where the pilot flying stays heads-down and passes control to the heads up pilot only if the latter sees enough to align, flare, and land, is used with variations in the military and in Europe.

They park and shut down. Rod can feel himself working up into a slow burn, and he still doesn't know why or at whom.

I don't want to be Captain America or Ace McCool. Fuck, I'm not even the Captain. Talk about dumb.

Rod realizes he is angry mostly at himself. But Roscoe is not blameless.

He's been sitting there like a useless cunt. The fucker. He's the one who's along for the ride.

The speakers crackle.

"Air Arcadia 613, Saint John Radio. You on?"

Roscoe grabs the mike.

"Go ahead for 613."

"What was your visibility on landing, 613?" the radio operator asks. "Center wants to know."

"Oh, we had, oh . . . a dozen lights or so . . . say half a mile," Roscoe drawls.

Then it is Rod's turn to talk to Saint John Radio. He copies the new sequence reports for Freddy and Saint John. Saint John is officially ¼ mile. Good enough for takeoff, if you have a takeoff alternate. But Freddy is wide open: scattered cloud and 15-mile visibility and a brisk northwest wind: the cold front is through. Freddy can be their destination and their takeoff alternate: it is close enough.

Roscoe looks at the weather Rod has copied down.

"Good," he says. "I'll fly this one, if you don't mind."

Saint John to Freddie is a ballistic trajectory up the river. Takeoff on 23, punch into the clag on rotation. U-turn. Level at twelve thousand four minutes after takeoff. Call for all the checks. Roscoe's briefing consists of:

"Yeah, should be able to do a visual . . ."

The airway does a ninety-degree turn to the left, following the river. If you cut the corner you're over the Army Base and you could be shot at.

They are already in a thirty-degree bank, trying to regain the 097 degree radial of the Freddy VOR.

"Air Arcadia 613, cleared for an approach at the Freddy Airport," calls Center.

"Air Arcadia 613, cleared for an approach at the Freddy Airport," Rod reads back.

Fuck, are we high or what?

Rod sets 2100 feet, the airway Minimum Safe Altitude, on the Altitude Alert. He glances at Roscoe's DME, tuned to the Freddie VORTAC.

"Seven from the VOR," he hints.

"Huh?" says Roscoe, looking up. "Ahh, leaving twelve. . ."

Roscoe bangs the throttles closed and yanks at the Speedbrake handle. Rod feels his body surge against the shoulder harness as the aircraft pitches forward clumsily. He keys his mike.

"Air Arcadia 613 leaving twelve for the approach."

Something is wrong. Boy, are they ever going down. Worse than the stories he heard about the Clunk. Or the Voodoo. More like the Zipper . . . Rod is looking around the cockpit.

Fuck!

Rod's head is screaming.

The Speedbrake handle! It's all the way back! Up, back, and up! The Ground Spoiler position! Fuck!

All day the world outside has been a limited one: the slope of the nose down to the radome and the bolt where the wiper attaches to the fuselage. Sometimes rain hurls itself against the windshield and streams back along the side window. The world beyond is grey. Shifting, sliding lumps and planes of grey. Sometimes in the densest cloud the sliding stops and the world is still as the sky holds one homogeneous shade for minutes at a time. It is like that in these last seconds. Eyes say you are not moving, but gut says you are falling out of the sky. Then they plunge through the surface of the front. Like a rounded wave hugging the surface, the cold air is rolling in, lifting the foggy warm air over it. It is like emerging from the face of a forward-leaning cliff. They can see forever, the landscape unfolding before them, the wind whipping streaks of blue-grey on the river, the airport a toy airport seven thousand feet under their nose.

"Gear down," calls Roscoe.

Leaning forward, Rod protects the gear lever with his left arm.

"Not with the spoilers out."

He points to the placard next to the gear lever: *Do not extend gear with Speedbrake in use.*

"Air Arcadia 613, you gonna get down OK?"

Rod imagines the scene in the radar room at Moncton Center.

"Can we do a couple of 360's?" asks Rod.

"Air Arcadia 613 cleared as requested. No traffic behind you."

Rod points to the Speedbrake lever, way back and up on the pedestal, where it should only ever be after landing or during a Rejected Takeoff. The Ground Spoilers position.

"Ease 'em back in," says Rod in a voice he doesn't recognize.

Roscoe starts a right turn. He grasps the release on the speed-brake lever and pushes forward. The lever snaps down onto the Max Speed-brake position. The aircraft lurches up, flying again.

"Gear down," calls Roscoe for the second time.

This time Rod's finger stays on the placard.

"One or the other. Not both."

Roscoe looks over at Rod. Rod shakes his head. Roscoe grips the release again and retracts the speed brakes. It is a little smoother this time.

"Gear down," Roscoe says once more.

Rod snaps the lever down. It is noisy: they are just under V_{LO}, the max gear operating speed. They are also above 250 Knots, the speed limit below ten thousand feet.

"Slats and Flap 5," calls Roscoe.

Rod can feel the deceleration and hear the groaning and the thud as the leading edge slats extend and hit the stops. He hears one beep from the Stab Trim as Roscoe thumbs the switch on the yoke.

"Air Arcadia 613, contact Freddy Radio 126.7."

"Air Arcadia 613, 126.7. Good day."

"Visual on 33," drawls Roscoe.

More beeps from the Stab in Motion alert.

The airport is under the nose again as they emerge from the 360-degree turn. Roscoe levels out. He is slowing, staying high, but dumping their kinetic energy. They are slowing through 250 Knots, legal again.

"Flap 15," calls Roscoe.

Rod puts his hand on the lever but waits until they slow through 240, making his point. 240 is max speed for 15 flap.

"Flap 25."

"Flap 40."

Roscoe is being more careful now, waiting for each V_{fe} before calling. They are fluttering down like Kleenex, engines at idle. It is still going to be tight. By the book, the engines should spooled up to 1.1 EPR with flaps extended. Rod changes to 126.7, listens for a few seconds, and keys the mike.

"Freddy Radio, Air Arcadia 613, right base for 33."

"Roger, Air Arcadia 613. Wind 290 at 20 gusting 35. No reported traffic."

That wind's gonna help a bit. 'Specially if he keeps it slow . . .

"Let's spool 'em up at 500 feet," Rod says aloud to no one in particular.

Roscoe is flying now. He looks like he knows what he's doing: hugging the river, giving himself room for that right turn onto final, resisting the urge to push the nose down. The wind is helping. It is probably more westerly up here, and stronger. They are plunging through six hundred feet, starting the turn to final.

"Sink rate," says Rod evenly. "Ya better spool . . ."

"Yeah, yeah," Roscoe answers impatiently. But he stands the throttles up a couple of inches.

Nothing happens for what seems like a very long time. They are rolling out on final at four hundred feet, the VASI coming into view, white over white, the upper lights rapidly going pink. Rod feels the yaw as the left engine spools up to 1.2 EPR. He waits for the second, opposite yaw. Whew!

"800 feet a minute," Rod calls. "Looking good."

The VASI is red over white. On glideslope.

"Wind two nine zero variable three two zero," calls radio. **"Speed two-fife gusting four-fife."**

They are down. A bit of a lurch to starboard: Roscoe hadn't pushed it quite all the way straight. But not bad. He can fly if he puts his mind to it. They taxi in and shut down. Just one more leg home.

Rod feels Roscoe looking at him.

"Ya know, it's really OK to have gear and speed brakes ...", Roscoe begins. He nods at the placard. "All that means is ya can't, yer not supposed ... I mean, the mechanism, the linkage, it could ..."

"It could extend the Ground Spoilers," Rod breaks in. "Like you had. Like the DC-8 in Toronto six years ago."

Rod tries to look Roscoe in the eye. It is iffy whether they are getting a lock. Rod presses on anyway.

"If it's OK with you, Captain, I'd like to go by the book. Just do it like the book says."

Rod hesitates for a split second.

"That way we're ready for the Sim," he adds, smiling broadly.

He isn't sure how he has summoned up the smile after the day they've had so far, but there it is.

Roscoe isn't immune. He smiles slightly, then lifts his chin and picks up the Wall Street Journal.

"Right you are. Wanna fly the last leg?"

The Players

The Twentieth Century

Snake

IN DEEPEST TRANSYLVANIA in a remote and scary castle there are screams: birth pangs. A spirit had moved on the earth nine months earlier but it is certain neither that he was flesh nor that she of the screaming had been a virgin.

The birth was normal during the dilation of the cervix. The army of midwives (there were three) left no doubt about that. Their meticulously kept diaries (independent and since compared by scholars) exhibit an almost identical record of dilation vs. time along with comments from the principal (between screams). Only the brief delivery was unusual.

There was no crowning, no urge to push. There was the amply documented approach to ten centimetres and then – birth! As Mom said, both then and later ad nauseum, *He just slipped out! Like a snake!*

Indeed, as the midwives recorded, he was a long, slender infant.

There the trail goes cold. It is unclear exactly why although there are bits of evidence, widely separated and unverifiable, which hint at a connection with the Count: he of the unusual appetite.

Nothing is known of the infant's upbringing, of his training, his predilections. He surfaces fully mature and trained as a lawyer, in Arcadia: specifically in Montreal at the firm *Strike 'em Yell at 'em*. All we have is testimony from a few law students who ran into him in a peripheral way at law school or as students articling at *Strike 'em*.

Boy Wonder

A WORLD AWAY from Transylvania another boy, of pre-school age, wanders along a city street. Frantic parents call the police with a description and it isn't long before he is spotted walking purposefully with a small suitcase. In the squad car he is cheerful and chatty and delighted to discuss his mission: I'm going to the airport. I'm going to fly Continental Flight 2712. To Los Angeles. It leaves at 1430 hours.

Growing up, he of the small suitcase moved through the world with his father's diplomatic postings. Now they are back in the 'States and his eclectic interests and twin 800's on the SAT have tweaked the interest of some good colleges: he has been accepted at Ivymore. Meanwhile Dad has helped along his undiminished fascination with airlines. At home they subscribe to *Airline Honcho*: Boy can follow the exploits of his twin idols, Horace Homer and Panhandle Pete.

AIRLINE HONCHO

January 23, 1978

WASHINGTON – In Senate hearings this week on airline deregulation, Patriot airlines was represented by Panhandle Pete, Patriot's Senior Financial Vice-President. Mr. Pete's testimony at the hearings was what several senate aides termed "colourful".

"My company is in business to make money," he said in response to a question put by Senator Cannon (D. Nevada). "and frankly, this proposed legislation is going to put airlines out of business." The questioning then heated up with Senators quoting from think tank tomes as to the myriad benefits of deregulation, led by lower fares. They then pressed Panhandle to retract his previous response.

"I'm not saying that the industry will die," he answered. "all I'm saying is a lot of airlines are going to die. And if anyone makes money in this business ever again it will be a fluke."

At Ivymore Boy Wonder's studies are exploratory. He is good at math and takes two courses per semester. In Sophomore Year some of the math topics lead to computer science and he is briefly bitten by the bug, learning Lisp and Prolog. But his unofficial work is keeping up with the exploits of his airline idols, especially Panhandle Pete, who has now become President of Patriot Airlines. As a curriculum requirement he takes a history survey course and reads about the South Sea Bubble. Something clicks in his head.

Boy likes reading about Pete's innovations in the airline business and then musing on them as he walks through campus. His mind has been occupied with the hub and spoke system recently put in place by Patriot. In his dorm room he combs the *Official Airline Guide*, the telephone-book-sized volume that contains information on the world's airline flights. He wants to see in his mind's eye the passenger's view as he arrives in Dallas or St. Louis and transfers to an onward flight. He wants to understand the logistics of passenger and baggage transfer, of gate assignment and, he realizes, the effect that weather or Air Traffic Control delays have on operations like these.

Panhandle continues to impress not just Boy Wonder but the industry at large. He is becoming the trendsetter, the fashion maven, the Miss Manners of movement. Boy hangs on his every word, combing the newspapers and business magazines for any scrap of information on Pete, no matter how small. When in his senior year the time comes to consider his next move he is decisive, applying only to the best business schools. Oddly, he is wait-listed by the nearby Wartorn School but accepted by the Brahmin Business School.

AIRLINE HONCHO
May 20, 1981
Miles Club at Patriot Air

Patriot Airlines surprised and galvanized the industry today with the announcement of its Miles Club 'frequent flier' program. Panhandle Pete, the company's CEO, said passengers will be rewarded for their loyalty: by flying Patriot they accumulate 'miles' which can be used to purchase future trips or upgrades.

Reaction in the industry was swift. Speaking for Sigma Airlines, CEO Horace Homer said their own Frequent Flyer Program would be launched "within the next couple of months."

Boy is excited by his admission into the prestigious Brahmin MBA program, but he is more excited by Panhandle Pete's latest gambit. Walking the campus paths that June his mind goes over and over the ramifications of Pete's move. VFR, Visiting Friends and Relatives, is a modest part of airline traffic. By far the largest category is business travellers, most of whom are middle managers flying on the company dime. Boy gets more excited thinking about it. And do those managers pay the tab? No! Will they be rewarded? Yes! The miles accumulate in their personal accounts! He finds himself walking faster, then slowing, then almost marching as he discovers the next step in Pete's logic. Basically, those 'miles' are kickbacks: manager chooses Patriot, pays with his company's money, and gets a kickback for himself. But also it's designed to make the perpetrator feel good. Good about his choice. Good about himself. That he's doing something smart. Better yet, this market segment, business travel, is not what you would call price sensitive. The individual isn't paying. But he's getting miles for his business travel, lots of miles. Kickbacks are an old business trick. But the implementation is genius!

Boy embarks on another campus loop. He hasn't finished putting this together in his mind. There was a Panhandle quote he saw not long ago, just a snippet in one of the newspapers. What was it? Something about the concept of getting something for nothing continuing to have a great fascination for people. That's the motivation, of course. Greed. Greed which is the most reliable of human motivations and can be counted on to turn the wheels of capitalism. But greed is one of the seven deadlies and kickbacks have a bad image in commerce even when they're legal ... that's the genius of it, right there, because the Miles Club is crafted for image, for good feeling. The perpetrator will feel not guilt, but pride. He is gaming the system, smarter than the next guy who has to pay for his ticket ...

Snake

LIFE IS GOOD as a partner. True, the workload is brutal but it's work he loves and hey, if you can't stand the heat then get out of the kitchen. Besides, he is now on the same level as the Prime Minister – well, just here at *Strike 'em Yell at 'em*, and only after the next election – because the man will be back in that office across the hall. The rolodex is already fat with Forwards and former Forwards. Now the challenge is to get to know just as many Backwards, because after the election, or the one after that, it's going to be Hurley Blarney – he'd lay odds on it. And he has to stay connected, because everything depends on knowing the minister.

What the interns and associates don't understand – even if they're billing over four thousand hours – is that clients who pay *Strike 'em's* rates (and certainly the partner rates) expect more than a solution, more than fitting in, more than working the system. If you're going to be a partner here you'll have to at least play the system like a Stradivarius. Hell, he thinks, for my clients I'll circumvent the system entirely, whether that's what they expect or not. Because those who don't see the need right away can be tempted. *Can always be tempted.*

Bullshit!

The North Atlantic – September, 1979

Cameron

"CAMERON? DICK IN CREW SKED. You're going to love this, buddy. Freighter. London layover. Second Officer is Hapless. Former Navigator. Captain's Bird of Prey."

Cameron is excited. This is his first trip on the DC-8. Overseas. Europe. And he has heard of Bird. Fires everyone, apparently.

Things move quickly the next afternoon. No sooner has Cameron introduced himself than the three of them are pushing their way out of the briefing room and hustling downstairs for the cab ride up to Mirabel. Bird nips at their heels like a sheepdog. It seems as though he can't wait to put some distance between them and the trappings of Flight Operations. Downstairs he quickly shoves Hapless into the front seat of the cab and gets into the Captain's seat, the right rear. Cameron walks around the back and installs himself in the left rear.

Once they are underway Bird wastes no time.

"How long you been on the '8, Cameron?"

"This is my first trip, sir," Cameron begins. "No, my second. First as First Officer."

"They drafted you as an S.O.?"

"Yes, Captain. Last weekend."

"Fucking idiots." Bird looks at him . "Call me Bird. Who checked you out?"

Cameron tells him. Bird grunts. It sounds like an OK sort of grunt.

"We're going to be heavy. This time of year it's horse meat. Seven pallets of dead horse. The frogs fucking love horse meat. It's going to be tight carrying enough gas."

Cameron can see Bird turning this over in his head. A brand-new unknown as F/O. Horse meat. Bad weather.

When they get to Mirabel Bird greets the guys in the loading dock.

"How's it going, guys?"

"Good, Captain. OK. We'd be ready now except we gotta take one pallet off."

"Says who?" growls Bird.

"Dispatch. Called up and said you're carrying six tonight."

"Whatterya going to with the seventh? Leave it here to fuckin' rot?"

"I don't know, Captain. Dispatch just said take it off."

Bird shakes his head.

"They just don't get it," he says. "We're in business to make money, right?"

Heads nod.

"Leave that pallet on there."

He nods to Cameron and Hapless.

"Get on board and do the checks. And don't start fueling 'till I get back."

Bird walks away toward the flight planning area, muttering under his breath.

"Stupid fucking assholes. Think the horses are going to care if we have to stop somewhere… Jesus…"

Cameron does the cockpit check and aligns the IRS's, but inserts no waypoints because he doesn't have a flight plan. Hapless is fussing at his panel. It sounds too purposeful. Cameron gets up, ostensibly so he can hang up his coat but in fact to see what Hapless is up to. Sure enough, the fill valves are open and he has the bugs set at full mains, full alts, and there is pressure in the lines.

"Uh, Hapless?"

"Yes, Cameron?"

"You know the Captain said not to start the refuelling. Not 'till he gets back."

"It's OK. I'm not. Just getting set up."

"But your fill valves are open. There's fuel going in."

"Well, sure. But full mains, full alts. We always have that going overseas. Never changes. You can count on it. You can put money on it, Cameron. Couldn't find a safer bet."

"Um. Point is, maybe we're not going overseas."

"So. Captain's going to defy the Company? Not go? I doubt …"

"No, no. Of course we're going to Paris. But we might stop on the way. For fuel."

"So, what's the big …"

"We'll be over Max Landing Weight if you let much more go on there."

Hapless twists off the main tank refuel valves and toggles off the alts.

"Exactly. Max Landing Weight. That's what I was saying. Why, two weeks ago I was flying with Captain Cubby and he said the same thing. Max Landing Weight. Just like you said. Imagine? Is that a coincidence or . . ."

Cameron has his coat on and the cockpit door open.

"Going to do the walkaround. See you in five."

Twenty minutes later Bird is back, clutching a flight plan. He hands it to Cameron.

"We're going via Stephenville. First leg's yours."

Cameron looks at the weather. Pouring rain. Gusty southeast wind. 400 overcast. It will be a Back Course on runway 10. He remembers flying the ADF to that runway on the DC-9 with Past Peak.

Bird gets Hapless going with the refueling. Cameron and Bird load the INS waypoints. It is close, but they are ready by sked departure.

Bird doesn't say much. Cameron and Bird are both perusing the weather maps, thinking about this leg and the next one to Paris. Gradually the lights below disappear under cloud cover. Then it starts to get bumpy. Cameron is thinking about the approach. He isn't going to fuck it up like that time with Past Peak.

He has more experience now. By the book, he has to go in to the beacon (*DitDahDahDah, Dah*) and do a Procedure Turn. That will add five or ten minutes to the flight even if he does it right.

But coming in over the bay, over water all the way, there is no reason not to do a DME/Radar descent onto the Back Course and go straight in. Even though that option is not depicted on the approach chart.

Cameron thinks about it. He'd have to start down soon – the wind up here is still westerly – a tailwind.

It is as if Bird can read his mind.

"When are you going to start down?" he growls.

Cameron explains the DME/Radar option.

"…start down at about 130 DME," he finishes.

He looks over at Bird. His face looks scarier than ever in the dim glow of the cockpit with its spotlights and sharp shadows.

"Good," says Bird. "When the weather's bad, get down early. Don't fuck around."

Evidently Bird approves of the straight-in-over-the-bay plan. That's a relief. Now Cameron can just concentrate on doing a good job. He starts down. So far so good.

"How are you going to intercept the Back Course?" asks Bird.

"I figure this track will cross it just outside 20 DME," says Cameron.

Bird says nothing. That is good, Cameron guesses. Cameron slows to 250 knots and starts down from 10,000 feet. He calls for the In Range Check. On the radar the bay and the peninsula show up clearly, with other shadows in between. Rain showers. Some of them heavy, by the look of it.

"ADF confirm you're going to intercept?"

Not quite a growl or a snarl, Bird's voice is certainly loud. Cameron has always been a little shy in that respect. He will learn to speak up, to make sure he is heard clearly.

"Yes," he says, in the loudest voice he dares. "Laying off to the left and increasing. Any minute now."

Sure enough, here it is. And the INS is a huge help. He uses it to pin their track on 104° as they close on the localizer. Their heading is about 120°. Sure blowing south up here.

Now it is raining harder and getting really bumpy, but things are going fine. Cameron has this one nailed. Going to be a crosswind landing, though, and this is not a DC-9. He will have to be careful not to scrape a pod. Just push her straight after the flare; keep those wings as level as you can.

The marker is about a mile away.

"Before Landing Check," calls Cameron.

Bird grabs the gear lever and puts it down. It is noisy. Cameron is still not used to the noise on the DC-8 with the nose gear doors open. The Master Caution light comes on. *Shit, what's that?* He glances up at the panel.

Spoiler Pump.

Oh boy. That's a no-go. I just looked at it the other day.

The 8's hydraulic system is a dog's breakfast compared to later systems. It is as if it was designed, then frozen in stone, and subsequently other requirements came up. Extra bits were added. The spoiler pump is one of these added bits.

In gusty crosswinds like tonight the early 40-series DC-8's were slow in roll response, so on the larger 50 and 60-series 8's the flight spoilers come into play when the wheel is displaced more than 40 degrees. The flight spoilers then supplement the ailerons, improving the roll response at low speeds. The spoiler pump comes on automatically when the landing gear is down. That explains why it only showed up now, with the gear ...

"I know what it is. I have control," calls Bird.

Cameron feels a stab of disappointment. A new airplane, a challenging approach, and he is on track to ace it. After a second or two, though, the disappointment mixes with relief. There are a lot of new factors in play here now, with the spoiler pump out. Cameron isn't sure he knows all the implications and there is no time to spool up. He gets back into PNF mode: alert and thinking ahead, hoping he is aware of everything.

Bird reaches down between his knees and holds the spoiler pump switch to Override. Bird and Cameron watch the Spoiler Pressure Gauge. Cameron can just barely see it below and to the left of the Standby Horizon on Bird's panel.

Nothing. Bird lets the switch snap back to normal.

"Pump's shot," says Bird.

What about the Ground Spoilers? thinks Cameron. They will need them as soon as they touch down. The spoilers kill the lift of the wings, putting more weight on the wheels. Without them, on this wet runway, it will be like landing on ice.

Cameron remembers there is a way to get pressure to the ground spoilers from the main hydraulic system. *Works only on the ground, I think.*

Bird nods to Hapless. His voice is even louder than normal.

"Hapless! Ground Spoiler Power Switch! Alternate!"

Hapless fumbles around on his panel. You can tell by the rhythm he doesn't know what he is doing. Bird turns his head. There is a green light on the left side of Hapless' panel.

"NOT THE STANDBY RUDDER POWER, YOU IDIOT!

"TURN THAT OFF!

"IT'S THE ONE ABOVE IT!

"GROUND SPOILER POWER!"

Cameron sneaks a look over at Bird. He is smiling. Hapless is still fumbling.

"It's lockwired, Captain."

That's right, thinks Cameron.

"WHAT!?" bellows Bird.

"I can't move it. It's lockwired closed."

Oh, oh, thinks Cameron.

Now Bird has a wide grin. He is flying like the ace he obviously is. The wheel is hardly moving as they bounce around. The LOC needle is pinned in the center. It looks as though it has lost power, except there is no *Off* flag.

"I KNOW IT'S FUCKING LOCKWIRED!

"IT'S SUPPOSED TO BE FUCKING LOCKWIRED!

"NOW BREAK THE FUCKING LOCKWIRE AND TURN IT ON BEFORE I BREAK YOUR FUCKING NECK!"

Bird's grin is even wider. They are breaking out, right on track. They are at 400 feet. You can't see a heck of a lot. Bird pulls his Rain Removal Lever.

"Whoooshsh."

The DC-8 has a pneumatic rain removal system instead of wipers. Basically it just blasts hot bleed air from a nozzle onto the outside of the windshield. Cameron follows suit.

"Whoooshsh."

Now he can see the runway lights – off to the left, because they are crabbed to the right into the wind.

Cameron wishes he could have a film of this approach. The runway lights are surreal through the rain. Then the landing lights are gleaming off the wet asphalt. The flare and de-crab are as good as it gets. Now they are floating along, power at idle, perfectly aligned, the right wing down just a hair so they don't drift. The right gear can't be more than an inch off the runway.

Bird turns toward Cameron, still smiling. In a voice louder than any he has used so far tonight, he bellows:

"REVERSE!"

Cameron hesitates. Reverse is not to be used until the aircraft is on the ground. But they are floating . . .   He is pretty sure the Ground Spoilers will work, although he hasn't actually turned in his seat to make sure Hapless has got that switch up. Besides, in the 60-series 8's you can pull the inners into reverse to use as speedbrakes, although not on approach . . .

What the fuck, he thinks. *We're an inch off the ground.*

He snicks all four into idle reverse. A second later they are on, as smoothly as only a wet runway can arrange. The blue Spoiler Extend light comes on. Bird pulls the engines up to about 1.4 EPR in reverse. They use hardly any braking.

The rain is coming down in buckets. Bird does a U-turn on the runway and they taxi back to the terminal ramp. It will be years before Cameron realizes he actually does have a film of this approach – in his head. It is something he will carry with him into retirement.

Cameron starts thinking about the next leg. They will be heavy. Good thing they didn't use much braking – the brakes will be cool for this Maximum Gross Weight takeoff. They won't be climbing very fast.

Holy shit. Cameron thinks of the terrain. They will be taking off toward the east. The ILS on the other end, on runway 28, has a 4 ½ degree glideslope. The norm is 3. Even 2 ½.

The approach to 28 is along a valley which slopes down toward the airport and the sea. The glideslope is steep because with a normal glideslope you would be down in the valley, with the mountains on either side level with your wings. And at the weight they are going to be tonight she won't climb any 4 ½ degree angle, that's for sure.

The re-fuelling truck is waiting. So is a new flight plan, brought out to the aircraft by a cheerful station guy who has obviously driven to the airport specially for this flight.

"Here ya go, Cap'n. Some Jesus wet, eh boy?" It sounds like 'buy'.

Bird smiles.

"Thanks," he says. "Yes, sir. Ain't a fit night out for man nor beast."

Guess I'm the beast. Cameron is almost blown off the air-stairs. But the air is fresh, a curious mixture of fresh and salt water smell that lifts his heart. *You know you're alive out here.* The brakes are indeed cool, barely steaming in the wet. The fuel guy has his ladder placed in the shelter of the wing.

Back inside Cameron shakes out his coat and hangs it up to dry. He slides back into his seat. Bird has been busy. They are almost ready to go. Cameron pulls out his ILS 28 approach chart and holds it in the glow from his spotlight.

"That's right," says Bird. "Good job. It's going to be tight. Here's how we're going to work it."

In the future there will be takeoff limits on runway 10. But tonight there are no limitations, no guidance. You just have to know what you're doing.

"You'll tune the Juliet beacon," continues Bird. "Make sure you monitor the Morse until we're through 5000 feet. I'll be tracking the beacon and the localizer and using the INS track. There are also these hazard lights…"

He points at the chart, to some starburst symbols north of the localizer track.

"We'll be able to see them, the first two, anyway. They'll be off the left wingtip. We'll stay at Takeoff Power until we're by. Then max angle climb. Takeoff flap until here" – he points out beyond the beacon – "or until 4200 feet."

His finger is on the sector east of the Juliet beacon.

"OK?"

Cameron nods.

"Yes sir," he replies.

It is exciting. He can feel the weight in the way she unsticks on rotation. She flies, but she does not leap into the air. She shrugs the weight onto her wings and bends to her task, willingly, but deliberately, as if to say, *This no walk in the park, you know.*

She hesitates in ground effect as the gear comes up. Then they are labouring upward, clawing for altitude against the rising valley floor.

Through the rain Cameron sees the hazard lights slide by off the left wing. He is listening to the Morse Code in his headset identifying the Juliet beacon: *DitDahDahDah...* pause... *DitDahDahDah,* over and over again. Then they are in solid cloud, bumping along with that damped-out ride peculiar to very heavily-loaded aircraft.

The Juliet beacon slips by. Finally, 4200 feet and flap retraction. *Whew!*

The North Atlantic Track structure starts just off the eastern coast of Newfoundland. Gander and Shanwick Oceanic Centers publish these tracks daily so that they can accommodate the maximum number of flights as close as possible to the Minimum Time Track. That track in turn depends on the position of the jet stream. As the flaps come up and the tension of the takeoff eases, Cameron is at once aware that he still has to get the Oceanic Clearance.

They have filed for Track Charlie, the third one down from the north. They have asked for Flight Level 330 and Mach .805 (80.5% of the speed of sound).

Cameron leaves Bird flying and talking to the low altitude controller on the number one VHF radio. He goes to the number two and negotiates with Gander Oceanic. They are a popup over The Rock, climbing up under the synchronized squadron of aircraft heading for the track system, coming from New York and Boston and Chicago as well as from Arcadia. The squadron already has its Oceanic Clearance.

"Air Arcadia 586, Gander. Ready to copy Oceanic?"

Bird listens on his number two with the volume turned down. Cameron keys his mike:

"**Gander, Air Arcadia 586. Go ahead Oceanic.**"

Cameron writes, concentrating hard: '48 North Fifty West; 49 North 40 West; 50 North 30 West…' *That's Track Charlie, so far so good.* But the zinger comes at the end:

"**Flight Level 280, Mach decimal eight two.**"

They will burn a whole lot more gas. Cameron will have to figure out how much.

He holds his clipboard up in the pool off light from his spot so Bird can see it. He points at the FL280 and the Mach 0.82. Bird nods. Cameron reads it back. Well, that's it. The track, at least, is as requested. They won't have to reprogram the INS.

Cameron gets out the Performance Book, a yellow plastic 8 ½ by 11 ring binder. Some of the guys have taken to slipping centerfolds from Playboy in with the charts. Previously these pictures were only to be found wadded up under the little covers over the rudder and aileron trim knobs. But since a new Check Pilot produced a memo warning about extraneous material on the Flight Deck, the Performance Book has fattened.

Cameron leafs through to the Fuel Consumption at Cruise, Mach 0.82 page. He finds the intersection of their weight and FL280. *Correct for temperature*, says the chart. Cameron glances at the RAT (Ram Air Temperature) gauge and finds ISA (International Standard Atmosphere) + 2.

He corrects the fuel flow. It is about 10 percent higher than planned. Will they have to land again, say at Shannon? Cameron notices Bird is spinning his wheel, the circular slide rule that sits in pilot's shirt pockets. He wonders if Hapless has twigged.

Cameron sets up the number two HF radio for the weather broadcast. He looks at the clock. It will start soon. He puts a fresh sheet of paper on his clipboard and writes down the stations he is interested in – Paris, Brussels, London, Shannon – leaving big spaces to copy the actuals and the forecasts.

He turns up the volume. The background is there: a rocket ship blasting off from the bottom of the sea. Then as the clock's second hand ticks into position the eerie voice with the Irish lilt begins reading the weather.

Cameron works hard at screening out the rocket noise as he copies. The weather is more or less *the shits*, as some of the guys say. Shannon is holding, but Paris and Brussels are forecast to go down in fog at dawn. *The way things are going with the gas, we can't hold an alternate longer than Brussels for Paris. Shannon will have to be our Ace in the Hole.*

Cameron passes the weather over to Bird. He reads, nods, and hands it back.

Now they are nearing 40 West. First the Alert lights on the INS's come on. Cameron goes through the drill, writing down time and fuel and wind and confirming track and distance to the next waypoint. He watches the autopilot turn to the new heading. Then he keys the mike.

"Gander, Gander, Air Arcadia 586, position."

No joy. Just that otherworldly noise. Cameron looks at their Oceanic Clearance, where he has copied their primary and secondary HF frequencies. The secondary was one lower in the family. Makes sense. It's night. Sun is low. Cameron switches to the secondary.

"Gander, Gander, Air Arcadia 586 on 4724, position."

There is is! Weak, but readable. A tiny voice with an unmistakable Rock accent, but sounding like it has been processed through compressors and squishers and equalizers and wawa boxes:

"Air ArccccsshhcccffffsttatesixGander, go ahead posssscchhcct."

Hoping for the best, Cameron presses harder on the mike switch and speaks as clearly, loudly, and slowly as he can.

"Air Arcadia 586, four-niner north four zero west 0231, Flight Level 280, estimating fife-zero north three zero west 0322, fife-zero north two zero west next, Mach dezimal eight two, wind three one zero diagonal niner fife, fuel on board seven eight dezimal six, forward to company. NOSIG."

Cameron strains to hear the readback. It is there. It is OK. He keys the mike again.

"Air Arcadia 586, that's all Charlie."

He clips the prehistoric mike back into its wire holder. With luck he won't have to pull it out for another fifty minutes. Then they'll be halfway across, more or less. Cameron turns down his HF volume so it doesn't drive him crazy. He can still hear transmissions, and anyway they can SELCAL the aircraft if he misses something.

Now the noise is the white hiss of Mach .82 air sliding around their shoulders and the remote whine of the cabin compressors and the separate white hiss of their exhaust blowing out the cockpit vents. And a new, more irritating pollutant: Cameron can hear a mechanical-sounding whine that sounds like four robots yodeling around a very sharp G above middle C. He experiments with the knobs on his audio panel. The yodeling goes away if he takes off his headset. It almost goes away if he turns all his volume knobs down to zero. He thinks about it for awhile. It is still there because he is monitoring 121.5, the emergency frequency, on VHF and sort of monitoring 4724 on HF.

In the relative quiet he is suddenly aware of intense activity behind him. He manages to sneak a peek.

Hapless is hard at work. In their brief acquaintance Cameron has never seen him so engaged. He is lettering in a column of the Fuel Log.

Of course. 40 West is the big, the major, the important fuel check. The one I just forwarded to dispatch.

The Air Arcadia Fuel Log is a thing of beauty. Legal size, but turned sideways into landscape mode, it has rows and columns and carbons so three copies of each flight's numbers are produced, each on a different-coloured paper. The Second Officer fills in a column for each waypoint. Hapless has almost finished the one for 40 West. Now he is inscribing numbers in the last two boxes: *Fuel Over Destination* and *Fuel Over Alternate*.

A feeling of foreboding overcomes Cameron even before he can become conscious of why. There is a rustling behind him. Hapless taps him on the shoulder.

"Cameron? Can you pass this up to the Captain?"

Cameron carefully takes the proffered journal. His left hand has to hold the previous flights' pages where Hapless has bent them back around the spine to better display tonight's labours. The page is a work of art. Hapless could be a forger. His penmanship is exceptional, striking. Cameron catches himself staring at it and quickly passes it over to Bird.

Bird focuses his spot on the page and almost immediately starts to smile. Cameron strains to see the bottom line, the FOD prediction. As far as he can see, in Hapless' masterpiece they are fat. Plenty of gas. It looks like Hapless has just copied in the numbers from the flight plan. The whole Mach 0.82 FL280 thing has just blown by him.

Bird is smiling broadly. The corners of his mouth, making shadows on his chin in the spotlight, curl upwards in an evil leer. He starts wadding up the fuel log, destroying Hapless' chef d'oeuvre. This is not an easy task. A new log is close to an inch thick with its cardboard covers. But fuelled by righteous indignation, Bird is up to the task. His big strong hands rip and crumple. The masterwork and all ancestors of this flight and the blank pages of its not-yet-conceived progeny succumb bit by bit to the Captain's wrath. Finally, with the log reduced to a projectile-worthy wad, Bird grabs it in his right hand and throws it backhand. In a voice that sets a new volume record for the evening, he yells:

"BULLSHIT!!!"

It is an exultant cry. The backhand is powerful. The wad hits the top of the cockpit door and opens up, raining down crumpled pages and carbons. Hapless is out of his seat, down on his knees, gathering up the pages. He is making little hurt cries:

"Oh, oh, oh, oh."

Bird has settled back in his seat. He looks very happy.

§

As the sun rises so does the quality of the HF reception. Cameron uses a higher frequency and copies the weather: Shannon is still OK and so far neither Paris nor London has fogged in.

Now they are visual in the daylight, starting their descent into Paris. The French controllers, loquacious in their own language, stumble in English. Cameron is working hard to make sure everyone is on the same page with their clearance.

"Affearmateave, AeroArcadienne, deerek Melun. Reepeet, deerek Melun."

Bird shakes his head.

"Always a fuckup."

They park the airplane and get a lift over to the passenger terminal. The deadhead to London is with British Continental. The aircraft is a Tripod, Britain's answer to the Trijet.

The flight is overbooked. The agent politely brings up the idea that perhaps one of you gentlemen, being pilots, wouldn't mind riding in the Flight Deck, that way we'll get everybody on. Bird looks

160

like he is going to growl but Cameron loves the idea. Comparative cockpit culture. He volunteers.

The Commander is a middle-aged gent who is also known as P1. Two younger guys are called P2 and P3. P2 sits in the right seat and P3 behind, but apparently they are qualified for both positions and switch around. Only the Commander ever says anything much except *Yes, Commander* or *No, Commander*.

At first it appears that it is P2's leg. He does the takeoff, levels off over the Channel and plugs in the Autopilot. Then instead of, *Pre-Descent Check, please*, it is the Commander who rolls up his sleeves and exclaims:

"I say, shall I do an immaculate letdown?"

The Commander hand-flies the descent and approach through clouds. As they near minimums Cameron finally understands: they are doing a version of the Pilot Monitored Approach, where one pilot flies the aircraft with reference to instruments only and the other stays heads-up, acquires visual contact, and takes over control for the landing.

"Approaching Minimums," says P1.

"Visual," says P2.

"Minimums," says P1.

"Visual, Landing, says P2.

The whole operation has been an eye-opener for Cameron. That is just as well because otherwise his snoring might have been a distraction.

As he reconnects with Bird and Hapless, he finds that British Continental has lost one of Bird's bags. Bird is left with his flight bag and the fifth of Bell's scotch he picked up at the duty-free.

When they get their room keys at the hotel Bird motions Cameron to wait. Hapless says goodbye and gets on the elevator. Bird's instructions are succinct:

"Sleep two hours. Set your alarm. Meet me in my room at 3." He waves the bottle. "We'll have some of this."

Cameron sets the alarm in his room and the one on his watch. It is confusing, not because it is hard to figure out but because he is so tired and the sun is in the wrong place. The earth has rotated under him and he is no longer connected to it.

He sleeps. When the alarms go off it is like surfacing from a hundred feet under water. He doesn't know where he is. It just seems wrong: wrong that he should wake up; wrong side of the bed to put a wall; wrong everything. There is a mechanical warbling in his ears. He shakes his head. The warbling is still there. He looks out the window. There are voices in his head that won't go away. Like last night. The yodeling. It was the generators. That sharp G, 400 Hertz. When they moved the audio panels outboard to make room for the INS's. The lines not shielded. Interference. He looks at the desk, the telephone, the lamp. Looks for his suitcase and shoes. Plugs, weird-looking plugs...

Of course, he thinks foggily. *London.*

It is ten to three. *Better get dressed. Splash some water. Wake up.*

He walks down the stairs to the floor below and knocks tentatively at Bird's door. It is already open a crack. There is a bellow from within:

"Come in. I'm on the phone."

Bird is still dressed in his uniform shirt and pants, minus the wings and epaulettes. *Right, his bag. Doesn't have his bag.*

Bird motions for him to sit down on the couch. He puts his hand over the mike on the phone:

"British Continental put me on fucking hold," he says.

He already has a tumbler of scotch in front of him. He makes a move to pour one for Cameron, but before he gets the stopper out of the Bell's Scotch he is talking into the phone.

"Not a problem," he says politely. "Especially now you've found it. When? Before five? Yes, that's fine. Thank you very much." Short pause. "Yes, you too. Bye bye."

He rings off. He reaches for the empty glass and pours Cameron what must be four or five ounces. He holds up his glass.

"Cheers," he says. "First today."

"Cheers," says Cameron.

"Kid, you're OK," says Bird.

He is looking at Cameron with those eyes of his. It is almost as if he really has a proud curved beak and wings with aileron finger-feathers and talons that are the stuff of rodent nightmares.

Cameron says nothing. He imagines the field mouse hearing the almost-vocal exhalation of the red-tail's flare in the instant before he strikes, the finger-feathers spreading and making a descant to the wing-wake. How the mouse understands and accepts that it and the bird are manifestations, limbs of a larger life.

"But ya really fucked up last night," continues Bird.

Cameron snaps from the meadow and the mouse back to last night. He races over his whole history with Bird, all eighteen hours of it. He thinks he knows.

"Ah, you mean in Stephenville. When you called for reverse and we weren't on the ground."

"That's right," says Bird.

Cameron screws up his courage. *Tell it like it is.*

"I was thinking of a lot of stuff. What if Hapless didn't get that switch up? The ground spoilers alternate. We'd hydroplane. And I knew we were an inch off the ground…"

Bird smiles that smile of his. Cameron again channels the field mouse.

"Right," says Bird. "Good."

Bird of Prey, Captain without epaulettes, terror of the skies, swirls scotch in his bathroom tumbler. He looks happy.

Cameron inclines his head slightly, exposing the back of his neck. He understands and accepts. He sees the magnificent flapping of the red-tail's wings after he has the field mouse in his talons. He hears the hawk's shrill, grating cry, like a scream.

Bird channels the hawk, speaking in short bursts.

"Just remember."

"Don't fly to please me."

"Fly to please yourself."

Bird raises his glass and holds it out.

"Cheers," he says.

The Times They Are A-Changin'

Montreal – December, 1986

Arcadia

I AM AFRAID, FATHER. I am not sure why, because Chauncey has done well and now he has moved to Chairman and found me Pierre, my new president. Pierre is a technical whiz. Right here in our house he invented *Flight Data Acquistion and Recording Systems* and guided us through a revolution in Information Technology. We can be proud, Father.

We have been solving problems, too. For example it seems only yesterday I was afraid for a pilot strike as the Big Twin was introduced. But Boing in their wisdom built three-crew flight decks and two-crew flight decks and finessed the certification and wooed Untied Airlines like a Casanova and I feared they would travel and woo me as well and whisper in my ear in their down-south accents things I knew were not so but it seems looking back I took a breath and our Ministry of Movement was onside saying yes, now two-engine over water is fine and two-crew is fine and suddenly not only the Navigator but also the Flight Engineer and even the Second Officer are history, Father, vanishing with our beautiful DC-8's and their special flight deck which I am embarrassed to say renders them somewhat difficult to unload.

My Pierre is moving along too, Father, on the question of my independence. Thanks to him it is no longer a taboo subject, even though the Backwards are in power. Hurley Blarney himself did not rule it out! So this, too, may come to pass despite my worries.

Could it be Barley Loam? We joined them, Father, just after I spoke with you last. Leasing airplanes has given us more financial flexibility. But is that enough?

Recently we have been struggling back from the brink, as Chauncey puts it. He says our profits are marginal. But are they not still profits? Chauncey and Pierre say our debt is too high; we need more equity. But it is only the government who may invest in us, as things stand. Pierre says he has talked to Hurley Blarney and Hurley agrees that we need more equity pumped in but he is afraid Arcadian Pacific and Pure West will howl so he hesitates.

Still, I have a sense of foreboding.

AIRLINE HONCHO
December 13, 1986

Pure West Buys Arcadian Pacific

In a surprise move, Pure West Airlines (PWA) has bought Arcadian Pacific Airlines (AP) for $300 M (Arcadian). Calgary-based PWA is much the smaller company, having approximately one-third the number of aircraft and one-third the number of employees as AP.

PWA sold the bulk of its fleet of B737's to Barley Loam Aviation and leased them back the same day, yielding $250 M in support of the all-cash deal.

> AP had been struggling recently after absorbing Yippieyieyay of Halifax and Air North of Montreal.
>
> PWA plans to operate the two companies separately for a while, meanwhile positioning the combined operation to compete more effectively with Air Arcadia.
>
> Government-owned Air Arcadia is twice the size of PWA and AP together.

Arcadia

ADVENT AND THE DARK TIME are upon us, Father. Once again I feel as I did when my Ben was taken from me. When was that, a decade ago? Once again now the coloured lights hold no promise and the dread thickens within me. Whence does it spring, Father?

Why have I never worried about money before? Did you, the greatest industrialist this country has known, worry about money? For eight years deregulation has been law south of the border. Eight years the Forwards have been saying a Crown Corporation must not act like a deregulated airline. But now suddenly Hurley and the Backwards are giving the nod to all these swallowings-up: Yippieyieyay and Air North by Arcadian Pacific and now AP itself plucked from the tree for a mere $300M by a prairie upstart one-third its size!

More and more often, Father, Chauncey and Pierre speak of the market. The Market! What is this thing we must defer to – worship, even? Is it not enough to do good work? Not enough to proudly accomplish the mission set out in our charter?

Perhaps we feel a change before we know it. Perhaps we sense a presence before we see it. Is this so, Father? Is that why my senses nag at me with visions of radar blips appearing and disappearing and even merging? If I appeared must I disappear?

Now I am talking with you, Father, I can see that I do fear The Market more than anything. That The Market and only The Market will determine my fate fills me with fear. That it may not be what I do or how I take care of my people or what I do for our country or its people, but only some balance sheet, some bottom line, some clinking of coins that drives my destiny. Was the only purpose of your enterprises that they should make money?

I was your first enterprise, Father. And what am I? An uneasy amalgam of people and airplanes? Is that it? Perhaps what I really fear is not The Market but my own mortality. Just as you brought me into being The Market can snuff me out.

What am I, Father? Like you and my dear people, mortal? I know you shake your head but does not a corporation stand at least in metaphorical relation to a person?

And do I not see, Father? Do I not feel? Am I not the sum of my dear people?

I am they, Father; yet they are not mine.

Through them I know the value of work: honest work where the individual heart attaches itself to labour for a common cause – my cause, Father! Their hearts pump for me, their life's blood runs through their veins for me. And through them – through them and only them, Father – I am alive. They give me thousands of eyes to see and hearts to feel and I do, Father. I see and I feel. And more yet – I know in an inchoate way there is more – yet I cannot name it.

For I am they, Father; yet they are not mine.

No, Father. They are not mine. Not mine to do with as I please. For why does each one work for me and honour me by believing in me? Why, it is of course because honest work feeds them. Feeds them in a way that is more precious even than the pay that I deposit in their accounts. But there is more yet: the pay in their accounts puts a roof over not just their heads and food in their mouths, but also shelters and feeds and clothes and educates their families and children.

I know, Father, because I see and feel through their eyes and hearts.

Most of them have a partner; almost as many have children; a sizeable fraction of those have a spouse who is home with the children, raising them, sheltering them, keeping them safe from the fray until they are grown enough to take on the frightening fray in their turn. So their father or mother who works with and for me has an enterprise of his or her own which although not on the scale of mine endeavour is nevertheless arguably more important still – certainly so in the aggregate of all peoples. So when he or she returns home after a day with me can I begrudge him or her a home life? Begrudge, when even as he or she returns home others have arrived to keep a shift, such that I am never alone? I should say not, Father. Indeed, I am honoured that a portion of the work of their hearts is dedicated to me, to my well-being.

For I am they, Father; yet they are not mine.

Through their eyes I see, Father. And what precious beauty! Can you imagine the joy in my heart when I peer through the eyes of their souls at the jostling humanity lined up at my counters and feel through the skin of others the biting winds and sleet on my winter ramps? Or especially – as I have scores of flights in the air always, through the day and the night – basking in the setting sun over the cloud tops and then nosing through the wet grey into dusk and rain or snow and threading between unseen mountain peaks that I see in my mind's eye because yesterday or last week the sun was shining and the snow glistening on those same peaks and I could see to the horizon in every direction and at altitude that is two hundred miles, Father!

Through the eyes of my pilots I know these threads of space left by my flights; they vary only by oceanic track or minimum time track or shortcuts and direct-to's or by runway in use. I know these threads, I exist in them. Indeed, they are my very veins, channelling my aircraft and my flight crew and my passengers. Through my people these threads are part of me.

For I am my people, Father, yet they do not belong to me.

I am these moments of wonder, Father: when Orion guides me to the Blessed Rock on a winter evening and I know I will hear the cadence of the Newfie speech when the door opens in Torbay, or when I glide around the cemetery on the LGA expressway visual, pulling mild G's to clear downtown Flushing; or as I again experience the minute or so of almost-panic as So-Cal cajoles me into a too-tight slot on one of the four southwest parallels at LAX: as any or all of these course through my awareness I am alive, Father! I am myself and present and I am happy and alive! The beauty of the world has fed me.

Can you then say truly, Father, that your firstborn is insensible to beauty? That she has not a soul?

Searching For Love

June, 1987

Rod

R OD FEELS HER LOOKING at him, seeing him as a magnificent animal. A sunshine smile spreads on her face and her brown eyes hold his. A warmth is spreading through his body. Something about the last few days has made him hungry for human contact.

He goes through the Captain's briefing to the Purser. She listens, occasionally tilting her head to one side, her eyes expertly keeping the channel open.

"Say, Rod? I guess this is some kind of check, eh?"

Lisette is beautiful and smart. She is also very good at her job, as he knows from previous flights.

"Yeah. Captain final. If all goes well."

"Congratulations!"

He exhales, almost laughing. The cycle is not over, he's not a captain yet, but thanks to Lisette the tension of the last few days is easing.

"Well, we'll see. Maybe after this leg."

The smile and the toss of her head is still with him as he settles into his seat.

"So tell me, Rod ..."

Rod is bent over the console, flipping the speed book. He sets it to 86,000 pounds and sits back.

"Sorry. Go ahead, Miles."

"So, let's say the fifth floor is down. Their backup won't come up, either. So load control is going to have to do everything by hand. There are going to be delays."

Rod takes a moment to think about where this is going.

"OK, yeah. What kind of delays?"

"Well, they're having trouble finding anyone who remembers how to do it ..."

"But Miles, they have to know how to do it. They can't hold that job unless they do. And by the way, we know how to do it, too. Only the charts are no longer in the manuals. They were when I joined." Rod remembers Miles was on the course just ahead of him. "When we joined."

"Anyway, they just put out a *FURther information AT* for four hours from now."

"Four hours ..." *He wants me to say I'd sit here for four hours?* "Well, in four hours we wouldn't be legal to finish the flight to Montreal. We'd have to pull the plug. Stay here in Charlottetown."

"So that's what you'd do?"

Rod looks at Captain Miles, trying to catch a hint of a smile, trying to find a way wiggle them both out of this without getting awkward or illegal. Nothing. Miles is nothing if not serious.

"No. We'd figure it out ourselves and go. I figure it out for myself every leg anyway. As a backup."

"So you're saying you'd go? With no load figures?"

Rod takes out his pen. On a clean sheet of notepaper, the pad stuck in the map clip on the yoke, he prints in caps *ZFW. Zero Fuel Weight.* As neatly as he can. He learned that from Mr. Matt. Centered, above that, he writes, *621.* Their flight number to Montreal. Also from Mr. Matt.

"We have the count from the purser. Fifty-two. At two hundred pounds per, with baggage, that's ten thousand four hundred. Sixteen in gas. Empty we're fifty-nine something. In round numbers, that's sixty, a little less, plus a bit more than ten, say seventy."

He leaves a bit of space after the 'ZFW' and writes '70,000'. Very neatly. Uncharacteristically neatly.

"With the sixteen in gas, that's eighty-six thousand."

Rod points at the speed book.

"So these speeds are good."

There is something coming off the DataLink printer. Rod tries not to look. Unnecessarily. Miles is already shielding it with his left hand. As the printer stops Miles rips it off with his right, glances at it, and stuffs it into his shirt pocket.

Four minutes to departure. *Paper was the right size. Gotta be the load numbers.*

Miles looks over at Rod.

"OK, but how are you going to get the C of G? The stab setting?"

In his head Rod covers the bases quickly.

"Two things. Two minutes." Rod smiles at Miles. "Be right back. Hold the fort, Captain."

Rod gets up from his seat and puts on his cap. He opens the door and steps into the entryway/galley area.

"Hey, Rod. Everything OK?"

The warmth and gratitude return. He smiles.

"Yeah. Fine. We should leave on sked in about three minutes. Just wanna have a look at the passenger distribution. Is it normal? I mean, they're not bunched up anywhere?"

"No. They're all over the place. Have a look."

Rod tries not to make it too obvious as he looks back and scans the cabin.

He steps into the entryway door and holds up a finger to the ramp guy.

"Gotta go talk to the lead for a sec. And – thanks."

In a few seconds he is down the air-stair conferring with the lead. *No, no cargo at all today. Mussels not in season, you know. Just one bag of mail. Suitcases. Divided fore and aft. By connections or no.*

In a few more seconds he is back in the left seat and can hear the whirr of the air-stairs being retracted. He buckles up and puts on his headset. He looks over at Miles.

"**Before Start Checklist**, please."

Miles obliges, closing the windows and setting the checklist down flat on the glareshield.

"**Before Start Checklist Complete**."

"OK, Miles. So I checked the passenger distribution. Normal. Talked to the lead about the cargo load. Just luggage and one bag of mail. No cargo. Evenly distributed."

"So how are you going to get a stab setting out of that?"

"Yeah. So we're mid-weight, even distribution. About as normal as you can get."

The stab-in-motion horn gives one beep as Rod adjusts the tailplane.

"Middle of the green band. That'll be fine. At least well within the acceptable range."

"Ground to cockpit. All ready down here, Cap'n."

"Roger. Brakes set. Starting engines, two and one."

With his left hand overhead on the starter switch and his right on the HP Cock, Rod again tries not to notice as Miles takes the paper out of his shirt pocket, squints at it, shoves it back in and leans over the pedestal to look at the stab indicator. It is hard not to notice because in the cramped cockpit the top of Miles' head is almost in Rod's left armpit.

If it's close he's going to let me go and either flunk me or not. But there's no way he's going to let me see those load numbers.

Rod calls for the After Start Check. Miles is strictly operational. OK, we're going.

"Revert to hand signals. Thanks for the turn, guys."

"Roger. Reverting to hand signals. Good luck, Cap'n."

How the hell does he – Lisette!

Sure enough, the lead is smiling as he waves them off, finishing with a thumbs-up. Rod spools up to breakaway thrust, then lets her roll forward a few feet before he smoothly winds the wheel hard right.

"Clear right."

Miles' head is out the window, his left thumb held up above the pedestal. As she gains momentum in the swing and starts moving ahead Rod brings the throttles back to idle. Now she is rolling down the ramp away from the terminal building. It feels good. *Gonna enjoy this leg, whatever happens.*

Through the rotation and takeoff the trim feels exactly right. There is no traffic, and the climb to FL350 is smooth, the visibility outstanding. Both Rod and Miles look out their windows. Oddly, it is a way to stay present in the operation. And at cruise, Miles seems to have relaxed. That's new, too. On each flight leg before this one he began a round of twenty questions as soon as they called level. Now he seems to be ruminating, drifting into some other sphere.

The Northumberland Strait drifts by underneath them.

"In September I'm going to Toulouse."

"Toulouse? Toulouse, France?"

"Yup. Going to spend a few months at Bus Industries. On assignment."

"Wow. That's going to be interesting, I'll bet. We're getting the Bus, right?"

"Yes, sir. We get the first one next January. With luck I'll be flying the delivery flight."

Rod manages some small talk about French food and wine. It is enough to bring Miles' ruminations to the surface. It seems there are going to be two of them on this mission to Bus Industries. They will take a course and get their ratings and be listed on the crew of the test flights of our first aircraft and generally represent Air Arcadia. But their main task will be to write the airline's Standard Operating Procedures for the new machine.

Check Pilot Miles makes no further demands. The flight is smooth, VMC, and normal, and their conversation refers only tangentially to what Rod hopes is his Command Final. In one of the quiet moments during the descent a thought forms in Rod's mind and lingers for a moment: *Whatever he says or does, remember you're doing good work today.*

Slowing at ten thousand feet Rod calls for the In Range Check and their interaction becomes strictly operational. Rod is flying by hand, enjoying carving in over the refineries and setting up for 24 Left. As he intercepts the localizer he sees out of the corner of his eye that Miles is ripping something off the printer. Probably he asked for another ATIS, to see if anything has changed. Here comes the glideslope and he's taking flap, decelerating slowly and enjoying the dynamics, trying to time it so he doesn't have to push the power up beyond the regulation 1.1 EPR until he calls for the Before Landing Check.

Rod waves his thumb over the throttles.

"By the Mike."

Miles makes the by-the-book response but he's looking out his window, toward Cartierville Airport. *Don't know if he's going to give me my epaulettes but this is fun.* In the slight crosswind he pushes her straight early and slow just for the pleasure of feeling her move. There isn't much turbulence from the hangar row. She settles prettily on her right main.

As they finish the rollout with power back to idle reverse Rod remembers the DataLink printout from back by the refineries. Miles hasn't put it down by the Speed Book on the radar where they would normally put an ATIS.

They taxi in and shut down. From the stories Rod has heard, some of the guys get their epaulettes at beer call on a layover. Others get them right here, after the Shutdown Check.

Miles rummages in his shirt pocket.

"Here, Rod. This came for you while we were on approach."

Rod reads the crumpled paper. *Rod please call Crew Sked on arrival.*

"So, Rod. Let's go up to the office and debrief. See you up there."

Check Pilot Miles disappears up the bridge. It takes Rod a minute or two to get all his charts back in his flight bag. As he puts on his tunic in the cockpit doorway, a pair of big brown eyes looks around the corner.

"So?"

She looks delicious. Rod wants to give her a hug.

"Don't know," he smiles. "Maybe I find out upstairs. We're gonna debrief."

Lisette shakes her head.

"What a jerk. Of course you passed. And he's trying to make you sweat?"

"S'OK. I'm not worried. If not today, then another day. With someone else."

"Good."

The sunshine smile spreads on her face and the brown eyes again hold a lock on his.

"Congratulations, Captain."

The warmth surges through him. He surrenders, taking in her energy, knowing this is simple human generosity and nothing more.

"Thanks, Lisette."

§

In the hall Rod glances at his watch. Shit! I can't believe I spent forty-five minutes in there with him!

He is heading for the briefing area, the closest place other than the office where he can phone. He takes out the crumpled paper again. It still says, *Rod please call Crew Sked on arrival.*

The briefing area is almost deserted. The six o'clock wave of departures has begun. Most of the crews are already on board. *They can't be sending me out. I'm out of time.* He dials the number.

"Sked Dick."

"Hey, Dick. It's Rod. In off 621. Got a message to call you."

"Rod! Captain Rod! Hey, Buddy. Congratulations!"

"You heard? Shit, I hardly know myself. You're not going to send me out?"

Rod realizes he is still clutching his captain's epaulettes in his left hand.

"Hell, no, buddy. We're a humane employer. Guy's gotta have a few beers on a day like this. But I'll tell ya, buddy, it sure is good news. We're minus captains for the rest of the month. Tell ya what, I'll give ya tomorrow off so you can get shitfaced. Then I'll have something for you."

"Yeah, OK. Thanks, Dick."

"Wait, wait! Don't hang up. Don't ya wanna know why you called us?"

"Uh, sure . . ."

"Well, there's a buddy a yours trying to get a hold of ya. A Colonel O'Riley. Got a number here . . ."

Shit, it's Brendan. Colonel? Rod dials. It's on the south shore, by the look of the number.

"438."

The voice is unfamiliar.

"Hello. I'm calling for Colonel O'Riley. It's his old friend Rod."

"Yes, sir. Right away. He's expecting your call."

Rod can hear the phone being put down on a hard surface. Then muffled voices and shuffling.

"O'Riley."

The voice transports Rod back to his wedding.

"Brendan. It's Rod. Are you in town?"

"Ah, can it really be you, Ramrod? Through the mists of years, is it?"

Since Rod and Susan's wedding there have been Christmas cards with brief notes. Brendan has never mentioned his rank. At the wedding he was a major.

"Congratulations, Brendan. Colonel."

"Your voice is music to my old ears, Ramrod. Thank you."

"So – 438. Are you over at St. Hubert?"

"That I am. Payin' a visit to the Reserves."

"Could we get together? It sure would be good …"

"Indeed. That's what I was hopin'. I've got to be at NDHQ. But tomorrow afternoon, only …"

"Wonderful. I'm at the airport. The other one. Dorval. I'll come pick you up. Should be able to get there in half an hour, this time of day. Maybe thirty-five minutes."

"Well, now you needn't be puttin' yourself out, Ramrod. There's transport around here. Staff car, if I …"

"No, really, Brendan," Rod interrupts without knowing why. "You're at the Garrison, right? Off – what's it called – Lisette, Liette …"

"You're close, old man. It's rue Leckie."

"Oh, of course. Rue Leckie. Look, Brendan. Give me 40 minutes. I'll call Susan, tell her you're staying the night. There's a room for you. The drive'll do me good. It's been quite a day. We'll have some time to catch up."

"I can feel you're het up, me lad. Take it as slow as you want. When you get here I'll be waiting."

There is a noise on the line, a cough or a sniff.

" … and thank Susan. I'm grateful."

§

There's the Victoria Bridge and St. Lambert and he remembers this tacky intersection in Le Moyne and then the sky opens out

180

a bit and he's on the 116 on a long straight with the train tracks on his left and it all comes back, getting his multi-engine rating at St. Hubert and meeting Cameron and his first flight on the DC-9 with Al Lank except now there are more buildings everywhere and he doesn't recognize anything and how do you get across the train tracks to the airport?

Eventually there is a St. Hubert exit and Rod takes it and there is an underpass he doesn't remember but it gets him on the other side of the tracks. Chemin de la Savanne looks right and then he's on the airport at the button of 06 Left so he just has to run north a bit and there's rue Leckie and he comes through its little 'S' curve and suddenly there's Brendan standing on a patch of lawn beside the hangars.

Before he knows what has happened Rod has slid the car to a stop in the gravel beside the pavement and is out the door giving the colonel a bear hug. He steps back to look at the man, the uniform, and is suddenly embarrassed. Conscious of his own blue uniform, he looks around to see if anyone has seen him fail to salute higher rank. Brendan is laughing, looking over Rod's shoulder.

"Jasus, Ramrod. I am sure as hopin' you put that shitbox in Park."

Rod looks behind him. The Skylark's driver's door is hanging open, the engine running, dust still afloat in the breeze in a small cloud. The cloud is drifting forward, giving the illusion that the car is creeping backwards. It looks disreputable. It is twelve years old and hasn't been washed since last fall. Perhaps it is the exhaust leak in the right header pipe, making the 401 cubic inch V-8 sound like an off-kilter four. Suddenly the whole day breaks loose in his chest and he is laughing, laughing to the point of tears.

"Brendan, Brendan! It's a miracle you're here."

"Ah, I can see you'll have some stories for me, Ramrod."

"Let me take your bag . . ."

"I'll just stick it in the back seat . . ."

Rod has moved to the back of the car and is searching in his pocket.

"You'll have trouble opening the boot, Ramrod, unless you've a spare set . . ."

Rod looks at his empty hand, at the open door, at the rumbling tailpipe, and at Brendan, who is looking at him with unconcealed amusement.

"Oh, my God . . ."

Rod breaks into a fresh fit of laughter, relief flowing through his chest and down his arms to his fingertips as he reaches in and turns off the ignition and pulls out the keys.

"Oh, I'm sorry, Brendan. I don't know what . . ."

Rod has managed to open the trunk. He sets Brendan's bag down beside his own brain bag and overnight bag and closes the lid. Still laughing to himself, Rod fishes in his shirt pocket. Brendan smiles at the offering.

"Congratulations, old man. Come on, let's go celebrate."

§

Rod has his aviator sunglasses back on. The Friday traffic has faded at 1930 hours but the June light has not. The colour-neutral strength of midday is turning gold; there are a few orange fringes on the western horizon. Rod has his sun visor down. The Skylark is rumbling evenly at highway speed.

On a hunch Rod has turned left on Boulevard Taschereau and run down to the Champlain Bridge, thinking of the rush-hour configuration on the Victoria Bridge: three lanes outbound and one inbound against oncoming traffic on that narrow deck. With the challenge of navigation and Montreal driving there has been little opportunity for them to explore the last thirteen years more deeply than a few touchstones in their lives; indeed, it feels like boulder-hopping a few hundred yards down a creek, landing in the forest on the opposite shore and not knowing where you are.

The twists and dips of highway 20 through Ville St. Pierre need Rod's concentration as he powers through without changing the note of the V-8. Then they emerge into the sky on the long straight through Lachine with the double set of train tracks on their right.

Brendan has just settled into what he expects will be a run into the West Island when Rod eases into the right lane and the V-8 burbles on closed throttle, slowing them from cruising speed as they run down the exit ramp at 55th Avenue. The light at the underpass is red.

"Jasus, Ramrod. Are we close? I was expectin' you'd be out further . . ."

"Yeah. Two, three minutes. Depending on the lights. We're on fifty-second."

The light changes. Rod turns left under the highway and rides the Skylark hard up the hill. The lights at Sherbrooke and Victoria wait for them and Rod swings left on Victoria and takes the next right at fifty-third. After a few stop signs they are on a boulevard, coming to a stop at the lake.

"This is lovely, old man. Are you near the lake?"

"Yeah. Not on though. A block away. More or less."

Rod swings through a U-turn onto the other side of the boulevard and then hangs a right onto a little cul-de-sac. Three boys and a dog vacate the street at their approach and then crowd around the Skylark as it stops in the driveway.

"Dad! Dad! Brendan says you're bringing Brendan."

The younger two are doing chin-ups on the driver's door.

"Is that Brendan?"

"Yeah, guys. This is Brendan. Brendan, this is Patrick."

Rod nods to the larger of the two heads peering in.

"And this is Liam – careful of that mirror, Liam. You're getting so big you might just pull it right off . . ."

Brendan chuckles as he lets himself out and circles the car. He introduces himself to the tallest of the three, whom he takes to be his namesake.

"Dad! You've got four stripes!"

Rod laughs.

"Well on my shirt, anyway."

"Indeed, Brendan. Well done. Your Dad is a captain."

Susan has appeared during the exchange.

"Congratulations, honey. And Brendan. Congratulations to you too."

"Susan. Look at you. Motherhood makes you more beautiful than ever."

"Oh, Brendan." Susan blushes. "Come in. I'll show you your room."

"Dad! Dad! Mom says we can stay up 'till 8:30."

"Yes, Liam," says Brendan, the oldest. "We get to have dessert while they have their drinks. Then we get ready for bed and I read you your story."

"He doesn't have to read me a story. I can read."

"Yes, Patrick. Of course you can," says Susan. "Maybe you can read Liam a different story."

§

"So then he says, 'OK, Rod, let's say you had a full load. Would you still have gone?' So I say, 'Sure. Ninety-five people at 200 per, with baggage, etc. etc. . . .'"

"I see. So it's twenty questions, is it? See what it would take to make you decide not to go?"

"Yeah. But I'm having trouble taking it seriously. Trying not to laugh. I mean, I'm not going to re-create the entire forty-five minutes, but then he starts talking about anvils . . ."

"Anvils?"

"Yeah. Like in the blacksmith shop. Only a whole bunch of them. All in the forward compartment. All in the aft compartment."

"Mother of God, he's getting a bit hypothetical, is he not?"

"Well, yeah. So I start with how you can't carry anvils in the first place. Not unless they are crated so as to distribute the load, tied down to withstand G forces – otherwise they'd just punch through the floor. In fact, if you looked up anvil in the freight shipper's manual . . ."

". . . you'd find you couldn't ship 'em at all . . ."

"Exactly."

"And it's not at all relevant to your particular job, Ramrod. Pilot. Captain."

"Yeah. Well, only in a glancing sort of way. But I did answer Miles. With what I thought was relevant to my job. I told him I wouldn't carry those anvils, but if they were in the forward compartment I might not have enough stab or elevator to rotate, and on landing – if it did fly – I certainly wouldn't have enough stab to take 40 Flap, or even 25, I'd go directly to slats and flap 15 because it's close to balanced, just one beep nose-up on the stab . . ."

"Jasus, Ramrod. This is rich. So what does he say?"

"Nothing. He just sort of nods. So I go on and explain the flying implications of the anvils in the rear compartment. How the longitudinal stability would be drastically reduced and even go negative, making the aircraft impossible to control in pitch." Rod snorts. "But I left out the part about how it would save the company money. Less down force on the tail, less drag, less fuel burn."

"Oh, don't you worry yourself about that, Ramrod. They'll be gettin' to that sooner or later, if they haven't already. Seating people more to the rear, up to the C of G limit. Somebody will get a big bonus, or at least a big pat on the back, for proving how many millions the company will save with their idea." He looks at Rod. "Maybe you should write a letter, Ramrod. Submit it. Take the credit."

It takes a second for Rod to see his old friend is tweaking him. He sighs. Brendan continues.

"You know, old man – I knew Miles. Knew of him, at least. Major Miles. So I'm somewhat aware of him. Who he is, and all. But who is this Pedro you were talkin' of? That's goin' with him to Toulouse?"

"His mother is Argentinian. Father mixed Eastern European, I think. Apparently he's fluent in five or six languages. Russian. German. As he as in French and English. Although you'd never know listening to him in English. He's always slangy, riffing on stuff."

"An easy-goin' sort of guy."

"Yeah. People call him Captain Fuck."

Brendan snorts into his beer.

"He's pretty blue in French, too." Rod pivots back to today's villain. "So Miles was a major?"

"Aye. That he was. Rose to his rank, as they say. As have I."

"Brendan! I – I mean, you've . . ."

"Had a fine career in the military . . ."

"Yes!"

"I've enjoyed it. But I fear there is a rank we all rise to and it is our own."

"But ..."

"Fear not, old man. All for the good. I am where I am for what I have to do. And if I were to climb further up the ladder I wouldn't be doing it anymore."

The day, the week, slide slowly from Rod's shoulders. It is quiet out here. Susan is putting the boys to bed. His old friend makes room for him, giving him space. He thinks of Brendan taking care of his pilots. He could see that dedication even back then, in 417 Squadron.

"Taking care of your boys."

"Indeed. Though they are girls now as well."

Lisette. Taking care of him today. Though he is a boy.

"Yeah. I guess I hadn't thought – we have girls here at the airline, but ..."

"Not to wonder. It has been a quiet thing. Back in '80 we opened up pilot courses to civilians. Not enough interest inside the forces, can you believe? So it started quietly."

Brendan sits, letting the silence expand. It is a peaceful thing, two people letting their thoughts and dreams merge into a common space.

"Girls. You know Brillo, one saved me today. Well, helped me. A lot."

"Lisette, could it be?"

Rod looks astonished.

"Brendan! How?"

"Easy, Sherlock. Remember what you called rue Leckie?"

Rod reddens. He recounts the afternoon's events, leaving out the incredible warmth. Brendan seems to have understood anyway.

"But by the time we arrived I remembered. I've seen her with her significant other. She's …"

"A girl."

Rod sighs.

"Yes. Why was she so good to me?"

There is a single chirp from a cricket, somewhere out in the fading light. Brendan looks out over the lawn, as if to interrogate the cricket.

"You are a person, are you not?"

It is the end of civil twilight, the sun some time since fully gone beneath the western horizon. More crickets are starting to join the first in song. The old friends sit on the patio looking south, in the direction of the lake. A bright star suddenly appears. It hangs above the houses on Boulevard St. Joseph. They sit quietly, contemplating the star. A minute or two goes by. Then the star starts veering west and disappears, leaving in its place a flashing red beacon.

"Probably one of our flights. DC-9 from New York. On the Plattsburgh arrival. Landing lights on at ten thousand. Then a left turn at Napee, setting up for the sixes."

"Or perhaps simply a sign."

Rod suspends his thoughts and listens, remembering their Friday night beer call seventeen years ago. He thinks of Kozy hitting the ridge at 480 knots. He wonders where Brendan's head is.

"Do you remember, Sherlock, how you solved Kozy's crash for me?"

"Yeah, sure."

"You're in no small way responsible for my career."

"What?"

"Indeed. Thee, O fighter jock god. Do you remember the Buffalo bringing the mucky-mucks?"

The pools of light materialize in Rod's head, the Buffalo pivoting, one prop slowing.

"Yes. Sure."

"Remember you spoke about the new mission for the Lawn Dart? The nuclear lob?"

"Yeah."

"I took your insight and presented it to the mucky-mucks. I hope you'll forgive me."

"Brendan, I'm honoured you could use it."

"Bless you, Ramrod. I'll tell you something."

Brendan sits, looking at the southern sky.

"I have a bad feeling about this mission to Toulouse. Perhaps it's just because I've had a chance to observe – and to participate in – some of this high mucky-muck decision-making."

"And these two . . ."

"I can hear some of their reasoning. Pedro is a linguist. He'll blend in and understand everything. Has a sense of humour. He'll balance Miles' seriousness and dare I say self-importance."

"Makes sense, I suppose."

"But looking deeper into the personalities I can see trouble. Miles is a man on a mission. He has a very strong sense of his own manifest destiny. And then there's – well, look at yourself, Ramrod, after – what was it? – two days with him? He couldn't not promote you. But did he leave you stronger as a result of your time together?"

Brendan sips his beer.

"Well. I'll not get into that. But he left it to others to congratulate you. Lisette, who by fortune happened to be there. Susan, bless her.

The boys. But this mission with Miles and Pedro. What will it be, months?

"They're leaving in September. And the first delivery is in January."

"Look. I don't know Pedro personally. But I like the sound of him. And I fear for him."

"What?"

"Forgive me, Ramrod. You know how I go on. It's just . . . I look at the two of them and I fear for both of them. And, not incidentally, old man, for the outcome of the mission. Perhaps we should leave it at that."

Still more crickets are joining the mating chorus. A light breeze is springing up from the south-southwest. It takes Rod a minute or two register the infrequency of a freshening at this time of night, when thermal mixing is over for the day. *They're going to have to switch back to the 24's.*

Susan has materialized in the dark. She puts down a bottle and three glasses on the little patio table.

"Boys asleep?"

"Liam. The others are still reading."

Susan tilts the bottle as if to show the label, but there isn't enough light from the kitchen to see much.

"I got this for Rod. When he started his captain stuff. I thought we'd celebrate."

She pours into the three snifters.

"I didn't know we had snifters . . ."

"Well, we do now. Cognac, too. I hope you like it. It's a VSOP."

"Oh, sweetie. That's . . ."

"Congratulations, honey."

Susan lifts her glass.

"And what a pleasant surprise *to* be celebrating two promotions. Or is it more? Are there ranks between Major and Colonel?"

"There's Lieutenant-Colonel."

They clink glasses and swirl and sniff and sip.

"Oh. That's lovely, Susie. Thank you."

The cognac slithers down. Warmth engulfs them. The June night cradles them. The crickets sing on, searching for love.

Slow Call

Montreal and Quebec City – New Years Eve, 1987-88

Cameron

BREATHING HARD AND SWEATING under his overcoat and uniform, Cameron drops his bags near the door of the briefing room and steps over to examine the Surface Analysis Chart on the wall. It offers nothing to ease his mind. There is a low a hundred miles or so north-northwest, up beyond Mont Tremblant. A cold front, curving down from the low, looks like it is near Petawawa, so Ottawa and Montreal are still in the warm sector. The warm front is pretty much north-south, between Montreal and Quebec City.

He has been expecting something like this. In the barely four months since he got his fourth stripe, the flying has been more or less routine. Sooner or later our Arcadian weather has to throw him a challenge.

Cameron steps back for the big picture. There is a big high – a capital 'H' on the chart – hanging over Sept-Isles and the Gaspé. At the door from the hall John appears with an odd smile and moves toward the desk.

"Cameron. They just call you for this?"

"Yes." He looks at his watch. "Twenty-five minutes ago. Weird. One leg to Quebec City on New Years Eve? So . . . how about you?"

"It's my block. Started in Windsor this morning. Captain booked off. A half-hour ago."

John puts a sheet of Sequence Reports and Terminal Forecasts on the desk in front of Cameron. Ottawa: wind 250 at 10 gusting 15, Temperature plus four. Montreal: 240/12, +5. Both places forecast to remain the same until the passage of a cold front around midnight local time. Trois Rivières: 100/15G18, -4. Weather 4 OVC 1 ½ ZL. *Shit! Freezing Drizzle! If that front keeps moving east, that's Quebec City in what? Two hours? Three hours?* Cameron puts his finger on CYRQ.

"John. You see that?"

"Yeah. I think that's what spooked Réjean."

"You mean he was going to do this flight?"

"Yeah. They didn't tell you?"

"Just said they had a last-minute bookoff. So . . ." Cameron looks at the Flight Plan. "It's still got his name on it. He have a party to go to?"

"No. I don't think so. He was arguing with dispatch. Wanted them to cancel."

"And they wouldn't?"

"No. And they pointed out that delaying the flight, which he could do, wouldn't help anything."

"Well, they're right about that."

Cameron steps back to the Surface Analysis Chart and puts his finger on Trois Rivières.

"This blob of freezing rain is heading for Quebec City. We've got – what? - two hours? Maybe three if we're lucky? Speaking of which, when's sked again?"

"Five minutes ago. And, by the way, the passengers are all on board. Full load. I just talked to station."

"Shit. Like it's a fait accompli. So what did Réjean say to dispatch?"

"Nothing. He didn't argue with them any more. Just got off. Then he said a few choice words in French. Then he dialed Crew Sked. As it was ringing he looked at me and said, *Piss on this, hostie.* Then he booked off."

Cameron smiles, thinking of Réjean in a snit.

"So, John. What do you think? Worth a try?"

"Sure. I'm single. I bid the block for this layover. New Years Eve in Carnaval-Town."

"Well, I like the gas. Alternate Ottawa via Montreal with an hour's hold . . ."

"And if we go now we'll stay ahead of that freezing drizzle."

§

On descent Cameron calls for the field report. Runway 06-24 snow removal in progress. Runway 12-30 100% snow covered, 3-5 inches, drifts 8-10 inches. The bad news is that on the last hour's sequence the snow has stopped.

"So, John . . . if we get a hold – for the snow removal – let's let 'em know we'll also want a JBI[1] before we commit."

"OK."

"And a weather observation from the tower, if possible. I don't like it that the snow has stopped."

---

1   The James Brake Index measures the traction the tires will get on the runway. See **Glossary.**

They are first in line but the plows are still on the runway. John reads back the holding clearance:

"**Roger. Air Arcadia 532, Hold West on the localizer at SouthShore, right turns, maintain three thousand fife hundred. Expect Approach Clearance at two one three zero.**"

John relays the request for a JBI and a tower observation.

"**Air Arcadia 532, Clearance correct. JBI truck will follow the plows on their last pass. Expect JBI and tower observation before passing Final Approach Fix.**"

Entering the hold, they ask for and receive clearance for 10-mile legs. Cameron is flying on autopilot, using the heading bug. They have slats and flaps 15 and have slowed to 160 knots, ready to start the approach.

"John – could you watch for icing? And also keep an eye on the **RAT**?"

As they level at 3500 feet on the first outbound leg there is no precipitation visible in the landing light beams, just cloud of varying density. The windshield-wiper bolts, the icing indicators, are clear. The **Ram Air Temperature** reads minus 12 C. A couple of minutes later, as Cameron starts the turn inbound, John calls:

"OK, Cameron. We're picking up ice . . ."

"OK, Wing Heat ON. What's the **RAT**?"

"Shit. It's way up. Minus 3."

The Flight Deck is silent on the inbound leg. As they start the outbound turn, John speaks up:

"Hard to tell about the icing, Cameron. No worse. But the **RAT**'s back down to minus 12."

Cameron waits until he's established outbound. He'll try a heading of 235 this time.

"It's what we were afraid of. We're at the front. We're playing with it. It's here a lot faster than we thought."

A minute later John says, "We're picking up ice again - and the **RAT**'s climbing . . ."

"Gotta remember to do the tail before the **FAF** . . ."

"Yeah. OK. I'll try to remind . . ."

"Air Arcadia 532, Cleared for the ILS 06 Approach. JBI check in progress."

"No time like now . . ."

Cameron reaches up and presses the Tail De-Ice button.

"Roger, Air Arcadia 532 Cleared for the ILS 06 Approach."

"Tail Heat on."

"Rog . . ."

"Gonna go the length here – get under the glideslope, give the tail heat time to cycle . . ."

"OK."

Cameron watches the glideslope go from the bottom to the top of the scale. The **RAT** is up to minus 2. He sneaks a glance at the windshield bolt.

"Shit. Icing's worse this time. Better turn in soon . . ."

Turning inbound he moves the autopilot Nav Selector to **ILS**. He is pleased to see the 235 heading has worked out: soon the Nav/Loc annunciator goes from **Arm** to **Cap** and they intercept the localizer smoothly, with no jerkiness or overshoot despite the presumed tailwind during the turn. Almost immediately the glideslope starts to move down. As the glideslope annunciator changes to **Cap** and the autopilot commands the initial pitch-down to intercept the glideslope, Cameron calls for the **Before Landing Check**. The wind up here is east or southeast: they are already heading 070 to hold the **LOC** course of 063; as they slow the drift angle is going to increase. At 2000 feet Cameron calls for Flap 25, and as the aircraft and autopilot settle down he calls for Flap 40. He wants to be stabilized as much as possible when they go by the Final Approach Fix.

Cameron, right hand on the throttles, catches the airspeed as it sags smoothly to final approach speed. He glances at the heading: 074. More than ten degrees of drift! For some reason old Teddy comes into his head. He remembers flying with old Teddy into Sydney on a dark Swamp night. How the weather was worse than forecast and Teddy froze and he had to talk him through it, cheerlead him through it; how his adrenaline was pumping not only with the stark reality and danger of the approach, but also with the necessity to act immediately even though he was not flying; to either get his Captain to fly safely or command him to do a Go-Around or to take over control and do the Go-Around himself . . .

. . . and then less than a year later Teddy was gone. And it was this approach! No, the ILS was off, so he had to do an ADF approach off the QB beacon. Limits 450/1, and the weather was ILS limits, 200 ½. And more: the beacon is offset from the runway center line. Final Approach Course 068. Apparently old Teddy just flew it anyway, hit the runway, then went off the side onto the grass and slid to a safe but muddy and embarrassing stop in the weeds. According to witnesses he got himself out of the airplane and walked away, never looking back at his crew, his passengers, or his career.

"Air Arcadia 532, ready to copy JBI and weather observation?"

John picks up the mike.

"Roger, Air Arcadia 532, go ahead . . ."

"Runway 06-24 JBI dezimal two zero, weather observation three hundred overcast, visibility one mile in light freezing rain, temperature minus fife, dew point minus six, wind zero niner zero

at 15 gusting 20, altimeter two niner four fife.”

Cameron visualizes the rest of the approach and landing. Touchdown on the right main, tracking straight, cross controls held as the nosewheel comes down, looking good; into reverse, slowing through 100 knots, nose starting to swing right into the wind, more left rudder: no use, she's going, she's swinging, reverse is starting to pull her back off the left side of the runway, ease back to idle reverse, she's still on the runway but sliding sideways, nose thirty degrees right, pointed into the wind; try to ease her back with rudder, with nosewheel steering: nothing.

We're too slow for aerodynamic controls and there's no traction for steering or brakes, there's the Alpha taxiway going by, I'm looking right at it, what a good view; the runway slopes down from here all the way to the runway 24 approach lights, we're going to accelerate if anything from here . . .

Cameron is sweating. Teddy froze. Cameron can't freeze.

“**Go-Around, Flap.**”

Cameron pushes the power up smoothly to 1.90 and hits the Go-Around switch with his palm. Disconnects the autopilot. Flies up into the command bars. *OK, it's gonna be climb straight ahead to 3300, then right turn and intercept the 090 radial of the YQB VOR . . .*

“**Positive Rate.**”

Cameron extends his right fist, thumb up.

“**Gear Up.**”

The altitude alert honks.

“**Twenty-three for thirty-three . . .**”

“**Air Arcadia 532, on the Missed Approach . . .**”

“**Roger, Air Arcadia 532, say intentions.**”

“**Flap 15. John, let's get a clearance back to Montreal . . .**”

§

Thank God for SOP's. Flying the Missed Approach just like we briefed five minutes before. Thank God for crews who work together. Thank God for the altitude alert. Thank God for everything that helps us keep it together.

"Ah, John? Did you get a chance to send the Diversion message?"

"Yup. Back on the Missed Approach."

The altitude alert sounds.

"**One-nine-oh for two-zero-zero.** Thanks. That should wake 'em up in dispatch. Get 'em working on our options . . ."

Cameron levels at FL200 and lifts the autopilot latch lever.

"**Cruise Check.**"

"**Roger. Air Arcadia 532, level two-zero-zero.** Hey, Cameron – here's something from dispatch . . ."

Cameron reads the message. **A blocking high** over Gaspé has stopped the system, which appears to be rapidly occluding . . . *Shit. Of course. Why didn't I see that possibility?* . . . the low is backing up toward Val d'Or and Ottawa is already under the occlusion; wind 120/15 and light freezing drizzle, suggest Alternate BTV via YUL . . . *Yeah. Makes sense. South is the only good option unless you go way west of the occlusion. So, Montreal?* . . . Montreal wind 100/10G15 temperature plus 2, switching to an ILS 10 operation; Burlington 500 overcast, temperature plus 6, wind 240/20 . . . *OK, good. Twenty knot crosswind no matter which way we land in BTV but it's dry and in the warm sector.*

Cameron hands John the message and gives him time to read it.

"Shit. Ever feel like you walked into a Venus Flytrap?"

"Yeah. I guess Réjean could read the tea leaves. So. . . let's set up for ILS 10 Montreal. And dig out the plates for Burlington.

And John – could you compose a nice message to dispatch? You know, confirm BTV via YUL and thank them and ask them to keep sending us info?"

"Sure, OK Cameron. By the way, the ATIS just says due to rapidly changing conditions ..."

" ... weather will be issued by approach control."

"Yeah."

"Sorry about your Quebec New Year's, John."

"Hey. No matter. Montreal's not so shabby either. You know, the Main, the Old Port ..."

"I don't know about Burlington ..."

Shouldn't a said that. Remember about one leg at a time.

" ... anyway, first we do the ILS 10. Wind's right down the runway, at least."

"And it's still above freezing."

"Right."

Cameron works on staying in the moment. It helps to keep the picture of a VFR day in your head as you bump through the cloud. Outside it is shades of wet grey with the water streaming along the side windows making a rudimentary angle-of-attack indicator, but inside your head you see the Richelieu River underneath as you turn left off Victor 352 to a 252 heading – wait – it's usually a 245 heading on the arrival for the sixes, so you'll have to correct the picture for this ILS 10 arrival which you rarely do, so no, you're not staying south of the river, aiming at La Prairie and Candiac and Delson; no, you're crossing the river obliquely and you're going to overfly Verdun and LaSalle and cross the river again at the Lachine Rapids and wind up at the mouth of the Chateauguay River where you'll turn right to 285, paralleling the runway and crossing Lac St. Louis and running the length of Île Perrot before they pick you off and turn you in to intercept . . .

With the approach briefed and the **In Range Check** done Cameron visualizes the partly frozen lake beneath: whitecaps churned by the southeast wind lapping over floating chunks and islands of ice; now the grey outline of Île Perrot appearing so it's time to slow to 200 knots and get ready to take flap.

"Air Arcadia 532, level three."

Hope we're number one or two. Want to get this sucker on the ground before . . . OK, there goes the glideslope, may not be long . . .

"Roger, Air Arcadia 532, turn right zero-one-zero, slow to 160 knots."

"Slats and Flaps 15."

"Roger, Air Arcadia 532 turning right zero-one-zero, 160 on the speed.

"Flaps 15 selected, 15 indicated."

The stab-in-motion alert beeps. Cameron spools the engines to catch the 160 knots.

"Temp's good up here . . ."

"Yeah. Plus five, six . . . let's hope it hangs on . . ."

"Air Arcadia 532, turn right zero-seven-zero, cleared for the ILS 10 approach."

Cameron is hand-flying. He wants to feel everything this time. Make it work. He turns the square knob on the Flight Director to **ILS**. *Talk to the weather gods. It's like talking to dice. Here comes the glideslope . . .*

"Before Landing Check, please . . ."

"Air Arcadia 532, contact tower one-one-niner dezimal niner."

"Nineteen-nine. See ya." John switches to tower. "Air Arcadia

532, ILS 10."

"Roger Air Arcadia 532, cleared to land runway 10, wind one hundred degrees at ten gusting eighteen, altimeter two-niner-fife-two, runway ten JBI dezimal three two at temperature plus one, urea treated."

"Air Arcadia 532, cleared to land runway 10, copy weather."

"Flap 25."

"25 selected. 25 indicated."

"Plus one."

"Yeah."

"Flap 40."

"40 selected, 40 indicated, Vapp 132."

"Gonna take half the gust. Say, 136."

"Sounds good."

"I like the point three-two."

"Yeah. And the wind's down the runway."

Cameron waves his right hand, thumb up, over the throttles.

"By the beacon. Uniform Lima."

"Twelve-fifty. Two-niner-fife-two inches set."

The DC-9 has a nice solid feel as it bounces in the gusty air. So far got it nailed. Hang in there, baby.

John takes a glance out his side window.

"Startin' to get a little ground contact . . ."

"Good. Urea treated. Hang in there, urea."

"I'd piss on it myself if I was there . . ."

Cameron reacts with something between a laugh and a choking

cough. He is clinging to that localizer and glideslope like a drowning man.

"**Hundred above.** Some lights."

"Rog."

"**Minimum. Runway in sight.** Lookin' good . . ."

"**Landing.**"

The wind is indeed almost down the runway. Cameron nudges the nose a little left and under-flares, chopping the power as he does. He doesn't want to float, and he absolutely wants to get those main tires spinning. It takes quite a bit of energy to get those wheels from zero to a hundred and thirty knots. Cameron doesn't like the look of things as he breaks out visual; there is some kind of precip. *Hang in there, urea.*

As long as the wheels spin up he'll have anti-skid where it counts. If they don't he's screwed, because the anti-skid computers deduce groundspeed from what the wheels spin up to. It will be the next generation of aircraft before the system has an independent groundspeed source available.

The touchdown is satisfyingly solid. He nicks the levers into idle reverse. Once he has the blue lights he starts feeding it in; by the time the nosewheel touches they are spooling. He sets 1.4 EPR as a start. Going by the Echo Taxiway they are slowing through 80 knots. Cameron tries the brakes. *Yes!* He brakes moderately and steadily, holding the reverse, now as they get close to taxi speed he leaves the reverse in, spooled at 1.1, *don't want to give it up just yet . . .*

"**Air Arcadia 532, clear right at your discretion. Exercise extreme caution. Ground reports taxiways very slippery. Temperature zero, light freezing rain.**"

Cameron caresses the nosewheel steering. She really doesn't want to turn away from the wind. He takes her toward the left side of the runway as they approach the Delta Taxiway at a walking pace. She'll swing through the wind only of he gets the sideways momentum up. He feels for little pieces of traction with the nosewheel and uses them to slowly build that sideways movement of the cockpit. He aims for the centerline of the Delta and almost gets it, oozing through onto the ramp. No urea treatment in here. She is a large boat and he is trying to bring her into a tight port on a windy day. She drifts. There are no brakes. Cameron is playing the reversers for both thrust and steering.

"John, this is amazing. Let's start the **APU**. We may have to shut 'em both down . . ."

John reaches up for the **APU Master Switch**, the mike in his other hand.

"Ground, Air Arcadia 532, very slippery here, no gate yet, need to hold somewhere . . ."

"Roger, Air Arcadia 532, proceed at your discretion straight ahead into the de-icing area, let us know how long you'll need."

John gets on the radio to Company while Cameron dances with the reversers. It is touch and go but surprisingly enjoyable. They are on the ground. Safe. Pumped with adrenaline. Just not at the gate. If he drops a tire into the mud it's a letter on his file. He remembers the FAA rules about low flying: *OK, but not nearer than 500 feet to any person, vessel, vehicle, or structure.* Well, he's on the ground so he doesn't need 500 feet but still, better not to slide into anything, mud included, if he can avoid it. But he's not playing with death here. And he can learn so much, get so much experience in a few minutes . . .

It is all mildly intoxicating.

"Air Arcadia 532, ground."

"Roger, go ahead for 532."

"Company says they won't have a gate for you for twenty to thirty minutes."

"Roger. We just confirmed that as well."

"We may have to get an aircraft through the de-icing bay before that. Are you able to maneuver to the North Hold Area?"

"Standby . . ."

Using one engine in reverse, Cameron manages to start a swing away from the wind. She is skating sideways, directly at the North Hold. The scene is unfolding in extreme slow motion.

"APU going?

"Yeah."

"Traction is nil. I'm afraid if I shut 'em down we'll drift off the ramp into the weeds by the runway."

"Shit."

"Yeah. Call company and ATC. Explain. Tell 'em to scramble a truck with the big metal chocks. And also a tractor with chains. We're going to need a tow in."

Cameron experiments, learning how to influence the direction of travel and how to stop. The latter is achievable, but only with her butt pointing into the wind and both engines in idle reverse. There is no way he's going to get her pointing into the wind again. By now they are in the North Hold Area and close enough to the edge of the ramp. Every once in a while she does a little skid and edges closer. Time to stop fooling around.

"OK. I'm just going to concentrate on holding our position. Reverse thrust is all we got."

"Truck with chocks is on the way out. They'll plug in a headset. Tractor might take another five."

"Thanks, John."

§

Here he comes. He parks a safe distance away. He is out of the truck and sliding, skating, holding the long headset cord in one hand. *Please don't fall.* He disappears under the nose. Cameron presses the Intercom button on the audio panel. Makes sure the volume is turned up.

"Ground to cockpit?"

There he is. He sounds winded.

"Cockpit to ground. Got to keep 'em running or we're gonna slide. You OK?"

"Yes, Captain. I'm standing clear to the front of the nosewheel. She's twitching a bit like she wants to weathercock. Nosewheel's moving sideways up to six inches."

"Roger. We can feel it. Can you stay clear if she starts to spin?"

"Affirmative, Captain. When I feel she's steady I'll signal my men into the mains with sand and chocks."

"Roger. Be careful."

"John. Keep a hand free. Be ready to shutdown both engines."

"OK, Cameron."

The wind is increasing. She is shaking, dancing in place to the rhythm of the gusts.

"I think she may pivot, Captain. The wind is shifting south and increasing. I can see the sock from here."

Cameron looks out front. He can see the ramp guy out ahead of the nose, his curlicue cord extended. The nose starts swinging left in nightmarish slow motion. The ramp guy is following, slipping but staying upright.

"S'OK, Captain. If I can't stay clear I'll drop the headset . . ."

"And if I lose sight of you I'm gonna shut down both engines . . ."

She continues her stately pirouette. Now she's pointing at Gate 41.

"Captain, she's starting to drift back. You've got maybe a hundred feet before the mains go into the grass . . ."

"Roger, thanks. I'm going to go into forward idle. Let me know if she starts coming toward you and I'll shut 'em down."

The dancing whirl continues, the rotation rate picking up perceptibly. She is pointing at Gate 5. The ramp guy is still out there ahead. His cord is stretching. Cameron nicks them into forward idle. The cord slackens. Cameron keeps his eyes on the ramp guy, willing him to stay in sight ahead.

"Cam. I just got the wind. One forty at twenty gusting thirty. We're swinging through one-seven-zero now . . ."

"Thanks, John. Cockpit to ground. How's she look? You OK?"

"Yes, Captain. Forward idle's good. She's holding her ground."

She swings lazily through one-four-zero and then back in small oscillations. She is a large and expensive weathervane. She dances in place.

"OK, Captain. She's steady as she goes. My guys are gonna go in."

"Roger. I'm standing by to shut 'em down on your command."

Two more trucks have materialized, one ahead of each wingtip. Two guys emerge from each truck, each carrying a small sandbag and a chock. They are sliding, crablike, toward the main gear.

"Lookin' good, Captain. She's staying in place. My boys gonna chock her."

It is a minute, but it seems longer. Cameron tries to remember to breathe. It gets harder after the four guys disappear. *In. Out.* He can still see the guy with the headset. *In. Out.* Deep breaths. *Playing with death again, even on the ground. You aren't out of the woods until she's parked and shut down. In. Out.* She's dancing but holding her position.

"OK, Captain. We've sanded behind the mains and put chocks there. When you shut down she should drift back. Then I'll get you to set the brakes."

"Sounds good. I'll wait for your signals. First shut down both engines. Then set brakes."

"Affirmative, Captain. OK, shut down engines."

"Roger. You got it, John? Numbers one and two engines off."

John presses the little silver safety buttons on the black HP cocks and flips them down to OFF. The sound of the engines winding down is briefly audible over the noise of the wind.

"She's starting to drift back, Captain. Looks good. OK, set brakes."

Cameron can feel a little bump just after he finds the braking threshold with his toes. He pulls the parking brake knob on the top of the steering tiller wheel and lets go the toe brakes. The knob stays up. He taps it to make sure it springs back up.

"OK, brakes set."

"Looking good, Captain. The guys are putting the chocks in front. OK, chocks in."

"Everybody OK?"

"Yes, Captain. You'll see them in a second."

Cameron counts them as they slide slowly upwind to their trucks. They stop occasionally to sprinkle what's left of their sand ahead of them. If they fall in this wind they'll just slide right back under.

"I'm gonna stay plugged in, Captain. A tractor with four-wheel chains is on the way."

Cameron exhales.

"Thank you. You and your crew. I'd like to meet you and thank you in person when we get her on the gate."

"Be my pleasure, Captain."

The heavy tractor's chains bite into the ice on the way to Gate 5. The tow is a non-event. At the gate, when the parking brake is set again and the main door opened, the flight is technically, officially, and even practically, over.

§

Released from the demands of the last three hours, Cameron falls into distraction. He is barely able to navigate through the terminal basement to the elevator. He has sent John on to find his Montreal New Year's party. The faces and voices of the lead and his crew still command most of his attention as he presses the UP button. They are still alive, these people. He rides up to the fourth floor.

He parks his bags near the door of the briefing room and wanders in. Why is he here? There is going to be nothing new in his mail folder, not on New Year's Eve. Nothing new anywhere, for that matter.

"Cameron. You knew him."

It is Hélène, the dispatch clerk. Sweet and generous to a fault. There is something in her voice though, a sadness.

"Who, Hélène?"

"Pedro. He's – come see. This just came in."

Hélène pins the notice to the board. *Pedro collapsed and died today in Toulouse, apparently of a massive brain hemorrhage.*

"Oh my God."

"Yes. He was a fine man, wasn't he, Cameron? We'll miss him."

"I can't believe it."

Cameron reaches out to the counter for support. Images of Pedro displace those of the ramp lead and his crew. Pedro's unhandsome, acne-scarred face was never experienced as unhandsome if you were inside his bubble of fun and goodwill. Nor was his sharp and dirty tongue the least unpleasant if you were within range of his infectious laugh.

Pedro is gone. It doesn't seem possible.

Cameron reaches into his shirt pocket and pulls out his mini-log. Folded in today's page is the DataLink summary. He spreads it out. He reads his day in numbers: *Gate to Gate, OUT to IN, YUL to YUL: 2:34. Airborne, OFF to ON: 1:26. Fuel Burn 9.2.* Nine thousand two hundred pounds. For no practical purpose.

The shadow of mortality passes afresh, dimming the numbers on the page, calling to order the taken and the not yet taken, demanding accounts from each and all.

Cameron smiles. He thinks of the utter uselessness of today's adventure. Pedro would have liked it.

From The Heart

Halifax – September, 1991

Grumpy

THE CHRYSLER PULLS UP to the stand. He shuts her down and gets out, looking at the view. To the west the sky is open. It is if he is on a balcony overlooking tiers of parking lots which fade into forest. *Right there was supposed to be the new Airport Hotel. Dead as a fucking doornail.*

"Grumpy! Whaddaeyer doin' in the pickup spot? I didn' call ya. Crew's not gonna be out for five minutes, at least."

"Did I say I was picking up the crew?"

"You know yer not supposed to be up here, boy. Not 'till I call ya."

"Alex is picking up the crew."

Grumpy jerks his thumb over his shoulder, back to where the cabs line up.

"He's waiting in the line like a good boy. Until you call him."

"Yer not pickin' up the crew?"

"That's what I'm trying to fucking tell you, Larry."

"So whatteryer doin' here?"

Grumpy turns and walks to the back to the Chysler. Opens the trunk.

"I'm askin' you a question, wiseguy."

"And I'm answering your question, Larry."

Grumpy reaches into the truck and pulls out the sign he made this morning. Big. Eleven inches high and more than two feet long. Black on white.

"Know who this is?"

"Mr. Homer? No. What the fuck does that have to do with anything?"

"It's who I'm picking up."

"Who. Homer?"

"Yes, Homer. Mr. Horace Homer. Know who he is?"

"Sure. Homer. Big fucking deal."

"Well, he's the President and Chief Executive Officer of Air Arcadia."

A tall man is crossing the street with a girl. He looks at the sign and catches Grumpy's eye. He smiles and nods. Grumpy retreats to the back of the Chrysler, opens the trunk, and puts away the sign, now redundant after its moment in the sun. Larry makes his own retreat.

"Grumpy? I'm Horace Homer. And this is my daughter, Felicia."

"Pleased to meet you, Mr. Homer. And you, ma'am."

Grumpy puts their luggage in the trunk and opens the curbside rear door.

"I'm afraid it's no limo, sir. I hope you don't find it too cramped."

Horace makes no move to get in.

"I like this small-body Chrysler. What engine do you have?"

"It's the 318."

"One of the best engines in the business. I have one down in Georgia. In a pickup."

"It's reliable if you take care of it."

Horace smiles.

"As we are."

Horace turns slightly to look directly at Grumpy.

"Thank you for agreeing to show us around. I know I'm taking you away from the Air Arcadia crews for the better part of three days."

"We've got 'em covered, sir."

"Thank you, Grumpy. Perhaps while I'm here we can get to know each other. Please call me Horace."

§

Rolling off the bridge the next morning Grumpy tosses a quarter into the bin, still doing 15 kmh. He heads out past the lights and up the hill on Nantucket Street. Loops around the little triangular park and heads north on Victoria. Makes a right on Woodland and with a left dives into the small streets of North Dartmouth. The Chrysler pulls to a stop in front of a small clapboard house.

"Born in that house."

The passengers are silent, contemplating the sidewalk, set back from the road and heaved with tree roots; the steep front lawn with its three levels as it terraces up from the walk; the small house with what must be its tiny rooms, and the mature trees and overgrown landscaping.

"Grumpy, you said your Mom saw the explosion?"

"July 18, 1945. Mom's pains started that day."

He shuts down the 318 and gets out. Felicia and Horace follow him onto the bumpy sidewalk. He gestures across the street.

"Nice place to grow up. Can't quite see it from here, but those houses back onto Little Albro Lake. When I was a kid most of those houses weren't there. It was wild country. Paradise for us boys."

"I can see that. Makes me think of my own childhood in west Georgia."

"Grumpy, the day of the explosion – your Mom went into labor? Was that with you?"

His memory is pulled from the 1950's to the family stories of 1945.

"Yup. Guess you could say I saw the explosion, too."

"What? How could you?"

Grumpy laughs.

"When I was born – just after midnight – ammo was still going off." He gestures northwest. "The depot was about there. On Bedford Basin. Put on a hell of a fireworks display. Mom could see it out of the window." He pauses for a breath. "Mom must have told that story – oh, I don't know how many times."

Grumpy looks back at the upstairs front window.

"Tracer bullets kept going off 'till maybe three, four in the morning. Like they were celebrating me. Or her."

"Two huge events in her life came together. No wonder she told that story."

Something in Horace's voice dissolves Grumpy's reserve.

"There's more. Mom was born December 6, 1917."

"Was that the other explosion?"

"Yup. That was the big one. SS Mont-Blanc collided with SS

Imo in The Narrows. Mont-Blanc was full of explosives. Biggest explosion in history before Hiroshima. So they say. A lotta people died."

"And your Grandma? Where was she?"

"She was lucky. She was down in Sambro. I guess we were all lucky. Grandma, Mom, and me."

"Sambro was far enough away?"

"It's on the tip of the Chebuckto. The peninsula west of Halifax."

Grumpy points his other arm southwest.

"Maybe 25 kilometres away."

"Not so far."

"No. Broke all the windows. But nobody died down there."

"That must have been a terrible shock."

"Well, yeah. They had no idea what was going on. Then Mom was born and it started to snow. Sixteen inches the next day, the seventh. They moved into the kitchen and draped blankets over the doors."

"No way for news to get to them . . ."

"The Old Sambro Road was closed for a week. They heard from a fisherman. He'd been up near Portuguese Cove. Saw the mushroom cloud. Still didn't know what caused it."

"You are tied to the land. You and your Mom."

In the silence bird song emerges: two thrushes singing, calling to each other with their imitative songs. Grumpy sighs.

"Yes, and to Air Arcadia, for good or ill."

§

Halifax – December, 1991

The sun is going down unseen. Citadel Hill, looming to the northeast, is disappearing. The grey is getting deeper. A light snow is falling, relieving the darkness, dusting the old woman standing beside the grave. He walks directly to her and opens his arms.

"Oh, Grumpy. He was like a son to me, he was."

"Yes, Agatha."

He holds her for a few moments in a bear hug.

"Oh, you're a warm one, Grumpy. I'm feeling the cold in my old age."

Agatha re-arranges the large wool muffler to close gaps where the cold seeps in. She is surprisingly upright for her eighty-five years. Strength of character props up her fragile frame.

In a few more minutes the employees of Buzzy's Cabs are all there, gathered around the deep rectangular hole in the earth. The snow seems to be seeking Agatha out. Her muffler has turned white, white as her hair.

"Thank you. Thank you all for coming. For coming to pay respects to our dear Squeaky. You know you are all my family."

Father Quinn is approaching, climbing the last slope of snowy grass. He takes his place at one end of the grave.

"Bless you, all of you, for showin' up. On such a night as this."

The sky is now quite dark. But the snow gathers in the faint light from Robie Street and Spring Garden Road as it filters through the trees. Gathers it in and holds it, surrounding the mourners with a tent of light.

"Did you want to be saying something, Agatha?"

"Just what you said yourself, Father. Thank you for showing up. And thank you, Dear Lord, for giving Squeaky the strength with which he bore his illness. May he be an example to us all."

Father Quinn opens his black book to the place kept by the silk ribbon. He holds the book open but does not read.

"Amen. We remember Squeaky as he was before the illness took him. Young and bright still, even as he grew into a man. His voice like an angel in the choir. A man of no pretense and no complaint. Even after the Good Lord took his voice he would squeak only praise for everything around him."

Father Quinn looks at the old lady, the head of Buzzy's Cabs.

"Agatha, forgive me if I remember your dear departed husband Buzzy. And if I remember how the two of you took in this child all those years ago and brought him up to be the fine man he was . . ."

Men with shovels materialize quietly out of the snow.

". . . thou shall eat bread, until thou return unto the ground; for out of it wast thou taken: for dust thou art, and unto dust shalt thou return. In the name of the Father, the Son, and the Holy Spirit . . ."

The shovels reveal more black earth with each plunge into the white hill. The sounds of earth and shovel and of earth and coffin are muted by the falling snow. The mourners straggle back toward their lives. Father Quinn slips and topples into Grumpy, who manages to disengage his arm from Agatha in time to hold him up.

"Oh, heavens . . . thank you, Grumpy. And I'm thinkin' – for Heaven's sake – I forgot to ask you to speak . . ."

Grumpy makes sure the three of them are upright and on safe ground. He pulls a paper from his pocket.

"No, Father. It's all right. I forgot too. And all I was going to say . . ."

He holds the paper so they could read it, had there been enough light.

"… Horace called me. He heard somehow. Wanted to extend his condolences to you, Agatha. And to everyone."

He gives the piece of paper to Agatha.

"Our customer. Our only customer. Bless him."

She folds the paper into her muffler, protecting it from the snow.

"A winter's night, that it is."

"Can we give you a lift, Father?"

The priest waves away the offer.

"Thank you, no. The walk will do the old bones good."

He heads off down the sidewalk, toward the rectory. Grumpy hands Agatha into the Chrysler and closes the door. The 318 burbles to life. The entire executive of Buzzy's Cabs glides off into the night.

In Her Prime

AIRLINE HONCHO

March 22, 1995

Taking Off For New Horizons

Air Arcadia's Annual Report was issued yesterday, ending months of speculation about the company's financial performance. The bottom line is a significant profit for the airline after four straight years of painful losses. Credit for the turnaround, according to nearly everyone interviewed, belongs to Chairman and CEO Horace Homer. Mr. Homer was not available for comment before we went to press. Aides are not surprised, saying that Mr. Homer can be very visible during times of crisis but avoids the limelight when things are going well.

The turnaround has a number of key components, according to those interviewed. First is a leaner, more responsive management. Two years ago the airline had twenty-six vice presidents; this year's Annual Report lists sixteen. Communication has been streamlined: Mr. Homer places high value on quick decision-making. This has borne fruit in the airline's aggressive response to the opportunities presented by the 1992 Open Skies Agreement. Air Arcadia has opened thirty new point-to-point Transborder routes, as well as a new Pacific route to Osaka, Japan.

Employee ranks have also been thinned by retirement, attrition, and judicious hiring freezes, bringing the crucial employees/aircraft ratio to a respectable 110/1.

Clues to Mr. Homer's management technique can be found in the text of the Annual Report, which refers to the employees' expertise and experience as enormous, intangible assets that Air Arcadia will rely on more than ever as it takes off for new horizons. Significant, too, is the new Share Ownership Plan. Buying shares is made easier and more attractive for employees with payroll deduction and company matching funds. As the Report states, chances are the employee serving our customer is also a part owner of the airline.

Arcadia

I AM HAPPY WITH HORACE, FATHER. Where I lack, he provides. Where I wander, he guides. Where I am blind, he sees. He is my pilot, deftly nudging me toward his true intent before my volition has a chance to turn my head. It is as though his intent has become mine; we are one. It is a wonderful feeling.

Yet it is more than that. Markets may buffet me but they bedevil me no longer, Father. They are as the motion of the air, the wind and the storm. They are my medium, my sea, my womb-fluid. I exist in them as I exist in the skies.

After all, I am privatized. I am a public company. Anyone can now buy a piece of me. My shares are trading every day. I have a place in the world!

As I speak with you I remember your lessons. Perhaps they come back to me now because I am ready for their wisdom. It is as if your words of years ago – I was a teenager, Father – are stored somewhere in my being and now play back of their own volition.

I remember especially your explanation of corporations. Of our reason for existence. I hear your voice comparing our purpose to what you called a barn-raising. Of how the self-sufficient, hard-working farmer can alone do most of his life's work but how raising the rafters of a barn exceeds even his prodigious energy.

Oh, how your eyes would glow! Though I was only a child I remember their fearsome gleam as you would conceive of something that had to be done for our country. And how that something could only be accomplished by a corporation, by a bringing-together of people, capital, energy, and ideas. And yes, ideals. Those too, Father. I remember you saying just that. Ideas and ideals. Templates born of dreams. Patterns to guide the energy of the people and to put the capital to work.

You were in your prime. The War and the Peace were making huge demands on you. I see the arc of your existence, stretched longer by those demands. I see your gifts, kept fruitful for decades.

But what about me, Father? I am merely one of thy many progeny, conceived for a purpose. I shall continue as long as I am able, adapting my talents to the times, being the airline our country needs. But I sense I am at my peak. Am I about to I start that inevitable descent, maneuvering toward a Final Approach for which I have no chart?

How silent you are!

Part II

On Course Again

Cameron

"Hey, Cameron. You're on the Bus!"

Freddy pushes past him, trying to get to the elevator.

"No. Can't be. You're – you've got to be kidding …"

Freddy is still moving, risking his right arm to get the doors to re-open. He turns and smiles through the narrowing gap as they close.

"Don't have to believe me. Look for yourself."

The Flight Planning area has changed in the twenty-two years since Cameron was on his first course. The long counter has gone, along with the Dispatchers and the Crew Schedulers. They have their own offices now. The Dispatchers are in Toronto, in some rental space on Airport Road. They are just a name on the AFPAA and a voice on the phone. Still, Cameron remembers some of them.

The room is empty except for the crowd at the new U-shaped counter around the Facilitator's work area. Cameron parks his bags and walks over.

"Cameron! Cameron! D'ja see you're on the Bus?"

Courtley's voice reaches him from somewhere near the counter.

"That Courtley? No. I haven't. Can't believe it."

"Here. I'll pass you the page. Can't move, anyway."

A hand is waving an 8 ½ by 11 sheet of paper. It works its way back via another hand. Cameron reaches for it. It is the last sheet of the new Montreal Bus Captains List. His name is on the bottom. Number fifty-nine out of fifty-nine. Cameron stares at the Course Date: January 23, 1995. Fuck! That's Monday!

§

Breakfast is always Cameron's time, and breakfast in the Airport Hilton is good. Scrambled eggs and sausage to order. Potatoes. A bit of fruit as dress-up. Good bread for the toast. Real orange juice. Decent coffee.

It is 7:15. Cameron is packing it away. Two rules for learning: a good sleep and a good breakfast. His waitress is the French-Canadian girl with the lopsided smile and the funny walk. *She was here when Ken was checking us in the Sim on the TriJet. How long ago is that? Twenty years, anyway. Glad I could get to that hockey game of Jeff's yesterday. It was tight, getting to the airport. Whole weekend's a blur. Hard on Leslie. Everything is changing so fast.*

§

"You going to the Sim Building, sir?"

"Um, no. Ground School. Never been there. I think it's near the Sim Building."

"Yes, sir. Just behind it. If you can wait a couple of minutes, I've got one more for the Sim."

Should know this guy's name by now. He's been here as long as that waitress. Cameron looks around, playing *spot the pilot in civvies*. He tries to do it without looking for brain bags. Use them only as confirmation. The young guy pretending to read The Globe. Zero business aura. Can only be a pilot or a cop. Sure enough, there's a brain bag at the end of the couch.

Cameron glances at his watch: 8:04. No sweat. He looks up, toward the Front Desk and the alcove leading to the elevators and the first-floor rooms. *Ken always stayed on the first floor, now I think of it. Didn't like to waste time in elevators. Or maybe it was because it was the smoking floor.* A familiar face is rounding the corner. The name, although not on the tip of his tongue, emerges. Winnipeg based. From the TriJet course in Seattle. Gabriel. Cameron smiles.

"Gabriel. It's been awhile. How you been?"

"Well, I'll be . . . Cameron! Never know who you're gonna meet in the center of the universe."

"How's the family, Gabe? I remember you had a baby girl?"

"Got five of 'em now. That baby's drinking age. And you? You had a boy, I remember . . ."

"Yes. He's in his last year at university. And two more boys. Youngest's about to turn fourteen."

"I guess it has been a while."

The young pilot/cop has materialized beside them.

"Cameron? This is Peter."

"You guys in the Sim?"

"Yup. Two and three check. Today and tomorrow."

"Excuse me, gentlemen. Are you ready to go?"

Ignacio. He has a name tag now.

The van pulls out into the morning traffic. It is a slightly hair-raising prospect but Ignacio stays calm and doesn't take chances. They come to a stop at the lights at Jetliner Road. Six lanes of traffic are moving briskly across in front of them, heading to and from Terminal Two.

"So Gabriel, you guys are on the Bus already? How long you been on it?"

"Six months. This is our first Sim since checkout. Not looking forward to it. At least we're going to have the old procedures."

"The old procedures?"

"Yeah. Starting soon it's gonna be a whole new deal. Bus POM."

"Pom?"

"Yeah. Pilots' Operating Manual. POM. The word according to Bus Industries."

"So, ah, what are we using now?"

The van pulls ahead smoothly, keeping pace with the hordes charging toward the 427 underpass.

"We're using Air Arcadia procedures. Minted right here at the airline by Miles."

"Oh, yes. I remember now. Miles and Pedro."

"Yeah, Pedro croaked. Miles got to do what he wanted. Now Pedro's name is on a brass plaque on the galley bulkhead in aircraft 201."

Death takes its moment of silence. Terminal 3 is moving past on their left. The Dawn of First Class Travel.

"Gabe. You're not looking forward to the Sim?"

Gabriel sighs.

"See, there's been a few guys flunk. Not the course. The six-month. Complacency, supposedly. And there are rumours . . ."

"Rumours?"

"Remember how we would never see MOM in the Sim? Well,

maybe not never, but it was rare. Now they're all over the place."

"Observing?"

"They're doing rides now. And turning up the heat."

The traffic on Airport Road is almost up to highway speed. Ignacio begins the maneuver that always brings Cameron's heart into his mouth: moving to the left lane and then signalling, slowing, trying to gauge when to cross in front of three lanes of oncoming traffic. Ignacio times it right. He swerves left onto the spur of Silver Dart Drive beside the Sim Building and right into the driveway.

Cameron is nearest the sliding door. He opens it and gets out.

"Nice to see you, Gabe."

"You too, Cameron. Maybe I'll see you back here in six months."

Gabriel and the young pilot/cop use their cards to buzz open the doors of Purgatory.

Ignacio drives around the back of the Sim and into the centre of a big U-shaped building. Trucks are everywhere, backed into the loading docks that take up most of the inner façade. The ground school is hidden away like a trendy club. The van stops in front of a set of shabby glass doors.

"It's on the second floor, sir. There's an elevator. It will make sense when you get up there."

"Thanks, Ignacio. Oh, how do I get back to the hotel?"

"Just give the front desk a call, sir, and I'll come right over. Or ask Suzy. Her desk is right there when you get off the elevator."

The elevator door opens on a different world. The freight dock is gone. This is corporate décor, executive level. A striking blonde is smiling at him from behind her desk.

"You must be Cameron? Right. Here's your course file. Rob, your partner, just arrived. And you're going to go through with Quietly

Ambitious. You know Captain Ambitious?"

"Um, yes. Sure."

"He's in a meeting on the other side. Be here before lunch. Tom is his partner. He's in there with Rob."

Quietly is in Training or Standards or something.

"Oh, and Cameron? John's your instructor, and Barney wants to have a word with you before you go in. I'll call him."

"Sure."

Barney the Brit. That's right. He's the head of Ground School now. She picks up the phone.

"OK, Cameron. Barney's ready for you. Just head down the hall that way. You'll find him."

"Thanks."

The indicated hallway stretches fifty feet or so ahead. The narrow hall appears to open out into a larger room up ahead. *This a bit of a hike. Maybe I'm walking around Garth's suite.* Once there the larger room is actually another, wider hallway with office doors on each side. It is perpendicular to the narrow hall. Cameron turns the corner.

"Cameron. I wanted a word ..."

Barney gestures into his office. Closes the door behind them.

"Please sit. Won't take long."

Barney looks nervous. But then he always looks nervous.

"Cameron, this is a bit awkward. I don't know if you've heard, but ..."

Cameron shakes his head.

"... but MOM has, well ..."

Cameron nods.

"I did hear something. New procedures?"

"Yes, yes. Exactly. New procedures. I'm afraid we're all in a bit of a flap. Just got the word this morning. Half hour ago. Don't know what we're going to do."

"And I – we – are going to use the new procedures?"

"Yes. That was the word. Problem is, we don't have them. Not yet, anyway. But MOM is insisting. You guys are going to be the first – look, I'm awfully sorry if you've been boning up at home for weeks learning the old stuff. I'm afraid . . ."

"No, no. Not at all. I just found out about the course on Friday. There were no books avail . . ."

"Of course. Of course. I had forgotten. This has all happened so fast. Of course. No. Of course you haven't. All the better, then. You'll start with a clean slate. That's the ticket."

"Barney, pardon me. You said you didn't have the procedures? But they're Bus procedures, right?"

"Yes, yes. Precisely. Bus POM. Only I don't have a clue what they are. I'm going to have to spend this week trying to get hold of a copy. That's what I wanted to say. Apologize. Thank God we've got two weeks before you start the Sim. Anyway, sorry. That's it."

"Is Captain Ambitious also . . ."

"Yes, yes. Absolutely. He knows, of course. That's probably what they're meeting about over there. I'm hoping he'll help me – us – get ahold of them . . ."

Cameron stands up.

"Thanks for the heads up, Barney. But like you say, don't really need 'em 'till the Sim."

"Right."

"We'll learn fast. Clean slate, and all."

"Exactly. Right. Good-O. Well, you're off to see John. Thanks for understanding, Cameron."

"Sure. Ah, where are we?"

"Oh, sorry. Of course. Classroom A. Down the hall on the left side."

§

Mornings are soporific in the extreme: WICAT lessons pursued in the dark, alone with your computer terminal. Technically, this is light years ahead of the old AVCAT but in human terms it is worse. Cameron remembers the old YOU ARE WRONG! slide. At least it would make you laugh. He stays awake by trying to ace it, jotting down notes during the presentation, stopping the flow if he needs more time to write. He draws diagrams. He makes sure he has the names right. FCU. Flight Control Unit. When the questions come he is ready. Still, it is not enough. After breakfast he can get through a couple of topics before he either drops off or feels like he is about to go nuts. Then he goes for a pee, gets a coffee. Chats with whomever. After that it's one topic, max, before the next break. Maybe it's just as well. He saves his crib sheets, sticking them in the ring-binder with the relevant aircraft systems chapter, just after the divider. The manuals are huge. Their foot-square covers and three-inch spines are barely enough to hold half of the aircraft system chapters.

On week two Cameron gets a pleasant surprise. During one of the afternoon class sessions John passes around a new, smaller binder. Still twelve by twelve but with a 1½-inch spine.

"These are for your POM Bulletins, guys."

He is strolling around again, handing them rubber-band-bound half-inch stacks of blue sheets. Tom, Quietly's partner, speaks up.

"POM, eh John? So when do we get the POM procedures?"

234

"Aw, Jesus, guys. It's all POM. Your aircraft systems chapters. These bulletins. Tomorrow I'm going to hand out the FMGS. Volume four. Fits in a one-and-a half like this. On Thursday there's another three-incher for the Abnormals. And you want more?"

Quietly stands up. He is tall and blond; heavyset without being overweight.

"Tom, I share your frustration. We all feel the same way. Am I right, Cameron? Rob?"

Quietly continues in his firm voice.

"Barney is working hard to get advance copies of the Normal Procedures. So are the Bus people in the office. It may be touch and go. But we will have them in hand before we start the Sim. You have my word on that. The good news is you can study Volume Three, the Abnormals, as soon as you get them."

"Thursday morning."

"Right. Thanks, John. You can study them because they will be as written. Verbatim. Exactly as they appear on the Electronic General Actions Director. The EGAD is now the Bible."

Quietly sits down. He looks slightly flushed. Cameron has the rubber bands off and is stowing the POM Bulletins in his new binder. There are forty-seven of them. Some interesting stuff here. *Reversion to Speed/Mach – V/S as a result of an FCU altitude change whilst in ALT*. This will be deleted at the next FMGC modification standard in early '92.* Wonder if that has anything to do with the A330 crash . . .

"So, guys."

John is back at the blackboard.

"Let's talk about a total hydraulic failure. Of course, it's not gonna happen. Haw, haw. In fact, in those Abnormals you're gonna get, there isn't even a procedure for Triple Hydraulic Failure. So the question is, just for the sake of argument – haw, haw – you got no hydraulics at all. You got any flight controls left?"

Rob puts his hand up.

"I don't think so. All control surfaces are hydraulic. No hydraulics, no control."

"But wait. What about Mechanical Backup?" Quietly asks. "You can still control the rudder and the stab. Fly it that way."

He looks alarmed. His colour has risen.

"Well, that's right. Mechanical Backup. But is that gonna save the day? I mean – haw, haw – in this scenario."

Cameron flips through the hydraulics and flight controls chapters, trying to find the reference. He puts his hand up.

"Whatcha got, Cameron?"

"Well, I'm not sure. But take the stabilizer. It looks like these three electric motors take orders from the ELACS and the SECS and command the Green and Yellow hydraulic motors that move the stab. But if there's no Green or Yellow . . ."

"Yeah. You're on to something."

". . . and over here, under Mechanical Backup, it says, Mechanical Backup permits the pilot to control the rudder and stabilizer following the temporary complete loss of electrical power."

"Electrical power. But not hydraulic? I can't believe it."

Quietly's voice has lost its firmness. The colour in his face glistens with sweat.

"OK, guys. It's four-thirty. Time to call it a day. As you know, you're welcome to do more in the WICAT if you want. Get ahead of the program. But as for me, there's a beer with my name on it when I get home. And as for the procedures, it's like the man said: *Procedures are for the instruction of fools and the guidance of wise men and being neither*, haw, haw . . ."

Cameron remembers that joke from the last time he had a course with John. *When was that – the 'nine? the L-1011?* John's laugh is more congested. *Another heart attack?* That would explain the slightly slack skin, the wet lungs.

Rob and Tom say goodnight and start their commute. Cameron heads back into the cafeteria area. One more coffee. One more topic before beer call. Quietly is there ahead of him, pouring.

"Cameron. Glad you're here. Want a coffee?"

"Yes, please."

Quietly pours into Cameron's offered cup. His hand is shaking slightly.

"You are Rob are gonna be a good team."

"Thanks. Yes, I think so."

"I'm impressed by how you guys know the book already. There's a lot of it, isn't there?"

"Yes. It's huge. I guess it's the new generation. Fly by wire. There's as much software as hardware. More, even."

"Yeah. You're right. You know, I was shocked today. That without hydraulics you're SOL."

"I wasn't sure about that. But I guess they're more concerned about designing to a loss of electrics – or more to the point, electronics. Lightning strikes, for example."

"Yes."

"And none of the newer aircraft have any backup if you lose all hydraulics. The Boing BigTwin, for example."

"Yeah. Guess I'm behind the times. Stayed on the DC-9."

"It's got the tab controls."

"Say, Cameron …"

Under the lights Cameron can see the moisture lingering on Quietly's face.

"… this situation – well, it's a bit awkward. I think maybe I hadn't realized just how awkward until this afternoon."

He looks up at Cameron.

"The procedures?"

"Yes. But there's more. Although MOM is insisting that you be the first – well, us; but actually, you, because Tom and I will be second – although they're insisting, they are being very slow in approving our …"

"The new procedures you're writing?"

"Well, I'm not going to go into all the politics, but yes. And I think I just saw how we have to do this."

He stops, looking at his coffee cup.

"It's gonna be straight POM. Just that and no more. I'll see you get it absolutely as soon as possible. But that's not all."

Quietly turns and walks to the window. An Air Arcadia Bus is taxiing down the Alpha for 24R.

"Pretty. That's us in a month or so."

The Bus disappears around the corner.

"Cameron, what I was going to say – well, there's the Sim Sked, too. I don't know if you follow these things, but the bean counters …"

He takes a sip of coffee. Cameron waits.

"… there's fashion in these things. They come and go. We've had Sim courses as high as fourteen sessions. Then somebody has an idea how to pare down the budget and it's twelve. Or ten. And now, at what turns out to be the worst possible time . . ."

Cameron can't help speaking.

"It's less? I mean, fewer. Than ten?"

"Yes. The plan is eight sessions with your Flight Instructor. Plus the ride. That's nine."

"Wow."

"Yeah. Frankly, Cameron, I'm embarrassed. Worried, too. Because we're all in the same boat."

Quietly is looking out the window again. Cameron doesn't rush him.

". . . it's a lot easier to get more Ground School Sims. Different budget. I'm going to talk to Barney. Try to bring it up from eight to ten. The idea being when we're in there with John we get to fly it around VFR some every day. Just to get used to it. Before the shit hits the fan. I'll talk to John, too."

"Good. That makes sense. Thanks."

"Yes. The other – the Flight Sims – that's harder. But Cameron . . ."

Quietly looks him in the eye. Cameron feels the new calm of it, as if a crisis has passed.

". . . I'll be a day or two behind you. I'll be right there in the Sim Building. I have an office there. And if you feel you guys are getting behind – if you need more time, for any reason – let me know right away. OK?"

"Yes. Sure. Thanks, Quietly. That's – that's very generous . . ."

"Yeah, well."

"Thanks. From me and Rob. We appreciate it."

Nightmare

Montreal – December, 1998

Arcadia

I HAD AN UGLY DREAM, Father. I awoke shivering and sweating with the ugliness of it.

It started with a vague numbness. But slowly I realized that I could no longer feel my people. They were slipping away from me. I was turning into an object, Father. It was horrible.

That was when I noticed my body. I know we have to accept the fading of our beauty as we grow older, Father. I understand that and I have accepted it. At least I have thought about it. But this? It was as if it was not my body at all, except it was, only there was more of it, parts that were totally unfamiliar. It was as if – as if there were another ...

Never mind. Can you hear me, Father? Say something! Comfort me, dear Father. The tears are running down my cheeks.

In my dream you could not hear me, Father. My voice was not heard at all. I was speaking, at first calmly and politely and then I was crying and finally shouting, screaming into nothingness and going blind as well as my people slipped away from me.

I was sliding down a slope, pulled by the ugliness attached to my body that was not even my body but another body, so unmentionably attached, so ugly. They were talking – talking about me and making decisions about me. I heard them and shouted *no!* but they couldn't or didn't hear. For them it was as if I did not exist except as a construct – something on paper but not even having the dignity of an idea.

Then the cutting. I was on a table, a metal table. I was happy because they were going to cut her away and I would get my body back. Anyway she was dead so it didn't matter, just cut her away and be done with it, I thought. At first it stung. The pain didn't go away but it no longer meant anything when the shock took over. I saw what they were doing. They were cutting me into pieces and packaging the pieces, trying to make them look nice, like a bouquet of flowers or a cut of meat. I saw the pretty package my leg made, all gussied up to look like it had a life of its own and my hand in another package and my kidneys, so valuable on the open market in their high-tech organ-donor freezers and on and on it went with me bleeding on the table and the pretty packages going out the door and the money rolling in and I woke up afraid and damp with sweat.

I am awake now and see it was a dream. But still I know that to Boy Wonder and his crowd I am not real the way they are. They can do with me as they please. I have nothing to say.

This Corruptible

Calgary – January, 2000

Derek

THE DRIVE FROM AIRDRIE is too fast. Derek wants to keep it slow, but then another eighteen-wheeler roars by him and the visibility drops to near zero in snow. When he can see again he picks up his speed but that's too fast for what he can see and he slows down again, only to be passed by another truck. Good thing it's two thirty in the morning.

Derek thinks about the early shift. First departure is Flight 201 to Vancouver, a Bus at 0630. He thinks about the late shift, which he was working until last Friday. Flight 201's airplane comes in off the late Toronto, somewhere around 0100. It's usually the last airplane dumped on the station overnight and if it's a snag-heavy night it's more than the shift can do to get to them all.

Oh, well. That's what he's here for. He's got three hours to get her logbook clear.

Out of exasperation more than anything Derek gets off the highway at Balzac and turns east. He turns south on Range Road 293. It's one of his little ways. The narrow range road turns into the Métis

Trail, taking him down to Martindale. From there he can cut west on 80th Avenue, pretty much direct into the airport parking lot.

By the time he parks the pickup he's grateful he got off the highway and stayed on the high ground. It's snowing hard as he walks in to the terminal. He hangs up his parka and walks through to the cramped space they use as an operations room. He thinks about how different this is from the military – maintenance here at the airline is not a prestige department. He's a ramp rat with a licence. He looks at the scribbles on the green board. Yup, Aircraft 257 out on Flight 201. Snag in the book. Not done. Nor is the log book anywhere around. He walks back through and puts on his parka.

On the Flight Deck Derek can see his breath. The only illumination is from the light standards on the terminal, and they are lost in snow. He reaches up and pushes the green light on the overhead panel to turn on the external power and some cockpit lights so he can read in comfort.

ELAC 1 PITCH FAULT on departure out of Toronto. Suspect split elevators due tailwind while parked. Reset OK.

Could be, Derek thinks. But better check all the maintenance codes.

He dives deep into the nested series of maintenance pages in the EGAD, looking at ELAC 1 and its history. There it is: three error codes, all S-series – sensor related. **S009 L ELEV INVAL. S019 L ELEV ELAC 2 CMP. S087 L ELEV ERROR LOCK.** This ELAC has disqualified itself. Not going to reset today.

Derek grunts, sticks the log back behind the Captain's seat. So far, an easy morning, touch wood. There's an ELAC spare on base. Just change it out and he's good for a trip upstairs to Tim's for a coffee. Well, as soon as they open at five.

§

Derek looks like a snowman as he opens the ramp door into the terminal. He is carrying the ELAC he removed from Aircraft 257.

The paperwork is done. Now he just has to erase 257 from the green to-do board and he can go upstairs for that coffee and doughnut. It is almost five.

He still has his coat on when the door opens. He startles visibly – he is alone on this shift until 0600. He turns to see Captain Ice Pick in hat and tunic, no overcoat or boots, black shoes shined. He knows Captain Pick. At least he knows who he is, because he sees Pick often. Pick lives here in Calgary and commutes.

"Good morning, Derek."

"Good morning, sir."

Derek is trying to figure out what Pick is doing here. He's early for Flight 201. But that's Ice Pick. A half-hour early is not that unusual for him, come to think of it.

"Derek, I've got a favour to ask of you."

Derek's mind flashes back to Cold Lake, where he spent his career. For some reason he thinks of Colonel O'Riley, of how he made Derek feel not intimidated or uncomfortable, but rather at ease and secure in the presence of higher rank. He's not sure about Pick.

"I'm doing a check ride this morning. Flight 134. Is that an ELAC you've got there?"

"Yes, sir. Off Fin 257. Pitch Fault."

"Excellent. I want you to put it on Fin 213."

"Sir . . ."

Derek involuntarily moves the ELAC behind his butt, trying to make it less visible.

"Nothing to worry about, Derek. We're going to push back, but then we'll taxi back to the gate. One way or another. And you can change it back."

Ice Pick pauses. A smile forms on the face under the gold-braided hat brim. He moves his arms, posing, putting the broad four-stripe sleeves into prominence.

"Just a maintenance action. And I'll owe you one."

The Italian Stallion

Montreal – September, 1998

Cameron

CAMERON SCANS the packed room. Two rows ahead, Jean-Luc is talking to a stranger.

Born Leader taps his mike and stands up.

"Ladies and gentlemen. It has come to our attention that there are unauthorized personnel in the room. They must quit the premises before the meeting can begin. I ask anyone without a badge to please leave at once. And pilots, I direct your attention to the security procedures. Look around you. Challenge anyone you don't know. Thank you."

Cameron looks back toward Jean-Luc. He is talking to a tall, lanky man. An intruder? Herc and another big guy are approaching them. Herc is six-foot three and a bear, but somehow in spite of the menace he looks as though he is concerned for the welfare of those he is about to dominate. Maybe it's the walrus mustache . . .

There is an unreality running through these weeks. I've never picketed before. There has never been security like this at union meetings. The media have never cared about us. It is the most beautiful September. You can see for a hundred miles. It is like a dream.

"...yes. There are limitations to Train to Standard. For example. If a pilot fails an upgrade to Captain, he has to wait twenty-four months before bidding it again. Four bid cycles. Anything else? Yes? Next in line?"

"Hey. Fern Enthuser. Captain on the BigTwin. All I'm getting out of this is a suitcase every two years. I mean, where's the money? I go on strike for almost two weeks so far for a suitcase? I say go back to the table and get some money."

Didn't thank the Negotiating Committee. Those guys have been at it more or less twenty-four seven for a week. This thing is going to pass, I can feel it. We want to go back to work. That Picture of Born Leader and Boy Wonder has been all over the media. And Rod saw them snap it. The two of them standing stubborn, getting in each others' faces.

" ... so does that mean if we go back to work next week there'll be no cut in our pay?"

"Thank you, Fred. Yes and no. You will see no difference on your next paycheck. Or on any paycheck until you retire. Your cash flow will be unaffected. Previously you were paid on the 17th for the previous month's work. Now you will get an advance on the first of the month. The advance will be deducted from your 17th paycheck. In effect you will be paid for your work two weeks earlier than before. Does that answer your question?"

"Yeah. I think so ..."

There is general laughter. Relief. Everyone in the room has been trying to plan for two weeks with no income. This thing is going to pass just for that pay thing.

It has been a long meeting. Born Leader has been at his most charming and patient, encouraging the Negotiating Committee to engage the room. Even the windbags have been accommodated. Cameron moves forward as they exit, trying to get into Jean-Luc's orbit.

"Eh, Cameron. Ça fait-tu ton affaire?"

"Yes. Long meeting, though."

"Oui. Et productif. À part ces hosties de bavards dans la queue, tabarnac."

Cameron laughs with relief. Rod is suddenly beside them.

"So, whaddaya think?"

"I think it's gonna pass ..."

"'Cept Garth gonna hate dat Train to Standard."

"Yeah. He's old-school military."

"How do you mean?"

"Oh, just that it's chain of command. One way down."

"Ça va lui donner un réveil brutal, hostie."

"Yeah. No more *World According to Garth*."

"You think he really didn't know what was going down in the Failure Center?"

"Probably not. Too busy agonizing about policy."

"So Southern Gentleman ..."

"Yeah. Probably had no clue, either."

"Hosties de cons."

They round the corner into the covered breezeway that leads out to the circular drive. The air is ambrosial. The low-angle September sun dresses to advantage flora, fauna, and the designs of man. A crowd of pilots has never looked more magical. Even Bad Dog looks angelic.

"Hey, Baddy. What's going on?"

"It's Enrico. I just can't fucking believe it."

"What?"

"I mean, you'd think with all the security material we've handed out, with the press hounding us, that he'd at least have a clue . . ."

"How do you mean . . ."

"He's living proof pilots are all rich assholes."

Bad Dog snorts, turning away.

"Check it out for yourselves. Words fucking fail me."

They move closer, trying to get a glimpse. A stunning red sports car is revealed. Standing beside it is Enrico. His toothy grin gets wider with each question.

"Yes, a Ferrari. The prancing horse. The Italian stallion."

"It's an F-355 Spider. That means convertible."

The top is down. The parking job is notable. Since the display area was intended to be a one-lane semi-circular dropoff, strictly no parking, Enrico has graciously driven the right-side wheels up onto the sidewalk so cars can get by. The crowd, however, has eliminated that option.

"380 horsepower. Yeah. That's right. Three-eighty."

"Zero to sixty? Book is 4.2 seconds. But I've got the F-1 transmission. Yeah, just like the Formula One cars. Use these paddles here. Lightning fast. I could probably do better than 4.2."

The crowd starts to thin out.

"Nice car, Enrico."

"Thanks, Cam."

"So, whaddaya think? You gonna vote for the package?"

"Fuckin' right. It's a good deal."

"Dere's no money, you get une hostie de valise, an' you're on da Boing. Hey, tu t'en fous, tabarnac."

Enrico vaults carefully into the driver's seat. It fits like a glove. The 355 cubic-inch V-8 roars into life and settles back, burbling as only V-8's do. Enrico smiles at the admiring crowd.

"Hey, by the way, Jean-Luc. This contract is perfect for me."

"'Ows dat, hostie?"

"Train to Standard! I'm gonna bid the left seat on the next bid. On the Bus!"

The V-8 starts to rev up in bursts. The crowd stands back, wary of toes. The Ferrari creeps forward, edging toward the roadway, about to drop off the curb. *He's gonna scrape something.*

But no. Rico finds the wheelchair ramp with the right front wheel and rolls smoothly onto the asphalt. His crooked teeth flash in the sun. He is moving his mouth but the V-8 drowns it out.

"What'd he say?"

Baddy shakes his head.

"I dunno, Cam. Something about four stripes."

Cueball

February, 1995

Cameron

THE WALKWAY is up. The Sim is dancing on its jacks, waving around like the head of a drunk making a point. The jacks make a noise somewhere between a groan and a whoosh.

They are watching from the balcony, trying to interpret phase of flight out of this crazy dance. These guys are running late. They should have been out of there ten minutes ago. An alarming noise seeps out of the box.

"Sounds like an engine fire."

Sure enough, the nose of the box yaws left, then right. The nose dips. There are coupled gyrations in roll and heave. Cameron stares at the walkway, which is raised at a forty-five degree angle, pointing up at the Sim.

"We're looking for a big heave and then a slow pitch forward. The heave's the landing. The pitch forward is the deceleration."

John's right. There it is. Must've been an engine fire on short final. Bet they're busy now. With a sigh the Sim settles back, level on its jacks. The room is quiet.

"So, John – if you do a really smooth landing there's not all that heave?"

"That's right, Rob. Haw, haw. Yours're gonna be greasers. Still get that decel, though. Unless ya roll her out with idle reverse and no brakes. She's pretty realistic. You'll see. She's certified to Level 4."

With another long sigh the Sim settles on its jacks, losing about two meters of altitude and coming level with Cameron's end of the walkway. Its door opens and a man appears, shrugging on his suit jacket. He nods to the three of them and presses a button by the door. The walkway groans and descends, the metal railings erecting as the platform goes level. Suit man walks across and brushes past. There is movement inside the box.

Two sweaty, wild-looking pilots cross the walkway, clutching brain bags and jackets. They nod to Cameron. The older man whispers as he goes by. *Sorry, gotta go. Didn't do a shutdown check.*

John and Rob look down at Cameron from the balcony.

"Go ahead, Cameron. She's all ours."

Cameron puts a tentative foot on the walkway. *Walking the plank. That's what it feels like. Those pilots looked like living corpses.* His feet on the plank make a metallic, hollow sound. He walks into the box and plunks his brain bag down on the Captain's seat, goes back toward the entry door, and hangs up his sports jacket in the little alcove. He opens the brain bags's top flaps and lowers it into the tray on the floor to the left of the captain's seat. He retrieves his headset and the new Bus adapter one of the techs in avionics made for him last week. This is his first time in the cockpit, his first encounter with the real space of it. He thinks of another first time, twenty-two years ago. Al Lank. Rod. That little seat in the door frame. The acceleration. The pushover to level at three thousand.

"Alright, guys. I'm going to set you up in Toronto. CAVOK day.

No, I guess it's evening. Haw, haw. No traffic. No abnormals. Hey, no worries. Sixty tons. Here's the load figures."

Cameron and Rod adjust their seats and rudder pedals. They check their oxygen masks.

"Captain on oxygen."

"First Officer on oxygen."

Their voices, trapped inside the masks and amplified over the intercom, sound like they need oxygen.

"Go ahead, Cameron. You start. You'll each get a half-hour, forty-five minutes of VFR circuits. We'll do that for a few days until you're happy with it."

"Thanks, John. We really appreciate it."

"No sweat. I'm going to work in my curriculum somewhere. Haw, haw."

Cameron starts the POM cockpit check. It seems simple after the routines he is used to. He feels like a conjuror, waving his hand across the overhead panel in the sequence suggested in the POM diagram, looking for lights. If there is a light in the switch, push the switch. The light goes out. Fuel pumps, for instance. They are off, or would have been if the previous guys had done a shutdown check. Push the button. The pump starts. If all is well, the pressure comes up and the light goes out. When he is done there is a single light on the panel, a green light showing that External Power is connected.

"Never seen that guy before. Probably MOM. Haw, haw. So how'd he know I'm just a lowly Ground School Instructor? I'd been a Flight Instructor he woulda apologized for taking fifteen minutes of my time. But no. Brushes past. Barely a glance. How'd he – oh, of course. The Sim schedule. He knew this was a ground school session. No sweat if he runs over. Fucker."

John mutters as he sets up his instructor's panel.

"OK, Cam. When you guys are ready, let 'er rip."

Cameron looks at Rob. Smiles.

"You set?"

"Sure. Let's do it."

"OK, Before Start Check, please."

John plays purser, the ramp lead, Air Traffic Control and if necessary, company radio or dispatch. Cameron calls for pushback. This Level 4 is pretty realistic, just like John said. They call it dusk. Dusk without the beauty. But you can see everything, including the texture of the ramp surface moving beneath you as you push.

"Starting Engine 2."

The Fully Automated Digital Engine Control does its thing. Neat software. But the flight control software is what I really want to see. He taxis out to 24L, noticing the heaps of dirty snow beside the taxiway. Nice touch. It's winter outside and in the software, too. Those Sim Techs are good. No wonder Jim Kirk made a point of knowing them.

"You're free to use the autopilot if you want, guys. But you're not going to get any stick time in the Flight Sim. Except for the single-engine ILS. Haw, haw."

Cameron has selected midway on both height and tilt on the left armrest, the armrest behind the sidestick. 5E is the setting. He's going to try the thumb and finger technique. There is no crosswind this time, so there should be no roll on liftoff. He squeezes the stick back with his third and fourth fingers. She rotates prettily and lifts off. Amazing! I can feel Normal Law wash in!

"Positive Rate."

"Gear Up."

Cameron opens his fingers tentatively. She is rock-solid as the gear doors open and the wheels come up. With his thumb he nudges her down from fifteen degrees nose-up to twelve. He glances over and sets climb thrust. She just sits there and accelerates.

"Flaps Zero."

He can feel the slight sag and the quickened acceleration. She sticks at twelve degrees nose up. Thumb on the inside of the pole. Push over into a thirty-degree left bank.

"Select Speed 200."

Rob reaches across the FCU. He selects 200 and pulls. Cameron watches the speed bug turn cyan and jump down to 200 knots. He hears the power coming back. Thumbs the back of the pole to push level at 3000 feet. Rolls out on crosswind.

"Visual 24 Left. In Range Check."

Rob is busy. Cameron starts the turn to downwind. He watches the airport slide by on his left.

"Flaps 1."

"Flaps 1, 200 Selected."

Where's S Speed? Oh, shit. He's right.

"Thanks, Rob. Speed Push."

Cameron watches the speed bug turn magenta, drop, and acquire the 'S' label. He hears the power come back, the autothrust seeking the new target speed. All new stuff. But wait – the approach phase has to be activated to get S Speed. Rob musta done it. Then I'd have had green dot. Wouldn't need selected speed. But we should talk when we . . . you know, this is a lot of fun. Cameron turns a close base leg. Why not? See if we can throw this thing around.

"Gear Down. Landing Check."

Not a lot to do there. Arm the spoilers.

"Flaps 2."

"Flaps 2, F Speed."

Yeah, talk the stuff on the PFD. This is like point and shoot. Whoops, speed's coming up and power's at idle . . .

"Flaps 3."

"Flaps 3, F Speed."

Cameron carves around to final at 500 Above Ground Level.

"Flaps Full."

"Flaps Full, Vapp 132."

A squeeze with third and fourth fingers checks the rate of descent as they settle onto the Visual Approach Slope Indicator glide slope. The power comes up to hold Vapp. OK, here we go. Breathe. Flare. Ease the thrust levers back. Don't let the nose drop. There it is – the nose-down trim winding in – OK, squeeze with third and fourth, hold the nose there . . .

"Nice one, Cameron. First time lucky! Cleared to taxi back to the button. Now we can do some touch and go's . . ."

§

Jeff's team has disappeared into the dressing room. They have lost, 5-2. Jeff has played well on defence but the team's forward lines are not strong. Jeff doesn't complain.

Cameron and Leslie are hanging around behind the seats in the chilly arena, talking occasionally with the other parents as they drift by. Suddenly Cameron is conscious of a deep pain running down his left arm. He moves from foot to foot, trying to change the alignment of his spine. Is this back trouble again? No, more likely neck with this arm stuff. Shit. Moving, he shrugs his shoulders, moves his neck. The deep pain becomes tingles and aches. Better. Last big back episode was when? I was on course. My captain course. Doing a walkaround, inspecting a 'nine in the hangar. Bent over to get under the wing. Tried the chiropractor that time. Aahh. That bloody pain again!

"Honey, what's wrong?"

"Pain in my arm . . ."

"I can see it in your face. What'd you do? Do you know?"

"Dunno. 'Cept it's like the pain in my legs when . . ."

"Oh, your back. You say it's in your arm?"

"Yah."

"I wonder, could it be neck?"

"I think so, maybe . . ."

"Here. I've got a couple of Advil in my purse. Don't want you to spasm up."

"OK. If I hold my head just . . . I can make it ease off . . ."

"C'mon out to the lobby. It's warmer. You know, the only thing that has really helped you with your back things is physio. And the exercises she taught you . . ."

"But where are we gonna find . . . I mean this weekend . . ."

"Susan knows a girl who comes to the house. I'll call her."

§

The van comes to a stop at Jetliner Road. Six lanes of Monday morning traffic move briskly across in front of them, intent on their purpose.

"You'd think the traffic would be better by now. It's ten thirty."

"Yes, sir. It's Monday morning. Monday morning and Friday night. The airport is crazy."

"Boy, you're right about that, Ignatio."

259

Cameron realizes he is doing the double-chin exercise. Chest out, head back, chin tucked in. It helps. Right now he just has a bit of tingling in his left hand. Oh, well. They say the Flight Sim is mostly on autopilot. Except for the single-engine ILS, he said. John. What a godsend.

They are moving again like horses out of the gate at the clang of the bell, charging toward the 427 underpass. Susan's physio lady. Thank goodness for her. Gotta keep the stress down this week.

The Dawn of First Class Travel is sliding by on their left. That day Rob drove me back to the hotel and we had a beer. That helped. We just talked Normal Procedures. Normal calls. Made them up, sometimes. But if we're a team, an unbreakable team . . ."

Ignatio executes the left turn onto Silver Dart Drive.

"Nicely done, as usual, Ignatio."

"Thank you, sir."

With a sigh, Cameron buzzes himself into Purgatory.

§

It is 11:59. With a dying sigh the box settles on its six jacks. A shirtsleeved man emerges blinking into the light. He looks vaguely familiar to Cameron, although no name accompanies the recognition. However, shirtsleeves is well known to their instructor.

"CueBall! Thought I'd better get my ass out of here on time!"

"Good of you, Foster. We've got a lot to cover."

"Hey, I don't envy you trying to do a course in eight sims. I think those bean counters have finally gone totally frickin' nuts."

"Well, Foster. I'm not going to argue with you on that."

Foster presses the button and the walkway descends. Two almost-normal-looking pilots emerge behind him, putting on their sports jackets.

"Go ahead, Cameron. Rob. Get yourselves set up. Just going to have a word with Foster."

The plank leads from the bottom of the balcony stairs into the dark maw of the Sim. Cameron walks bravely into a world now inhabited by men fighting political battles meaningful only to themselves. Battles that could nevertheless clip Cameron and Rob on the shoulder and send them spinning into oblivion.

Cameron lingers by the door to hang up his jacket and welcome Rob and pull in some of the light from the world outside.

"Hey, Rob. We'll just stick to the POM. Speak the words on the PFD. We'll be fine."

"OK, Cameron."

Cameron smiles a smile he doesn't entirely feel. But he means what he says.

"We're a good team, Rob. We can do this."

They settle in. Seats and rudder pedals adjust. Oxygen masks and intercom check. Cameron decides to wait for CueBall before beginning the cockpit check proper. Might as well get it all out up front.

The shaft of outside light disappears. The hydraulics beneath stir as CueBall turns on the motion, lifting them on six jacks into the neutral position, ready for action. He works quickly at his instructor's panel. The PFD, ND, and EGAD are coming alive. Looks like where? Cameron zooms his ND back. Ottawa!

There is a scraping as CueBall swivels his seat so it is facing forward and then slides it up to the back of the pedestal, between Cameron and Rob. Like where I was sitting on the 'nine between al Al Lank and Rod. CueBall reaches into his pocket and pulls out a six-inch-long cylinder. He pulls on the ends and with five distinct clicks the slender cylinder extends into a thirty-inch pointer. It looks like something he has snapped off somebody's car. He raps the center of the glareshield.

"OK, guys. Let's get off to a good start. What I like to see, right away, as soon as you sit down, is check the batteries, check the oxygen, then go over to the..."

"We've already done the seat and rudder pedal check, and the oxygen and intercom. I thought we'd wait 'till you sat down to do the rest."

"OK, fine. So start with the batteries . . ."

"Ah, excuse me . . ."

"What?"

He taps his pointer on the battery switches.

"Batteries. Check the batteries."

"Excuse me, Captain CueBall, but the Ministry of Movement has required us to use the Pilots' Operating Manual procedures. That begins with the flow."

"The what? The flow? What in the . . ."

Cameron offers a crumpled Xerox sheet – the page of the POM which has a diagram of the flow.

"Yes, they call it the flow."

Cameron raises his right arm, pointing to the upper left section of the overhead panel.

"It starts here with the IRS switches."

He continues the flow, his hand waving magically over the panel, making it dark. CueBall has the flow between thumb and forefinger, dangling it as if it were a piece of dog shit. He lets it go over the pedestal. Rob catches the fluttering page with an eye for its future and their own.

§

"I don't know, Cameron. He's angry. I can feel it."

"You're right. He *is* angry."

"But what can we do? This is crazy. Anyway, I heard something today. You know Dan Keen?"

"Sure. Check pilot from Winnipeg. Saw him a couple of days ago. He asked me what we were doing for procedures."

"He's been into everybody's office. Asking the same thing. Getting everybody's opinion."

"He's a good guy, you know. Very serious. Good pilot."

"He's the first recurrent to use POM."

There a tension in Rob's voice.

"What? Today was his ride, right?"

"Yes. He flunked."

"Dan? No . . ."

Cameron has his finger tips on his temples, shaking his head.

"Yes. His F/O told me. In the can. Just before we left. He was pretty upset."

"Jesus."

Cameron signals the waiter.

"Have one more before you go?"

"Shit, Cameron. I shouldn't. Sure."

"Let's get some nachos. We'll make a plan."

§

Rob sips his second beer. He is making short work of the nachos. Cameron is thinking out loud.

"So who do we have to please, here? I mean really, push comes to shove?"

Rob chews.

"Not CueBall. Sad to say, he hardly counts in this, except for the downside. I mean, his license isn't on the line like ours are, but if we flunk he looks bad. He could lose his instructor status. And he didn't even have a copy of the POM. This was sprung on him worse than it was sprung on us."

"So who . . ."

"Not the company. MOM is leaning on the company. That's the battle. We're just pawns in this game."

"God. I'm starting to feel sick."

"You know Bird of Prey? Ever met him?"

"Once. When I was a Second Officer on the Tritanic."

"So you know who I'm talking about. You know what he told me?"

Cameron relates a short version of the trip across the pond with Hapless and the horse meat.

" . . . so he says, *Cameron, don't fly to please me. Fly to please yourself.* And I thought I knew what he meant. I did, sort of. But today . . ."

"Today. You mean – you mean Dan Keen?"

"Yes. Absolutely. Dan Keen. That was his mistake. Trying to please someone else."

"So we . . ."

"We please ourselves. No one else. Well, maybe MOM. MOM has to think we're OK."

"It's still scary. CueBall's angry, Dan just flunked. It's not a good atmosphere."

"No, it's not. But CueBall's scared. Probably more than we are. He can teach, but he can't guarantee we're going to pass. His ass is on the line. Shit, everybody in the Company is probably scared, V.P. on down. But we've got a lot going for us."

"We're a good team."

"Yes. And we're doing fine. We have a copy of the POM, so we know exactly what it is. It's a pretty spare SOP, right?"

"How do you mean?"

"Take the Standard Operating Procedures, the Normal Ops, of the last aircraft you were on. The 'nine, right?"

"Yes."

"So how does the POM compare?"

"It's short. There's not much in it. Easy to memorize."

"Right. It's not even a full SOP. It's Bus Industries's recommendation to its customers. Along with its other recommendations, like start training with Autopilot and Flight Directors off, and verbalize everything that pops up on the PFD. And we're doing all that, no small thanks to John ..."

"Yes. But we're kinda making stuff up ..."

"Darn right. But what can they say? The only thing that's in writing is the POM. So we make an operation on top of that."

"Yeah. That makes sense."

"And there is something else we've got going for us. Quietly Ambitious took me aside. He seemed really embarrassed that the Flight Sim was going to be only eight sessions and the ride. He said, if you guys feel you don't have enough time, if you're getting pushed, come tell me right away. I'll get you more sessions. Whatever you need."

"Wow. That's nice."

"I'd like continue these debriefings after each Sim. Not after the eight to midnight next week, but ..."

"Sure. Yeah. Like if something comes up and we haven't got it quite right or something . . ."

". . . we can write our own script. Keep our act tight."

"That goddamn car antenna pisses me off, though."

Cameron laughs his two-beers laugh.

§

They are cranking the gear down. The procedure is **L/G Gravity Extension.** Though Cameron is flying, CueBall has suggested Rob take control for a few seconds so Cameron can feel what turning the crank feels like. The Blue and Yellow hydraulic systems are out, leaving only the Green system. Gear is Green. So why crank the gear down? To maintain system integrity, it says. They have deployed the RAT, the little propellor under the fuselage that drives a small generator and a Blue system hydraulic pump. No dice. Still no Blue System pressure. Ditto for the Yellow System: the electric pump doesn't restore pressure. Lines must be damaged somewhere, leaking fluid. Not going to risk doing something as large as the gear with the Green System. What if there are leaks in the gear lines? Then we lose the Green System, too. Then it's no flight controls. Game over.

They have worked through the INOP SYS list on the EGAD. Cameron is trying to fly and remind himself of the big stuff. To sort the wheat from the chaff. Right now it feels fine. Like nothing is wrong. But we're one broken green line away from disaster. That's why it says, LAND ASAP.

"Flaps 3."

"Flaps 3, F Speed."

"OK, Cameron. Looking good. So we'll do a touch and go off this one."

Touch and go? Fuck you, CueBall.

"No, we just free-fell the gear. And we have two hydraulic systems out. This will be a full stop."

"No, no. Don't worry. I'm going to reset all systems as soon as you touch. Just stand up the thrust levers and be prepared to rotate…"

"Flaps Full."

"Flaps Full. Vapp 134."

The pointer comes out. The fucking car antenna. Taps the EGAD. Tap tap tap.

"All this'll be normal as soon as you touch."

Cameron feels the steam coming out his ears.

"With respect, Captain CueBall, you are the instructor, I am the Captain. This will be a full-stop landing."

Cameron can hear the five clicks as CueBall collapses the pointer. B b b b brat. Then a blessed silence descends. Breathe. Gentle, early flare. No holdoff.

"No Reverse Number 2."

"Roger. Number 1 Idle Only."

They are going to make the Delta taxiway. Easily. Cameron squeezes the brakes just enough to click off the autobrake.

"Manual Braking."

"70."

"Roger."

Cameron keeps the idle reverse on number one until they have slowed to a walking pace. They turn off on the Delta and then right onto the ramp. Cameron brings her to a stop and sets the parking brake. It holds. There is pressure on the gauge. Accumulators OK, I guess. Leak somewhere else.

"OK, Rob. Let's ask 'em for a tow-in. Just to be on the safe side."

Rob tries, but it is not Company who answers. They can feel the heat from the third seat.

"Jesus, Cameron. Now there's no way we're going to be ready. No way in hell. I mean, it was tight to begin with, but now . . ."

The car antenna is extending and retracting. B b b b brat. B b b b brat.

"And by the way, what the fuck do think you're doing? I'm the one in charge of the syllabus. It was hard at twelve, it was really goddam hard at ten, and now they fucking want eight. And you, apparently, don't give a flying fuck one way or the other."

B b b b brat. B b b b brat.

"You're fucking up my whole operation. There's just not enough time left. And if you think I'm going to recommend you guys for the ride when we haven't finished the syllabus..."

B b b b brat. Tap tap tap. B b b b brat. Rob has moved to the right. Expecting the switch on his neck, perhaps.

"Fucking MOM is going to have a shitfit . . ."

Cameron is inspecting the Ottawa Terminal Building. He can hear the whine of the idling CFM-56 engines. When they added that front section on the terminal there was a little step up. As if the architects or the builders didn't quite . . . CueBall is working at his panel. The EGAD is clear. All systems normal. Cameron clears his throat.

"Um, CueBall, I should have mentioned it . . ."

"Uh huh?"

"Well, first, of course we don't want to be recommended for the ride if we're not ready. But Captain Ambitious – you know Quietly?"

"Yes, yes. Of course."

"He said he knew eight Sims was tight. I was to let him know if we were having any problem finishing in time. I mean, comfortably."

"And, what? He'd get us another? More?"

"Yes."

Cameron notices motion on his Navigation Display. The world is slewing around. He looks out. It is disorienting but fun. They slide sideways, skidding down the Alpha and across the snow-covered grass as they re-position and re-align. They come to rest on the button of runway 25.

"OK, guys. New airplane, new day. 60 tons. Same numbers. Set 'er up and we'll go."

The Failure Center

Spring/Summer 1997

Rod

"Well, I was just gettin' to that."

Rod can hear Brendan breathing on the other end of the line.

"You see, Ramrod – the reason I'm calling – would you be my best man?"

"Brillo! No shit! You're tying the knot?"

"That is indeed the plan ..."

"That's great! Of course I'll be your best man!

"Thank you, Ramrod. Thank you. Her name is Teresa. Teresa Barbarossa. She is a redhead. And it's soon – June 27th. Just six weeks away. I know you have to bid and all. Do you think you could get it off?"

"Shit, Brillo. I'll book off if I have to. Never mind, I'll quit if I have to. I'll be there."

"Well now, don't be gettin' too radical. I'm going to need you in position ..."

"I'll get it off. I'll bid Reserve. Get the 27ᵗʰ – what day is it?"

"Saturday."

"I'll get Friday to Monday as my G-Offs. Where?"

"Not far. Ottawa. Well, Hull, actually. She's a Québecoise."

"With a name like Barbarossa?"

"An Italian Quebecer. Speaks all three like a song, she does."

"Wait'll I tell Susan!"

"We're hoping Susan and the boys can be there. How are they all, by the way?"

"They're great. Growing up."

"Yes, and little Liam would be fourteen now, if I'm not mistaken."

"Yes. Right. And Patrick's about to go to his Senior Prom. Brendan's at Queens."

"I look forward to seeing all of your young men."

"And me to meeting Teresa! But what was that about keeping me in position?"

"Well, yes, tall one. I've just been accepted at your airline. I was thinkin' to get your advice from time to time. While I'm on course, and all."

§

The view from the patio of the Oak and Acorn foreshortens the row of approach light stanchions. The old friends sit looking up at the undersides of the crossbars, as if approaching the glideslope from underground. The setting sun is playing among the bars. To a pilot the effect is surreal.

"Jasus, Ramrod. If you looked up and saw that out of the window, you'd piss yourself."

As if in answer a mighty roar eclipses their world. The sky becomes aluminum, all greasy underbelly and dangling wheel trucks. As if frightened by their drunken vision, the pilot adds power, yaws, and pitches up. Their sky tilts alarmingly. No further witticisms are possible for another fifteen seconds.

Reversers roar in the distance.

"Like to see how that turned out."

"Yeah. Looked iffy."

"Too much fockin' around."

It is a beautiful May evening. Venus has just appeared in the wake of the setting sun. A brave thrush ventures his song from the trees on Meteor Drive.

"It's a wonder God's creation can still exist amongst the likes of this . . ."

"Yes."

The thrush sings again. It is the same motif but with an extra beat on the end. *Never seen Brendan quite like this. Changing careers at fifty. On course on the Bus. Getting married in less than a month.*

"You've got a lot on your plate, Brillo. How you doing?"

The old Brillo looks him in the eye.

"Thank you, Ramrod. You're a godsend."

"Well . . ."

"No, I swear to you. Do you know what just came into my head?"

"What?"

"You remember the day you were promoted? You came to pick me up?"

"Sure. At St. Hubert."

"That day – ten years ago, is it? Nine? You were a bit beside yourself, if you recall."

"Yeah. Guess you're right. I remember how I couldn't open the trunk of the Skylark . . ."

"Yes. You'd had a day. But thanks to your kind inquiry, I can see this time it is myself who's not all of a piece."

With a roar the sky is again a hundred feet above their heads. This sky has a cleaner, painted belly and fewer wheel trucks. It holds steady as it flashes over them. The drift angle is apparent. Rod points up.

"Bit of a south wind coming up, by the looks of it."

"What?"

"South wind."

"Yes. Looked like a good landing coming up."

They wait for the sound of the reversers. It does not come.

"Idle reverse, maybe. Knew he had that one taped."

Rod lets a beat go by.

"As do you, Brillo. You'll see."

"Well, I am no longer a young buck . . ."

"Yeah. Know what you mean. Hey, would you rather go inside? The chairs are more comfortable."

Brendan shifts on the picnic table bench.

"No. Sore butt's a small price to pay. Stars are about to appear. And the landers give me time to reflect. Adjust a bit."

He gestures about.

"This is fine indeed. Thank you for draggin' me out."

The air is filled with promise, still warm as the sun's disc flattens on the horizon.

"Hey, with a layover here I couldn't not try. So – how are you liking the course, so far?"

"Well, the first two weeks . . ."

"Yeah."

"But now, on the Bus course – John's a treat."

"Yeah, I liked him, too. So did Cameron, a couple of years back."

"Poor devil sounds like a consumptive, though. Reminds me of some of the tales of the old country."

"Yeah. His heart, I think."

Another aircraft soars by, its landing light beams stabbing the near-darkness.

"His heart. Yes, indeed. He takes good care of us."

The reverser noise is distant and normal.

"Say, Ramrod."

"Yeah."

"You still got a glow on for accidents? Like you had for those 'eights, years ago . . ."

"Sure."

"I'd like to know a wee bit about the Bus. Seeing I'm going to fly it."

"OK. There haven't been that many on the Bus, but there's a lot to learn from each one."

They talk them through: Mulhouse, Bangalore, Strasbourg.

"There's mods out to fix up some of the crew interface stuff. Like Bangalore: now I can see if your Flight Director is off. My PFD will say 1FD- instead of 1FD2."

"Yes, that's already in the training modules."

"And Strasbourg, too. They're changing out the fleet now. I think it's called CPIP2. Should be done by the time you get on line. It's more instinctive. FCU now says -3.3 if it's Flight Path Angle, and -3300 if it's Vertical Speed."

"Big difference. What's CPIP2?"

"Continuous Product Improvement Program."

"Bus Industries spin."

"Yeah."

Landing lights stab the darkness half a heartbeat ahead of the roar. Then for another heartbeat the stars disappear.

"Amazing, is it not? How easily we are confused . . ."

"What?"

"Oh, I just mean – by a slight oversight in design, maybe . . ."

"Yeah."

"Ramrod. Explain to me this fockin' ALT Star."

"You're thinking of the BigTwin crash."

"Yes. But more than that. I happened to hear it was rolling around MOM. Right after the crash. Couple of years ago."

"Well, the guy to talk to about that is Cameron. He had it on his ride. Two years ago. Just over."

It takes a heartbeat this time. The lights are chased by a different sound: the beating of big paddles. A Dash-8 floats over, the thuds changing to a deep-throated whisper. It seems benign after the big jets.

"You know, Brendan . . ."

"Uh huh . . ."

"I just thought about how you felt back when Pedro went to France with Miles."

"Yes."

"Then I heard more about what happened later. About how MOM finally had a lever in QuickTrain."

"Exactly so."

"Then Cameron went through. He and his F/O were the first to do POM."

"And he passed, did he not?"

"Yes, but as he says, it was by sheer luck. The day before the ride he heard rumours that MOM was going to use ALT Star."

"And he had time to prepare ..."

"Yeah. Not much. They did it over beer the night before the ride. They even figured out where it was going to happen."

"Sounds like some of your Sherlock stuff. How'd he do it?"

"Well, they knew the BigBus crash happened right after takeoff. The test pilots had 2000 feet set as the cleared altitude, and it was climbing like crazy, so altitude capture mode – ALT* – engaged as soon as the gear was up. They were about 20 degrees nose up. Then they failed an engine, as per their plan."

"Only they hadn't cleared it with their software guys."

"Yeah, really. So Cameron figured the closest scenario MOM could come up with was a missed approach. One with a low altitude. Then they'd force a go-around, wait for the high rate of climb, and cut an engine the instant they saw ALT Star."

"Makes sense. So you said they even knew where?"

"They didn't know for sure. But they looked at all the approaches in Toronto, Montreal, Ottawa. It was a slam dunk."

"Spill it to me, Sherlock."

"Ottawa 25. It's a bugger, anyway. Back Course. Beacon's offset.

FAF is close in. And – this is the kicker – the Missed Approach Altitude is 2500."

"Bingo. And it was?"

"Yes."

A roaring jumbo blots out the stars. It makes them jump. The Dash-8 and the lull have led to complacency.

"So what'd they do? Push to level off?"

"No. Remember, they didn't have CPIP2. It was out but we didn't have it yet."

"There was no push to level off, I gather."

"No. Lots of stuff was different. No V/S on the PFD, for example. So you'd have to look up to dial in a vertical speed. Cameron figured the only sure way was to kill the autopilot and fly by hand."

"So he was rehearsin' in his head, the way you used to do."

"Yeah."

"And they passed."

"Yeah. And the MOM guy in the debriefing congratulated them on their handling of ALT Star."

"Good for them."

"Yeah. Really. I'm glad I waited a year."

A corporate jet whistles by overhead, its lights twisting in the sky as it adjusts its drift angle.

"South wind looks to be pickin' up."

"Yeah," says Rod. "I think Cameron's through with wide open equipment bids."

§

Cameron

Occasionally the stars align. Cameron thinks back to that phone call a year ago when they asked him. He had said no when they tapped him to be a Check Pilot, so he wasn't expecting another call. But this was different. It was a new job, flowing from the existence of Level IV simulators. Now a pilot transitioning from another type gets his rating in the Sim, and his first flight in the real airplane is a line flight with passengers.

So he said yes, and for a year he has been a Line Indoctrination Training Captain, or LITC. Now the hours at cruise go by in a blink because he is doing what he loves best – having a conversation about systems and techniques and technical arcana.

He pulls his training clipboard out of his brain bag. Opens it and stares at the front page of the AATF 1101 – Pilot Line Indoctrination. He is looking for blank lines, items he hasn't initialed. There aren't any. He flips the form. He has listed the legs of their four-day cycle, except for this Montreal-Vancouver leg and tomorrow's direct home. He has written Very High Standard Demonstrated Throughout diagonally through the five categories of skills.

"Brendan. Have a look. We're done with the official curriculum. And I'm telling it like it is. Just gotta sign it and send the teletype when we get back tomorrow."

He hands the form to Brendan, who scans it and hands it back.

"Thank you, Cameron. It's a pleasure working with you."

It is one of those fine August days that bless Arcadia. CAVOK from The Rock to Vancouver Island. The wheat fields of Saskatchewan slide eastward below them. Cameron looks ahead, trying to see if that emerging line of white is water vapour or granite in disguise. He watches for a few minutes.

"Hey, I think that's the Rockies."

Brendan stares for a minute.

"Yes. I believe so. We are enjoying a treat today, are we not? The beauty of our Arcadia spread out beneath us."

They watch the white line again, looking for growth, shape. *Still, it would be embarrassing if that's just cloud.* Cameron looks down at his ND. About twenty east of Empress. He looks at the windowsill, where his book of approach plates is fastened. He has adapted his binder so it fits on either windowsill. Each flap has a rivet and a 1 1/4-inch hole. The rivet goes in the map clip, the hole lets the binder cover slip over the window handle. He peers at Strip 25. OK, then about a hundred to Calgary and then another hundred and a bit to WELFF. Say, 230 miles. Yeah, could be. He stares ahead again. The white line is thicker and has grown jagged peaks on the top.

"**Air Arcadia 129, call Edmonton Center on 134.22.**"

"**Roger, Air Arcadia 129, Edmonton 134.22.** See ya."

Cameron checks in with Edmonton and fills in the AFPAA abeam Empress. He settles in his seat, watching the snow-covered line of peaks reveal itself and scanning the foothills for the smudge that will be Calgary. He punches FLT PLN on his MCDU and glances down at the bottom lines. The Estimated Fuel Over Destination is 3.1 tonnes. All is well.

"You know, Brendan, I've been meaning to ask you. It was ten years ago, right after we got promoted. You were in town and celebrated with Rod . . ."

"Indeed. I remember it well. A fine night."

The Rockies. Unmistakably. And the smudge. There it is, painted on the brown foothills.

"Rod said you made a prediction."

"I remember. I don't know that I would dignify it with that size of a word. I had a feeling."

"About the team going over to Bus Industries."

"Yes. You see, I knew Miles in the service. Ambitious, to be sure. But more than that. A sense of his own importance. A strutting popinjay. That's how he came across."

Brendan's ears are red. Cameron pushes past it.

"And you said you feared for the mission?"

"From what Rod told me about Captain Pedro, well, I had a feeling it wouldn't work."

Cameron looks at the smudge. It is beginning to resolve itself into a city with spires. Cameron stares at a spot north of the spires, waiting for the airport to appear.

"Stupid stuff is going on. Starting from then."

It comes out of nowhere. Brendan waits to see where it leads.

"You know that Insert we just got on MDA? How we have to add fifty feet? And call *Hundred Above* at a hundred above fifty feet above the published MDA?"

"Oh, indeed."

"Well, isn't that fifty feet – for recognition and reaction, say – already built in?"

"Technically, no ..."

This is not the answer Cameron expected. He stares at the spot, waiting for that north-south line which will be runway 16-34. He feels his cheeks reddening.

"You're saying we can't sag below MDA ...

"Yes. It has to do with glideslope or not – you know, Decision Altitude versus Minimum Descent Altitude ..."

Brendan looks abashed.

"No – go on, Brendan. I'm starting to realize I don't know what I'm talking about."

"For now let's just say that MOM's move and the airline's reaction have left us in the dark."

Cameron struggles to decode Brendan's diplomacy. The north-south smudge appears.

"It's condescension, isn't it, Brendan? We pilots can't handle it?"

"You're right ..." Brendan pauses, uncertain. Cameron is, after all a representative of management and also, when it comes to that, of MOM. "But I am afraid, Cameron, it is because your company – oh heavens, our company – has been informed that any pilot who sags one foot below the published fockin' MDA on a missed approach will fail the ride."

"Just like that?"

"Just like that."

The long smudge of 16-34 has been joined by the shorter one of 10-28. There is even a tower and a terminal building.

"Jesus."

"Indeed."

Cameron presses his left temple against the side window. He follows downtown as it slides by, obscured by the tiny heating wires in the pane. He remembers this town in 1973 when on layovers he stayed in the tallest building in town, the cylindrical, eight-story Foothill Summit. That was before big oil came to stay. He sighs.

"Guess I'd better get you set up for the approach. The new ATIS should be out."

"Would you mind if I programmed it? I'll talk it through and you can see if I'm thinkin' about it in the right way."

"Sure. Of course."

§

"Would this be where you're leadin' me, Cameron?"

Brendan has spotted the sign in the window. They are descending a steep block of Helmcken in Yaletown.

"Rod did tell me that you would appreciate a place that served draft Guinness."

They climb the steps from the street to the sidewalk.

"There's a patio. What do you think?"

"Yes. Truly a beautiful evening. You'd not rather be in?"

"Beer'll taste better out here."

The waitress gestures toward a table for two by the railing.

"What can I bring you, gentlemen?"

"A pint of Smithwicks, please."

"Ah, Cameron. I can see you are an aficionado of our Irish ales. Make it two, please."

The sun already has a golden glow as it sinks toward English Bay. Today's crew, the pilots of AA129/17, slide into relaxation. They study the Yaletown cityscape. The diagonal parking. The black two-inch pipe railings along the elevated sidewalks and stairs. The boardwalks that were loading docks in their day, protected by awning-like roofs hanging from diagonal braces above. Their beer arrives.

"Cameron, allow me to propose a toast. To a Line Indoc that is truly a pleasure!"

The first gulp is exquisite after a day at altitude.

"Hey, you F-18 guys take to the Bus like ducks to water. And that approach and landing today was a thing of beauty."

"Thank you, Cameron. For the acknowledgment that there is beauty in our work."

That view out the windshield as the glideslope was coming down. Sitting in a bowl of mountains. The Fraser River meandering out from underneath us, only to split before it reaches the Sound, its arms embracing emerald Sea Island, 26R a bright chalk line on the greensward by the water's edge.

"I can see it in my mind's eye. The final approach."

Cameron loves it, all of it. The steadiness. The perspective that doesn't change. The runway that just gets larger and larger until the flare. How the nose comes up and stays steady, power off and airspeed decaying, angle of attack increasing to the stall. The kiss and the settling as the spoilers deploy.

"I can see the landing. It was beautiful."

§

The day's last light rounds the corner from Davie.

"What rank is Teresa now?"

"She's a Lieutenant-Colonel."

The Magritte moment is almost past. Their glasses are half full and half empty. Cameron drums his fingers, tapping each right against its matching left."

"Brendan, this time I'm the one with a bad feeling. It's not just the 50-feet thing. It's the failure rate. Not the other types. Just the Bus. In the Sim."

"On the initial?"

"No. Pretty low there. Normal. No, it's on the recurrents. Mostly the six-months, but it's everywhere."

"Ouch. I'd better be watching myself this next while. How many? What's the rate?"

"Well, it has been thirty percent for more than a year. Last month it was a third."

"Mother of Jasus. I'm glad I didn't hear of it. Before they stuck my own self in the box just now."

"What's that doing to our confidence?"

"Your pilots' confidence is your airline's asset."

Cameron looks out at the evening, at nothing. Brendan lets the silence sit.

"The guys are joking about it. There's two types of Bus pilot. Those who have failed a ride and those who are about to fail a ride. It's not funny. They're good guys. They're being devalued. And for what?"

"For a fight that has nothing to do with them."

Cameron refocuses.

"But it should be over, Brendan. We did the POM when I went through two years ago. That's what they wanted, right? Isn't that what it was about?"

"It was indeed. Ostensibly, at least."

"You think there was more to it?"

"Who knows. But even if that were the only issue, we know there was a fight. And a poor body died in it, rest his soul."

"Pedro."

A sense of loss overtakes Cameron.

"Captain Fuck."

"Yes. And now I've seen his tombstone with my own eyes."

"The plaque in aircraft 201."

"Yes."

"So – that somebody died, that Pedro died – that has some

relevance to this fight?”

“So I believe. And it’s not just because there was an unfortunate death. Anytime there is damage to a person the conflict persists.”

“Why are we still at war, Brendan?”

Streetlamps have taken over. Stars are visible in the slices of sky between the buildings.

“Do you know a – a check pilot, I believe – called Peevish Pete?”

“Sure. Not well. Big guy. Bit of a loudmouth.”

“I witnessed an incident involving him. I was in the hallway. In the Sim building. At the end of one of our sessions. Pete was there. Mouthing off. And the object of his disparagement was a MOM inspector. Cocky little guy.”

“Navajo Joe.”

“Yes. That’s the name. They were trading schoolboy slurs.”

“I believe Peevish started the exchange by pointing out that MOM were in the Sim Building by invitation. That they were guests. That they could be asked to leave.”

Venus is barely visible over the buildings at the end of the block.

“Oh, oh . . .”

“Which inspired Navajo Joe to explain exactly how MOM had the airline by the short and curlies – he said, *we could shut you guys down tomorrow.* By then his voice was rising. To a bit of a squeak.”

“Oh my God . . .”

“Which only infuriated Pete all the more. You know the staircase at the end of the hall? Leads down to the front door?”

“Sure . . .”

“Well, it wasn’t that difficult, the size Pete is. He grabbed Joe and spun him around so he fell on his rear end and dragged him along by the arms, wiggling like a hooked fish, all the way down the hall and down the stairs. At the landing Pete dragged Joe to his feet. Propped him up against the front door. Then he reached for the latch, kicked the door open, yelled *Now get out!* at the top of his lungs, and pushed Joe so hard he staggered over the whole of the concrete and went down in the gravel of the drive. Pete shouted after him *And fucking stay out!*"

Venus has set. Cameron bends his head back and looks up. *That bright one. Vega? Maybe that's Hercules beyond it to the west . . .*

"You know, Brendan, when a pilot fails a ride . . ."

Brendan inspects the remains of his Guinness.

". . . well, he's lost his job, really. It's like getting divorced or losing custody of a child. It's a disaster. After you fail you're no longer qualified, so you have to deadhead to home base and wait."

"Yes. And perhaps have a taste too many of the sauce."

"Sure. And then you're hung over and feeling miserable and waiting for the Chief Pilot to call. And maybe if you're lucky Barbara from Planning calls saying she's scheduled you for a re-ride so at least you know you're going to get another chance . . ."

"The failure doth murder the cock."

"Yes! That cockiness you have to have. To do the job."

Cameron tilts his head back. Vega gleams at him. Who's that up top? Deneb? Tail of the swan?

"You know, Brendan . . . the Sim Center. Its real name is the Training Center. And what is its purpose? To train. Give our guys experience dealing with emergencies. Give them the confidence they can handle whatever comes."

"Can I get you guys a couple more of those?"

Cameron catches Brendan's eye.

"No, thank you. We're going to call it a night. Could you bring us ..."

"The check? Sure. Right away."

She disappears inside.

"That fricking building. You know what a lot of the guys are calling it, Brendan?"

No answer is immediately forthcoming. Brendan is dealing with dregs and foam. He sets the glass down and looks up, as if to allow matters to proceed.

"They're calling it the failure center."

There is disgust in Cameron's voice. He looks away, ashamed, then up at the heavens. Bright Vega beckons, a siren of the skies.

Walking the Plank

Toronto – March, 1998

Captain Everyman

"You have all your papers, gentlemen?"

Asshole. Just because he's from the Ministry Of Movement he thinks he has to be all fucking formal. Look at him shuffling our papers!

"Captain Everyman. Do you have your radiotelephone license?"

Radiotelephone license. When did I last lay eyes on that? 1975?

"Yes, of course. Gotta be here somewhere . . ."

Don't even remember what it looks like . . . Hah! Here it is!

"Thank you, Captain. And First Officer Guy. As you know, I will be keeping your papers here in your files until after the ride. Then, if all goes well, I will sign them and give them back to you."

Jesus. Rub it in, will you?

"Treat this as you would any line flight."

Yeah. Like you MOM guys have ever flown a line flight.

"There will be no multiple failures. We will have plenty of time to complete the scenario. Just take your time and do it by the book."

No multiple failures. That's what they always say. Then the shit hits the fan and you're on approach and you can't remember all the stuff that's gone . . ."

"Here's your flight plan, your AFPAA as you call it . . ."

Now you're making fun of our in-house stuff? Do you even have flight plans over at MOM?

". . . so get on board and start setting up. We're in number two. I'll be there in a few minutes."

Probably has to take a crap. Well, fair enough. Guess that makes him human. But don't get your hopes up. Number two. That's the one around the corner. Some of the guys say number two is bad luck. That's gotta be bullshit. They're all the same. The Sim Techs do a pretty good job . . .

"Gerry! The walkway thing is up. I can't find the switch to get it down."

"It's over on the box, Guy. Catch 22. Can't get there from here. Hang on, I'll call the Sim Techs . . . you just pick up this phone . . ."

§

"Sorry, guys. They were working on it last night. If you ever need it again, there's another switch over here . . ."

The Sim Tech flips the switch.

Look at that walkway coming down! It's like we're on a pirate ship. And that sucker's the fucking plank. And guess who gets to walk it while Heavy Henry's in there sitting on the crapper. Least we're not blindfolded.

§

"Thought you guys would be ready to go by now."

"Plank was up. Walkway. Had to call the Sim Tech."

"No problem. We have plenty of time for the scenario. Go ahead with your cockpit check."

OK. Here goes the flow. How many times have I learned this check in the last three years? Same airplane. Same airline. But the check keeps changing. First the old procedures. Then POM. Then amendments every other month. Memorize whatever horseshit they want you to memorize. Say what they want you to say. Then they change their minds. Forget what you knew. That stuff you used to say. It's no good anymore.

"OK, I'll be ATC, Company, ATIS, and Pedro, your In-Charge.

Pedro's on a plaque in aircraft 201, dummy. Never mind. Stay cool.

The box groans and heaves, a beast rising from slumber. It steadies, quivering slightly on its six legs.

Motion's on. OK, here we go . . .

§

"Power Loss"

OK. Continue rotation. Gonna be lower. Twelve and a half. Nail the swing with rudder. Balance her out. Use the nice blue slip thing. Good girl. Climb.

"Positive Rate"

"Gear Up"

Nice baby. Now ease her back to the departure heading. Good. Wasn't far off. I musta nailed the rudder.

"Autopilot 1"

Now get my 400 feet . . .

"Heading Pull. EGAD Actions."

291

Thank God I saw those dials unwind. Caught it. So far so good. Fucker could'a waited for the second takeoff . . .

"Idle"

Check the blue thing. The whatsits target. Reach back. Make sure that's the rudder trim you've got. Tweak a little more on . . .

"Off"

"No damage I can see, Captain. N1 and N2 still spinning. Oh, and 1500 . . ."

"Thanks. **Vertical Speed Zero.**"

C'mon, baby. Accelerate. Atta girl. . .

"**Flap 1**"

Good girl . . .

"**Flap Zero**"

"Standing by with Engine Relight Procedure . . ."

"Oh. Ah, **Stop EGAD.**"

"Gerry, ya got green dot . . ."

"Ah, thanks. **Altitude Pull. Speed Pull. Max Continuous Thrust.**"

"**Air Arcadia 446, what are your intentions?**"

§

Captain Everyman stuffs the last of his loonies into the hot-drink machine.

"Whadaya like, Guy? Coffee?"

"Oh, you don't have to – a hot chocolate. Thanks."

A cup drops down. The machine whirrs and groans. A small stream of brown muck is joined by a larger stream of clear liquid. Most of it winds up in the cup.

"Here ya go. Coffee for me. I know it'll make me pee but what the hell."

The groanings and squirtings repeat. A couple of quarters rattle out in change.

"Buck twenty-five each. Fucking highway robbery."

"Thanks. We need the blood sugar . . ."

The basement room is long and narrow, constricted by the simulator bays along the west wall. Their view is of the stems of neglected shrubs out of windows barely above ground level. They are alone.

"Where is he?"

"Dunno. Guess he doesn't fraternize with the troops."

Guy wanders around with his hot chocolate, looking out each of the two doors.

"Nope. Can't see him."

"Good. We can take our break in peace."

"So. Those guys have never flown the line, right?"

"Doubt it. But they have the EA-32 rating. So I guess we have to respect them."

"Sure."

"But I sure don't like their attitude."

Guy snuffles into his hot chocolate. He looks up and smiles.

"I'm with you on that."

§

The plank is down. The maw beckons.

Heavy Henry is here. Sitting at his console. Probably brewing some really bad shit.

"OK, it's a station stop, gentlemen. We were in Ottawa, as you recall. Flight 446 is continuing to Montreal. Your leg, First Officer Guy."

§

Yeah, I know. There's a requirement to see us fly a single-engine ILS by hand. Guy's handling the fire fine. We did the EGAD, secured everything. He did everything like he was supposed to. Suggested we continue into Montreal. Good call. I made it official, talked to everybody. We've done all the checks. Now he just has to show he can fly the sucker down the ILS on one engine. Just forget about the asshole looking over our shoulders. What the fuck does he know, anyway? Go, Guy. Do your thing. Then we'll be out of this fuckin' sweatbox.

OK, there's the LOC . . .

    "Localizer"

OK, now don't forget to fly it by hand . . ."

    "Glideslope's alive . . ."

    "Roger"

Don't forget, now . . .

    "*Tweet tweet tweet.*"

Good. There's the cricket . . .

    "Autopilot Off"

Good boy.

    "Roger"

    "Glideslope"

    "Missed Approach three thousand, set."

Just hang onto her, baby.

    "By the Mike"

"Fourteen-eighty. Two-niner-eight-two inches set. Air Arcadia 446, by the Mike."

What's that whooshing sound? Wind? No, steady as she goes. Feels like we're sinking, though. What the fuck? No, on glideslope. Got this feeling Henry's up to something. The fucker. Nothing on EGAD. What's that clunk? Gear was down before the marker. Still got three green. Look around. Everything's OK. Where the fuck is our landing clearance?

Fuck! It's the motion!

"Ride's over, gentlemen. I'll see you in the briefing room in five minutes."

Heavy Henry gets up out of his seat. Light floods the sweatbox as he opens the door. He puts his fat finger on the fat button. The plank whirrs and whines as it comes down. Heavy walks across. He doesn't look back.

Jesus! There was nothing wrong with that approach! But the fat fucker is flunking us! I don't believe it!

"Shit. Sorry, Guy. No clue what it was. Your approach was right on the money."

"You think he's gonna flunk us?"

"That's sure as hell what it looks like. Shit. I gotta pee real bad."

"Really? You think we failed?"

"We're gonna find out in five minutes. Gotta go. See ya in the can."

§

Heavy Henry is sitting behind the desk. Their files are open in front of him. They take their chairs, submissives.

"Well, gentlemen."

OK, let us have it.

"Captain. Generally a good ride with you flying. A few minor points, but I'm not going to waste time here."

What's this? Fucking shit sandwich?

"First Officer Guy. Do you remember the controls check with you flying?"

"Um, I guess so . . ."

"Where were your feet during the rudder check?"

"My feet?"

"Those are linked controls. When the Captain does the rudder check, you are to follow through, with your feet on the pedals. Your feet were flat on the floor. That's an automatic failure right there, but I thought I'd give you guys the benefit of the doubt."

There it is. The word. It's out and bouncing around the room. Fucking failure. Boing boing boing.

"Then you were setting up that last approach. After the engine fire. Captain, you declared an emergency."

No shit. I mean, for fuck's sake . . .

"Yes – I wanted to scramble the trucks – that is, ah, you know, I wanted the fire trucks to be there when we touched down . . ."

"Of course. But Captain, do you remember what information you need to include when you declare an emergency?"

"Ah, sure . . . nature of emergency, intentions, souls on board, and . . . and fuel."

Fucker's just sitting there looking at me. Guess I didn't get it right. OK, think of the book. Bring it back verbatim.

"Anything else?"

"Ah, yes . . ."

C'mon, it's in there somewhere . . .

" . . . um, passengers, fuel on board, ah – yeah, and HAZMAT."

"That's right. Hazardous materials. Did you have any?"

Feel like a cornered rat. OK, think. What'd he give us at the beginning of Guy's ride? 60 tons, trim 1.5 nose down, I'll give you a minute to set it up . . . That's all. That's all he said. No mention of HAZMAT. So it had to be earlier. On my ride. Yeah. There was something on that first leg. A load sheet he had typed up. And there was HAZMAT. But that was three fucking hours ago! But wait. Did he ever say, *new airplane, new day*? I mean, everybody always says, *new airplane, new day*. Everybody. Except maybe he didn't, the fucker. So what was it? Can't remember the name. But it was flammable. A tiny quantity or it wouldn't be legal on a passenger flight. Asshole!

"Yeah. I mean, way back there, we had some, ah – tolua . . . propo . . . nazarene – I don't remember the name. But that was a different flight! We were in Toronto!"

It's no good. Look at the fucker. He's holding up those small pieces of blue paper!

"As I recall, I never said that you no longer had that Hazardous Material."

Look at him wave those licenses back and forth! He looks like a fucking fat lady fanning herself.

"So it was still on board. And you didn't mention it to ATC. You risked the lives of those rescuers."

Listen to his voice. That righteous conviction.

"They could have been killed . . ."

. . . feel like my nuts are in a vise . . .

" . . . because you didn't inform them of that flammable material in the hold. You didn't tell Dispatch you had flammable. And you didn't call CANUTEC."

"Yeah, my cell phone was turned off."

What the fuck. My re-ride won't be with this shithead, anyway.

"So I'm going to hold on to these."

Heavy Henry waves the licenses.

"You'll be getting a call from your Chief Pilot . . ."

A Vision

August 20, 1999

Boy Wonder Named CEO at Air Arcadia

Boy Wonder will take over the CEO chair at Air Arcadia starting Monday.

Southern Gentleman, the previous CEO, has resigned effective immediately following a short and troubled tenure. Last year's pilot strike cost the company $250 M and resulted in a loss for the year. Blizzards in January knocked out operations at the company's hub. Perhaps most critically, the airline's stock has taken a big hit, bottoming last month at half its value a year ago.

Boy Wonder, 39, arrived from Sigma along with Southern Gentleman as part of Horace Homer's staff. Insiders credit Mr. Wonder's tough stance during the strike in his gaining the inside track for this job.

Arcadia

A NEW CHAPTER, FATHER! I do not know how I feel.

When I lost my dear Chauncey I was sorely grieved. Then Horace, the great gift of my life, came and rescued me and inspired me as has no one save you, Father. And he left me in the hands of a good man. But this good man has not been able to stave off disaster. He has not steered my ship clear of storms and whirlpools.

So what now? Where will this puppy, Boy Wonder, take me? Of his intelligence and his keenness I have no doubt. Why do I feel uneasy?

A picture opens before me, Father, and I know not whence it comes.

A new millennium approaches. With the tumbling of the fourth digit comes accelerated change: technology wondrous to behold, transforming the daily lives and habits of our people. I am already flying GPS direct more often than I should. Children no longer play or socialize but instead disappear into their virtual games, killing soldiers at an inhuman pace. Adults prioritize their mobile devices over their fellow beings.

But nay, Father. It is not the technology. Jet engines did not ruin me. Neither did inertial navigation pull blinders over my eyes. Even television has not ruined my people nor rotted their brains.

No. It is something human, social, timeless. It is about people, my people, but it is more consequential to the enterprise, the company, the corporation. More consequential to me, Father!

You see, it is I who am fast becoming virtual. In the business schools I am a case study. I am an abstract entity to the young, the best and the brightest of them, who have been seduced by the lure of the Business School and its MBA, for them the key to financial rewards, to a life of affluence merited – well deserved, they would say! – because of their superior intelligence.

I fear, Father. I fear for my life when this vision comes to me. For Boy Wonder has it all: the youth, the intelligence, the keen, the Brahmin Business School diploma.

I fear the disconnect, Father. I fear this version of meritocracy where the intelligent feel they are anointed and disconnect from their fellow beings. I fear their work, as they virtualize the corporation.

I fear that in their quest to make their visions of themselves real, they will sacrifice our mutual enterprise and all we have striven for together.

This is what I see in my vision, Father. Is this the sight? Is it real? Or is it only my troubled imagination?

Bottom Dealing

Toronto – October, 1999

Rod

THE INBOUND IS running late: gate arrival estimated at 21:08 local. Flight planning done. Got the ALPAA. What time is it? Got an hour to kill, even if we're at the gate when she arrives.

"Hal. You hungry?"

"No thanks, Rod. Still full from that meal on the last leg."

"Yeah, me too."

"Just saw Jean-Luc out there. Says the bid's out."

"Isn't it early?"

"Yeah, supposed to be tomorrow? Ennaway, Jean-Luc said they just put it up."

They walk through the passage between the flight planning area and the crew lounge. Usually pilots are sprawled across chairs and sofas, reading crumpled sections of newspapers others have left behind. Now the sofas are empty and the pilots are clustered up against the inside wall of the lounge.

In Montreal the list comes out in a 3-ring binder. In recent years the individual sheets have been placed in plastic sleeves. But here in Toronto, the Center of the Universe, even that presentation would be torn to shreds in minutes. Instead, the 8 ½ x 11 sheets are taped to the bulletin board that covers the entire inside wall. Four-by-eight sheets of plexiglass are then screwed down over the paper, completing the security. Jean-Luc emerges from the scrum.

"'Ey, tall boy. Viens voir."

"Hal says it's out."

"Fuckin' right, hostie. Viens voir, comme je t'ai dit. Enfin, Jean-Luc, sur la liste des commandants."

"Congratulations!"

"C'est précoce, hostie. Mais tout de même, merci."

"How do you say? J'ai aucun doute? Ça me fait plaisir de t'imaginer commandant."

"C'est bien dit et très gentil. Mais 'garde donc c'qui est aussi sur la liste."

"Who?"

"'Garde."

Rod looks where Jean-Luc is pointing. Slightly below his own name on the Montreal Captain's list.

"Shit."

There is a moment of silence. Hal slides into a space near them.

"Hey, congrats, Jean-Luc. And someone else, did you guys say?"

Rod puts his finger on the space a few below Jean-Luc. Hal reads, then turns, facing them. His face is red.

"Bottom Gun?"

It is a reflective moment. The crowd has thinned. Both Jean-Luc and Hal are looking at Rod. Rod looks back at the list.

"Well, shit. All I'm gonna say is, they're gonna be gunning for him. Poor Enrico."

"Gunning, Rod?"

"He's got a t'ick file."

"Yeah. He's generated a lot of paper, that Rico. Now me, when I retire, I want them to say, *Rod who?*"

"So how come his file is so thick?"

Jesus. How do I get out of this?

"It's not that he's a bad pilot. When he puts his mind to it, he can do a decent job. It's just that he's scared just about everybody at one time or another. Including check pilots, unfortunately."

"Why?"

Why? Fuck, why do pigs fly?

"Don't know. Don't understand it. I mean, he's fun to be with. Good guy."

Rod moves toward the couches. Picks up a section of the Globe and Mail. *Said too much already.* Hal and Jean-Luc follow and sit down where they can look at the back of the Globe.

"Le Train to Stan Dard, c'est bien mais ce n'est pas suffisant. Tout de même: comme on dit, *Quand une bonne occasion se présente, faut en profiter.*"

Rod peers over the Globe.

"Aie, là. I start to h'admire d'is fucker. Tiene cojones."

§

Calgary – January, 2000

Enrico

HE PICKS HIS WAY across the four lanes of asphalt between the hotel and the terminal proper, trying not to slip. It is snowing, as last night's forecast said it would be. His leather soled shoes have zero grip on this slick surface. His raincoat is packed in his suitcase.

Today is the day for Enrico. He has been working his butt off for close to three months, going through one hoop after another and he hasn't tripped yet. It would be a shame if he fell on his ass today.

He makes it to the other side of the road and into the terminal and out of the snow with just a few slides of the soles. Today is the Command Final, the line trip with Check Captain Ice Pick. This is the last hoop. He'd have to be pretty dumb to imagine that today will be a breeze. They haven't got rid of him so far and if they're determined to do it today is their last chance.

§

It is still snowing. Enrico takes one swipe with the windshield wiper so he can see out front. The ramp is white. By the way the guys are walking, it is slippery, too.

"Uh, Ice . . ."

"Yes?"

"We're going to be closing up in less than ten minutes and I don't see any de-icing trucks around. Call the station and see what their plans are."

"Sure, right away."

"Oh, and tell them we'll want an over-spray of Type IV. We've got to taxi all the way to 34 . . ."

"OK, will do."

Enrico turns up his number two VHF so hear can hear the station's reply. They are very sorry. They will get on it right away. A crew is available. Should still be a sked departure.

"So Enrico, if they give us this Type IV over-spray like you requested, will we have enough time to taxi down to runway 34?"

Enrico picks up the ATIS, fresh off the printer.

"They're calling it one mile visibility – temp's minus four – so according to the table it's light snow, but just barely. Hey Ice, dig out the charts, would ya, and give me a Type IV holdover at this temp? I'll make the announcements."

A de-icing truck has moved into place ahead of the right wing.

"Ah, Enrico, I've got it here . . ."

Ice Pick holds up the green Type IV (Green) for use only in Arcadia chart.

"For moderate snow with Type IV at minus four it says 25 to 55 minutes."

"Thanks."

So he gives me the moderate snow numbers. When I told him it was light. Yeah, and good luck getting out to the the button of 34 in 25 minutes. Spray on the gate. Then push back in this slippery shit. Then taxi two miles. Fuck.

Ice Pick looks out his window.

"Looks like they're starting to spray the right wing."

"Thanks. Let me know if you see 'em start the over-spray. The green stuff."

"Will do."

Enrico looks down into his flight bag. He has a five by eight piece of cardboard with his personal checklists on it. He squints at the Before First Departure list.

Flight Attendant Briefing. Cockpit check. Emergency briefings. De-ice P.A. OK, did all that. *Logbook.* Yeah, looked at that. *Load.* Any minute now. *FMGC's Route, Perf, Flex?* Yeah, no flex. De-icing.

He looks up. He can see Fin 213 reflected in the windows of the terminal. It is hard to be sure with the bridge blocking part of the view, but it looks like the fuel truck has gone and a de-icing truck has taken its place. So why did I have to ask for de-icing? That's not procedure here. Station de-ices on gate. And it's not as if it isn't obvious. It's snowing, for fuck's sake.

He glances over at Ice Pick. He has the board. Or is that his board? Probably taking notes. Nothing operational, that's for sure. Not going to get much help today. Maybe I should brief him that I expect him do his First Officer duties? No. Too aggressive. Just keep an eye on him.

He glances down at his checklist again.

Flight Attendant Briefing. Cockpit check. Emergency briefings. De-ice P.A. Logbook. I looked at it. Started the entry for this flight. Wait. Wasn't there some maintenance action here?

Enrico reaches casually behind and pulls the logbook out of its metal receptacle on the back of his seat. He turns to the Journey Log as if that is what is important. Checks that he has written *I. Pick* in the Captain box as well as the flight number and station for this leg. As if it is merely a reflex, he turns the book over and opens up the Maintenance Log. Clean machine. No snags the last few days. Except last night, or when was it? He looks at the time in the log. 1125Z. What time is it now? 0700. Plus seven for Mountain Standard. 1400Z. 1125Z is this morning! Two and a half hours ago. He scans the page again, but carefully this time. Number one ELAC changed. No related snag. Just maintenance action. He snaps the book shut and swings it into the tray behind him without looking. Just a twist of the wrist. Three pointer!

"Ah, Enrico – looks like they're starting to spray the Type IV on the right wing."

Enrico punches his timer.

"OK, got it. Thanks."

Just play the game. Go by the book, and then some. See what comes.

"Ground to Cockpit?"

Enrico punches his INT button.

"Cockpit to Ground. Go ahead."

"Captain, we are beginning the application of Type IV at this time."

"Roger. Thank you. And let me know when you're done and the trucks are clear and you're ready to push."

"Will do, Captain."

"Oh, and we won't be starting engines on the push today. Too slippery. We'll wait 'till the brakes are set after the push."

"Roger, Captain. I'll pass that on to the lead."

§

"Air Arcadia 134 approaching the Golf. We have ATIS Charlie."

"Air Arcadia 134, Calgary Ground. Proceed via Golf. Hold short of runway 28 for landing traffic."

"Roger, Air Arcadia 134, hold short of two-eight."

Enrico takes it slowly around the corners. He could feel the tractor slipping a little back there on the push. He brings Fin 213 to a stop before the hold line on Golf, sets the parking brake, and looks at his timer. Shit! 13 minutes already! Good luck making it all the way in twenty-five minutes. He looks out to the left. Landing lights are stabbing the snow, rocking slightly in the turbulence. She is pointing right at them, crabbed into the crosswind. It is the competition, a BestJet Boing.

The BestJet jock lands it firmly and not quite straight. It rocks as it settles on its landing gear, spoilers up. As it passes them the buckets open and it disappears into its own private squall, the snow kicked up by reverse thrust.

"Air Arcadia 134, cleared to runway 34 via Golf and Charlie, cleared across runways 28 and 25."

They are on the Charlie, coasting downhill at idle thrust. It is a Christmas card view. The rolling high plains are white. Enrico thinks of the prairie dogs whose playground this is. Are they asleep now? Or fucking away in their burrows? He looks ahead and to the right. He can make out the hangars down where the terminal used to be, so long ago. Good. More than a mile away. Visibility is still at least a mile. I can ask him to pull out the Holdover Chart and give me the time for light snow. But not yet.

"Before Takeoff Check"

Ice Pick leans forward and puts his middle Finger on the tab for the first item on the mechanical checklist.

"Flight Controls"

Enrico pushes the Pedals Disc button on the steering tiller and holds it with the heel of his hand as he works the rudders.

"Rudder Left, Rudder Right, Neutral"

"Check"

"Ailerons Left, Ailerons Right, Neutral"

"Check"

Enrico glances down. Ice Pick is checking the control position indicator on the EGAD to make sure that the controls in question are returning to neutral.

"Elevators Up, Elevators Down, Neutral"

"Check"

Enrico feels the slight shudder in the airframe as the elevators cycle. The chime sounds. In his peripheral vision, notices the glow from the Master Caution light.

Ice Pick reads the EGAD.

"*F/CTL ELAC 1 PITCH FAULT*"

A smaller, virtual Master Caution comes on in Enrico's brain, clicking facts together into a suspicion. But he knows what he has to do right now. Without even looking at the screen, he calls:

"EGAD ACTIONS"

"It just says Crew Awareness."

Enrico slows the aircraft to a crawl, still looking straight ahead.

"Is that all?"

"Well, OK, it says *Pitch Function is achieved by the other ELAC. CAT 3 Single Only.*"

It is like it is being squeezed out of him.

Hasn't mentioned the Minimum Equipment List, the fucker! He'll trap me any way he can.

Enrico looks out at the snow. Peaceful. Shit, I'm getting upset. Can't show it, whatever I do . . .

"Ah, Ice – ask ground if we can stop here for a couple of minutes. And look this up in the M.E.L."

Enrico knows that an ELAC 1 PITCH FAULT is not a No Go. He also knows you can sometimes fix it.

"Air Arcadia 134 cleared to hold position on Charlie. No one behind you."

Enrico brings Fin 213 to a stop and sets the parking brake. Ice Pick is fumbling ineffectually with the M.E.L., a nine-inch by twelve-inch by five-inch thick tome with hard, heavy covers. It weighs a ton. Ice is leafing through it, trying to find the section on flight controls, presumably. Yeah, and he's not that fucking stupid.

"Ah, Ice – I think if you look in the front you can see right away if it's a No Go or a Return to Gate. You know, in that alphabetical listing."

It's a Return to Gate. Went through it last month on line indoc with Gary. *Insert 128. C/B Computer Reset Procedures.* You can reset the fault if it was caused by a tailwind blowing the two elevators in opposite directions before the hydraulics come up, like on engine start.

Ice Pick takes his advice and turns to the front of the book.

Messy procedure, though. All kinds of bells and red lights. Not today. Besides, wasn't it number one ELAC that was changed this morning?

"Captain . . ."

And now the fucker is calling me Captain. Jesus. Is there no end to this shit?

"Ah, Captain, I found it. It's a Return to Gate."

"Very good."

Very good? Where'd I come up with that? I sound like a fucking limey.

"We're going back to the gate. Get us a clearance and then call the station as we're taxiing in. I'll talk to the people before we move."

§

Time has slowed. The virtual Master Caution is still glowing in Enrico's head. He has kept Ice Pick busy arranging the maintenance action and the next de-icing. He has decided that the passengers

312

will remain on board. He has briefed the purser. He has asked Ice Pick to start the APU and told him why. And they are still not at the gate.

Ice switches to apron control as they enter the ramp from Golf. They are headed back to A14, the gate they left half an hour ago. Enrico feels for traction with the tips of his toes. He thinks of how the anti-skid kicks out at 20 knots ground speed.

"Ice, stand by to shut down both engines at my command. Shouldn't be necessary, but . . ."

"Roger. Standing by."

OK. Lined up. There's four knots. Try . . .

There is a satisfying little tug from each main gear as his toes test for grip. He is fully present, mind racing, as he eases her into berth. There. Brakes set. He shuts down the engines and calls for the Parking Checklist. Gotta keep him on board, is what I gotta do . . .

He grabs the logbook and enters the snag for the ELAC, and hands it to Ice Pick.

"Here, Ice. Finish off the details for me. Then stay on board and co-ordinate with station. Call the fueler. I'm going down to talk to dispatch and get a new flight plan. Tell the fueler I'll have numbers for him about ten minutes from now. You co-ordinate with station for de-icing. See what we need."

Enrico stands up and puts on his tunic and hat. He manages a smile.

"OK, you're in charge here. See you in fifteen."

He heads up the bridge, but detours out the side door and down the stairs to the ramp. Still greasy. Go slow. Don't fall on your ass.

In thirty seconds he is across the short space of ramp and into the door twenty feet in front of their nosewheel. It opens on a corridor. He walks in and enters the first door on the left, putting on his best toothy smile.

"Hi everybody!"

The Station Operations Control command room is like a mini-Houston. There are five or six people with headsets sitting at consoles. Lots of buttons and TV screens.

"I'm off 134. At gate fourteen."

One of them bites.

"Sure. With the attempt. The controls snag."

Enrico aims the full force of his smile at him.

"Yeah. I just want to hook up with the maintenance guys. Describe what happened. Save some time, maybe."

The SOC guy nods his head toward the door Enrico came in.

"Next door down. On your left, if you're facing the ramp. Unless they're out there already."

"Thanks," grins Enrico.

He walks toward the door, waving a *Thanks!* gesture. As if in afterthought, after a couple of paces he turns and focuses his smile on the SOC guy again.

"That the same shift that was on earlier this morning?"

The SOC guy hesitates a second. At least he doesn't look suspicious or doubtful.

"I guess so. Depends how early. First guy comes on shift at three."

Enrico broadens his already wide smile.

"Thanks, guys. Take care."

The smile vanishes as he turns the corner. Three. That's ten Zulu. So it's the same guy. He ducks into the door on the left. Nobody. Just walls of manuals and a microfilm reader. He turns and heads for the door to the ramp. The cold, snow-scented air is intoxicating as he opens the door. There they are. By the Electronics Bay Door, just behind the nosewheel. His foot slips as he steps off the curb onto the ramp proper. It is not a back-wrenching slip, just close enough to put fear in the body. Shit! Slow down, Rico.

There is a pair of legs hanging out of the fuselage just behind the nosewheel, a stepladder set where the legs would be if the attached hips weren't perching on the sill. A guy in winter maintenance garb is standing at the base of the ladder, handing up a large-format ARINC avionics box.

Enrico walks to the base of the ladder, turning on his deluxe smile again.

"Hi guys!"

Two grunts, one from inside the fuselage.

"I guess ya got a spare ELAC, eh? That's great."

More grunts.

"That's great. Get us out of here. I'm sure that's what you want."

No grunts that time. Just silence. Then movement and breathing from inside. An identical ARINC box noses out of the hole.

"Here, Herb. The UNI off. Tag's attached."

Herb shifts the unit to his left hand. More shuffling from inside. A hand emerges.

"Here's the tag from the UNI on. Go up and start the tests while I close up. Start the paperwork. I'll be there in a couple of minutes."

Herb disappears up the outside stairs to the jetway, still carrying the offending ELAC. The fuel truck has arrived. The fuel guy has his ladder out and is hooking up.

Enrico waits. Herb's buddy's feet feel for the ladder. He eases down, closing the Electronics Bay Door. He turns around to find Enrico, all teeth and extended hand.

"Hey, thanks for getting on this so quick."

Enrico grabs the reluctantly extended hand.

"I'm Enrico."

"Derek."

It is more of a mumble than an acknowledgement. Derek moves to get on with his work. He doesn't look at Enrico, but grabs the ladder and moves off toward his truck. Enrico follows. He waits while Derek stows his tools.

"Hey, this is great you guys had an ELAC in stock on the base. I'm on a check ride with Captain Pick. It'll be great if we don't have to cancel."

He pauses to give Derek a chance to turn around and look at him. To see the smile focused on him. To see the burning eyes looking straight into his. Enrico feels the power of his gaze working. It feels good, even though he prefers using it on women.

"How many ELACS do you normally have on station?"

There is a pause. A bit too much of a pause.

"None," says Derek hesitantly. "I mean, one. We had one last night until . . ."

Enrico widens his smile and holds Derek's eyes.

"Sure. So . . . whatever. This unit you took off just now – where did it come from?"

"Fin 257."

"Where's 257 now?"

"Went to Lotus Land. Flight 201. Six-thirty."

Fin 257 has two serviceable ELACs. So the one they took off 257 must have been on my airplane.

"And the UNI on. Let me guess. Before I go upstairs and check in the logbook."

It is not difficult to hold Derek's gaze. He is like a deer in the headlights. The fear is rolling off him. He could be fired for this. He could lose his license. You don't install a snagged unit on an aircraft. Not one that's going flying.

Enrico puts his hand on Derek's shoulder.

"Don't worry. This isn't going anywhere. It stops with me."

Enrico nods upward, toward the Flight Deck.

"And him. He asked you to do it."

It is a statement. There is a barely perceptible nod.

Enrico squeezes Derek's shoulder and gently pushes him toward the bridge. Enrico heads for the fuel truck. He turns to see Derek looking at him from the stairs.

"Don't worry," calls Enrico, over the ramp noise. "It's gone. Buried."

§

The snow has stopped. Sun is poking through the clouds. Enrico has time to look for prairie dogs as they coast two miles down the Charlie between shafts of sunlight. They roll onto 34 and up to FLEX Thrust in one smooth, continuous movement. They lift off and climb through wisps of lingering low-level cloud.

At cruising altitude the pace of the operation slows to a crawl. Plenty of time to catch up on this and that. Ice Pick rummages in his flight bag. Ever the helpful First Officer, he pulls out a Flight Crew Report form.

"Well, Captain, I guess we'll have to explain the delay."

Enrico makes no move to take the form. He is looking at the winter landscape. Diefenbaker Lake is visible ahead and to the right.

"Nice view."

317

Enrico is looking at the lake but he is thinking of how the UNI numbers match. Of how this airplane, Fin 213, is back to the same state as is was when it came in last night.

"Yes."

Enrico turns further so he is looking at Ice Pick.

"Funny thing."

"What?"

He waits until Ice Pick turns and their eyes lock.

"That delay was caused by removing a perfectly good ELAC this morning and putting on a snagged unit."

Enrico waits again. He leaves plenty of time for the realization and its implications to percolate through layers of previous calculation.

"So I imagine I can leave the Flight Crew Report up to you?"

Another heartbeat or two.

"That is, if one is required?"

Temptation

September 23, 1999

Jade Widens Bid to Include Air Arcadia

In a surprise move, Ziggy Birnbaum, the swashbuckling CEO of the Jade Corporation, today initiated what amounts to a hostile takeover bid for Air Arcadia.

He had previously been negotiating in partnership with Patriot Airlines to rescue the ailing Pacific Airlines International, which in its previous guise as Arcadian Pacific Airlines had swallowed numerous Arcadian airlines before being itself swallowed by Pure West Airlines and renamed.

Bay Street suspects Jade has fronted Patriot to smooth over the 25% limit on foreign ownership.

It is further believed Mr. Birnbaum intends to merge the Arcadian airlines and that the government favours the arrangement.

Boy Wonder

"Respectfully, sir, I think we should look at getting some outside help with this."

"But who, Larry?"

Boy's eye is caught by a Convair 580. Probably in from La Grande Rivière. He has been re-arranging his office to showcase the view of the final approach and the touchdown zone of 24R. His desk is angled so arrivals emerge over his right shoulder, flare just over his phone, and settle to earth behind the fake inkwell. The 580 looks like a butterfly in today's gusty north-west wind.

"It's gotta be someone good."

The pilot is fighting it a little too much.

"No. Good, yes. But also hard. Ruthless, even."

He adds power and tries again, settling acceptably but way long. The nosewheel is just coming down abeam the Echo. Boy looks back at Larry Tennyson, his Vice-President, Legal Affairs.

"Larry, you're a Montreal boy. McGill, right?"

Larry nods.

"So you know the scene. Who do we talk to?"

"Well, sir. I don't think you could do better than call Strike 'em Yell at 'em."

"Former Prime Ministers, right?"

"Well, yes sir – but . . ."

"But that's not who we want. OK. So who's the hard-ass?"

"Snake. He might be able to help us out."

§

"Strike 'em Yell at 'em. How may I direct your call?"

"Maître Snake, please."

"May I ask who is calling?"

"This is Larry Tennyson, Vice-President, Legal Affairs, Air Arcadia. I'm calling on behalf of our Chief Executive Officer, Boy

Wonder. I'm afraid it's rather urgent. Is he available?"

"Hold the line just a moment if you would, sir. I believe he's in the office."

§

The round table is behind a discreet screen in the Executive Dining Room. The table was Boy's idea. It is an Arthur sort of thing where he is king but his knights are willing to speak their minds. It is nestled into the north-east corner of the seventh floor, counterpoised with Boy's corner office on the north-west. The view overlooks the cantilever trusses of the line hangar and the threshold of runway 24 Left and continues up to the Oratory. Boy stares at the little cleft between Westmount and Mount Royal that is Côte des Neiges.

"So you think a legal challenge . . ."

"I do. They have prepared this very carefully, but you can't ever get the government to fully . . ."

Snake pauses, sipping his coffee, weighing how much to say.

"Let me put it this way: the Minister hasn't proposed a change in the law. Not yet at least."

The silence draws Boy back from Côte des Neiges. Larry looks pregnant with speech.

"Excuse me, Maître Snake. May I ask which law exactly?"

"Of course, Larry. The Arcadian Public Participation Act."

"The foreign ownership."

"Yes."

Boy nods toward the Oratory.

"You can make the case Jade's just a front?"

"Not in so many words, no. But if I were to . . ."

Snake uses his index finger on the handle to twirl his cup in the saucer.

"...if I were to point out Air Arcadia's Montreal head office and the commitment to bilingualism in its charter ..."

The cup makes another turn.

"... and bring the case before the Quebec Superior Court."

Distant reverse thrust noises penetrate the seventh floor glass. Boy looks out involuntarily, then looks back to the table, reddening slightly. The landing aircraft is of course invisible behind the line hangars. Larry beats him to it.

"Implication ..."

"... can be powerful, Maître Tennyson. As I am sure you are aware."

Snake has said what he has to say. He sits, looking composed in his Armani suit. The venom is already circulating in the blood of the prey. There is nothing more to do.

Boy sits up straight.

"I won't beat around the bush, Maître Snake. I am here to run an airline. If this Jade bid succeeds ... well, Air Arcadia will be part of World Unity – that's one of Ziggy's conditions. And when he's done I won't recognize the airline I've been working for these last seven years. I'll be out of work two months after I take office."

Boy looks out the window in time to catch an Air Arcadia Bus over the numbers, just beginning its flare. It sinks behind the hangars.

"I'm sure I don't have to tell you I want to fight this bid."

There is a barely perceptible nod.

"You could be my eyes and ears in Ottawa. If we get through this challenge there are sure to be others ahead. Most of our big decisions will involve the government, one way or the other."

Boy pauses, glances toward the runway, looks back.

"Come aboard, Maître Snake. Vice-President of Tactics and Strategy. Reporting directly to me."

§

AIRLINE HONCHO

November 5, 1999

Quebec Judge Declares Jade Bid Illegal

After an autumn of high drama, Judge Hugo Touchette today effectively ended the Jade Corporation's bid to acquire and merge Arcadia's two largest airlines.

His ruling affirmed the primacy of the 25% foreign ownership rule in Arcadian corporate law. Ziggy Birnbaum, Jade's CEO, withdrew his offer without comment.

Airline Honcho has learned that Maître Snake, formerly of Strike 'em Yell at 'em, played a large role in Air Arcadia's legal representation.

It is not yet clear where the government stands on this issue.

Light floods the corner office in shades of grey. Outside most of the brown decaying vegetation is hidden under the dirty crust of last week's snow.

Thank you, Boy.

Boy grimaces. She's talking to me again, he thinks. The high cirrus is grey. There is no discernible arc to the sky; on the northern horizon the high cloud merges with the snowy high ground of Laval, formerly Île Jesus.

I do thank you, Boy.

323

"Not me. Snake."

It's all grey. Why did I get a grey carpet? Why am I talking to her?

What's wrong, Boy? We're safe. We can get on with life.

Boy stares at his hands. It is like an embarrassing love affair you don't know how to end. What can he say? And why doesn't he feel better, even exuberant? Never mind. Look ahead, at the next threat. Do your job.

BestJet, the buggers. Never liked that Slimey Limey much. Anyone can make money in real estate! And now teaming up with this Dirk Cruise: they're starting to be dangerous. Same model as Old West. Point-to point. Quick turns. No unions. Most of all, that cheeky upstart image. We're new, we're quick, we're fun. You'll love our spirit and you'll love our prices. All that shit. And if that's not enough, Slimey is exploiting Arcadia's western alienation theme as a subtext. Pulled it right out of politics and remade it for commerce, the bugger.

I'm lean, Boy. Ready to take them on. Don't worry. We can do it.

"Not that easy."

Gotta stop talking to her. Cut it off. Snake would . . .

Oh, so that's it! Snake!

"He saved us, Arcadia. We'd both be gone if it weren't for him."

Boy struggles back into the landscape of business issues, which have taken on a more acute reality in the last couple of months. With Ziggy out of the way they are unavoidable. He squirms in his seat. There's still a lot that's good, though. We're at 110 employees per airplane, where Horace took us. Lean enough to compete, it's true.

Snake is not my president. You're my president.

"I'm CEO."

*Whatever. I'm your job. You can't cut me out. You saved me, not Snake.
You hired Snake.*

"Don't know the politics. I have to listen to him."

Can't serve two masters, Boy.

Boy's intercom buzzes.

"Yes, Laura?"

"Maître Snake to see you, sir."

Snake is slim, erect, and elegant. He is not handsome, but the suit
looks like it cost ten grand.

"Always good to see you, Maître Snake. Let's talk strategy."

Why does he make me feel uneasy?

Boy leads his Vice-President for Tactics and Strategy to the strategy
corner, the 24R view corner in front of his desk. A small table and
two matching chairs furnish the space. Danish modern. The airport
view opens out before them. Still grey on grey.

A Boing SmallTwin in Patriot colors is touching down. Boy winces
involuntarily. Snake gestures dismissively toward the SmallTwin.

"No longer a player, Boy. Not up here in Arcadia. That's over."

"No small thanks to you. That was brilliant, taking the case before
the Quebec Superior Court."

In his mind the SmallTwin morphs into BestJet colors.

"You know, BestJet could become a major pain. They're using this
western alienation angle…"

We can compete, Boy . . .

Snake gestures as if he is brushing away a harmless bug.

"It's true they've got a political angle. But they're pissants. Let
them overextend, then we'll crush them."

We don't have to crush them. Just compete with them. We'll do fine.

Snake's confidence momentarily disarms Boy. He is aware of an Air Arcadia Bus rotating and lifting off. He's light. Probably Toronto. Or LaGuardia.

"Boy, I'd like to talk about Pacific Airlines International."

No, Boy. No way. We're done with that.

Boy looks up, surprised.

"You think they're a problem? Terminal III and The Dawn of First Class Travel? Have you ever seen such an inane ad campaign? I think they're down for the count."

She's a fat old bitch, Boy. Don't touch her.

Snake nods. He pauses for a moment, looking serious, like he is thinking this thing through.

"Down for the count, yes."

Snake re-arranges the Bus BigTwin model on the table.

"Down for the count, and not quite out."

The BigTwin model changes heading again under Snake's expert guidance. It swivels until it is pointing at Boy.

"Between down and out there is opportunity."

Noooo!

Boy squirms, loosens his tie.

"Sure. We'll pick up the pieces. Like the Asian and South American routes the government parcelled off to them."

Yes. That's the idea, Boy. Tell him.

"I'm not sure it will be so easy, Boy. The Forward Party doesn't like job losses. They may not just stand by while Pacific slides. They may try to save it."

There are multiple puffs of smoke as a stretched Boing BigTwin touches down. Pacific Airlines International.

"But what about the foreign ownership rules?"

"Good point, Boy. But rules are flexible. Especially if you're the government. So don't count out Patriot or even Jade. But the Forwards could wind up helping us."

Be careful, Boy. Be careful of the Forwards. Be careful of MOM.

Snake smiles.

"The buzzword, by the way, is *Made in Arcadia*."

"I've heard the minister talking about that."

"They're serious. That's what they want. A right here at home solution. But they also want it to be a private sector solution. There's an election coming up. They don't want to blow it with an airline fuckup. They'd rather not be involved at all."

We're not the government, Boy. We don't have to help them solve their problems.

"You know, I've just been working through our business issues."

Boy is suddenly flooded with the sense of Horace's initiatives running out, running their course. He feels the weight of command resting on his shoulders, of the need for new ideas. He feels the effects of the low stock price left to him by Southern and of the agonizing autumn just ended. He feels the weight of the debt.

"OK, I see where you're going. We buy 'em out. The Forwards don't have to change the rules. A Made in Arcadia solution. But business-wise, I've got issues with that. Those guys are fat. And their debt is huge. I don't like it. We've got enough of that already."

Snake nods approvingly.

"You're right, of course, Boy. There are problems."

Don't listen, Boy. He's trying to suck you in.

Snake looks out the window. Boy follows his gaze. A BigBus is on short final: the twin, a magnificent-looking machine. It looks as proud as a hawk riding thermals, looking for prey. The landing is effortless. Puffs of smoke materialize from where the tires were a moment before, spinning up at touchdown. It is like the dive on the other side of a quiet bay, the diver already resurfacing as the sound of the splash reaches the observer. Here it is the speed of the aircraft, not the speed of sound, that produces the effect. The hot rubber takes a second to condense into smoke, and the wheels have already moved on.

The BigBus is going to make the Echo.

"Nice airplane. What's it doing here this early?"

Boy bites.

"Positioning for the Paris day-tripper. Leaves at 11:05. We're running it against France 511. I didn't think they could stop that quick!"

"Magnificent machine. Magnificent airline."

Look out, Boy. He's hypnotizing you. Don't look . . .

Snake turns to watch the BigBus enter the Echo. He swivels back, elegant even seated. He's like Fred Astaire in that chair.

"But it could be bigger. Much bigger."

Snake stands up. He walks to the window and paces, his fingers on his chin.

"Boy, you run a wonderful company. A billion-dollar company."

The pacing stops.

"But it could be a two-billion-dollar company. World-wide route structure and virtually no international competition."

No, Boy. Don't do it. Don't fasten me to that fat old bitch!

Boy's gaze out the window is unfocused. The BigBus twin has

vanished. He is getting sweats and chills as he struggles to stay in the here and now. Be strong. She's not real. Loosen your collar and get down to business.

"Please go on."

Boy, listen to me! He's setting the hook . . .

"You'd have eighty percent of the domestic market. All the international routes. And I think we can lose their debt." Snake pauses to let that sink in. "The Forwards really don't want bankruptcy and layoffs. They'd be prepared to make it easier for us if we can keep people employed."

Boy shakes his head.

"I don't know. Put us together and we're bloated. We should be able to downsize if we have to. And putting those two cultures together – the red and the blue – that's not going to be easy."

Not easy – Boy, it's suicide! Think of it! If you were asking me to marry the fat bitch, that would be one thing. But you're going to say we're the same person? You're asking me to be her?

Snake nods.

"Right. They've got too many on the payroll. But they're not kids. Most of them are getting a little long in the tooth. I'm sure we could package some of them – maybe a lot of them. And in the near future you're going to need most of them to keep things going during the transition."

He's talking like it's a done deal. It's tempting. Eighty percent of domestic and virtually a hundred percent of international.

Yes, Boy. He's talking like it's a done deal. Doesn't that tell you something? Who's CEO here, you or Snake?

Enough clout to just run BestJet dry on certain routes – like their bread and butter routes out west. And a two-billion dollar company!

"Yeah, I suppose we could downsize slowly, once we got the

operation merged. But ... merging those two cultures – I'm afraid we're going to lose something, something intangible ..."

Boy! You're saying I'm intangible?

Snake smiles his thin smile.

"You could look at it that way, Boy. You could say that the culture would change. But there's another way to look at it. We've had this discussion before: how the legacy airlines, great though they are, are hobbled by the unions. They can't keep their costs down, and the upstarts are going to come in and kick their butts. But I remember a thesis – a Brahmin Business School thesis – where it was pointed out – brilliantly – that there was a connection between worker culture and union strength."

Boy nods, biting the nail of his left little finger.

"So. The blues."

His voice is almost inaudible. He is talking to himself.

"Mix the reds and the blues. They hate each other."

Now you're going after my people?

Snake nods almost imperceptibly, looking serious and respectful.

"... eighty percent of the payroll is union ..."

Boy remembers the photo. The famous photo that was in all the papers during the strike. The photo that played such a large part in getting him to where he is today: Boy and Born Leader toe to toe, heels dug in, chins thrust forward like bulldogs. He sees now what he didn't see then: that moment was, in a way, the end of goodwill.

You are going to let me die?

Boy's voice breaks as he tries to speak normally, to speak to Snake instead of talking to himself. He clears his throat.

"I see lots of possibilities. But I still worry that we're going to lose something, something that's not in the numbers ..."

Snake manages to smile and look concerned at the same time.

"The soul of the airline?"

Boy looks startled.

Uh, well . . ."

You're going to pay his price, aren't you? But listen! We're in this together. Give him my soul and you're giving him yours.

Snake nods.

"You know, Boy, nothing in this life is free."

El Exigente

San Francisco – January, 2003

Proud captains irk Adolf.

What drives him every day is that he is not the captain. When he studies, which is not just before the Sim but before every line flight, he is seeking not knowledge for himself but humiliation for others. True, should a captain show enough respect Adolf might not unleash the full power of his scorn. He might go along for a whole cycle, letting things ride, letting good enough alone.

But at the merest hint of command arrogance it's look out, left seat. Traps can be laid. Adolf is adept at feigning concurrence, for example. The captain might duly consult on a decision, be confident in the unity of the team, and meanwhile Adolf is storing a unilateral decision on his mental checkride sheet.

On layovers he spends hours writing, organizing the day's mental notes into longhand briefs. He assembles files for problem captains. Monthly, or sometimes weekly, he goes through each file, deciding which are ripe for presentation to the brass.

Seniority is such shit. The idea that he must learn from those with more experience is ridiculous. And waiting for his turn is a waste of time. Especially since it is obvious that intelligence is the only true scale on which to measure merit. And having intelligence makes taking them down so much easier. The poor fucks don't suspect a thing.

Take that arrogant bugger with the toothy grin, for example. Can't wait to fatten that file. Just one leg with him and it's obvious he's one of those who should go down, making more room on the left seat lists. Talks about his flight, his airplane. As if he, Adolf, is chopped liver.

Can't bid to fly with him, though. He's on reserve. This may take a while.

§

Enrico

They are chasing the sun at FL350, trying to stop time. The red disc has been hanging there for the last half-hour, slowly losing its bottom edge.

How fast would they have to go to keep that sun from setting? What is the circumference of the earth? Twenty-five thousand miles? And here they are at about forty north latitude. Say fifteen thousand. So they'd have to do fifteen thousand miles in twenty-four hours to hold the sun still.

Enrico pulls out the Jeppesen wheel he got when he joined and still carries. It's one of the things Adolf has been ridiculing. Distance over time. 15/24 = 625 knots. Nope. Not in this direction. Saw that groundspeed once, though, going to Newfoundland. Just cooking along with 200 knots on the tail. Except we were going east, speeding up time. Can't fucking win.

The cycle sounded so attractive three days ago when Crew Sked pitched it to him. Four days, very productive, last layover downtown in SFO. San Francisco! How could he turn that down? Should have asked who the F/O was. But would he have remembered this guy?

How fast it all turned to shit. That bad weather in the Swamp. His arguments with Dispatch trying to get more gas or multiple alternates. How Adolf undercuts him at every opportunity. Even calls Dispatch on his own.

Dispatch was sure pissed at him tonight. Couldn't make out, over the phone, what the fuck was going on. The awkwardness, the pauses. Something wasn't right. Someone looking over the dispatcher's shoulder? A Supervisor?

Anyway, the result is he can't get a fucking drop more gas. So he gives up and goes with the flow, which happens to be Sacramento plus 10 minutes hold. Of course then there's a thirty-five minute taxi out to runway 05, slippery as hell, and no way is he gonna shut one down, even though Adolf is getting on his case. All the time he's thinking, if Adolf was in the left seat he would let him try to taxi out on one engine and see what happens. Let him slide off the taxiway, the stupid fuck.

So Air Arcadia 759 uses double the planned fuel to taxi out. And then Toronto Center keeps them down at FL290 until Detroit. More gas down the tubes.

§

Enrico punches FLT PLN on his MCDU and glances down at the bottom lines: two point zero. Two tons. Shit, that's barely Sacramento and no hold. Fuck.

Maybe he shouldn't have asked for an hour's hold. Maybe he started too high. Maybe he should have asked for a different alternate. But what? Reno, maybe. Back when he was doing his left seat it was Gary who told him, he remembers, about the valley in winter. How they always give you KSMF, Sacramento, and often there's ground fog and it's not forecast. Learned some stuff from Gary that came in handy. Like about the ELAC Pitch Fault. Wouldn't be sitting here today if it weren't for that.

Of course he explained about KSMF and ground fog to the dispatcher, but of course the dispatcher wouldn't listen. The forecast is fine, he said.

Enrico picks up the board, looks at the dispatch clearance on the AFPAA flight plan. The dispatcher's name is Foster. Foster! Isn't that the same guy he was arguing with over the Moncton alternate two nights ago? When Adolf was giving him such a hard time? Jesus I'm stupid, he thinks.

The sunset seems to have picked up speed. Only a fingernail paring of red disc is clinging to the horizon. Enrico glances at the groundspeed: 422 knots. No – haven't slowed down. Wind's more or less the same. He peers out front. Nothing better to do. Adolf hasn't said three words since they left Toronto.

He keeps pulling out that second clipboard of his and writing, so it feels like a fucking checkride. The bugger is pissing him off.

The sun is gone, sinking behind the Wasatch Range. Salt Lake is up ahead to the right. Enrico is thinking how it will be pitch black in a hour and how they're not making any gas.

§

"Bay Approach, Air Arcadia 759 level two-two-zero with India."

"Air Arcadia 759, Bay Approach, after Modesto proceed via the Locke 1 Arrival, Kilo's current."

"Air Arcadia 759, Roger. Locke 1. We'll get Kilo."

"Kilo? What the fuck happened to Juliet? Lock one? We're a mile from Modesto!"

"Yeah. Maybe they've shifted to runway 19."

Enrico struggles with anger and I told you so, trying not to lose focus. He notices Adolf punching keys on his MCDU.

"Wait. If they have shifted, ya better get the runway in first. Get the ATIS. I'll dig out the chart."

Enrico riffles through his Standard Terminal Arrival charts.

"OK, got it. Locke 1. It's the same after Modesto until GROAN. We've got sixteen miles. No sweat. But it's a runway 19 arrival."

"Yeah. Here's Kilo."

Adolf rips it off the printer and reads it before handing it to Enrico. Then he starts changing the arrival and landing runway in the FMCG. On autopilot, Flight 759 turns right at GROAN, its next waypoint LOCKE. Unseen ahead in the solid cloud and rain is Mount Diablo, poking up to 3849 feet.

"**Air Arcadia 759, Bay Approach, holding clearance when ready to copy.**"

Enrico holds a hand up across the pedestal.

"I'll get it."

"**Bay Approach, Air Arcadia 759, unable more than one turn in the hold. Say delays.**"

"**Air Arcadia 759, Bay Approach, estimating twenty to thirty minutes for runway change. Say intentions.**"

"We can't hold thirty minutes. We don't have enough fucking gas."

"**Air Arcadia 759 requesting clearance to alternate KSMF.**"

"**Standby . . .**"

Adolf looks up from his work. There is challenge in his eyes.

"We're loaded for the Locke 1 and 19L, Captain."

"OK, good work. Now get the ATIS for Sacramento. Load that

in the Secondary."

"Our destination is San Francisco, Captain. The passengers don't want to go to Sacramento."

"Jesus."

Enrico punches FLT PLN on his MCDU. He points to the Estimated Fuel On Board over destination.

"See that? What's a half-hour hold? One point one? One point two?"

He points at ATIS Information Kilo for San Francisco.

"You want to land in five hundred overcast, one mile visibility in light rain and fog, with no alternate and six hundred kilos in the tanks? Are you fucking crazy?"

"Air Arcadia 759, Bay Approach, ready to copy?"

Enrico thumbs his push-to-talk.

"Go ahead for Air Arcadia 759."

"Air Arcadia 759, Bay Approach, cleared to Sacramento Metro via direct Concord, Concord 1 Arrival, contact Bay Approach one two fife dezimal two-fife. Sacramento Foxtrot is current."

Enrico reads it back.

"You got Foxtrot?"

Adolf nods, hands it over.

"OK, set it up."

§

Air Arcadia 759 levels at ten thousand. Mount Diablo is behind them. The arrival jogs left, turning north toward Marysville. Travis Air Force Base slides by underneath. They are still in cloud.

Enrico glances at the FLT PLN page. Touchdown on runway 16R

is 22 miles away. Fuel at touchdown will be 1.2 tonnes.

It's VFR in Sacramento. Why are they still in cloud?

"Air Arcadia 759, descend to six thousand."

The turbulence begins as they leave ten thousand. Below and to the left, Lake Barryessa signals the eastern edge of the coast range and the beginning of the great valley. Suddenly the air is smooth. They have left the cloud behind. Stars appear above. A waning gibbous moon sits above the Sierras to the east.

Air Arcadia 759 passes ELKOE and turns slightly left to 340° for the downwind leg.

"Yeah, it's wide open."

Adolf is staring down to the right, looking at the parallel runways 16-34 at Sacramento Metro.

"Air Arcadia 759, descend to three thousand."

Enrico starts the descent, looking out his own side window. Tiny cars are crawling along the I-5, heading west, then turning northwest parallel to the coast range as they pass by the lights of a town. With his attention back in the cockpit, where all is normal, the hairs on the back of his neck suddenly bristle and he looks out again. He stares at the tiny cars and the lights of the town. He watches a car, follows it by the town. The splotches of brightness from its headlights on the pavement go from sharp edged to fuzzy to just a glow and back again. Now he can see that some of light from the town is just a glow.

Ground fog. Radiation fog. As the day's heat in the valley radiates out into space through the clear skies, the air in contact with the ground – just a shallow layer because at this time of night there's no wind and no mixing – chills to the dew point and fog forms, sometimes very rapidly. It's a super suck-in because on final approach you see the runway until the flare. Then, as you settle that final few feet toward the runway, the visibility suddenly goes to zero.

"Air Arcadia 759, turn right zero-seven-zero for base leg, report runway in sight for a visual 16R, no traffic."

Adolf isn't worried.

"You have the runway, Captain?"

"Flap 1. Yeah. Got the runway."

"Air Arcadia 759, cleared a right visual 16R, contact tower one two fife seven, goodnight."

"Flap 2. Gear down. Landing check."

Turning final the approach lights on the first stanchion are fuzzy. The lights on the rest of the towers, the VASIS, and the runway lights are clear. Fucking horseshoes. Just hang in for another two minutes.

§

On the ground it is a completely different hassle. Dispatch is catching up, sending them the frequency for the Jet Center who in turn are negotiating for a gate. Meanwhile there is a full load of passengers who are rapidly realizing they are not in San Francisco.

Enrico is steamed. His heart is beating from the adrenaline of a near thing. When he was a First Officer he didn't care about how much gas they had when they landed. Not his problem. But now his mind is racing. Where would he have gone with his 1.2 tonnes of fuel if this place had gone down? Reno? Vault up over the Sierras and Tahoe and glide in on approach praying the engines don't flame out? Set up for a CAT II on 16R here in Sacramento, do an autoland with autobrake medium and just sit there as the world disappears at 100 feet and hope they are still on the centerline of the runway when they come to a stop, and get violated and lose his license? Go direct to San Francisco and declare an emergency and get priority and land on 19L in rain and fog with no alternate and

300 kilos in the tanks and go through the LOW FUEL checklist *AND* get violated *AND* lose his license?

Fuck.

The gate is ready. They taxi in and shut down.

"So Adolf. Datalink Dispatch or get a VHF patch or whatever. Get a flight plan for SFO with a good alternate and an hour's hold. Co-ordinate with the Jet Center. I'm going to make an announcement and do the walkaround. Do the cockpit check. Your leg to San Francisco."

Enrico just wants to get out: out of the cockpit, out of the airplane, out of the terminal. He gets the gate door code from the ramp guy, writes it in his hat and takes the bridge three steps at a time. He walks out to the tail of the airplane.

The skies are ablaze with stars in the clear air. The moon is a little higher over the Sierras, barely past full. Enrico studies the brilliant disc with the slightly flattened right side. Squished, he thinks. Give it another few days and it's going to look like a breast, a shining breast with no nipple. He breathes deeply, trying to calm down, trying to get rational. It's hard, because it's like flying with Ice Pick on his ride. It's a battle.

The walkaround is not by the book only because he starts and finishes at the tail. Enrico is meticulous, looking at everything, thinking about each issue. It is a calming exercise. The brakes are so cool he can touch them. There is no wind, not a breath, so the fans are not rotating. He thinks of doing a walkaround in Torbay where the wind is over twenty knots, blowing into the tailpipes, and the fans are rotating backwards, making that almost-musical clink-clink-clink as the cool blades move in and out in their sockets at the top and bottom of their rotation. The gas truck is rolling up, parking under the left wing. He strolls over.

"Hi. You got a fuel slip yet?"

"Yes, Captain. Won't take long."

"How much does it say?"

"Four point zero."

Enrico feels his heartbeat surging again. His face feels tight.

"Great. Please don't unhook, though. There's going to be a revision. I'll be right back."

He walks slowly back to the bridge, working it through in his mind. Fuel in Tanks plus Burn. Somewhere between 2.2 and 2.5. That leaves barely back here plus ten, twenty minutes. Maybe there's a real close alternate like San Jose. But it's raining in the Bay Area.

He climbs the exterior stairs to the bridge and fishes for the cheat sheet in his hat. Fuck it's dark out here. He pulls the paper out of his hat and moves it so the moonlight shines on his latest entry: 4157. He punches it into the lock on the bridge door. By the grace of somebody or other it opens.

As he rounds the corner he is staring into the eyes of a J-Class passenger, one of several crowded into the galley area. He puts on his wide, toothy grin.

"Won't be long, sir. Excuse me."

He pushes past into the cockpit and closes the door. Adolf holds up what looks like a flight plan.

"They just brought this, Captain. I'm setting it up."

"Great. Could I see it for a sec?"

Enrico scans the AFPAA, looking for the important stuff. Alternate: KSMF. Holding fuel: 800 KG. Twenty minutes. He looks down at the fuel clearance, looking for the dispatcher's signature: Foster. Fuck! The bastard. He's still on shift?

"Adolf. Did you talk to dispatch?"

"Yeah. Patched through on Jet Center's frequency. He said they're still landing 19 in SFO. No delays. I told him it was clear here. He said the forecasts are still good. I've got 'em here . . ."

"Thanks. Be right back."

This time he takes the bridge steps one at a time, going through it in his head. He asked for a good alternate. So Adolf and Foster could maybe think this is a good alternate if they look at nothing but paper. But shit, he thinks, he asked for an hour's hold. And they have ignored him. Foster says there are no delays, so that is their reasoning in ignoring him. Yeah, OK, they have their story all set. But they didn't give him the courtesy of even discussing it with him. They just fucking did it and ignored him.

Who's the fucking captain? he thinks. I'm the fucking captain.

He walks slowly over to the gas truck.

"Hey. New numbers. Dial 'er up to 8.0"

"Yes, Captain. Here we go."

Enrico decides to linger in the moonlight and wait for the fuel slip, with its gallons pumped. Keep it in his own hands. He walks to the left wingtip and works through what he is going to do.

§

"Captain, they put on too much gas. Look – 8.0."

"So did you talk to dispatch again?"

"No."

It is a *no* with a rising inflection, a defensive *no*.

"You want me to call Jet Center? Get them to de-fuel?"

"No. We're going. You get the load?"

"Yeah, but it's no good. The fuel's wrong. So the C of G will be wrong, too. We can't go like that."

Enrico holds out his hand.

"Let's see."

He inspects the load sheet with its 4.0 fuel load. He calls up the Init B page on his MCDU. The Zero Fuel Weight CG field is blank.

"OK, Adolf. Watch and learn."

He enters the Zero Fuel Weight and the Zero Fuel Weight CG, then pages to the Datalink and enters the fuel upload in gallons and does the fuel upload crosscheck.

"After start we're going to check the Fuel Pred page. We'll make sure the fuel shows and the Gross weight is right. The C of G you see there in small print will have been calculated by the FMCG for the 8.0 fuel. That's what we'll use to set the stab."

§

The nice thing about the layover is the absence of Adolf. It is already midnight when they get downtown and Adolf says he is tired and going to bed so Enrico goes out to a strip club he knows and has a few beers and watches the girls. By three he is feeling pretty tired himself and although he knows he should be taking more advantage of the night he just can't. Doesn't have the energy.

Now as he wakes up the red light on the telephone is blinking with a message. It is from Don in Crew Sked. Adolf has booked off. Vancouver-based Steve has been drafted for the leg to Toronto and will join him at the airport.

Breakfast and the latte aren't sitting quite right. With no one to talk to in the taxi he starts to think. So Adolf books off. Why the fuck would he do that? And he doesn't call, either. That would be the courteous thing, no matter how sick you are. If you can call Crew Sked you can call the captain and let him know personally. Fuck, you'd call the captain before you called Crew Sked.

Just north of the airport, south of Candlestick Park, the 101 runs along the water's edge the length of a small bay. The traffic opens out in the long straight stretch and Adolf swims back into his mind, holding that second noteboard, the one he's always writing on. The egg and potato gets heavier in his gut as Enrico makes a logical leap: Adolf is not sick.

Enrico swallows a few times trying to calm the roiling in his intestines. He grabs a door handle as a black Mercedes cuts off two lanes of traffic trying to get to the I-380 cutoff. Shit! Not only is he not sick, but it's not even that Adolf can't stand to fly even one more leg with him. No, it's worse: he's going to the brass and he's going to claim this captain is not safe. Although, logically how could he say that and then the brass let him fly this leg? Doesn't make sense. Maybe he's going to wait until they're airborne before he calls. Oh, what the fuck, Enrico. Do your job.

§

The flight today is effortless. Steve is quiet but smiles a lot. He even laughs sometimes at Enrico's jokes. The four hours go by quickly and before long they are talking to Toronto Approach. Then they are chatting amiably as they trail their bags down the long halls in Terminal II and down the escalator into the customs hall. The crew line is not long so they start their goodbyes: Steve is on Reserve so he's going upstairs to the crew lounge to call Crew Sked. Enrico is planning a quick exit out of Customs and onto the escalator up to the RancidAir lounge. He wants to get home to Montreal.

Beyond Customs, in the baggage area, Enrico spots a pretty passenger agent he knows. He holds out his hand.

"Hey, Steve. Gonna stop and chat a minute. Pleasure working with you. Give my best to Vancouver."

"Yeah, likewise, Enrico. See you."

Steve joins the line inching toward the exit. Vanna has a couple of minutes and tells Enrico a story. They both laugh, and Enrico feels his stallion stirring. He is still smiling as he emerges out of the customs hall into Arcadia proper, the dark downstairs hall of Terminal II.

"Enrico! Got a minute?"

A tall, slender man in a business suit is standing, not quite in his path but almost, smoothing strands of hair over his bald crown. He looks uncomfortable, as if the suit is a disguise.

"Boss!"

"I know you want to get home, Enrico. I've made sure you're booked on the seven o'clock."

Enrico glances at his watch. Five thirty-seven.

"Sure, Boss. I'm going to miss the six o'clock, anyway."

Captain Boss Boss leads the way upstairs to his office. It is a modest room, more like a cubicle than an office, but it does have a window looking east over the tar and gravel roof of Terminal II. He closes the door.

"Enrico, we have a problem."

They sit. Boss hefts a large file and punks it down on his blotter.

"It's a large one."

He lays his long hand on top of the bulging folder.

"We're all human, and we have moments when we're not at our best."

Captain Boss Boss, Chief Pilot of the Bus fleet, rests his case, or at least that is the phrase that comes to Enrico's mind as Boss sits back in his chair and waits, although it is not immediately evident why he is waiting.

"True, Boss."

"I don't ride my pilots, Enrico. They are not all going to do the job exactly as I would. I ask them to stick to Standard Operating Procedures so we can all get on with each other and know what to expect. I ask them to do the best they can and stay safe."

"Sure, Boss."

"And you have, as far as I can see."

The room is silent for awhile. Enrico is surprised that the atmosphere is not tense, like flying with Ice Pick or Adolf. There is no disrespect emanating from Boss Boss.

"I especially want my new captains to find their way. So I try to stay out of the picture."

Boss's long hand lands again on top of the file folder.

"But I do ask that they keep a low profile. In that you have been less successful."

Again the room is quiet. Enrico finds he has room to think along with Boss. Boss pats the folder.

"I have been following this for a year or so. Do you remember a departure out of here last February? You were flying with François. Montreal Base."

Enrico thinks back. He was on vacation most of February. He got back from San Diego in the middle of a cold snap. Yes, he remembers. The bucking bronco.

"Yes, Boss. I remember. It was a ShortBus. It went crazy on me."

Boss waits. Nods once. Enrico can't imagine François ratting on him. He looks at Boss for clues.

"Excuse me, Boss, but how do you know about that? Did François?"

"No."

Boss turns and pulls his copy of the Flight Operating Manual from a shelf. He leafs through quickly to a blue insert.

"I'm sure you've seen this."

The insert is dated a year ago last fall. It describes Air Arcadia's data monitoring system. How data is downloaded regularly from each aircraft's Digital Flight Data Recording System and analyzed by computer. How excursions beyond certain normal flight parameters are highlighted for review.

"Reports from the Bus fleet land on my desk. A copy goes into the Captain's file. François had nothing to do with it. But that incident is not what concerns me. As I said, we all have our bad days."

Again the room holds a reverent silence. Enrico remembers the cathedrals of his youth: the banks of candles, the confessionals, the soaring ceilings.

"What concerns me, Enrico, is this accumulation."

It is clear he is referring to the bulging file folder in front of him.

"Not that any one report is something that calls for action on my part. Although admittedly you could have been more discreet in some cases. Perhaps polite is a better word. All these one-page reports from passenger agents and dispatchers and even some pilots. Usually some dispute where you pulled rank."

"Yeah. But I'm the Captain, Boss."

"Yes, of course. But a little humility can sometimes go a long way in building a command presence. I have studied this file and certain phrases stay with me. How you reportedly refer to the flight as "my flight" and the airplane as "my airplane." You speak of "my crew.""

"Yeah, Boss. Sure. But aren't they?"

"Well, yes, in a sense. But not literally. You don't own the airplane. Air Arcadia owns the airplane."

Boss looks suddenly uncomfortable and shakes his head.

"Well, we used to own the airplane. Today it's mostly the leasing company. But that's another story." Boss shifts in his chair. "You certainly don't own the crew. They are people you have been assigned to lead. Even there the In Charge is responsible for the back-end stuff."

"Sure . . ."

"Humility, Enrico. Just a hint. I recommend that you try to think of the flight as the *flight assigned to me*. Same for the aircraft and the crew. Your assignment, as an employee of Air Arcadia, is to lead a team. The First Officer, the Dispatcher, the Flight Attendants. Sure, you are the ultimate authority for that flight. But your job – your responsibility – is to make that team work smoothly."

Again the room is silent. Again Enrico feels the presence of the churches of his youth. The confessional. The fullness in his heart. The desire for forgiveness.

"I'm sorry, Boss. You're right."

He bows his head. He knows it is crazy but he is praying for absolution. Outside, every two minutes a jet roars, setting takeoff power. It is like a clock, ticking very slowly. Perhaps a clock feels like that to an insect. How many ticks can there be in the life of a gnat?

"Tell me about last night in Sacramento."

Boss listens carefully. At one point he hauls out a volume of his Aircraft Operating Manual and flips it open, referring to a page here and there as Enrico speaks. For his part Enrico is careful to stick to the facts and recount every detail to the best of his memory. He does, however, edit out the strip club.

Boss nods as the story ends.

"Enrico, I can't fault you on your operational decisions. Your handling of the FMCG to find the Gross Weight C of G is technically correct."

"Thanks, Boss."

"Where you fell short is in keeping your crew together. Although I'll admit Adolf is a special case."

"Yes, Boss. He . . ."

Boss Boss holds up a hand to stop him.

"I'm not going to talk about Adolf. That's his story and it will play out as it does. I bring up his name only to point out that he has tied my hands. The milk he's spilled and the way he's splashed it around leave me no choice but to act."

This time the silence holds an unfolding secret. Absolution, yes. The penance is pending, forming.

"You see how it is, Enrico. I am the boss and I have no choice."

Another couple of departures roar down the unseen runway. Two more ticks in the life of a gnat. Boss stands. Enrico follows his lead, head still bowed.

Boss pronounces the penance, unwelcome but deserved. Enrico will fly as a First Officer for a month. Supervised.

Absolution is there, hanging in the reverent air, available, the object of desire. Boss smiles.

"Go catch your plane, Enrico."

Joined At The Hip

Montreal – December, 2001

Arcadia

FATHER, IF I HAD SPRUNG thus from your loins I would have killed myself.

It is disgusting. I am disgusting. Joined at the hip to this fat blue bitch! I knew she was old and bloated but this is beyond my worst imaginings!

I try to walk; I waddle. I try to move south; I lurch west. I try to see through the eyes of my boys and girls; a veil of her vision, through the eyes of her boys and girls, clouds my sight. I want to beat the shit out of her. I want to cut loose this anchor and deep-six it. I want her to die!

Gotta get my breath, Father.

See, they are running around in the head shed. They have plans, they have schemes, but they don't know what they are doing. Out at the pointy end where our service meets the passenger things have gone for shit but they don't see it. They hear it through the media and then they run around some more.

Gotta get it together. Look on the bright side . . .

Boy is cute in his way, Father. I cannot say he is not one of us the way he watches airplanes come and go on the north runway. He does have some airline blood in his veins.

But the head shed feels different, Father. The Vice-Presidents have stopped talking. I don't know if they have turned cynical or they're just afraid for their asses. Well, excuse my language Father but what the fuck. How else am I going to say what I feel?

Maybe it is I who have turned cynical? Oh shit, try, Arcadia!

Terry and Smarts, bless them, are still trying. With great politeness and respect they present suggestions to Boy and he nods and sort-of listens but then he tells them the way it has to be. They, like good lieutenants, try to take care of their troops but he says no, it's like this. They bow and retreat and go back to their mechanics and pilots and try to make a silk purse out of a sow's ear. What it must cost them, Father!

So why is this boy Boy alienating all that is good in me?

Has he forgotten I exist? I am become as nothing to him. He listens only to Snake. Snake who is not one of us.

For Snake I am less than a name. I am a convenient symbol to hide behind. I am a brand to paste over his machinations. I am a dragonfly caught in his web, Father. My beauty is become dull, inert, empty. He feasts on my innards, extracting what he will for his needs. I am become a shell, a fragile carapace, an empty skin.

I am sorry, Father. I feel myself slipping. I do not know if I can hold but I must try.

AIRLINE HONCHO

December 18, 2001

Parliament Removes
15% Ownership Limit

Bill C-38, the Air Arcadia Public Participation Act, was today amended to remove the 15% ownership limit by individuals. The 25% limit on foreign ownership remains in force.

C-38, originally entitled the Air Arcadia Privatization Act, was passed when the Backward Party held power so that Air Arcadia could become a public company.

Since then the Forward Party changed the Arcadian Competition Act to allow the merger of Arcadia's two largest airlines.

It is not clear what today's development augurs for Air Arcadia, which has been suffering under the massive debt load incurred by the absorption of the failing Pacific Airlines International.

Boy Wonder

THE BRIEF DAY is fading. Snow is falling outside the corner office. Boy Wonder can barely see the landing aircraft as they touch down. They exist as almost-horizontal beams of light stabbing through the snow, rocking as the aircraft adjust for the gusty crosswind. He watches them as they flare, the maneuver made manifest by the beams lifting, pointing further down the runway. He likes the way each airplane disappears into its own private blizzard.

It has been a year. A year since he said yes to this merger, this bailout, this folly.

Yes, Boy. Folly is the word.

It has been nothing but trouble. The huge and exhausting public campaign last winter where he promised to fix everything pronto. Successful, sure. It has kept the complaining, critical media at bay. But for what?

Snake promised a two-billion-dollar company. He promised the Forwards would help dump Pacific Airlines International's three-billion-dollar debt. They haven't.

No, and I'm a mess, Boy. Look at me!

And then the goddamn twin towers. Shut down the whole operation for days, just like the goddamn strike.

Another flight flares, touches down and selects reverse thrust. He waits for the blizzard.

What would Horace say? Hell, what is Horace saying? He always keeps up with the industry. Knows everything. Chapter and verse. Just like his Bible.

He's praying for me, Boy. Everything I am is fading. How can I be me when I'm a fucking Siamese twin?

Yeah, and what is he saying about me, now? Boy, his protégé? Horace left a nice billion-dollar company that he trimmed into shape. Now I've got this two-billion-dollar mess. Shit, the company is going to lose a billion dollars this year. A goddamn record. Boy Wonder responsible for record loss at Air Arcadia. That sure looks good on the resumé.

§

Official sunset has passed. This day is gone and the length of day is almost at its perigee. In a few days it will be the winter solstice, the heart of the dark time.

Horace would say Advent. The coming of light and hope.

In two months the financial results for this year will be official. Boy has been sitting here for not quite fifteen months and he's going to have a billion-dollar loss. A billion plus, by the look of it. The Board is going to be baying for Boy's ass.

Yes. I'm bleeding to death, Boy.

So what does Boy have going for him? A lock on International. Snake was right about that. No real competition there: not for a while anyway. And Air Arcadia is in like Flynn with Starry Skies, thanks to all that travel and schmoozing Boy did a year ago.

You hear me, Boy. I know you can still hear me.

She's right. We're hemorrhaging cash.

Boy is suddenly aware of the wind outside. Is it just the sound, or did the window actually bow, yielding to a gust like the skin of a drum? He looks out. A huge shape is lurching in the wild weather. It seems to be coming for him. Can't be . . . He dives for the switch of his little VHF receiver, tuned to 119.9, the tower frequency. He feels like ducking under his desk.

It is a whale. He can clearly see the cockpit hump and the the four main-gear trucks dangling under the wing. It is way too close. It has drifted or been pushed south, almost to the parking lot by the look of it. The monster plane banks right, aiming the main-gear trucks at Boy's office as it sets course to avoid drifting into the building.

"Speedboat 75 on the Missed Approach."

"Roger, Speedboat 75. Say Intentions."

"Standby"

The whale's lights stab upward. It disappears into the snow, which has become horizontal. The windows are bending or vibrating or something. Suddenly there is a loud rattling, like a machine gun.

Again Boy feels like taking cover, but curiosity draws him over to the window. What is it, hail? He notices a glaze forming on the outside of the pane.

"Attention all aircraft: Dorval weather 2124 Zulu. Wind three zero zero to three two zero at three five gusting four eight. Ceiling indefinite one hundred obscured visibility one quarter mile in snow, ice pellets and freezing rain, thunderstorm embedded north, temperature minus two, dew point minus two, altimeter two niner two fife."

"Speedboat 75 requesting straight ahead to 3000. We're painting a rather nasty line to the north."

"Roger, Speedboat 75. Continue heading two four zero. Contact departure one two four dezimal six fife."

The frequency is silent. There are no landing lights piercing the weather. Boy remains by the window, fascinated by the fury of it. The machine-gun ice pellets come in waves, making a strange music. He puts his fingertips on the window glass. He can feel a slow pulse beating time to the music of the storm. This is nasty. Hope none of ours are on approach.

Boy jumps as the outdoors, pitch-dark without landing lights, suddenly gains a brilliant, jagged sun. A huge *CRRAACK* follows with no perceptible delay. The sound is loud enough to penetrate the panes of glass as if they are not there. Boy's vision retains the memory of the world outside lit up like the inside of a fuzzy ball. He shivers. The Headquarters Building feels insignificant.

Boy walks back behind his desk and sits down. There are no thoughts in his head.

You don't have to listen to me, Boy. You don't have to say anything.

Another wave of ice pellets attacks the window.

Sure I'm old. Yes, I'm ugly, thanks to you. So ignore me. Do your own goddamn thing.

Boy is afraid. The plate glass is pulsing like a beating heart.

Listen, Boy. I'm old and ugly but I have the sight. Like Father. Like Horace.

Boy is sweating profusely. He starts to shiver.

I can see. You are going to cut me apart to save your ass. But remember: if you ignore me and pretend you don't hear me you will be irrelevant. If I'm not real then neither are you.

The waves of rattling ice pellets gradually fade. Boy looks up. The runway lights are starting to re-appear, surreal in the glaze of ice on the window. A pickup truck is driving down the runway, stopping – or trying to – every quarter-mile or so. Getting a JBI, maybe. Boy watches patiently.

It is a dream. It is all a dream.

Larger trucks are on the runway. How long has it been? The snow has stopped. Maybe they're spreading urea. He watches the trucks move slowly up the runway.

The intercom buzzes.

"Yes, Laura?"

"Mr. Snake to see you, sir."

"Attention all aircraft: Dorval weather 2143 Zulu. Wind three zero zero . . ."

Boy reaches for the VHF receiver and switches it off. The door opens. Snake looks smart. Look at those shoes! You could shave in those toe caps! And the hankie matching the tie . . .

Snake holds out his hand.

"It's a red-letter day, Boy."

"Yeah? This weather . . ."

"Was that thunder a few minutes ago?"

"Yes. Did you see the lightning?"

"No. There was lightning? This is December, for heaven's sake. And I have a concert tonight . . ."

Boy gestures toward their strategy table by the window. There are a few aircraft visible on the taxiway. They look like cartoons through the layer of glaze on the window.

"No. Parliament. Did you see they've come through for us?"

"The debt?"

"No. I'm afraid they got us on that one. They're players."

"So . . ."

"You didn't see? It's in today's Honcho. Ownership . . ."

"They didn't lift the 25% foreign?"

"No, no. It's still there. The private."

"The 15%? What's it up to?"

"It's gone."

There is an aircraft moving on the runway. A takeoff. It creeps along, gathering speed. Boy squints, trying to focus. With the darkness and the glaze on the window it is impossible to see whose it is.

"Gone. So you mean an individual could own Air Arcadia. In theory."

"Yes."

Boy watches the rotation, up near the Echo taxiway. The lights sweep upward fifteen degrees and are slowly carried away into the overcast, into the sky, into the night. Boy tries to say something pertinent.

"That's only important if . . ."

Snake lets it sit for a minute. Together they watch the next blurry jet take position. There is time for Boy's quick mind to move ahead.

Bankruptcy. Private Equity. A holding company . . .

Snake nods knowingly.

"Exactly, Boy. We might want to think about an exit strategy . . ."

The Irish Bank

San Francisco – February, 2003

Cameron

It has been touch and go persuading him to come out.

They are crossing Union Square on a sort-of diagonal, heading for the corner of Post and Stockton. Cameron slows, deciding to hang back out of the pushing crowd until the light turns green.

"So where are you dragging me, Cameron? You said beer, right?"

"Absolutely. Good beer, too. You never been there?"

"What's it called, again?"

"The Irish Bank."

"Stupid name for a bar."

The light turns green. They flow across Post and up Stockton, chips caught in a fast-moving stream. Past the Grand Hyatt there are cross-currents: limos unload and important people demand to be exempted from courtesy and the laws of nature. Exasperated, Cameron signals a right turn and they cross at Sutter, heading east again toward the Embarcadero and the shadow of the Bay Bridge.

It is as if the current has spun them out into a side eddy.

At Grant Cameron turns north again. As they get closer he gestures ahead.

"That's a good landmark for the Irish Bank. When you see the Chinatown Gate, you're getting close."

Enrico smiles. It is a big natural smile unmarred by orthodontistry.

"So this Irish thing – it's in Chinatown?"

"No, just close . . ."

Cameron decides on the scenic approach, down Bush and into Mark Lane. The alley is shorter, but it is lined with garbage cans and usually smells bad. Maybe they'll stumble back that way.

Mark Lane seems to make a good impression.

"Hey. This feels like my family's town."

He looks around the confined space with appreciation.

"Where's that, Enrico?"

"Campo Basso. Little streets like this. No cars."

"Good food, I bet."

"Better believe it."

They go up the stone steps and into the cramped lobby. To their right the bar beckons. The room is not large but the bar is a nice one with stools and a couple of dozen taps. Some small tables with benches and chairs provide places to take drinks away from the bar.

Cameron gestures at the room.

"You want to grab a table?"

Enrico's eyes have taken in the barmaid.

"Hey, let's sit at the bar."

"Sure. Near the taps."

It is only once they are seated that Cameron catches on. She is not a stunner, at least not in a movie-star sort of way. But she has reddish hair and freckles. She's solidly built. She doesn't have a shred of innocence but her presence is warm and enveloping.

"What'll it be, gentlemen?"

"A Red Hook Extra Special Bitter, please."

"May I ask your advice?"

Enrico has aimed his smile across the bar.

"You look like you might be Irish."

"Well, sort of . . ."

"'Cause then I'd take your advice on what to have. Even over my friend here."

"Well, Red Hook ESB is a California Ale. Styled after an English Bitter. Hoppy but not edgy."

"So you are Irish . . ."

"Way back, yes. But I'm a city girl."

"San Francisco?"

"Yup. All my life."

Enrico has shifted on his stool. His body language is eloquent. Cameron can feel Enrico's rut reflecting back off Freckles.

"So would I like what my friend is having?"

"I think you would. But let me draw his and I'll give you a small glass. To taste."

She disengages herself gently. The room is almost empty. Locals have finished lunch and gone back to work. But the Arcadians are on eastern time and their work is done for the day. Or almost. Cameron is still working.

"So. I know I pissed you off this morning."

"Yeah. No shit. That was aggressive."

Cameron twirls his pint. Enrico would rather engage Freckles, but he has emptied his sample and smiled at her and she has brought him a pint of his own. Now she has moved on to a new customer. He is left with Cameron and the events of the day.

"Perhaps. But put yourself in my position. I thought I was going home today."

"Yeah? So what does that have to do . . ."

"Well, I was finishing off a student. It was her last leg: Toronto-Montreal."

"Girl, huh? Was she cute?"

"Enrico, you met her this morning. Remember? In Montreal."

"That chick in flight planning?"

"Yes. I was signing her off as an F/O. I introduced you."

"Oh, yeah. Right."

Cameron twirls his pint again.

"Enrico, I'm bringing it up because we were both angry. Maybe we should talk it through."

Enrico is looking down the bar in Freckles' direction but she is talking to a new customer. Cameron changes tack.

"So when did they call you for this cycle?"

"Last night."

"But someone from the office had talked to you before that. Told you they were going to set up a schedule for you . . ."

"Yeah."

"OK, look – I'm not going to beat around the bush. When we went to check in this morning in Toronto, the clerk had a message for me. Go see Boss Boss. So I tell Clara to go check the flight plan.

Get it ready for me to sign. I'll be back in fifteen, twenty minutes."

"So you see the boss."

"Yes. He's a good guy, Enrico. Best Chief Pilot I've ever had."

"Yeah. Maybe."

Enrico turns away from the far end of the bar. Looks at Cameron. Not quite in the eye, but almost.

"He just wants to bust my ass. They all do."

Be careful, Cameron thinks. Don't lie. A lot of them actually do.

"You know, maybe some of them do. I'm not saying you're in an easy position. But I think Boss Boss wants to help you. Give you a chance to make this go away."

Two men come in and join the guy at the end of the bar.

"He told you what he is doing to me."

"Could be what he is doing *for* you. If you take it the right way. But, yes. He's busting you back to F/O for a month. And for that month you fly with me."

"The whole month?"

Cameron laughs.

"'Fraid so. That's your penance."

"Jesus."

"Well, what I figure is, we might as well try to enjoy it."

"Jesus. They way you started the day with me, Cameron, I don't think so."

Cameron nods.

"You're right. I owe you an apology. I should have asked you to step out of the room. There were too many people who could have heard."

Enrico stares at his beer.

"Enrico, I'm sorry. I got angry. I lost it."

"Yeah, well. OK."

Three more people have come in. The noise level has gone up a notch.

"But what about the question, Enrico? Was I wrong to ask?"

"Well, what business is it of yours?"

"Seems to me it is business that has been assigned to me by my boss. He tells me you are to fly for a month as a First Officer. He tells me he wants this blizzard of paper to stop. He tells me to see what I can do. By the way, he did explain all this to you, didn't he?"

"Yeah."

"So I walk into Flight Planning this morning and I see you standing there with your four stripes and your Captain's hat with the scrambled eggs and your Captain's wings and how do you think that makes me feel?"

"Didn't think of that . . ."

"Even if you've thrown your old ones out you could have maybe just got a set of three-stripe epaulettes from the office. Just to show a little respect."

"You're still angry . . ."

"Yeah. I guess I am. We're going to fly a month together and you're going to pretend you're giving me a checkride? I mean, come on, Enrico. Who's in shit here, anyway?"

"Me, me. It's always fucking me."

Freckles is heading their way.

"Enrico, let me buy you another beer and we'll start over. You want to stick with this or try something else?"

"This. Red whatever. Pretty good."

"OK, guys. Two more Red Hook ESB's. Comin' up."

Enrico watches her draw the pints. It seems to relax him.

"Enrico, I know there are at least two people who want to help. To get you through this and out the other side. Let's start from there."

"Yeah. OK."

Freckles sets their pints down. Enrico watches Freckles as she moves away. He sighs and looks back at Cameron.

"Where do I start?"

§

They are halfway through their third Red Hook. Enrico has been talking energetically, emotionally; he has told the story of his promotion. Most of the time has been devoted to his Command Final out of Calgary with Captain Pick.

"What then? Nothing. He just signed me off. Handed me my epaulettes. Wished me luck. Looked kinda weird while he said it. There was no Flight Crew Report."

Cameron shakes his head.

"Jesus, Enrico. I find it hard to believe."

"It's true, though."

Enrico glances down the bar, perhaps to reassure himself that Freckles is still there.

"Then in February I had this bucking bronco thing out of Toronto. On the ShortBus."

"Bucking bronco?"

"Yeah. Windy day. We were light. She was climbing like a scalded cat."

"Cold day, too?"

"Oh, yeah. Minus 30 or something. First the vertical speed turned yellow."

"Wow. You were climbing, all right. That tape turns yellow at 6000 feet per minute."

"Yeah. We were way nose up. Then the F/O called airspeed and I look and it's way down near the hook and I still don't know what's going on."

Cameron is piecing it together in his head. He thinks he can see where the bucking bronco came from.

"So then – did the nose go down?"

"Yeah. Just pitched over like a lunatic. Seemed like zero G's. There was dust floating in the air."

Cameron takes a sip. If he had been there he would have needed it to steady his nerves. With Enrico's stories he is beginning to feel as if he were there.

§

Cameron has been trying to explain mode reversion. Enrico, though, wants to know about how Boss Boss found out about the bucking bronco. Through a pleasant beer fog, Cameron sees himself trying to teach technical arcana to someone who has just received an emotional kick in the nuts. It is going nowhere. He sighs.

"Hey, don't worry. Maybe tomorrow we'll talk more about verbalizing what's on the FMA."

Cameron knows it is too late, but he tries to see where Enrico's head has gone. The student isn't looking at Sarah. He looks hurt.

Cameron stops talking. The room has filled with the after work crowd. A group in the corner erupts with laughter. The noise level is making conversation difficult.

"Don't worry about it. We've had too many beers to be technical, anyway."

"What?"

Enough for one day, Cameron thinks. He makes a megaphone with his cupped hands.

"Hey. You wanna go eat?"

April Fool

March 28, 2003

Air Arcadia CEO Confident

OTTAWA - Boy Wonder, CEO of Air Arcadia, today responded to questions concerning the government's review of the 'pension holiday' the company has been enjoying during its merger with the former Arcadian Airlines.

"Our pension fund is is excellent shape," Mr. Wonder affirmed. "I am confident the regulator's investigation will confirm, and that the government report will reflect, my confidence in our funding of future obligations."

Boy Wonder

THE DULL, GREY DAY has crept into the corner office. A sense of dirty snow and last year's dead, dank vegetation filters in through the sealed, multi-pane glass. Even the ceiling is contiguous with the low, scudding cloud.

It has been another difficult winter. Rain, snow, and far too much mixed precipitation, as the weather guys like to call it. Yesterday's operations in Vancouver were a mess: missed connections, lost baggage, irate passengers. Because of rain. Rain? Since when does rain affect an airline's operations? Must have been some hell of a goddamn rain.

Boy scans the reports. Today the prairie airports have all slowed to a crawl in heavy snow. The storm is moving east. That would be OK except there is another storm moving up the east coast and there is a possibility they could join forces. Shit! Just one damn thing after another, as Grandpa used to say . . .

The intercom buzzes.

"Yes, Laura . . ."

"Mr. Snake to see you, sir."

Boy stands and walks out from behind his desk. Snake materializes, seemingly from nowhere. It is always a little startling. Boy nods toward the strategy corner.

"Come have a seat."

"Is it damp in here? Or is it my imagination?"

Boy laughs uneasily.

"You can feel the weather in here. Makes no sense, with this sealed-building design."

Their table and chairs seem exposed. Snake coils into his seat. Boy can see him staying there, hibernating, until Spring arrives.

"We're on schedule. Did you see today's Honcho?"

"Yeah. Doesn't leave us much time, though. Especially to put the fear of God in the unions."

Snake waves a hand.

"Don't worry. Everything's all set to go. I'm having Tuesday's date put on everything. Then when you give the word we'll roll the presses."

Boy settles in his strategy chair.

"So. April Fool, huh?"

Snake smiles.

"Taking it private, Boy. This is the first step."

"And Danny's still on board?"

"Yes. I went over it with him this morning."

"He's OK with thirty-three percent? For $640M?"

"Yes. Of course he wants to shed the bulk of our $13B debt."

"That's what the Arcadian Business Creditors Act is all about …"

"Exactly."

"What worries me a bit – the other one-point-three billion – how safe is that?

"Pretty much a done deal. ReichBank is on board for $600M. And the rest – well, it's not signed yet, but General Equipment Capital is a go, too. And if one of them gets cold feet there's no shortage of cash out there looking for private equity placement."

"And our – our exit opportunities?"

"Danny wants to keep us. He doesn't know the business like you do, Boy. So he's fine with it. $5M for me, $20M for you. If he still has his equity and either of us leaves within five years."

Boy thinks over the last five years. Well, four and a half, actually. Four and a half years and a one-billion company becomes a two-billion company and loses five billion. It's a record that would make anyone want to hedge his bets.

Snake shifts again so he is looking directly at Boy.

"And remember your thesis, Boy. How you figured out how to monetize the parts of a corporation. By separating them into value centres. This is a chance to try it. With no downside."

One of the scudding clouds has become saturated. It releases its moisture, craftily timing the drop to intercept the headquarters building. Boy watches as it hits his window and freezes, a droopy glaze. Shit! Turn to snow, goddammit!

"But the financial industry has to be on board for that, Snake. They have to be involved. Be part of the deal. We'll have to reserve some ..."

"Oh, of course. But you have it all right there in your thesis: we'll carve out the pieces, let them mature – got to time it right – then we'll have the holding company do an IPO on each piece in turn. Let everyone get in on the act. That'll bring in more cash."

"But some of it's for us."

A pickup truck races down the runway and jams on the brakes. Boy watches. The JBI truck. Not a good sign.

"Absolutely, Boy. The lion's share."

The pickup has skidded to a stop sideways on the runway. It accelerates slowly, re-aligning itself with the runway axis. What a goddamn crazy business!

§

AIRLINE HONCHO

April 1, 2003

Air Arcadia Declares Bankruptcy

MONTREAL – Air Arcadia attorneys appeared before Judge Simone de Pouvoir in Montreal Superior Court this morning to file for bankruptcy under the Arcadian Business Creditors Act, or ABCA. Roughly equivalent to Chapter 11 in U.S. law, the Act allows a corporation to seek protection from creditors while it re-structures for greater profitability.

Boy Wonder, President and CEO of Air Arcadia, stressed that there would be no change in daily operations.

"The merger and other market forces have necessitated a review of our corporate structure with a view to enhancing the value of our assets for all stakeholders," Mr. Wonder explained. "Today's filing will allow these positive measures to move ahead unimpeded."

Rod

IN EAST BERKSHIRE Rod pulls in to Saint's Qwik Stop to fill up on cheap American gas. Climbing the hill out of town in fourth gear he feels tired in that good way, relaxed and happy, coming down from exercise and adrenaline. He is listening to Vermont Public Radio.

Approaching the small border stop at West Berkshire, Rod turns down the volume.

"Ou demeurez-vous?"

"À Lachine."

"Vous êtes parti depuis combien de temps?"

"Depuis hier soir."

"Apportez-vous quelque chose?"

"Non."

The customs agent eyes his board in the back seat.

"Bonne journée de planche?"

Rod smiles at her.

"Bain oui, certain. Huit pouces de neige fraîche."

She waves him on.

"Jalouse, moi. Bonne soirée."

Rod pulls back out onto the road toward Frelighsburg. *Arcadia welcomes you. Speeds are in kilometers.* As he reaches to turn the radio back on he pushes the button for the CBC.

. . . and to the top business story of today: this morning Air Arcadia's Boy Wonder took the airline into bankruptcy, filing in Montreal Superior Court under the Arcadian Business Creditors Act. He was emphatic that normal operations would continue but further details about Air Arcadia's future were not immediately forthcoming . . .

Rod is stunned. He drives in a daze, through Frelighsburg, then Stanbridge East and along the river. As he turns left off the 235 onto Rang Kempt, the St. Lawrence Valley opens up ahead, snow from the long, narrow rectangular fields drifting lazily across the road. He thinks of riding this road on the motorcycle last fall, of coming up behind the farm wagon full of freshly-harvested onions. Of how he was overwhelmed by their powerful sweet smell, of how hungry he suddenly was.

He is hungry now, too, he realizes. And he should talk to someone. Especially with Susan away. He slows to 80 kph, finds Cameron in the directory, and pushes dial.

"Cam – Rod. Is this a bad time?"

"No, perfect. I just poured a beer. I guess you've heard?"

"Yeah, just now. On the radio."

"Where are you? It's been all over the news."

"I've been down at Jay. Great day, although I'm not feeling so good now."

"Oh, OK. So what do you know?"

"Nothing. Not a fucking thing."

Rod hears Cameron sigh into the phone.

"God, I don't know where to begin." He pauses. "Heard from Jean-Luc at 8 o'clock this morning. Woke me up with the news."

Rod shifts in his seat so he can drive and hold the phone a bit more comfortably.

"Yeah, and . . . ?"

"You remember he has a neighbour who works in maintenance? Jerry. Jerry Desmarais."

"Shit! Hang on a sec . . ."

The lights ahead have veered, aiming for him. Rod slows, flashing his high beam, pulling over as far as he dares. He knows these ditches along Rang Kempt are about ten feet deep, even though you can't see them now for the snow.

The headlights flash by.

Whew! That was close!

The car has slowed to 35 kph. It is tracking straight. The right front wheel bumps along, just off the pavement. The right rear drops off, too. Rod cautiously edges left. He doesn't want to drift the rear end into the ditch. There is a lurch and a shimmy as the right-side wheels regain the pavement. He takes a deep breath and retrieves the cell phone from the seat next to him.

"Cam? You still there?"

"Yeah, I'm here. Where are you, anyway?"

"Rang Kempt. Truck just about got me. Halfway into my lane."

"He didn't force you off the road?"

"No, I managed to stay out of the ditch." Rod accelerates back to 60 kph, the better to power through the drifts. "Maybe I better get off. I guess the bloody bankruptcy will keep 'till I get home."

"Look, Leslie and I were going to order pizza. Why don't you swing by and pick up Susan?"

"Susan's up in Toronto, visiting her folks."

"Come anyway. We'll get up to date."

"I'd like that. Thanks, Cam."

"OK – I'll set things up. Uh, Rod, you know you can get off on St. Patrick. Bypass the zoo in the Turcot Yards."

§

The traffic is light until just before the bridge. Then suddenly it is Cameron's zoo. Rod hates the lurch and go, the cutting-in, the every man for himself. All these microscopic actors turn into a natural phenomenon as they make their little self-serving decisions, hindering not helping the advancement of the whole, the aggregate of their actions producing mathematical complexity and beauty like waves on a beach. Except these waves are fast and brutal.

Past the Wellington exit Rod signals and merges into the right lane. Where the Jean-Lesage curves left, he goes straight, onto the St. Patrick exit. Rolling downhill, he passes the entrance to the Atwater Tunnel and comes to a stop where the road comes to an end at the Lachine Canal and St. Patrick Street. Waiting at the light, he feels calmer. Light snow is falling through the trees along the canal. The peace is welcome.

The Honda rolls steadily along the canal, past the Lachine harbour and the parks along the lake. The snow is still falling. It feels like Christmas Eve. After Dorval Rod works his way through the Pointe Claire maze toward Cameron and Leslie's house. He almost gets lost because he's used to approaching from the other direction, from the 20 and Cartier. But just when he starts to feel the tightness of exasperation he recognizes a corner and knows where he is. The map swivels ninety degrees in his head. He pulls into Cameron's driveway and climbs stiffly from the car.

"Woof!"

The ancient chocolate lab is lurching toward him. After the requisite bark of defence he starts wagging his tail.

"Hey, Hershey. How you doin', old buddy?"

Hearing Rod's voice Hershey wags more energetically. Rod scratches him behind the ears and under the collar and Hershey turns, presenting his butt for more scratching and almost knocking Rod down in the process.

"Hey, easy, old buddy. I've really got to pee. Let's go in. C'mon."

Leslie opens the door as they arrive. Rod gives her a hug and the two-cheek kiss they don't do in Ontario.

"Thanks for taking me in, Les."

"Not at all, Rod. Sorry about Hershey. The pizzas arrived five minutes ago so I figured it was OK to let him out."

"Hey, he's my buddy."

"So, Rod. You just heard?"

"Yeah. Down at Jay all day. Radio silence. It was . . ."

He looks up from undoing his boots.

"Les – you OK?"

"Yes. Fine. It's just . . ."

"The bankruptcy. What's going to happen to us . . ."

"Yes."

She is putting up a good front, but Rod can see the tears are close. He steps forward and gives her a hug.

"'S'gonna be all right, Les. They're not going to stop operating."

"I know . . ."

She sniffs.

"Maybe it's just that Cameron doesn't seem upset at all."

"Yeah. Guess men are kind of heartless sometimes. But we've had some warning."

"We have?"

"There have been bankruptcies down in the 'States. One airline has been in and out of bankruptcy twice."

Rod scratches Hershey's back and Hershey wiggles against Rod's knees.

"Les, can I use your . . ."

"You know where it is, Rod. Leave your stuff, get comfortable and come on back."

At the powder room door Rod feels her eyes following him. He turns and looks into her forlorn gaze.

"It's going to be OK, Les. For us it's gonna be – I mean, it might affect the pension."

Leslie sniffs again.

"Thanks, Rod. You make me feel better."

She takes a breath.

"We're in the family room."

§

It is a room that feels good to be in, cozy in winter and airy in summer. Windows on three sides make it feel like it is part of the back yard. The yard itself is surrounded by an out-of-control cedar hedge about twelve feet high.

"I drew you a beer, Rod. I didn't think you'd object."

Rod takes the pint glass with eagerness and a touch of jealousy. Cameron is a beer nut like they all are, but Cameron has gone a step further and constructed an under-the-counter refrigerated compartment in his kitchen, which houses two beer kegs. The plumbing rises directly to taps on the counter top.

"Thanks, buddy. That hits the spot."

"You took a little longer than I figured. Traffic bad?"

"Not so much bad as just nuts. I wound up taking St. Patrick."

Rod sets his beer down on the coffee table.

"Cam, before the truck almost hit me, you were telling me about a maintenance guy."

"Jerry. He was at headquarters, middle of the night, killing time, walking around."

"So there were no negotiations?"

"No. Nothing happening at all. So he walks by Boy Wonder's office and the door is open. Boy sees him. He says, *Hey, Jerry. C'mon in. I'm bored.* So Jerry goes in. Boy's sitting at his desk and there are stacks of documents everywhere."

Hershey has sidled up to Cameron and is giving him a an imploring stare.

"OK, Hershey. You deserve some, old man. Sit."

Cameron stands and Hershey sits up on his haunches, raising his head as if he is fixing to howl. Cameron takes careful aim, tipping the beer glass slowly to get a small, steady stream. The stream disappears down Hershey's gullet. Head thrown back, he swallows steadily.

"Cameron!"

Leslie appears, holding one of the pizzas.

"You're not giving him beer again! Some people might say it's cruelty to animals."

"Cruelty?" Cameron chuckles. "He loves it!"

Hershey makes a few expressive sounds and slumps down at Cameron's feet. Leslie sighs.

"At least you're on the tile, not the carpet."

Rod snorts into his beer.

"That's the best trick ever."

"They think they're pretty clever." Leslie smiles. "Say, you guys want to eat here or up in the kitchen?"

"Here would be nice," says Cameron.

"OK. We'll just have to watch Hershey. We'd better not leave the pizza alone."

"I'll stand guard," Rod offers.

"Good. Listen – you guys talk and I'll put it on. Jeff is going to come join us."

Leslie disappears into the kitchen.

"So it was Smarts who called them in. Jerry and Born Leader."

"Yes. This is where it gets murky. We don't know for sure, but it seems Boy Wonder told Smarts to call all these Union Reps in to get some more concessions so they could avoid going into bankruptcy. Supposedly."

"Supposedly?"

"Yes. You remember those stacks of documents in Boy's office? Jean-Luc said Boy actually invited Jerry to read them. Have a look, he said."

"And . . ."

"So Jerry reads them. Well, not all the way through. There were employee communiqués, files of legal papers, and press releases.

And they all said the same thing."

"Which was?"

"That Air Arcadia was going to go court Tuesday morning . . ."

"Today."

". . . yes, today. This morning. To declare bankruptcy."

"So the Union Reps being called in?"

"Didn't mean dick."

A young man's voice echoes down the stairs.

"Dad, can I have a beer?"

Cameron smiles. He raises his voice so it will carry up to the kitchen.

"Of course, Jeff. That keg's there to be kicked."

Rod takes a swig of his own beer, drifting back to their earlier conversation. Something in the story is bothering him.

"Smarts must have known."

"What? Oh yes. Vice President of Technical Operations. How could he not?"

"I dunno, Cam. I find that sad. 'Cause he's done a great job. Poor bugger."

Leslie comes down the steps with the other pizza. Jeff follows her, carrying his beer. He is a fine-looking young man, Rod's height or perhaps taller. Rod stands up to greet him.

"Good to see you, Jeff."

"You, too. It's been awhile."

Jeff settles into one of the chairs. Leslie sits down beside Jeff. She has cut the pizza into slices.

"This one's all dressed, and this one is vegetarian. Help yourself, everyone."

A companionable silence reigns. Outside the snow drifts down on the cedars, the branches occasionally shrugging off their loads.

Cameron reaches for another slice of pizza.

"Something else I heard from Jean-Luc."

"'Bout the bankruptcy?" Rod manages the question between bites.

"No. More like where the company is going. Somebody was just in Halifax. I forget who."

"And?"

"We're not using Buzzy's Cabs any more."

"No!"

Rod puts down his beer.

"We've been using Buzzy's since you and I joined!"

"It's the merger. Blue guy gets promoted in some department. Another Blue thing prevails. Another Red tradition vanishes overnight."

"But Buzzy's!"

Rod shakes his head.

"You know, the last time I was in Halifax I was talking to Grumpy as we drove downtown in the Chrysler. I asked him how long Buzzy'd been gone." Rod pauses. "You know Grumpy. How often will he actually turn down his country and western station? So he says, *Buzzy? Hah!* and exhales with a disgusted air and turns the radio off and I'm thinking, shit, I hope I haven't offended him and then he half turns in his seat and I'm starting to worry he's going to veer off the road and he says, *Buzzy! Jesus, man, Buzzy's been planted these twenty years ennaway. Where you been?"*

Cameron turns to Jeff.

"I can remember one night, late. The weather was on the shitty end of bad. Who was I flying with? I was about your age, Jeff. Must've been when we were brand new on the 'nine. We're going downtown, after midnight. The Captain says, *Buzzy, where can a guy get a drink this time of night?* Buzzy says, *There is some, Cap'n, but could be they're not to your taste, but ennaway, as yer here, have a taste of this.* He pulls a fifth of Arcadian Club out from under the seat and the Captain takes a swig, passes it to me and I take a swig and pass it back and the Captain passes it back to Buzzy and he takes a swig and passes it back again and says, *No need to stop the circle, gentlemen.*"

Rod and Cameron laugh. Leslie slides the last slice of pizza onto Jeff's plate. She disappears up the stairs.

"You know, Cam, another couple of years and we'll both be retired. Aren't you next year?"

"Yeah. Just over a year from now. Goes quick, eh?"

Cameron picks up his beer. The snow is suddenly heavy. The cedar hedges have disappeared.

"Remember when Audacious was in the Union? Years ago?"

"Yeah," Rod smiles. "That is years ago. Like when we were new. Captain Audacious. He was going places."

"He always used the same rhetoric. We were professionals. The Union was an association of professionals. We would never strike: it would be a withdrawal of services. So. Professionals? We're more like tradesmen."

"I've heard you say that before, Dad."

Rod laughs.

"I've heard him say it before too, Jeff. Hey, you guys see the snow?"

"Crazy!" says Jeff. "It's really coming down. Hey, Rod, I hear you were down at Jay. How was it?"

"Well, I'd say awesome if it didn't make you feel too bad."

"That's OK. I feel bad because I've only been down twice this year. Not because I missed today."

The snow is briefly heavy enough so that the family room feels like an aquarium being buried in a blizzard.

"Dad, did your degree help you get into Air Arcadia?"

Rod can't help it; he laughs.

"Sorry, Cam."

Jeff looks back and forth between them. Cameron shrugs.

"Maybe it helped." He reaches down and pats Hershey. "You can laugh. You had what they wanted in spades. Military training. Fighters. The best of the best. Preselected and ready to go."

Jeff turns to Rod.

"What'd you fly?"

"The Widow Maker."

"The Widow Maker? That's wild."

Cameron puts his glass down on the coffee table, leans back, and howls. The noise is somewhere between an abused band saw and a bull moose in rut.

"Wow," Rod laughs. "You got it, Cam. Where'd you learn that?"

Jeff looks puzzled and slightly alarmed. Rod and Cameron's explanations collide.

"CF-104." "Variable thrust nozzle."

Rod looks at Cameron.

"How'd you . . ."

"Been behind one for takeoff a few times," Cameron explains. "Sitting at the button. The noise is like something from another world. Makes the hair on your neck stand up."

"It really sounds like that?" asks Jeff.

"Yeah."

Rod turns to Jeff to explain.

"The variable thrust nozzle is wide open for takeoff."

Rod demonstrates with his hands, spreading his fingers like a flower. He whistles under his breath, changing the note as the flower closes for the evening.

"See, you use full burner for takeoff."

The flower opens again, Rod's low whistle following.

"What's burner?"

"Afterburner. That's where you spray a bunch of fuel in behind the engine for more power. Only you need a bigger exhaust pipe for it to work right."

"That's the nozzle ..."

"Right. Only thing is, if the nozzle sticks open for some reason you're kind-of screwed, 'cause then the engine develops only a fraction of its normal thrust."

Cameron has settled back in his seat. Hershey's head is on his knee. Cameron's hand is deep in the fur and loose skin on Hershey's shoulder.

"The nozzle wasn't the only thing that could kill you."

Jeff looks at Rod.

"Guys died?"

"Yeah. Can't remember exactly, except that we lost 110 aircraft and the Luftwaffe lost 110 pilots. Just a coincidence, those numbers. Probably half or more of our ejections were successful."

"How many of these airplanes did the Forces have?"

"Two hundred."

"And a hundred and ten crashed?"

"Yeah."

There is silence as Jeff digests this. Hershey, too, seems to be considering it. Cameron's eyes are half-closed.

"That's amazing. How did you survive?"

Rod smiles.

"I was lucky. I wasn't one of the first to fly it, so I could learn from other guys' scares."

Rod seems to get younger as Jeff watches. The exasperation and occasional bitterness that has crept in along with his grey hair is gone. He sits straighter, with his head held high, like the young officer he once was.

"I remember when I was in training at Cold Lake. What one of the instructors told us. *It's an honest airplane, the 104*, he said. *You make a mistake, it'll kill you.*"

"And you didn't make any mistakes."

Rod smiles, skimming back over thirty-five years.

"Who doesn't make mistakes, Jeff?"

"But . . ."

"Yeah. I'm still here. There are things. Stuff you have to know."

"About flying?"

"More about the airplane."

"About why it killed so many pilots?"

"Sure. But we wanted to fly that sucker. I mean, Mach 2 – who wouldn't? That butt-kicking acceleration! But we didn't want to die. That made the airplane really interesting."

"A matter of life and death."

"Yeah. It was. The 104 had these tiny wings. And it was heavy. So if you mishandled it – pulled too hard – it could pitch up uncontrollably. We lost some guys that way. And then there was the BLC."

Jeff waits.

"Boundary Layer Control. Blown flaps. For landing they blow some engine bypass air over the flaps. Lowers the approach speed by forty knots. Only problem is that it can come in asymmetric. Happened to me. Scared the shit out of me. Rolled me vertical. Faster than I'd ever seen that sucker roll. Thank God we had the procedure and I'd trained myself mentally."

Jeff's eyes are wide with attention.

"So how did that work?"

"Well, for that BLC thing, our procedure was to select landing flap at 1500 feet above ground, wings level, hand on the lever. That way, you had a chance to recover. We found an early report by a guy named Warren Hunt. He was on a delivery flight when it happened to him. He was at 800 feet, base to final in a forty-degree bank, and it rolled him past vertical."

"What happened to him?"

"He couldn't control the roll. Thank God he figured it was the BLC and he pushed the flap lever back to Takeoff and went to full burner and went with the roll."

"So he rolled all the way around?"

"Yeah. When he rolled level he was clipping sagebrush. The tower thought he had crashed."

"But he made it?"

"Yeah. And better yet, he wrote a report and Lockheed listened to it and that's why we had our procedure."

"But you also said you did mental training."

"Well, sure. Most of us did. I'm sure your dad's done it too. What I mean is that I went through that story in my head until it was engraved. I rehearsed the moves. I rehearsed them in the cockpit so I could do them in my sleep. Except when it happened to me I didn't roll all the way around like I'd rehearsed. I rolled back up. Because I could."

In the silence Rod rushes forward through time, seeing it all unroll, watching the years blur by as if in low-level supersonic flight.

"You know, your dad's right about it being a trade. No one knows it all. No one's an instant hero. You learn. You learn from others and then you teach. You're part of a – what's it called, Cameron?"

Rod's arrival into the present has brought his friend back from his dreamy haze.

"Guild."

With a whump audible through the glass a cedar dumps a large burden of white. The snow has stopped. A few stars are visible above the hedge.

"So yeah, you train yourself. You rehearse in your head. Cam – I bet you did before your Bus ride. To survive ALT*."

"True. Went through it with Rob."

"Rob?" asks Jeff.

"His F/O for the ride."

"For the whole course."

"Dad, what's ALT Star?

"I'll tell you the story sometime," says Cameron reluctantly.

"Altitude capture mode on the Bus," Rod says. "It's as important to us as BLC was on the 104. Bus Industries lost their first BigBus Twin to an engine cut in ALT*. It's something we pay close attention to."

Hershey heaves himself up and walks to the door to the back yard. He nudges it with his nose.

"Hey, you want out, boy?"

Cameron walks over and opens the door. There is a rush of cold air. The sky is ablaze with stars.

Family

New York – June, 2003

Enrico

THE CEMETERY FLASHES by underneath.

"Gonna take her, ahh, you know . . ."

The Bus-sired cricket chirps.

"*Bleep bleep bleep.*"

"**Autopilot off.**"

"Yeah. That's what I meant to say. Gotta keep her inside – what is it, downtown Flushing?"

Brendan moves both arms up to the glareshield.

"That's right. Flight Directors off?"

His fingers are poised above the switches, one in front of Enrico, the other in front of himself.

"What? Why?"

"Puts the auto-thrust in speed mode, old man. Yer in Idle Open."

"**Flap 3.** Oh, OK, sure . . ."

Brendan pokes the switches. Checks the FMA. After far to long to suit him, the power surges up, trying to regain the Flap 2 F speed. He selects Flap 3.

"Flap 3, Vapp 134, Autothrust Speed."

Enrico has her in a thirty-degree left bank. He has left it a little late and is pulling mild G's trying not to bust his airspace. They are descending through 400 feet; Enrico has corrected the rate of descent and the auto-thrust has nailed the airspeed. They roll out of the turn at two hundred feet, more or less on the VASI's.

It works out, the way things do.

"Reverse Green."

"Air Arcadia 749, clear left in Tango if able, ground point seven."

"Seventy knots. That was Tango. Sierra's comin' up . . ."

They have missed the Sierra, the last high-speed. Brendan discreetly adds some brake, bringing them to a crawl before the Romeo.

"Air Arcadia 749 turn left there. Repeat, turn left on Romeo. Zero four is active for departures. Traffic on short final 31."

Enrico negotiates the ninety-degree turn onto the Romeo.

"Air Arcadia 749, left on Papa, ground one two one dezimal seven."

Brendan switches and checks in.

"Air Arcadia 749, transition to Alpha at Double Golf, hold short of Juliet."

"Where in the . . ."

"Next right, here – then next left."

"OK, thanks . . ."

Brendan completes the After Landing Check.

"So why was he so steamed? I was planning to turn left at the runway anyway, and we had – what – another thousand feet after that?"

"Yes. Well, almost. It was just that we had accepted a LAHSO."

"What?"

"Land and Hold Short."

Brendan picks up the ATIS.

"See – Expressway Visual 31, Departures 04, LAHSO procedures in effect. Remember? He asked us. We said no sweat."

They are cruising up to the Juliet.

"Enrico, hold short of the next taxiway . . ."

"Oh, right. That the one? Thanks . . ."

§

Brendan

The room is agreeable. The tap selection better than adequate. And it does advertise itself as being an Irish bar.

"Never been to the Village before. This is kinda cool."

"Never? Has no one dragged you down here, then?"

"No. Maybe it's – well, maybe we didn't know how to work the subways . . ."

"What do you make of this IPA?"

"Good. I could have another of these. Where's it from?"

"Boston, I think. At least, that's where I made its acquaintance."

They have taken the F train from Rockefeller Center down to West 4th Street. Walked the few blocks down to 3rd and Sullivan.

"So how'd you find this place, Brendan?"

"My friend Rod. He knows I like the Guinness. When I joined he wrote out a little guide for me. You know, where to find it on tap, and all."

"You know Rod from the military?"

"Yes. We were young together. That was a long time ago."

The self-evidentiary nature of the phrase seems to have stalled the conversation. The barman senses the lull.

"How's those Hahpoons doin'? Would ya like anutha?"

"Yes indeed. Enrico?"

"Sure. Good stuff."

He moves off a few paces to draw their pints. The silence still hangs. He nods his head at them.

"So wheah you genumen in from?"

Enrico smiles, all teeth.

"Montreal."

"Oh yeah. Ahcadia. I thought I huhd an accent . . ."

He sets the new pints carefully on cardboard coasters.

"So you heah on business?"

"Yeah, sort of. We're pilots."

Enrico's pride is evident.

"The aihlines?"

"Yeah. Air Arcadia."

"Hey, welcome to New Yoack."

He moves down the bar to greet a couple of newcomers.

"Last time I was in an Irish bar like this was with Cameron. In

San Francisco. Weird name."

Brendan looks up from his pint.

"Can't remember . . ."

"Well let's see . . ."

Brendan pulls a small notebook out of his jacket pocket.

"See if Ramrod has it . . ." he mumbles. "Ah, yes! The Irish Bank, perhaps?"

"Yeah, that's it. Barmaid was . . ." Enrico smiles again at the recollection. "Very fuckable."

The observation has not moved the conversation forward. Enrico tries again.

"So I hear you married a real looker. High mucky-muck in the forces . . ."

"The lovely Teresa. Yes, she has done very well for herself."

"And you retired from the forces?"

"Yes."

"How come?"

"I had done all I could." Brendan takes a sip. "And – I was eligible for a full pension . . ."

"Yeah? That's great. So how come you're still working?"

More people are entering the bar. Brendan looks at his watch. Just after five. The working crowd.

"Good question. I'm not yet sixty. Our airline let me in. But I imagine it could be more than that. Like these people coming in – sure, they need the money – but it is the work itself, you see . . ."

"So you don't need the money?"

Brendan laughs.

"Need? No."

"So your wife – Teresa – she makes pretty good dough?"

"Bless her, yes. Good enough. Although the Good Lord knows money is not why we join the military . . ."

"But she's up there, right? I mean – um – what's her rank?"

"She's a Major-General. Works at NDHQ."

"What's that?"

"National Defense Headquarters."

"Major-General? How many stars is that?"

Brendan laughs again. Truly, there is no other option.

"Two. Except Arcadia has maple leaves instead. Two maple leaves."

"So you guys would be comfortable . . ."

"Truly, yes. And yet here I am drinkin' beer with you."

The noise level is going up as The Pinch fills with the after-work crowd. Very few singles: mostly groups of two or three doing a post-mortem on the day. Fragments of conversations drift by. Brendan nods his head at the room.

"We come out to drink beer and talk work. So do most people. Perhaps work is important to us."

"All the same – I'd retire if I could."

Enrico scans the room. The bartender and the new one, just arrived, are guys with bellies. The work crowd is divided, but the girls are all very much part of their group, talking animatedly. There are no single women.

"Would you then?"

"Sure. Get paid for doing fuck-all? Why not?"

As the first beers hit the conversations heat up. Mostly, there is laughter: *Did you see the look on her face? . . . And that's not even the funny part . . . So then Ted comes over and – get this . . . I think they're not going to renew. I just have this feeling . . .*

"Enrico, I know the company hasn't always treated you well."

"So did Cameron blab on me? About our flying together?"

"No."

Brendan pauses. He manages to catch Enrico's eye. It is only for an instant, but it is there.

"I will tell you straight out, Enrico, how I know the company hasn't treated you well. You see . . ."

Brendan begins with Derek's panicked phone call. He relates the story of Enrico's promotion from Derek's point of view. Enrico is drawn in, his face flushed with the emotional recollection of the day and the fear on Derek's face.

"Yeah. So Ice didn't do him much good either . . ."

"That would be one of your understatements . . ."

"And it's true – Ice did ask him?"

"Yes."

"So I called it right."

"Yes."

"It's funny. I feel relieved. But I don't know why."

"Well – just maybe – because you didn't bear false witness, even to him. I mean, you didn't assume something about Derek that wasn't so."

"No. I wasn't trying to screw Derek, if that's what you mean."

"True enough."

"And I told him it would stop with me. So how come he was so upset?"

§

They have made their way west on W. 3rd Street, past the Blue Note and the guys playing basketball in the court at Sixth Avenue. Strolled up the Avenue and hung a forty-five-degree left at Village Square, and continued up Greenwich Avenue almost to the Greenwich/11th St./7th Avenue conjunction. Brendan found this place last month through Rod's notebook and it was indeed as he said: comfortable, good value, home cooking.

Brendan looks around. They have been seated in a little raised alcove near the front which also houses the espresso machine. Last time he was behind the kitchen in what probably used to be a back porch. Presumably Enrico has found the bathroom using Brendan's instructions.

He stretches his neck to read the blackboard on the wall. There is the chicken breast thing he had last time. Also a boeuf bourguignon with green beans and fresh bread. He turns back and examines the espresso machine, but he doesn't see it. Instead he sees Enrico, the human being. Not one of our stars, he thinks. Nor would you accuse him of erudition or subtlety. But so very much himself and enjoyable to be with. Funny how a reputation takes on a life of its own.

With the scraping of chair legs on the wood floor the subject is once again before him.

"Real estate must be expensive in New York. That can – shit – it's even smaller than the one at the bar. I was thinking of a tall girl trying to sit down in there. She'd have to stick her knees apart a mile or she wouldn't fit."

Enrico grins lasciviously and chuckles to himself.

"Couldn't do much in there, though. A little tight."

He chuckles again.

"So what's for supper?"

§

"Would you gentlemen like to see a dessert menu?"

"Sure!"

Enrico has had the pasta special and pronounced it worthy. He is feeling mellow. He has just finished a disquisition on wine-making which Brendan to his surprise found fascinating. No added yeast, no sulphites. Start and control the fermentation with a copper-coil heat exchanger. Their desserts arrive.

"Some coffees, gentlemen?"

"An espresso. After. Give us five minutes. Brendan?"

"Yes. For me as well, if you please."

The waiter leaves them alone.

"So Brendan. I've decided. I'm going to bid the Boing."

Brendan puts down his fork.

"Where would you be sitting, then?"

"Bottom half. Maybe even bottom third. But not on Reserve."

"Not bad. And I imagine the money's better . . ."

"Better believe it. With this new contract anything that's not a wide-body gets paid shit."

A vision has seized Brendan. Enrico being led off to the slaughter.

"Brendan. What is it?"

"No, it's nothing."

The waiter is back in their alcove, brewing the espressos.

"C'mon."

"Well, then."

Brendan considers how to put it, how much to say.

"I just thought you might like to stay with family."

Sinking Ship

AIRLINE HONCHO

April 8, 2004

Triple Time to Pass on Air Arcadia Bailout

Danny Yung and his Triple Time Investments appear to be preparing to withdraw from the Air Arcadia re-financing consortium.

Although a meeting in London with Air Arcadia's CEO Boy Wonder last week was by all accounts a routine financial update, sources within Triple Time point to Mr. Yung's increasing restiveness over the issue of employee pensions, particularly pilot pensions.

"Pensions are a deal-breaker for us," explained Born Leader, Chairman of the Arcadian Airline Pilots Organization. "Our members have been paying into this fund their entire careers. It is their money."

For his part Mr. Yung sees the pension funds not only as current assets but as unfunded liabilities going forward.

Air Arcadia is looking to write off the majority of its $13B (Arcadian) debt before emerging from ABCA.

Boy Wonder

THIS YEAR SPRING is early. The landscape is parched and treeless. There is no water about. The powerful sun busily sublimes the last of the snowbanks at the edges of the parking lots and taxiways. It has taken the dormant vegetation unawares. Sleepy photosynthesis is rubbing its eyes, surprised.

The light outside is brilliant, sere, threatening. It is what one might imagine for the top of Everest, or somewhere in the Colorado Front Range. Boy watches the precise, brown-black shadow of the headquarters building. It has been creeping toward him across the employee parking lot as the morning sun rises higher. He can imagine himself in that shadow: a tall smudge in the top right corner. He is flowing into this building to hide. He is a sundial, as old as Stonehenge. For a moment he will disappear; he will cease to exist. Then it will be time for lunch. He can't believe the company has been in bankruptcy for a year.

Boy glances again through the Honcho article. He can't accept it. Only last week he was in London, pitching the latest numbers to Danny and his staff. There was no hint that Danny . . .

. . . or was there? Boy plays back the tapes in his head, listening to himself speak:

> *". . . remarkable results in an unprecedentedly short period of time . . ."*

> *". . . the coporatization business model . . . significant value creation . . ."*

> *". . . a chance for all stakeholders to realize . . ."*

Was it all a bunch of shit? Was that what Danny was really thinking? And now this new thing.

Boy walks back to his desk and picks up the report Laura brought him a half-hour ago. Apparently BestJet has had access to Air Arcadia passenger bookings for the last year or so. It seems a former

Air Arcadia employee is responsible. Boy remembers him: a Blue guy with attitude. How he resigned and Boy was happy to see him go. Bob Mole! I signed his package, too. What an idiot I am!

Exasperated, Boy presses the intercom.

"Laura? Could you come in here a minute?"

Laura is a tall and imposing brunette. She sits in her customary straight chair on the other side of Boy's desk, steno pad ready for action.

"To whom, sir?"

"Oh. Sorry, Laura. Not a letter. You know our employee travel website?"

"Of course, sir."

"Can you see our bookings?"

Laura tries to cover her astonishment. It is difficult. Even sitting down she has a strong presence. Boy blushes.

"Well, sir, anyone who has access to the site can see our loads ...

Boy struggles with the recognition.

"And our plans? Can they see our plans?"

"Well, no, sir. Not as such. But they can look at a city pair on a specific date and see what we're planning to operate and what the bookings ..."

Boy looks at his watch. Not noon yet. 'Course it would be one o'clock Daylight. Or thereabouts. He is still thinking about disappearing.

You can't disappear, kid.

Beads of sweat appear on Boy's forehead. He reaches up to rub what is left of his hair. The scalp is wet, too. He looks out the window. The shadow's edge is very close to the building.

"Did you see that Hired Gun has been trying to get hold of you?

I think it might have to do with this BestJet thing . . ."

"Really?"

"Yes, sir. He was very anxious to speak to you."

§

In a few minutes Hired Gun is in the office, explaining how Mole wrote software to access Air Arcadia's employee travel site. How BestJet have been using that software to steal proprietary information.

Boy gets up and moves to the strategy area. He looks out the window. The shadow has disappeared. It will be on the other side now, creeping toward the hangars and 24L. Any minute now that pitiless sun is going to shine into these windows. A ShortBus is touching down on 24R. LaGuardia, probably. Flight 745.

This is not important, Boy.

Hired puts forward a plan to deal with BestJet and signs up to deal with it. The plan sounds reasonable to Boy, but he can't stop thinking about how he has been blindsided by this.

It's a distraction, Boy. Pissant stuff. Something much bigger is happening.

Boy watches the next touchdown on 24R – a Whale. First to spin are the rear wheels on the body gear. Then, as those trucks tilt, their front wheels and the rear set on the wing gear touch. In a second or so sixteen puffs of smoke have spun up sixteen tires. In his head Boy sees the sixteen puffs drift together to form an image – a face. He has never seen her, but he knows it is Arcadia.

§

At lunch Snake isn't around. Unless Snake is out of town he is usually visible at lunch, coming around for a huddle with Boy on some topic or other. Boy feels uneasy as he eats his little custard cup and has another cup of coffee. He is thinking how he should lay off the coffee. With no distractions, his mind worries away at the BestJet thing.

BestJet is a distraction.

"More coffee, sir?"

Boy nods out of habit.

"Oh, just a half – that's plenty. Thanks."

He looks around the almost-deserted executive dining room. The waiter has disappeared.

Boy pushes back from the table and walks to the window. A nubbly-looking executive jet is approaching 24L. The light is an artist's dream. North, all-seeing, no glare.

All seeing, yes. Don't ask me how.

Or perhaps not – it's so strong the colours are bleached out. But there's something about that light.

Lunch sits like a couple of hockey pucks in that growing gut that he hasn't been taking care of. He knows he is deferring things: walks in the outdoors, health club membership, time with family. Happiness.

§

The corner office greets him. The sun shines in the big windows. The strategy table and its two chairs cast harsh shadows on the carpet. The light is blinding, threatening. Suddenly he knows: Danny is not the only one who's going to walk.

That's right, Boy.

The realization is strangely calming. Boy sits in his strategy chair, willing the spring sun to fill in the details.

He takes off his jacket and pretends he's on the beach. The radiation soaks into his body, baking away debris. An aircraft lands. Another. And another. He sees what he has done. No going back now.

Boy stands, puts on his jacket, and walks slowly to the outer office.

"Laura, has Mr. Snake been by?"

"No sir, I haven't seen him today, now that you mention it."

"Could you get him on the phone, please, and move my two o'clock stuff . . ."

"Yes, sir. I'll ring through when I've got him on the line."

"No. Just tell him I want to see him here. At two."

§

The door opens and there he is, looking resplendent in Armani.

"Boy, your door was closed. Not like you."

"No."

"I'm glad you called. I've been meaning to talk to you. I imagine you've seen this report from Security?"

"Yeah, not a pretty picture. Why weren't we faster on the uptake?" Snake smiles.

"Well, you and I have been pretty busy this last while. Actually, I got wind of it last week and put Corporate Security on it. They've got an operation going."

"They getting anything?"

"It's a bit early to say."

On an impulse Boy gets up from his desk and walks over to the window. The winnowing sun works on his shoulders again as he turns to lock horns.

Snake drops the security report on Boy's desk and takes a few steps toward him.

"By the way, if anyone asks you about someone stealing some garbage, you don't know anything."

Except you do know, Boy.

"OK, I know nothing . . ." Boy's high forehead starts to glisten. ". . . and you can co-ordinate with Hired Gun. I recruited him for it this morning. We're thinking of going public with this in a week or so."

And you know I can't help you anymore.

Snake's face tightens perceptibly. He pulls another, smaller sheaf of papers from his pocket. The smile is still there on his mouth but it has left his eyes. He takes the remaining steps and holds out the papers.

"I won't be doing a lot of coordinating. This is my resignation. Effective immediately."

Boy looks Snake in the eye. He makes no move to take the papers. He is going through the effect of today's desertions on their exit strategies. Boy's \$20M is gone, gone with Danny. So is Snake's \$5M. What's left for Snake is what's in his contract: termination, his or company option: three years' salary. That would be about \$2M.

"Yeah. Danny walks, you walk."

Snake keeps his mouth shut, but his small sheaf of papers speak for him. Held between his thumb and forefinger, it falls vertical and dangles.

"Very perceptive, Boy."

Snake twists his wrist palm-up so the subject document sticks up like a finger, a leaning tower. Boy steps forward a pace.

"You've done good work for us. Thank you."

He takes the leaning tower and stuffs it into his inside breast pocket.

"Accepted. So it's \$2M instead of five."

The smile returns to Snakes eyes.

"Better odds, Boy. Better odds."

There is a layer of alto-stratus moving in, muting the light.

Goodbye, Boy.

Short Course

October, 2003

Enrico

Truck after truck of California grapes unloads at the makeshift market on the corner lot. Tarps have been raised on frames, mainly to shelter the organizers from mid-October showers. They are scarcely needed: the cartons of grapes vanish down the streets and lanes almost as soon as they are unloaded.

Men with dollies stack six or eight cases and wave to each other as they pass. The cases are stacked on or near the back porch; there is precious little real estate because they are still coaxing the last tomatoes from the trellised vines. But the cases will not rest long there, either. From California Central Valley fields to eighteen-wheelers to corner lot to back porch to crushing vat takes less than a week.

In Ville Émard if there is a garden there is likely also a winemaker in the family who is recruiting family members and getting a day or two off work to get the must working. This year the trucks arrived Thanksgiving Friday night and Saturday morning so the weekend is consecrated to la vinificazione: Mamma plans big meals for three days and la famiglia are all there, working the vats and heat exchangers and gossiping and after dinner and coffee toasting with a little grappa and it's a big party.

Enrico arrives in time for Sunday supper; he has been flying for three days and he is ready to enjoy himself. Besides, he would never choose to miss a meal when Mamma is cooking for company. His timing is perfect: the grapes are crushed and the boxes hosed out so he grabs a beer and helps Uncle Angelo get the heat exchanger into the must and the warm water circulating; tomorrow morning there may not be a lot of hot water for showers but the must will be fermenting and soon the heat generated will be enough to keep the yeast happy and they can turn off the warm water for a day or half a day and then they'll have to start some cold water through to keep the fermentation from going too fast. Dinner is Mamma's eggplant parmigliana made from the backyard bounty and of course it is wonderful and she is proudly calling him *mio figlio capitano* as the grappa is passed around.

His ring-tone is Pavarotti singing a phrase of Nessun Dorma: *quando la luce splenderà*. He is laughing as he picks up.

"Enrico, it's Barbara in planning."

"Barb! How's it going, sweetheart? What, you working late?"

"Yeah. Thanksgiving Sunday. But I'm outa here after I talk to you."

"So what can I do for you, Barb?"

"You know you got the Boing BigTwin on this bid?"

"Yeah, sure. Saw it this afternoon."

Barb pauses, gathering her strength.

"The Chief Pilot called me this morning. He wants you on course tomorrow."

"Shit, Barb. Tomorrow?"

"Listen, I know you just got back, Enrico. But the Chief got me in here today to set it up. Short course. Three days WICAT. Eight Sims including the ride. Line Check."

"Jesus, Barb, I've been thinking nothing but Bus. I've forgotten everything I ever knew about the Boing."

"You still got your books?"

"Jesus, I don't know. Maybe. Somewhere."

"Look, Enrico. I know they're pushing it, so I'm doing what I can. I've got an up-to-date set of Boing books for you. I'm going to leave them with Barney."

The enormity of it washes over him. It's like Ice Pick only worse. Suddenly Boss Boss and the Bus and even Cameron look good to him. He's got another fight ahead of him. Starting tomorrow.

§

Last week wasn't so bad, considering the grappa and the Advil and the lack of sleep. Just hard to stay awake in the WICAT. Then three Sims and Sunday off so he can come home for a day. Then another Monday with a grappa fog.

Saturday he had been doing OK with the Normal Procedures and Emergency Recalls but this morning Bus stuff keeps creeping back in and confusing him. At the break he drinks a coffee and has a good piss and starts working again, reciting the drills in his head, trying to keep it all straight.

Friday's the ride so Thursday is the dress rehearsal and shit, it's all too quick, how can the bean counters even remotely believe eight Sims is enough time? But he's hanging in there, maybe by the skin of his teeth but he's there as the week progresses and the instructor is not trying to bust him, just teach him, and the First Officer is OK too, although then he was taken all the more by surprise when on Thursday the rehearsal was in the form of a Line Oriented Flight Training session and the F/O fucked up the ILS so bad that he, Enrico, had to take over saying *I have control* and land because they were in the middle of a smoke drill and he wasn't going to do a missed approach. But he figures that was what he was supposed to do, anyway. Not that, theoretically, there's anything you're supposed to do on a LOFT except land the aircraft safely.

Then they are in the debriefing room and the instructor is recommending some specific areas to bone up on before tomorrow.

"Oh, and one more thing, Enrico, before you go . . ."

"Sure."

"On the Missed Approach where you had the engine failure: nicely handled. I noticed that when you were cleared for the turn to crosswind you disengaged the autopilot and flew by hand for awhile."

"Yeah."

"That's fine. Nothing wrong with that. I just want to bring your attention to what happens if you hadn't. In an ILS Approach you have three autopilots engaged."

"Right."

"They have three-axis authority, so they take care of your engine-out rudder."

"Sure."

"But the minute you select any mode other than ILS you're down to one two-axis autopilot. I'd recommend you check the book. Go over it."

§

At the Hilton the van pulls up short of the door, behind another crew van. As Enrico hands Ignatio his tip he is distracted by the laughing girls piling out of the van ahead. He is thinking it must be an overseas flight, a big airplane, to have made that many girls that punchy.

He is intrigued. He strolls closer, widening his toothy grin, empathizing with their jet lag. But he is not quick enough to see her first.

"Ciao, Enrico! What's up?"

The stallion stirs. He and Cindy have a limited but memorable history.

"Hey Cindy! Where'r'ya in from? Overseas, I bet."

"Si. Roma."

"So you wanna catch a beer or something?"

§

Next morning the seven AM show time is way too early. He scoffed down a couple of donuts and a coffee in the Hilton lobby but he is still not fully in the aviation world. Cindy has a way of turning his head.

The briefing has a funereal feel. It is the Chief himself, which is a little odd. He doesn't say much. Enrico hopes it it just the early hour; after all, he doesn't feel all that voluble himself. He is paired not with this week's F/O but with another captain, someone he has never met and who hasn't yet met his eye. Apparently Enrico is to go first and then they'll switch seats.

So far so good. He has been meticulous with the Emergency Briefings and the airplane's quirks are starting to come back to him. He could get used to this. A widebody, after all, and the miracle of formula pay where size counts . . .

But he'd better concentrate. He waves his thumb over the thrust levers.

"By the NOAHA."

"2090, altimeter two niner eight two inches, Missed Approach

4000 set."

The decision to come back to Toronto is OK. Nothing wrong with it. Ottawa and Montreal flat on their asses all of a sudden. No point in wasting gas holding. So just bring her back here where the weather's not so bad. Land and consider your options. Of course that's what he wants, anyway. Yeah, and he's gonna give me some emergency on this approach, too. Get ready. Missed Approach is straight ahead to 1100 and then left direct St. Catherine, climb to 4000.

"Captain, I've got a flag on my localizer."

Enrico looks at his Primary Flight Display.

"Yeah, me too. OK, **Go Around.**"

He pushes the power up and clicks the Go Around palm switch on the thrust levers.

"**Positive Rate.**"

"**Gear Up.**"

OK, she's going good. Remember the Missed Approach Procedure. Left at 1100.

"**Engine Fire.**"

Fuck. This guy doesn't fool around. Take it easy. One step at a time.

"**Fire Drill.**"

"**Roger. Fire Drill. Thrust Lever, Idle. Number One Thrust Lever . . .**"

Enrico glances down at the quadrant.

"Idle."

"We're climbing through 1200, Captain."

Under stress a pilot's cone of vision narrows; he processes data only from the fovea. Enrico sees only the Heading Knob as he turns it left to 180°, pretty close to direct the St. Catherine Beacon, Sierra November, frequency 408.

He feels the simulator twist and jerk on its jacks. Nobody is saying anything. He looks back at his Primary Flight Display, trying to focus his fovea centralis on a useful image. He can't believe what he sees; it makes no sense. The line dividing the blue sky from the brown ground is vertical, tilting past vertical. The Vertical Speed tape is plunging down, lengthening. He looks up, over the glareshield, desperate to deny something he cannot believe. The sky is full of stars. Eight lanes of stars, moving quickly: four lanes east, four lanes west.

The sickening noise of the crash and the vision of highway 401 in the sky is still in Enrico's head as they file back into the briefing room. The Chief Pilot takes his position behind the desk. The penitents sit in the two chairs on the other side. Enrico sneaks a glance at his teammate. He seems unperturbed.

"Enrico, where is the Missed Approach Point on the ILS to 24R?"

At the Chief's question the teammate obligingly pulls his chart binder out of his bag and opens it to the Toronto 24R ILS. He points to the LOC/NDB box, note 3. Enrico is thinking of why this guy wasn't helping him, but he follows the finger and reads.

"MAP – threshold. The threshold, chief."

"Yes. According to the Arcadian Air Regulations, is it permissible to execute any turn in the Missed Approach Procedure before reaching the MAP?"

Enrico struggles to see the relevance of the question. All he can see – no, he can hear – is his putative teammate saying *We're climbing through 1200, Captain.* Right before he reached up for the heading knob.

"No, Chief."

"And were you at the threshold yet?"

"Don't know, Chief."

"I didn't fail the DME or the Glideslope, just the Localizer. You were two miles inside the NOAHA. 2.8 DME. A good two-and-a-half miles from the threshold."

Enrico doesn't reply. He sees, suddenly and clearly: this is a bust. This whole operation is basically a police action, a setup. The teammate most certainly is not a teammate – not on his team, anyway. He must be another check pilot with his own scripted part to play. He sees how the left engine was at idle thrust before he reached up for the heading knob. He remembers the instructor, yesterday, reminding him that as soon as he touches the Heading Knob or indeed anything, goddammit, the three three-axis autopilots drop off, leaving one measly two-axis autopilot to level the wings and leaving him, Enrico, the Pilot Flying, to do the rudder work balancing the failed engine.

The Chief says nothing about the autopilot or the crash, nothing about what Enrico could or should have done. His purpose has been served. He starts putting his papers away.

"Obviously, Enrico, this is a failure."

He snaps his briefcase shut and stands up.

"Of course your union will go to bat for you. Some sort of deal will be reached."

The Chief walks toward the door. The other captain has already grabbed his bag and backed out. As he goes by, the Chief turns for one last look.

"I recommend very strongly that you accept the deal as offered."

Home

Montreal – January, 2005

Arcadia

WELL, FATHER. Here I am in this fucking home, or whatever it is.

As for that fat useless blob of blue debt, I have ceased to care. The financial miracle workers could not cut her away, so here she is: dead and still attached. I push her around in that stupid trolley they have given me. Really, the only benefit to them is that I get to the goddamn toilet on my own. Most of the time.

My roommate – SnowTel, I think she said her name was – doesn't say much. Mostly, if she is not in bed, she sits in that chair over there and looks out the window. Days go by. When it gets dark she looks at the lights for awhile and then packs it in.

Nothing much is happening here. So I think of you and of MOM. I was your firstborn, after all. I suppose you were proud of me. Maybe you even loved me, in your own way. I wouldn't know, now.

Wouldn't know, either, what has become of my boys and girls. You see, Father, they cannot come to the home. They will not let them in, I guess. But I think of them, too. Well, mostly dream. When I sleep, sometimes it is OK. I dream of you, of MOM, and of my boys and girls and the times we used to have. I can't remember shit when I'm awake.

How did I get here, Father?

I don't even know if you can hear me. I feel you can, but your voice no longer reaches me. Perhaps it is the home, Father? Does it have lead walls, so nothing can go through? Oh, I know. I am not making any sense. I can no longer tell what is real and what is dreams.

Still, I wonder. Am I dead, like the blue bitch?

Probably not, more's the pity. I still wake up in this stupid room. People are always walking in and out, as if SnowTel and I were animals in a zoo. They come to feed us and clean our cage. I suppose they are just people, Father, earning a living for their families. But they don't see me, not really. It's always *we, we, we. How are we doing today, Arcadia? Do we have a dirty diaper? Wouldn't we like to take a nice warm shower and get all clean?* Shower, shit. Strip me and the inert blue bitch on her cart and hose us down in the tile room.

Did that keeno kid put me here? Is that what I hear you saying? I struggle to remember. Please, Father, keep talking to me. I feel I can hear you faintly. Or is that just my memory, calling in fits and starts? So speak, Father. Speak as though time and space did not exist. I would know more. I would cling to something, if I am to live.

I know I already had this blue bitch hanging to to me. And then the kid – what's his name – stopped listening to me. Pretended he didn't hear me. As if. He heard all right. I remember how I could make him sweat whenever I felt like it. Just whisper in his ear, especially when he was talking to that slender creepy guy. Not that it did me any good.

Yes, perhaps it was the young one. Perhaps he tired of my voice in his ear. He made his choice, to listen to Slim Creepy. He decided that I do not exist.

Sometimes when I look over at SnowTel and she's looking out the window I look out the window too and I see what she is seeing and it is airplanes. Airplanes up in the sky. Is that what I used to be about, Father?

§

I have been reading, Father. I have a few old issues of Honcho and the Financial Gazette.

I can't remember much so I read and look for my life. And Snowie's life too, bless her. For the last while I have read everything I can find about her. Why, Father? Because she has a story, too. And what a story! What a wild ride she has had!

You see, she made switches. No, not for railroads. Yes, of course – this is something new since your time, Father. You would not have heard. But do you remember telephone switches? Banks of electromagnetic relays and such? Yes. And the transistor – that had been invented, had it not? Well they have come together and evolved – she has made it so – into digital switches. The banks of relays are now software, Father, and Snowie led the way.

Right here in Arcadia she led and she grew and we were proud to have her here and have the world come to see what she was making and adopt and buy and copy – oh, especially copy, I think – and she prospered, Father. She would have caught your eye. She broke records for Arcadia with her phenomenal market capitalization which at one point made up one-third of the Toronto Exchange if you can believe it. She was huge, the biggest company in Arcadia. Everybody wanted to invest in her.

Sometimes Snowie looks at me when I talk to you, Father. I don't think it bothers her, she just finds talking curious, as a dog would. She hasn't said one word to me or anyone else in a long time.

She is not siamesed to a dead woman as I am, but in most ways she is worse off. Her fall has been more traumatic than mine own. No wonder the poor thing keeps her own counsel.

She is looking at me now. I'll read for a bit, and let her be.

§

She is looking out the window again, Father. So I can ask you. I found this the other day. Remember Airline Honcho?

AIRLINE HONCHO
April 1, 2003

Air Arcadia Declares Bankruptcy

MONTREAL – Air Arcadia attorneys appeared before Judge Simone de Pouvoir in Montreal Superior Court this morning to file for bankruptcy under the Arcadian Business Creditors Act, or ABCA. Roughly equivalent to Chapter 11 in U.S. Law, the Act allows a corporation to seek protection from creditors while it re-structures for greater profitability.

Boy Wonder, President and CEO of Air Arcadia, stressed that there would be no change in daily operations.

"The merger and other market forces have necessitated a review of our corporate structure with a view to enhancing the value of our assets for all stakeholders," Mr. Wonder explained. "Today's filing will allow these positive measures to move ahead unimpeded."

That is me, is it not? Air Arcadia? And Boy Wonder – that is the new guy who won't listen to me, who has to pretend I am not real?

So what does this mean, this bankruptcy? Does it mean that he is right, and I am not? That only he and the money are real and that my boys and girls and I are not real? That we are figments, dreams?

I should not complain. Poor Snowie, looking out the window all day. Her wild ride came to a sudden end, Father, and then she just kept falling. The market that had embraced her declared her worthless. She was liquidated, broken up for scrap like the Jetliner and the Supersonic Fighter. Recently I saw that some of her executives – former executives, I should say – have been criminally charged. Apparently they were cooking the books, trying to look good in the eyes of Wall Street, currying favour one quarter at a time.

MegaTwin Ops

Toronto – March, 2009

Rod

ROD PUTS HIS ARM out to steady himself against a window pillar. His eyesight isn't as good as it used to be. He can make out a large tractor that seems wrapped around the nosewheel of a very large airplane emerging from behind a wing of the terminal three hundred yards away. It could be their machine.

Flight 420 is planned as a MegaTwin with 350-odd seats. All the passengers and more are here at Gate 146, where the lounge was designed to hold two hundred. Susan is sitting on the low ledge by his feet. Several times someone squeezing by has jostled him roughly enough to almost push him into her lap.

He glances down at the ramp.

There is a great, hulking bridge, its two wheeled jetways sitting at odd angles. There is a regular tractor, parked where their aircraft's nosewheel will go. Other equipment is scattered about, some of it obviously inside the safety zone. There are no ramp guys in sight.

It is cold and windy out there, a blustery north-wester. Their flight from the west coast had snatch-flared, floated, powered up, re-flared, and run out most of Runway 33L before turning off on Runway 05. Rod thinks of how 33L is a tricky runway. The chart says it's an upslope, but that's just counting the ends. It's actually an up-and-down with a displaced threshold.

After three years of retirement Rod likes to feel he has forgotten the flying world. He and Susan still travel some, and as a passenger he can zone out and endure pretty well during a regular operation. He even sleeps through smooth landings sometimes. But anything abnormal in the operation brings memories flooding back.

He doesn't want them. He tries to banish them. He knows he will only be critical of how things are being handled. He doesn't want to go there. Let the young guys do their thing. But increasingly, the stories from the guys who are still working are less funny. Even the keen guys are saying they don't care anymore. Can't afford to and stay sane, they say.

Not Bad Dog, Rod thinks. Whatever anyone says about him, Bad Dog is the keenest pilot he knows.

Bad Dog has been on the MegaTwin now for two years. In typical Baddy style he got the books early and studied his butt off, so by the time he started course (one of the first, down at Boing) he knew more than his instructors. That's just the way Bad Dog does business. Once, in a rare moment, he confessed to Rod that he told the office he would like to instruct and had been rebuffed.

He is one of the boys, for sure. Just not one of the office boys. And that crowd has gone downhill as well. Bernie, the new VP Ops, is a self-serving twit with zero management experience or expertise. He can keep a seat warm, though, and suck up to the top brass for admission into the top ten, the elite few who hold shares in APPC, the Arcadia Private Property Corporation. Just last summer Bernie pocketed a $1.4 M bonus on one of APPC's periodic payouts. Hell, his total pay last year was $3.6 M, if Rod can believe what he hears.

He turns toward the desk. It is set out a bit, away from the window wall and the door to the bridge. A rope separates the bridge entrance from the area where he is standing. Two pilots are standing beyond the rope. Neither of them is Bad Dog. Rod recognizes the Captain but not the First Officer. A blue guy, maybe.

As he pushes slowly through the crowd toward the rope, he sees there is another, shorter, pilot standing with his back to him on his side of the line. Deadheading, he thinks. Deadheading crew.

When he checked this morning there were twenty-something open seats in J Class, even though the back showed full.

How quickly one forgets, he thinks. There will be a zillion crew trying to deadhead back to Montreal any evening, and today's delays will funnel them all into this flight. They will fill that huge J section because they have priority over retired employees, even those who have paid double for the J option.

Rod is closer to the rope. The three pilots are conversing earnestly. The deadheading pilot turns slightly. Rod smiles as Jean-Luc recognizes him.

"Mon hostie de tabarnac, c'est Rod! Comment ça va, mon vieux?"

"Hey, Jean-Luc!" Rod claps him on the shoulder. "Guess what? I paid double just so you can take my seat!"

Jean-Luc's face flushes.

"Calice! I tol' you about dat! Cocksuckers! Dey jus' tryin' to piss us off!"

Rod laughs and rocks Jean-Luc's shoulder.

"So, what's the latest?"

The Captain – Roland, Rod remembers – speaks first.

"Equipment bid's out."

"Any change for you guys?" Rod asks politely. He looks at the unknown F/O. He holds out his hand. "I'm Rod. Retired. Out of all this."

"Tim," says the putative blue guy, shaking his hand. "Nice to meet you. Retired, eh? I'm jealous. Me, it's status quo. Stayin' on the MegaTwin."

"Me, too," says Roland. "But I wouldn't mind getting back to Montreal."

"But on what?" Rod asks. "You're not going to down-bid, are you?"

The smaller BigTwin is the largest aircraft at the Montreal base.

"They put ten crews in Montreal on the new bid," says Roland.

"MegaTwin positions?"

"Fuckin' right, and I got one of dem. Number five."

Rod turns to look at Jean-Luc, trying to suppress disbelief. Jean-Luc used to fly with Rod all the time as his First Officer. True, Rod is now beyond senior, he is gone. He can't quite take it in.

Jean-Luc can't hide his glee. He is trying to make it an inward gloat, a private gloat. It isn't working.

"Can't bump him," says Roland, by way of explanation. "No openings on the base."

According to the contract, as long as the base stays steady or contracts, as it has been doing since Rod was a fresh-faced First Officer, there are no openings, and pilots who have bid off the base cannot bid back on. It is one of those arcane rules where seniority does not hold total sway.

"Takes your seat today, takes mine for the next year. What the fuck." Roland gestures toward the window wall. "There's our bird. Take care, guys."

Tim and Roland disappear down the bridge. Jean-Luc smiles the impish smile Rod remembers so well.

"Just doesn't want to hang around because he knows I gonna tease da shit out of him. His fuckin' F/O is senior to me and I'm holding dat hostie de baleine bimoteur at 'ome, tabarnac!" Jean-

Luc pauses to snort meaningfully. "He's gonna freeze his butt in that bridge, hostie." He jerks his head toward the window.

The tow has stopped fifty feet away, waiting for the tractor that was left parked in the safety zone. There is no sign of human presence on the ramp, save for the invisible driver in the tow tractor and his counterpart high above on the Flight Deck. The bridge still hasn't budged.

"Check that out, là. L'équipe. Don't see them? They're still on break, hostie. Roland n'a même pas regardé. He think that bridge gonna move. Il n'a pas demandé, he don't know shit. This gonna be the operation from 'ell."

Rod looks out the window. Sked departure was forty minutes ago. A solitary figure trudges, head down, toward the bridge stairs. If anything, the operation is becoming more random. At least nothing is nothing.

"Is it always like this?"

"Thank God, no. I'd be crazy, hostie. In the States it's contract crew. Get paid half, do twice de fuckin' work. The swamp, too. They're good guys. Even smile sometime, hostie."

He gestures at the window again. Three mittened, parka'd, hooded figures are standing near the abandoned tractor, gesturing, steam from their argument escaping downwind in wisps.

"I like that. First, you have to have a fuckin' conference. Not my fault. Not my crew. Your crew shoulda move da fuckin' tractor. Not my crew, your fuckin' crew. They're all at each other's t'roat."

"That's just here?"

"Fuck, no, hostie. Lotus Land is just as bad."

"What about home?" Rod feeds Jean-Luc's rant out of old habit.

"Des fois c'est mieux, des fois c'est pire, mais au moins ils parlent français, hostie."

The gate P/A system crackles limply, barely able to make itself heard above the murmur of the crowd.

In preparation for boarding Flight 420, RancidAir service to Montreal, may I bring your attention to the special procedures implemented by Air Arcadia for boarding this splendid Boing MegaTwin. Today, to facilitate the process, we will be using two bridge access points. As you enter the bridge area, you will notice that there is an intersection. Our J-Class, Pamper, and Super-Pamper passengers will be turning left at the intersection to go directly to the J-Class section of the aircraft. Our Welcome-To-The-Club passengers will proceed straight ahead to the Welcome Class section. I repeat: Welcome Class passengers must proceed straight ahead at the intersection.

There are more muted crackles and clicks from the P/A. Rod and Jean-Luc move slightly so they can see part of the desk area from the rear, including the rear of the agent handling the P/A. She is shuffling papers and has dropped the mike. She picks it up, throws her head back, and begins anew.

In order to make this whole procedure more efficient we will be forming two lines here in front of the desk.

The crowd has packed the gate area to the point that there is virtually no room to move anywhere.

The left line, closest to the desk, will be reserved for our J-Class, Pamper, and Super-Pamper passengers. The line on the right will be for the rest of you. You could help us now by moving back away from the desk so we can organize these lines.

"Rod, you connecting from the States?"

"Yeah, we started in San Francisco."

"You checked in with this broad yet?"

Jean-Luc nods his head at the girl at the desk, the dark-haired one who has been doing the P/A. The other girl, a pretty blonde, is conferring politely with passengers at the other end of the desk.

"No. It's all in the computer, right?"

"I know this chick – if you're not in her face you don't h'exist."

"OK, maybe I'll go see."

Rod gently elbows his way to the desk and stands politely, waiting for the dark-haired girl to look up. When she does he flashes his best smile and holds out his standby boarding cards.

"We're connecting from San Franscisco."

She waves away the standby cards.

"Go siddown and waitle I call ya."

It is almost a snarl. Rod works his way back around the counter to where he has been standing with Jean-Luc. The latter exhibits a satisfied smirk.

"Son of a bitch! You set me up!"

Jean-Luc laughs.

"I had to introduce you to this chick. I know her for awhile."

As if on cue, the P/A crackles feebly. Rod glances back toward the desk. The dark-haired girl stands proud, chin and chest high, preparing for another round as drill sergeant.

Your attention please, everyone.

She holds the mike away from her face and scans the crowd, waiting for compliance. It is not forthcoming.

All right everyone, listen up! There has been a change to the boarding process. I repeat, there has been a change to the way you are about to board the aircraft.

She scans the room again. A few people are looking in her direction. Perhaps it was the words *about to board the aircraft.*

You will recall that previously we described boarding the aircraft through two portals. It appears that one of these devices has frozen and cannot be moved up to the aircraft.

Rod glances out the window. Sure enough, the J-Class bridge is now in place but the other is still hanging down like a broken arm.

We will still, however, be forming two lines here at the desk. Once again the left line, closest to the desk, will be reserved for our J-Class, Pamper, and Super-Pamper passengers. The line on the right will be for our Welcome-To-The-Club passengers. Since we will be boarding by seat and row number, please do not come toward the desk or get in line until your row number has been announced.

"Rod, I got my seat. I'm gonna go." Jean-Luc grabs his arm and slowly pushes by him. "Good to see you, mon vieux. Bonne chance." He turns for a moment to look back with that maniacal smile of his. "Hostie," he mutters.

He is gone; the crowd has swallowed him like the whale swallowed Jonah. Rod makes his way slowly back to the window where Susan is sitting on the ledge, reading her book.

"Any news?"

"Nothing for us, yet. Although I think we should be prepared. We might not get on. There's a ton of deadheading crew. If we do get on it's probably going to be in the back, separated by miles."

§

It is as he thought. They have seats in the back, far apart. They have just called his cabin, row numbers that seem impossibly high.

He steps into the crowd, clutching his precious boarding card. It is like stepping off a boulder into the rapids. He is swept forward toward the blonde girl's station. She checks off seat numbers in the computer as she lets people through. Rod manages to get his passport out and open to the picture page.

"Fifty-four E," she says cheerfully, handing his documents back. "Have a good flight."

Borne along by the tide, Rod is channelled into the J bridge. As the current slows and then stops, dammed up by the sluice-way at the aircraft's door, he finds himself behind two middle-aged men in expensive overcoats.

"You'd think they'd say something," the taller man says. His suit looks even pricier than his overcoat. "But that bitch behind the desk obviously didn't know what was going on."

"You can't expect anything from Air Arcadia anymore," says the second man. He is dressed more casually in some sort of chamois leather jacket. "I fly BestJet now, unless . . ."

" . . . unless you don't have a choice. I know what you're talking about. These guys just don't give a – well, I won't say it." He makes a discreet but obscene gesture, almost dropping the leather gloves he is holding.

Rod maintains radio silence. He is thinking about his pension. The crowd shuffles ahead a few feet at a time.

The sluiceway dumps him into the middle of J Class. Rod has never seen this before. Alien pods angled at forty-five degrees to the axis of the aircraft. All singles. You won't be chatting with your wife and having a little party up here. There are dividers between the two seats in the center. The window seats, if that's what they are, are singles too.

As the tide carries him slowly back, he looks more closely. These pods recline into beds and close up for privacy. Rod is slightly alarmed that he didn't know about them. He read about something like this in the paper, but he didn't know Air Arcadia had any. It shows how out of touch he is.

The tide sluices into Welcome Class. Nine across. Three, three, and three. Past a divider with rest rooms and a small galley a new room opens out. He looks for a row number. Thirty-five.

The tide slows and stops. Rod puts his laptop on the floor between his feet so he can put his backpack on properly. He slung it over one shoulder thinking it wouldn't be long, but his back is hurting. Someone ahead is trying to cram a suitcase, a questionable carry-on, into an overhead bin that clearly has no room for a portfolio. A flight attendant works her way forward to the blockage.

"Excuse me, sir," she says, holding out her arms. "May I take that for you? I think there's some room a few rows back."

The perpetrator looks suspiciously at the flight attendant. He seems reluctant to let go. He makes one more half-hearted attempt to squish his bag into the shallow space and then slowly turns and looks at the flight attendant, who is still smiling courteously.

"I think we can find you a place for that bag, sir. Would you like to follow me?"

The offer to take the bag for him has evaporated. Probably she can read the perp and knows he isn't going to let go of it.

The tide ebbs again, sucking out toward the rear of the aircraft. They pass through another bulkhead, this one containing just restrooms. The next cabin is bigger than the previous cabins. It seems to stretch to infinity, like an outdoors vista, but on closer inspection Rod sees that the illusion is caused by the narrowing of the fuselage. He looks for a row number. Forty-eight. Fifty-four is near the middle of this big tail section.

He unslings his backpack and looks for some room in the overhead bin. He is beginning to feel spaced-out, unreal, even a little tight in the chest.

"Are you in here? I'll let you in."

It is the lady in 54-D. She struggles to get a handhold somewhere so she can get up. Rod's embarrassment goes up a notch.

"I can step over, if you don't mind."

He puts his laptop down on the seat with his headset case.

"That OK?"

"Oh, yes."

She seems relieved to be able to sink back into her seat. Rod steps carefully over her knees and goes through the Rubic's Cube moves to get the laptop under the seat in front, the headset case and the Times Magazine into the seat pocket, and his own butt into the now-clear 54-E. He is sweating profusely and distinctly claustrophobic. The cabin walls are closing in around him. He closes his eyes and tries to breathe deeply as he fumbles around his hips for the seat belt. He finds the two ends, untwists them, and snaps them together. He keeps his eyes closed. Earphones. He feels for the case and zips it open. He doesn't bother with the cable but puts the earphones over his ears and feels for the little sliding power switch. Not silence exactly but quiet, peace; the packed-to-the-gills cabin is not so immediate, not so pressing-into-his-head. Rod takes a few slow deep breaths and, eyes still closed, sleeps.

§

. . . ont trouvé les baggages en question et nous partirons dans les très bref délais. Nous vous remercions de votre patience.

It is the Captain. Rod recognizes the voice through the dampening tunnel of noise-cancelling and struggles to the surface. Shit, how long have I been asleep? He looks at his watch. Seventeen forty-five. Wow, I've been out for forty minutes, easy. This thing's now going on two hours late, and they've had an aircraft on the gate for an hour. What a fuckup.

Ladies and gentlemen, this is Captain Poirier speaking . . .

Rod takes off his earphones so he can hear more clearly.

It appears that there are several passengers who could not be boarded and of course in the interest of security we had to remove their bags. As you can appreciate on an aircraft of this size that process takes some time . . .

435

His mind snaps back two and a half hours and he sees with perfect clarity the turbaned gentleman in some uniform or other who was explaining to them as to a pair of dunces that of course they could not, they absolutely could not, place bags on the transfer belt because they did not have boarding passes, you know, and must only go three floors up to see an agent and get new boarding passes and then of course ...

The movie continues its playback and Rod sees himself putting on his best easy smile and explaining how they had come from San Francisco and how the bags were checked through and showing the gentleman the baggage tags and how the gentleman had relented and said oh, if you like and waved them on and Rod had triumphantly placed the bags flat, wheels up on the belt as you are supposed to do and there is the belt bearing them away into that little dark opening from which they WILL NOT RETURN and he sees clearly the yellow standby tags on their bags that he has failed to rip off, the standby tags that were quite properly affixed in San Francisco and which are now irrelevant and of course the guys downstairs are just looking for yellow in their understandable careless haste and of course their bags have been yanked.

The claustrophobia, sweating, and dizziness have faded with his nap. Rod pulls out a crossword puzzle to try to let his extreme frustration ease slowly into resignation. Roland is still speaking.

... now that we have removed the bags we will be able to push back in just a few minutes. We apologize for the delay and wish you a pleasant flight to Montreal. The weather there is light snow and a temperature of minus thirteen.

There is a murmuring in the cabin. Rod senses he isn't the only one newly awake. The murmurs resolve into comments.

" ... think he could have said something before this ..."

"Oui, oui, c'est normal. Le boarding process prend au moins une heure. Ce n'est que BestJet qui a le secret de partir à l'heure ..."

"I don't know how Air Arcadia thinks they can get away . . ."

"Le Chef de Service n'a pas eu un seul mot du Commandant . . ."

"Bain, il n'a rien dit non plus . . ."

The last two are sotto voce from two Flight Attendants walking down the aisle. Or maybe not so sotto voce. Rod understands just fine in his middle seat. He finds his pencil and starts working on the upper right corner of the crossword.

The pushback is at eighteen hundred. Two hours late. If he wasn't fully awake before, the engine start finishes the job. Rod has never heard anything like it. The anguished howl drowns out all conversation.

The lights blink as the first generator comes online and the howl begins again for engine two. Perhaps the APU is U/S and the howl is the world's largest air cart.

They are moving. Rod sees the sea of blue lights around the Bravo and the Alpha and the Alpha-Kilo and feels himself hurtling sideways as the big bird swivels on its triple main gear and the nosewheel turns south on the Bravo.

They take position. There is a brief wait. Then a little lurch as the brakes on the main trucks release a fraction of a second apart. The power comes up, making a whoosh that seems mild after the air-start cart or whatever it was. There are more sideways lurches as Roland or Tim counters the gusty crosswind, keeping the big airplane on the runway centreline. It feels as though they are hardly moving: an illusion, Rod figures, caused by both the size of the aircraft and the low Flex Thrust they are using. Rod's butt has hardly started down in the rotation and they are airborne, clawing into the sky on those enormous wings built to carry at least a third again as much weight.

§

...et que vos effets personnelles soient bien rangés...

Rod can feel the MegaTwin slowing to 250 knots and then starting the descent below 10,000 feet. Fed by sounds and inertial nudges, he is back on the flight deck flying the FRANX 3 Arrival to 24R as he has done hundreds of times. In his head he sees it all: the slowdown, flap extension, the intercepts of final approach course and glideslope. He closes his eyes and sees the alignment, the flare, the touchdown and rollout. He sighs as the big bird comes to a stop, obviously not at the gate. He listens to the In Charge requesting they remain in their seats. It is right out of the 351 Manual, the Flight Attendant's Bible, but somehow the familiar words have taken on a menace unintended by the author.

The flight has got him down. Rod doesn't get depressed often or easily but walking down the endless corridors of the new wing he realizes that something has got to him. Also, he's lost; he's never been right here before in an airport he spent his career walking through, his home airport, and whether it's that or the big airplane or the delay or the bags they've probably lost he realizes he feels bad, not just disoriented but depressed, too, as if any effort to deal with anything is going to be more trouble than it's worth. That dizzyness or claustrophobia from before the flight has returned with a darker component. He is trying to tell Susan that their bags are most likely still in Toronto.

"Don't worry, Rod. There's nothing we need tonight. Besides, they'll deliver them, no? Probably tomorrow?"

"Yeah, you're right. Don't know why it's getting to me."

"I knew right away something was. I could see it in your face."

"Maybe it's just that operation. Sure, there are always screw-ups, but you hate to see the company that's paying your pension ..."

"I know, honey, but it's like you always say, one paycheck at a time."

Suddenly at a bend in the corridor Rod knows where they are. His mental map display slews into position. This must be where the new wing joins – no, it's at the end of the wall where the new facade joins the old building. There's where we used to walk to old Gate 1, the RancidAir counter for so many years, so the stairs and escalators to baggage should be just behind, just around the corner.

The familiar ride down and the guard stationed at the exit from the Security Zone and the confidence that he knows exactly where he is eases Rod's distress. At the bottom of the escalator he can see right away that their bags will arrive, if they do, on Carrousel 1. The press of people around it is like bees on a honeycomb and thicker, four or five deep so that the carrousel itself has completely disappeared. There is no one around the others save for a solitary worker bee or two still inbound for the hive. Rod steers them toward number two so they can watch from a safe distance.

He notices another family who have sought relief from the crowd. They have staked out a spot behind a pillar along one side of Carrousel 2 and he sees they have a dog, a large golden retriever. As Rod and Susan invade his space he starts to bark, not in that reassuring way big dogs usually have but with a false bravado more characteristic of small dogs. Rod's instinct to go over and introduce himself to the dog fades. Now Mom, if that is who it is, is down or her knees trying to hush Toffee or Goldie or Honey. Rod can't seem to come up with male names for this dog, whose barking only grows more angry and insistent and annoying as Mom coos in his ear. Rod grabs a baggage cart and stacks the few items they have on it. He digs for their cell phone in his backpack and turns it on for the first time since they left home a month ago. He sticks it back in his pocket.

"I'll go over and watch the carrousel for awhile," Susan says. "Just in case."

§

Forty minutes later they are standing together in the long line at the lost luggage desk, Air Arcadia Baggage Services. The crowd has vanished from Carrousel 1. It has stopped turning, Rod notices, as he turns to inspect it once again. There is a weird buzzing in his pocket. The panic lasts only a fraction of a second before he realizes it is their cell phone. Ringing. Ringing? Who even has their number?

"Hello?"

"Rod?" It sure sounds like Cameron.

"That you, Cam?"

"Yes, been trying to reach you. Thought you might be back about now."

"Yeah. We're at the airport standing in the lost luggage line."

"I'm glad I got you."

Cameron sounds a bit breathless, like he does when he gets excited about something.

"I wanted to let you know about Trefor's captain party. Tomorrow. At the Moose. After hockey."

"I'm glad we're back for it. You know, I should go to hockey, too, if I can get my butt in gear."

"Oh, by the way – I called Brendan. Not your Brendan – Brillo. He's going to come to the party tomorrow."

Rod's dark fog lifts. He is in the mess at Cold Lake, drinking his first Guinness with Brillo, watching the bubbles descend. He is almost happy as he comes back to the present, accepting it all. He has retired. The dogs have died. The kids have moved out.

He breathes.

"Thanks, Cam."

All of Me

Montreal – June 5, 2005

Arcadia

IT IS A SUNNY morning, Father.

I am sitting up in bed, eating breakfast. It tastes good. There are leaves on the trees I can see outside. It looks like summer.

Have I been gone for awhile?

I am trying to get my bearings, now that I am awake and almost comfortable. Snowie is walking over to my bed.

The home. That is where I am and where I have been for some time. Snowie is my roommate. She is here now, silent as usual, looking at me with her great sad eyes.

What a comfort she is! She doesn't have to say anything – it is better not. She has been through such hardship, poor thing! It is coming back to me. From our country's largest market capitalization to obscurity in a heartbeat, her people corrupt and her secrets stolen. Seen by so many investors as *the betrayer*. Oh, poor Judas. I feel for her.

She is back by the window again, Father, but she has left me a newspaper – the *Financial Gazette.*

The Financial Gazette
May 22, 2004

APPC Unlocks Value

Boy Wonder, Chairman and CEO of the Arcadian Private Property Corporation, today explained his business strategy in a telephone interview with the Gazette.

"Ever since deregulation, the market has undervalued airline shares," Mr. Wonder explained. "With our cutting edge expertise in so many areas – aircraft maintenance and loyalty plans to name but two – we are optimistic that we can better unlock their intrinsic value as separate companies under the umbrella of APPC."

As Air Arcadia emerges from ABCA, it is expected that APPC will be a holding company for as many as a dozen pieces of the former airline. "I see them as a family of companies," said Wonder.

The financial community was quick to express its approval of the new business plan.

I read but I don't understand, Father. Too many initials. I keep having to go back to see what they stand for.

But now I remember the nightmare. It started with the Blue Bitch being attached and my people slipping away from me. And as memories come back I know these things did come to pass and I realize she is no longer here, no longer attached.

In the nightmare I was on the metal table and there was cutting. I remember almost cheering because they were cutting her away. *Hooray,* I thought. She's dead anyway. It won't hurt her.

Perhaps this has come to pass as well?

I just tried to move a little and it stings. My left side feels paper-delicate. I had better not move for awhile. But there is a sting on my right side, too – in back under my ribs . . .

Oh, Father! It is all coming back. Why did I cry out for consciousness? In the nightmare there were those high-tech organ-donor freezers or whatever they are. They were going to cut me apart and sell the pieces.

Have they taken one of my kidneys?

Will they take all of me?

Who Maketh Thee To Differ?

Montreal – March, 2009

Cameron

THE MOOSE SITS at the corner of a nondescript mini-mall. Across the boulevard, running alongside, is a landscaped greensward with artificial hills and a row of trees. Behind are the backs of townhouses, accessible from some Court or Crescent in the depths of Pointe Claire.

Today the greensward is a mess of dirty snow and ice. It is raining.

Cameron pulls in to the mini-mall lot and parks at the end opposite from the Moose, in front of the Couche-Tard, acting like this is a stealth operation. He hustles through the rain looking down, vigilant for black ice.

Inside the little vestibule condensation forms on his glasses. There is no one around. He steps out of the airlock into the tavern proper. The room is long and narrow, with the long axis parallel to the side street.

He peers into the gloom.

Down at the back, on the left, is a scene he recognizes. The crotch-height stainless steel counter that doubles as dishwasher and service bar. At the clean-glasses end of the washer a stalk sprouts to chest height. Several tap handles bloom from the bud at the top.

Cameron remembers the setup from his youth, when in the feckless years between adolescence and marriage he frequented the taverns of Montreal. In those days they were a man's refuge, particularly on Friday and Saturday, when the working guy got paid. Beaten down by his job and briefly free of Church and home, he could spend half his paycheck drinking with his fellows and cursing the boss and the system.

Then came La Révolution Tranquille. In the blink of an eye the Church lost its influence, the job had more opportunities and the boss was no longer un anglais, un bloke. Change for la taverne was slower. As business declined and women entered the job market the pressure increased. First a few high-end taverns appeared. Still beer, just beer, but food, or better food, and – women! Girls allowed! These new establishments called themselves Brasseries. You could take your girlfriend on a date. You could take your wife.

The waiter stands at the dirty-glasses end of the counter, loading a rack for the washer. Cameron recognizes him by his apron, a black leather tool-belt with a bib. There is a special strap for the bottle opener and four loose pouches. They used to be for nickels, dimes, quarters, and bills. That was when a glass was a dime, a bottle cost a quarter, and *une grosse* was forty cents. Tips were paid in nickels and dimes.

Cameron glances to the right. Trefor is talking to a shortish man with curly, greying hair. They are on a raised section by the windows, separated from the rest of the bar by a railing. At each end, two steps up allow access. Cameron climbs the steps at the near entrance and approaches the pair. They are both drinking Guinness.

"Trefor, Brendan – so you've met?"

"Well as a matter of fact we hadn't done. But we've been getting on famously, as you can see."

Brendan gestures toward their half-empty glasses.

"Would you be likin' one of these, Cameron?"

"I've got a pitcher of Rickhart's on the way, if you prefer . . ."

It is the first time the Captain has spoken. Cameron grabs them both by the shoulder.

"Oh, Tref. Congratulations!"

The waiter is suddenly standing with them, putting a pitcher and a half-dozen glasses on the table.

"Merci, Pierre. Et s'il vous plaît, un pichet à chaque table, à mesure qu'ils vont arriver."

"Bien sùr, commandant."

Trefor's cheeks redden.

"You'll have to be gettin' used to it, commander."

Cameron is already seated, pouring himself a Rickhart's. He raises his glass.

"To Captain Trefor!"

"Thank you, Cameron."

"And Brendan, retired! Congratulations! My God, I can't keep up with it all."

"Don't fret, Cameron. It's just that we're all old."

Trefor laughs.

". . . and I was just sayin' to your friend here that I have obviously retired too early, as I haven't had the pleasure of flyin' with him . . ."

§

Pilots filter in through both doors. They find Trefor, congratulate him, and wander off to get a beer. Cameron has left Trefor's table,

447

making room for the procession. He meanders, saying brief hellos. He watches as groups coalesce and drift apart. The platform is getting crowded.

Cameron walks down the two steps onto the main floor. *I never knew there were two doors to this place. More of the guys are coming in the back. Must be parking back there, too . . .*

"Cameron! How's Terry?"

Cameron turns. He recognizes a large, avuncular man perhaps a decade older than himself.

"Ted! Hi! You just come from hockey?"

"Yeah. Good turnout. Lotta the guys there today."

Before he retired, Ted held just about every position at Flight Operations Headquarters that wasn't a pilot or a secretary, including, for a period, Office Manager. Since then he has been busy as a general factotum for all Air Arcadia pilot things, including hockey and The Moose.

"Hey, did Rod play today?"

"Yeah. Did a great job on defence."

Ted looks around the room, perhaps to see if any of today's team are out of the showers yet.

"Hey, know who else came today? Haven't seen him in a coon's age. Played nets on no notice at all. We usually have three or four we can count on for goalie, but no dice today, so when Enrico showed up and volunteered . . ."

"Rico came? No shit?"

Cameron knows only the barest outline of what has happened since that month they spent together. How Enrico bid the Boing BigTwin and failed. How he was put on permanent medical leave. And how years later he was called back to go on course to re-qualify, only to be pulled from the classroom and told that it had been a mistake.

"Kid you not. Looks good, too. Grown a beard."

"Wow. Good for him. I guess they're all coming over?"

"Think so. Rod and Baddy were talking it up."

A burst of cold air hits Cameron's back. A boisterous group of men with high colour and wet hair are pushing through the back door.

"Hey, here they come now …"

Ted moves off. Cameron watches as Rod and Bad Dog find Trefor and push him around affectionately. There is much laughter.

§

Every table on the platform is full. The din of voices washes over Cameron, filling the room.

Cameron moves past the platform railing, trying to catch a few wisps of conversation. Suddenly another blast of cold air admits a Mutt and Jeff duo. Mutt, tall and mustachioed, is speaking rapid French in a nonstop blast of bonhomie.

The Jeff figure almost bumps into Cameron as Mutt pushes after him through the door.

"Aie, 'scuse, Cameron. Sorry, là, mais c'est c'qui arrive quand tu fréquentes cette hostie de girafe."

The room is filling to the point where navigation has become difficult. Currents and eddies bear people along. Some resist and cling to a chair-back or pillar as to a piece of flotsam. Cameron assesses the situation from his position near the draft handles. There is a definite right-to-left movement on the platform, up the front stairs and down the rear stairs. He decides to go with it.

Cameron allows himself to be caught in an eddy. He says quick hellos and manages not to stumble as he is borne up the two steps. The current takes him away from the railing, toward the window wall.

"Cameron!"

Almost hidden in the forest of bodies, Rod and Brendan are waving at him. They can't get up with the press around them, but there is a chair. Cameron manages to sit.

"Have some eats! Brendan just sprang for all of us. He's waving money around."

"Fiddle. It's only that Ramrod is concerned for my sanity . . ."

"I did say perhaps we ought to have a bite."

"I'll admit I have been tuckin' it away. As who would not after the stories I've been hearin'?"

Pierre's tray is drifting by in the stream. His arm puts a fresh Guinness in front of Brendan and retracts into the current. Brendan reaches for it and takes a gulp.

"Ah, me mother's milk . . ."

"Brendan's coming back to our place tonight."

Shouts emanate from a few tables over.

"Ah, friendship. A wonderful thing. As is the lovely Susan."

"Heck, maybe if I get a thing going here Susan will come and drive us both home. Wouldn't be the first time a couple of cars overnighted in the back lot of the Moose."

From the invisible, lively table, more shouts mix with cheers. Cameron swallows his bite of nacho.

"So Brendan. Stories?"

"Oh, indeed. Back when I was sober I managed to extract Trefor's life story."

"It's a good one. He told you about CEGEP de la Vieille Souche?"

Trefor's family emigrated from Wales when he was eight years old.

They were not well off to begin with, and then his parents divorced. When the flying bug bit Trefor saw that his best and perhaps only chance lay with the CEGEP de la Vieille Souche, the only Quebec community college to offer a full aviation program. As a citizen and resident he was entitled to apply.

The odds are steep. About twenty percent of applicants are accepted. Fifty percent of those wash out before second year. Fifteen percent graduate. About ten percent of graduates go on to careers with an airline.

Then there is the question of language. The CEGEP de la Vieille Souche is unilingual French. Trefor spoke some, but nowhere near enough to get by in that environment. So learned French. He applied to la Vieille Souche and got in.

"Oh, yes. And the part that did get to me, I confess – was he tellin' you about the ombudsman?"

"Ombudsman? No – what ombudsman?"

"Department of Education. Or whatever they're callin' it – Office de la quelque chose."

"Sure. No, he didn't . . ."

Brendan takes a gulp.

"Well. You know the third year, the fourth year – whenever it is they start to fly the Barons?"

"Sure. Nice airplane."

"So they say."

"So?"

"They tried to throw him out."

"Why?"

The lively table erupts in shouts. Cameron can hear *Whoa, Baddy!* *and Go, Bad Dog!* More shouts. They look over. Rising above the intervening heads and shoulders, Bad Dog's head appears.

"He's standing on the table!"

The din diminishes measurably.

"Listen up, plebes! 'Coute bien, les gars!"

The volume goes down another notch.

"I propose a toast. To my poor buddy who's on the hook for all this beer we're drinking. ARE WE DOING A GOOD JOB?"

The volume surges.

"Et c'est qui qui paie? C'est qui qui nous a bien soignés cet après-midi? C'EST À QUI CE PARTY?"

The volume surges again. There are shouts:

"TREFOR! TREFOR!"

Bad Dog holds up his arms for quiet.

"FUCKING RIGHT! And he's showed us a thing or two, remember. REMEMBER THAT, HOSTIES DE BLOKES. ET SOUVENEZ-VOUS BIEN, YOU FUCKING PEPPERS! Trefor, thank you. Merci, Commando."

Bad Dog hoists a full pint glass above his head. He looks like the Statue of Liberty. The crowd murmers. Bad Dog tilts his head back and chugs. He holds up the empty glass. Cheers erupt.

"TREFOR! TREFOR! TREFOR!"

"Will they be gettin' him to speak, do you think?"

Brendan is craning around, trying to catch a glimpse of his new friend. There are scuffles, exclamations. Trefor's head and shoulders appear, at about the same height as Bad Dog's.

"He's standing on a chair!"

Cameron flushes. His observation has been heard in the suddenly quiet room. Tall Trefor. Tall, lanky Trefor, with his quiet charm and a face that is his alone, full of character.

"Mes copains, mes amis – merci d'être venus. Je vous remercie tous, chacun. Thank you all so much for coming. I am grateful to you all. Amusez-vous bien!"

Trefor disappears. There is a brief roar and a few more shouts. The conversational din returns.

Their table is silent for a few moments. Cameron picks up the thread.

"No. I didn't know, Brendan. They tried to throw him out?"

"They did indeed. And for no discernible reason. He was doing well. In fact he was at the top of his class. It was a move of great stupidity . . ."

"Wait! Was that what Bad Dog – just now – was talking about?"

"The Lord shall cause thine enemies that rise up against thee to be smitten before thy face . . ."

Cameron stares at Brendan, wondering what to say.

"The ombudsman . . ."

"Ruled for Trefor. He stayed. Finished at the top of his class. Graduated . . ."

Brendan takes a gulp.

"Scripture frames the doings of us mere mortals."

The last is a whisper. He puts down his pint and crosses himself.

"I didn't know, Brendan. What a story."

"There's more."

Brendan has run out of steam. He nods his head sideways. Rod fills the silence.

"Enrico was in nets today. Played like a fiend. We had a good time."

"Yes, I saw Ted just now. He told me."

"He tell you about Enrico getting called back?"

"No. But I heard something about it. A few years ago. It was a mistake, or something?"

"Yeah."

Rod sits up straight. Again for a moment he looks like a young officer, a survivor of the Lawn Dart.

"Seems that – after you and I retired, Cam – a bunch of the older Blue guys decided they just didn't give a shit anymore. Beats me why – they made out like bandits on the seniority list – but there you go. Anyway, they began getting sick. There was this enormous bunch of them on General Disability, getting paid for doing nothing."

"That was their revenge, tall one. Locusts that they are."

Brendan returns to his Guinness.

"Anyway, so management in their wisdom decide to rehabilitate these guys. Call their bluff. So they review medical records and call all the dubious ones in to start class in whatever recurrent stuff they need to re-qualify. Needless to say there's been turnover in the office and no one remembers the deal they made with Enrico."

"Oh, my God. And he . . ."

"Yeah, exactly. There he is in class with a bunch of Blues. Monday, Tuesday, thinking he's smoked the system . . ."

"And?"

"Wednesday they come and pull him out of the class. Say there's been a mistake. Send him back home."

"Jesus. That's such – I don't know – such . . ."

Brendan grunts, shakes his head, and takes a large gulp. *I've never seen him drink so much . . .* It takes a second before Cameron realizes the curly grey head with its remnant of red is nodding, reciting, speaking to no one in particular.

"…not be puffed up against another. For who maketh me to differ from another? And what hast thou that thou didst not receive?"

Cameron watches, transfixed. Brendan lifts his face. There are tears in his eyes. He smiles.

"And shall I boast of these gifts as their author?"

In a sudden gust, rain spatters the window. Cameron looks out. The light is almost gone. Last October's grass has appeared, the dirty ice and snow worn away by the afternoon's rain.

"Yo, Brendan!"

"Well! Enrico! Have a seat!"

Cameron turns. Inches from his face, a large tooth-and-gums grin hangs in the air. As he stares, the grin's context fades in: a large and handsome salt-and-pepper beard.

"Cameron! Good to see you, man!"

Brendan moves enough so his chair squeaks against the floor.

"Pull up a chair, old fellow."

"We're putting tables together. C'mon. I'll help move yours."

Cameron can hear individual voices emerging from the din. He looks over his shoulder. The crowd has thinned and wearied. There are just a few people standing up. The tall Mutt figure is commanding one of the standing clumps, towering over the subordinate drinkers, clapping them on the back, telling jokes.

"Hey Rod! What are you guys, antisocial? C'mon. Move that fucking table!"

Bad Dog is forming his own conversational clump and it will include the honouree, Cameron sees. Baddy stands up.

"Cameron! Brendan! Good! We'll have a quorum."

Brendan gets up with surprising steadiness. He holds his pint in one hand and a pitcher in the other. Cameron moves some chairs out of the way. Rod and Enrico lift the table with its glasses and move it endways six feet to mate with Baddy's. The glasses and their cargo are intact.

"OK. Now, let's get down to business."

It has become a refectory table. Bad Dog holds sway like a medieval king, from the middle of one of the long sides. Cameron can imagine him tossing a rib over his shoulder to a patient mastiff.

"Have some food, guys . . ."

He waves at plates of nachos and wings. Some are slid down to their end.

"We don't want to get too drunk before we finish up the agenda. Speaking of which . . ."

He stands up and catches Pierre's eye. He grabs a depleted pitcher with his left hand and holds his right aloft, circling with two fingers in the *V for Victory* sign. Cameron thinks of the hand signals page in the FOM, of the *cleared to start engine* signal.

Bad Dog sits.

"OK, where were we?"

The short Jeff figure takes the cue.

"Tu parlais de Wall Street, hostie. Pourquoi, j'n'ai aucune idée. Ces choses-là me passent par dessus la tête."

"Well, that's my point, Jean-Luc. You don't have to be smart to understand that shit."

"Va shier, frenchy . . ."

"No, really. They'd like you to think it's fucking rocket science and they're so much smarter than you. But it's not and they're not."

"So, Bad. How come you're into all this money shit? You gonna be my advisor?"

"What, Enrico? You got money all of a sudden?"

"Sure. Retire next month. With my best five years it's better than General Disability."

"Well good for you. After all those assholes did to you. Hey, speaking of assholes – Roddy, did I tell you?"

"What?"

"They asked me to do Line Indoc."

"Well, finally. Good for you."

"I told 'em no. Too late. I told 'em I wanted to do it so I could fly with my buddies. Now they've all retired. Just too fucking late."

There is general laughter. Even Trefor chuckles discreetly.

"Hang on a sec . . ."

Pierre arrives with two pitchers. Bad Dog stands up and pays. Trefor tries to protest.

"No way, Tref. We've taken you for enough of a ride as it is. LISTEN UP, GUYS."

He casts a meaningful glance in the direction of Mutt's group.

"FREE LUNCH IS OVER. FROM NOW ON WE PAY. ÇA COMPRENS-TU, LES GARS?"

He sits. Jean-Luc pushes him on the shoulder.

"Comprends. Tu as raison, hostie. But why you have this hard-on pour la finance, tabarnac?"

"OK. Patience, 'tit-frère. Well, it started when that design company fired my brother. I started reading some shit."

"Yes. I remember when you told us about your brother. In Vancouver."

"The Swamp Pub, Cameron. It was pissing down rain. And then what happened?"

"April Fool."

"Right, Roddy. April fucking fool. So I've been looking into it. And now our Boy Wonder is safe in London with his money. It went down just like Jim said it would. Remember? Extract the value after it's already gone?"

Another gust of wind and rain rattles the window.

"Everybody's doing it. Or trying to. Everyone who's been to business school. It's the only game in town."

"What, hostie? Que est-ce qu'ils font?"

"All you gotta do, Jean-Luc, is invent some piece of financial hocus-pocus. And all of their rocket-science inventions have one thing in common."

"Bain, dis-nous le secret, tabarnac . . ."

"They lock in the profit for themselves and pass the risk on to the next guy."

"Like a pyramid scheme . . ."

"Or a Ponzi scheme. Except they're legal and above board. But they all do the same thing. Privatize the profit and socialize the risk."

There is a respectful silence.

"Moreover it is required in stewards, that a man be found faithful."

The words are slower. This is a sodden Brendan. The Guinness has permeated the flesh, but the elocution survives.

Enrico has assumed an attentiveness he usually reserves for women or food.

"What's that, Brendan?"

"It means, old man, that a man who has been given a trust must fulfil that trust. He must have some integrity."

"So that means Boy Wonder."

"Indeed, indeed." Brendan nods his curly head. "But it could as well apply to any of us."

"To us?"

Brendan lets it hang. The patter of rain on the window has become a roar.

"Fucking thunderstorm in March?"

"Could be fireworks . . ."

Sure enough, the heavenly welder strikes an arc. The window-rattling thunderclap is almost simultaneous.

"Brendan, that was from Corinthians, right?"

"Yes, so it was."

Brendan glances at Enrico with interest. Enrico laughs.

"It was the Jesuits. They gave up on me."

Cameron is caught between two conversations. He wants to hear about Enrico and the Jesuits, and he wants to hear Bad Dog in his conciliatory mode.

". . . it's just fucking human nature. But it's not all of human . . ."

" . . . so that stuff the Bible says about stewards, or jobs, or whatever . . ."

". . . of course it's a fuckup. How could a major financial meltdown not be a fuckup?

"What does the worker gain from his toil?"

". . . this is going to go on for years. Those mortgage securities are still toxic fucking waste. They haven't been written down on the books. We're still living in a fool's . . ."

This thunderclap and sizzling arc are simultaneous. Conversation stops. People look around, feel their bodies, check for damage.

"That was really fuckin' close!"

The Moose is not burning. The rain outside is steady.

"Hey, 'Ti-Guy. C'est ton char qui a pris feu . . ."

"Bain non, hostie. C'était toi qui conduisais . . ."

Enrico pursues his conversation with Brendan.

"So what does St. Paul say about work?"

"That everyone may eat and drink, and find satisfaction in his toil – this is the gift of God."

"What does it say about all my stuff? All I can see is that shit makes more shit . . ."

"T'is true. Shit begets shit. Well put, Enrico. We'll be makin' a Nietzsche out of you yet."

The table hasn't had a lot to say since the last thunderclap. Trefor, the honouree, speaks into the silence.

"I'm lucky. I have a job and I love it."

The rain is heavier. Brendan drains his glass. He is at that point in a session where drinking seems like a good idea for its own sake. He gestures grandly, sweeping in Rod and Cameron and Bad Dog.

"The bloodline of Bird of Prey himself."

He is pointing his empty glass at Trefor. There is an awkward pause as Brendan regains some composure. Jean-Luc leans in.

"Il a raison, tu sais?"

"Comprends, 'tit frère. We're passing it on ourselves, even without fucking Line Indoc."

Cameron raises his glass. It is heavy. The fatigue of much merrymaking is pulling it down.

"Here's to you, Trefor."

"Amen."

Brendan leaves his glass on the table. There is nothing left in it, anyway.

Rod stands up.

"C'mon, Brillo. Let's go home to supper."

Brendan stands. He nods to the refectory table. Words are superfluous. He walks with dignity down the steps and toward the back door. He pushes it open, admitting a blast of rain and stormy air.

"Jasus, Mary and Joseph. Truly a rain to float Noah."

It smells like spring.

Glossary

ADI	Attitude Director Indicator. Center of the Primary Flight Display.
APU	Auxiliary Power Unit. Small turbine, usually in the tail of the aircraft. Provides electrical power and air under pressure for air conditioning and engine start.
ATIS	Automated Terminal Information Service. Airport weather, runway in use, and other information are recorded every hour and broadcast in a loop on a dedicated frequency.
CAT I	An ILS approach to limits of 200 feet altitude and 1/2 mile visibility. Can be flown by hand.
CAT II	An ILS approach to a Decision Height of 100 feet. Must be flown by autopilot to DH.
CAT III	An ILS approach flown to a DH of less than 100 feet. Autoland must be used.
Datalink	Developed in the 1980's, this system sends text over VHF radio. The technology is similar to FAX over telephone lines. Airlines also use the system to automatically capture OOOI (Out, Off, On, and In) times and send them to the airline's computer systems.
DH	Decision Height

EGAD	Electronic Gee-Whiz Actions Director. Two screens in the center of the panel show all engine and systems information. All data is monitored and faults are displayed along with interactive emergency checklists. (This is a fictional, commercial-free version)
EFOB	Estimated Fuel on Board. The FMGC uses the route, winds, and other data to calculate how much fuel will remain at waypoints ahead, including destination.
ETA	Estimated Time of Arrival.
FLEX Thrust	Using less than full thrust for takeoff to prolong engine life. Thrust used is calculated based on weight, altitude, temperature, and runway length.
FMA	Flight Mode Annunciator. A strip across the top of the Primary Flight Display. Shows auto-thrust mode and autopilot (and Flight Director) modes. In other words, what the automatics think they are doing.
FMGC	Flight Management and Guidance Computer. Pilots enter flight planned route and altitudes. The FMGC continuously calculates projected ETA, EFOB, and aircraft weight for each waypoint using IRS and GPS inputs. FMCG also issues guidance commands to the autopilot.
FOB	Fuel On Board
FOD	Fuel Over Destination
FOD	Foreign Object Damage. Loose stones or other debris can be sucked into engine intakes or damage propellors.

FOM	Flight Operations Manual. Each airline must write and maintain one as part of its operating certificate. It spells out standards for all parts of a flight. Commonly known as the Bible.
GPS	Global Positioning System. This relatively recent navigation system uses a constellation of satellites to calculate position and altitude within an error of a few meters.
HSI	Horizontal Situation Indicator. This counterpart to the ADI sits just underneath or to one side of it and displays aircraft heading and position relative to navigation beacons or waypoints. With IRS and/or GPS inputs it also displays aircraft track, maps, and even radar or satellite data.
INS	Inertial Navigation System. Although invented in Canada in the 1920's, this huge advance in navigation was not commercially available until the 1970's, when it replaced the navigator on overseas routes. In a nutshell, a gyro-stabilized platform holds accelerometers in each of the three axes. The computer asks for a known starting position in latitude/longitude. The computer then integrates the accelerations to get velocities, and integrates those to get positions. Readouts include lat/long, track, and groundspeed.

IRS	Inertial Reference System. This is the modern version of INS. It has no moving parts except photons and electrons, so it is much more reliable than INS. The accelerometers are solid state, and instead of the gyro-stabilized platform there are three "laser gyros" one in each of the three axes. These are triangular quartz blocks which contain two laser beams moving in opposite directions. Any rotational acceleration in the plane of rotation (of the laser beams) means one beam temporarily has a longer route to travel. This results in an interference pattern proportional to the acceleration. In addition to the outputs of the INS, the IRS knows aircraft attitude.
JBI	James Brake Index The James Brake Decelerometer measures the traction a tire is likely to get on the runway. The result is given as a fraction of G, so a James Brake Index of 1 is a deceleration force of 32 feet/sec/sec, almost like landing on a carrier. Not that 1 G is attainable in practice on an asphalt runway: the slightest contamination – dirt, oil, fuel, water; or worse yet, snow, ice, or wet ice – will bring the traction down to a fraction of a G.

JBI (con't.)	The JBI is important not only because a landing aircraft needs traction to stop, but also because it needs to steer and to keep from being blown off the side of the runway in a crosswind. And if the equipment measures a JBI of 0.3, the pilot must divide that force between braking and side-force: if all of the 0.3 G is used for braking, any crosswind will drift the aircraft off the downwind side of the runway. Worse yet, if the traction is so bad that steering is compromised, the aircraft will weather-cock into the wind, so any reverse thrust will help pull the aircraft downwind into the weeds. There are charts and tables which help figure out the increase in landing distance; in practice most pilots have a number in their heads. Below that number they become exceedingly wary. Multiple factors can gang up on you, so the transition from a normal, controllable landing roll to the whole thing going to hell in a hand-basket can be very abrupt.
MCDU	Multifunction Control and Display Unit. This is the pilot's interface to the FMCG as well as other devices like the Datalink. It has a display screen and a full alpha-numeric (although not qwertyuiop) keyboard.
PFD	Primary Flight Display. This is the modern ("glass") version of the ADI. It incorporates the instruments that used to make up the "basic T", in the same relative positions. So the attitude display is in the middle with airspeed to the left and altitude to the right. It includes vertical speed and the "ball" portion of the old "needle and ball", as well as the FMA across the top.

RAT	To make things confusing, there are two RAT's. The Ram Air Temperature (also known as the Total Air Temperature, TAT) is what a thermometer reads in the air compressed in front of a fast-moving aircraft. It is higher that the still air temperature in proportion to the aircraft speed. Wings on supersonic aircraft get quite hot.
RAT	Ram Air Turbine. This is a small propeller which pops into the airstream in an emergency. It powers (usually) a generator and a hydraulic pump, on a bad day when all other sources fail.
STAR	Standard Terminal Arrival Route. This is a published procedure describing a route to be flown, as well as altitudes and speeds. The clearance is simply "Cleared via the HABBS 3 Arrival to 24R", saving paragraphs of description on a busy frequency.
U/S	Unserviceable. This is a standard shorthand.
VASIS	Visual Approach Slope Indicator (s). Two light boxes to the left of the runway touchdown point show red or white depending on the aircraft's approach angle. "White over white, too high. Red over red, you're dead. Red over white, just right."
ZFW	Zero Fuel Weight. This is the weight of the aircraft fully loaded for the flight, but without the fuel. It is useful because the weight of the aircraft at any point in the flight can be found by adding the Fuel on Board (FOB) to the ZFW.